CONCRETE EVIDENCE

"Mills delivers another action-packed novel that offers intrigue and an adventurous ride. . . . Well-developed characters, vivid imagery, and thorough research guide this story line every step of the way. Readers old and new will be left clutching the armrest as they quickly turn the pages racing to the end."

LIBRARY JOURNAL

"[In] the exciting latest from Mills . . . the confident plotting keeps the mysteries coming, and red herrings will have readers guessing the culprit through to the satisfying conclusion. Fans of Colleen Coble and Susan Sleeman will savor this thrilling stand-alone."

PUBLISHERS WEEKLY

TRACE OF DOUBT

"A well-researched and intimate story with some surprising twists along the way. In *Trace of Doubt*, Mills weaves together a tale of faith, intrigue, and suspense that her fans are sure to enjoy."

STEVEN JAMES, award-winning author of *Synapse* and *Every Wicked Man*

"DiAnn Mills took me on a wild ride with *Trace of Doubt*. . . . Filled with high stakes, high emotion, and high intrigue, *Trace of Doubt* will keep you guessing until the thrilling and satisfying conclusion."

LYNN H. BLACKBURN, award-winning author of the Dive Team Investigations series

"DiAnn Mills serves up a perfect blend of action, grit, and heart with characters so real they leap off the page. *Trace of Doubt* takes romantic suspense to a whole new level."

JAMES R. HANNIBAL, award-winning author of *The Paris Betrayal*

"*Trace of Doubt* is a suspense reader's best friend. From page one until the end, the action is intense and the story line keeps you guessing."

EVA MARIE EVERSON, bestselling author of *Five Brides* and *Dust*

AIRBORNE

"When DiAnn Mills started writing suspense novels, she found her niche. They are strong stories that keep the reader guessing. *Airborne* was filled with twists and turns."

LENA NELSON DOOLEY, bestselling, award-winning author of the Love's Road Home series

"Mills keeps getting better with each novel."

LAURAINE SNELLING, bestselling, award-winning author of *A Blessing to Cherish* and the Home to Blessing series

FATAL STRIKE

"DiAnn Mills has done it again! *Fatal Strike* captivates the reader from the first to last page. Deliciously detailed, this fast-paced romantic suspense novel creates an emotional roller coaster that keeps the pages turning as quickly as they can be read."

REBECCA MCLAFFERTY, author of *Intentional Heirs*

"*Fatal Strike* is a fascinating and page-turning suspense novel with fabulous characters and a touch of romance. Five stars from me! . . . The plot was full of suspense and plot twists and I was left guessing at every turn!"

SARAH GRACE GRZY, author of *Never Say Goodbye*

BURDEN OF PROOF

"DiAnn Mills never disappoints. . . . Put on a fresh pot of coffee before you start this one because you're not going to want to sleep until the suspense ride is over. You might want to grab a safety harness while you're at it—you're going to need it!"

LYNETTE EASON, bestselling, award-winning author of the Elite Guardians and Blue Justice series

"Taking her readers on a veritable roller-coaster ride of unexpected plot twists and turns, *Burden of Proof* is an inherently riveting read from beginning to end."

MIDWEST BOOK REVIEW

"Mills has added yet another winner to her growing roster of romantic thrillers, perhaps the best one yet."

THE SUSPENSE ZONE

HIGH TREASON

"In this third book in Mills's action-packed FBI Task Force series, the stakes are higher than ever. . . . Readers can count on being glued to the pages late into the night—as 'just one more chapter' turns into 'can't stop now.'"

ROMANTIC TIMES

"This suspenseful novel will appeal to Christian readers looking for a tidy, uplifting tale."

PUBLISHERS WEEKLY

DEEP EXTRACTION

"A harrowing police procedural [that] . . . Mills's many fans will devour."

LIBRARY JOURNAL

"Few characters in Mills's latest novel are who they appear to be at first glance. . . . Combined with intense action and stunning twists, this search for the truth keeps readers on the edges of their favorite reading chairs. . . . The crime is tightly plotted, and the message of faith is authentic and sincere."

ROMANTIC TIMES, 4½-star review, Top Pick

DEADLY ENCOUNTER

"Crackling dialogue and heart-stopping plotlines are the hallmarks of Mills's thrillers, and this series launch won't disappoint her many fans. Dealing with issues of murder, domestic terrorism, and airport security, it eerily echoes current events."

LIBRARY JOURNAL

"From the first paragraph until the last, this story is a nail-biter, promising to delight readers who enjoy a well-written adventure."

CHRISTIAN MARKET MAGAZINE

FACING THE ENEMY

DiANN MILLS

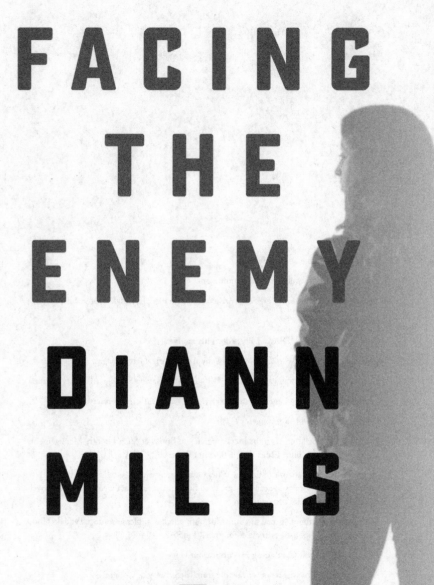

Tyndale House Publishers
Carol Stream, Illinois

Visit Tyndale online at tyndale.com.

Visit DiAnn Mills's website at diannmills.com.

Tyndale and Tyndale's quill logo are registered trademarks of Tyndale House Ministries.

Facing the Enemy

Designed by Dean H. Renninger

Published in association with the literary agency of Books & Such Literary Management, 52 Mission Circle, Suite 122, PBM 170, Santa Rosa, CA 95409.

For information about special discounts for bulk purchases, please contact Tyndale House Publishers at csresponse@tyndale.com, or call 1-855-277-9400.

Library of Congress Cataloging-in-Publication Data

A catalog record for this book is available from the Library of Congress.

ISBN 978-1-4964-5194-1 (HC)

ISBN 978-1-4964-5195-8 (SC)

Printed in the United States of America

29	28	27	26	25	24	23
7	6	5	4	3	2	1

In memory of Brett Morgan Egert:
February 2, 1977–July 29, 2021.

And to the family who loved him.

1

JULY 29
RISA

Twelve years ago, my younger brother fell into an abyss of drugs and alcohol. He chose his addictions over Mom and Dad—and me. Prayers for healing fell flat, but none of us gave up, proving our belief in unconditional love. Then yesterday he called, and my hopes skyrocketed. Trenton said he missed me and wanted to make amends with his family, beginning with his older sis. We chose to meet at a popular restaurant for a late dinner within walking distance of my apartment.

A knock on my cubicle jolted me back to reality. Gage, my work partner, towered in the entryway and grinned. "Hey, what's going on?"

The sound of his voice caused me to tingle to my toes. "Thinking."

"Obviously, you were a million miles away." His blue-gray eyes bored into mine, the intensity nearly distracting me.

I leaned back in my comfy, ergonomic chair. "My brother called."

"Trenton? The guy you haven't seen in years?"

"The same."

"And?"

"He wants to meet tonight for dinner, to talk about making amends."

Gage shook his head. "Risa, he has a record a mile long. He's planning on manipulating you, squeezing every penny he can get."

I picked up an old photo of Trenton and me as kids. Dad had snapped it while we were in our tree house. I swiped at a piece of dust, then replaced it beside my photo of Mom and Dad. "I must give him a chance. He's my brother."

"What if he's gotten himself in over his head and needs his FBI agent sis to bail him out?"

I bit into my lower lip. Gage's words had a level of truth, even if I didn't want to admit it. "I want to hear him out."

Gage stepped closer. "I don't want to see you hurt. Remember three years ago when he called you from a bar demanding money, cursed you until you hung up?" The soft gentleness in his whispered tone said more than friend to friend. "Think about canceling the dinner or let me go with you."

Emotion rose thick in my throat. "You mean well, and I—" Catching myself, I nearly said *love*. "I appreciate your concern. But I'll be fine. Want me to call you afterward?"

He nodded. "I can run by if you need to talk."

I peered into the face of the man I adored. "I will. Promise."

★　★　★

I arrived early at the restaurant to meet Trenton, anticipating his contagious smile perfected by an overpaid orthodontist. The phone attempted to keep my attention, but my mind swirled with how I wanted tonight to move forward against the reality of what had happened in the past.

The host approached me. Trenton walked behind him, towering several inches above the short man. I held my breath and stood, not feeling my legs, only my pulse speeding at the sight of my brother.

Trenton chuckled low, the familiar, dazzling, heart-crunching expression that had always touched me with sibling love. Clear brown eyes captured mine. Gone were the dilated pupils and bone-thin body. My brother held out his buff arms, and I rushed into them.

"Risa, you look amazing," he whispered. "Thanks for seeing me on such short notice."

"Nothing could have kept me away." I stepped back, noting the miracle before me. Telling Mom and Dad wasn't a part of tonight's plan, but I wished they were here. We'd all be blubbering. I swiped at a tear and feared a humiliating sob would replace my already-fragile composure. "I want to remember this moment forever." *Please stay strong this time.*

"Me too, Sis." He gestured to the booth. "Sit, and let's talk and eat."

I slid in and he took the opposite side of the table. A server presented us with menus and asked for our drink order.

"We'll have two Dr Peppers," Trenton said.

He remembered my favorite drink. No mention of alcohol. I breathed in deeply to steady myself. I wanted our reunion to be special, not me a weeping mess. "I've missed you."

Trenton cocked his head, and the mischievous brother from days gone by appeared. "I've been clean for four months. Working steady and enrolled in night school for the next college term." He took my hands, and his features grew serious. "But before I say another word, I'm sorry. I promise you, I'll never hurt you, Mom, or Dad again. Please forgive me for the mess I made of my life and dragging my family through the stench of it."

I'd heard this before, from his teen years into his twenties. Dare I believe our prayers had been answered? "I forgave you years ago. All we ever wanted for you is a healthy body and mind."

"Thanks, Sis. I know you've heard this 'I'm sorry' junk before, but I'm well on my way."

His words warmed me like a quilt on a chilly night. "I can see it, feel it. Why tell me first instead of Mom and Dad?"

"Great times with you growing up that never left me."

Memories rushed over me . . . The time we went camping by ourselves and it snowed. Birthdays. Christmases. All the treasured times I believed had vanished into the chasm of addiction.

The server returned with our drinks, and Trenton released my hands.

"Have you decided on your order?" the server said.

Neither of us had picked up our menus, but I often frequented the restaurant and ordered a vegan dish. Trenton opted for their pork chop and fixings.

"And I'll take the bill." He pointed at me. "No arguments."

"My treat when we have dinner again."

"Got it."

"You were about to tell me something about us."

He rubbed his palms on the thighs of his jeans. "Two things stand out. The first one happened when I was four, so that made you ten. You were watching me trying to climb an oak tree in the backyard. I was crying because my short legs couldn't swing high enough. Then I felt your hand on my shoulder. You boosted me up onto the branch. Climbed up with me. Not long after that, Dad built us a tree house."

"I loved that tree house. You had your space and I had mine."

"What I'll always remember is what you said to me. 'Trenton, I'm your big sis. I'll always help you. I promise.'"

I blinked back the ocean of hopeful tears. "Thanks. I remember our times in the tree house, our private little world."

"One more reason I contacted you. I was six and you were twelve. For three summers, Mom and Dad put me in swimming lessons, but I couldn't put my head underwater. Not sure why. You convinced Mom and Dad that you could teach me how to swim. So every day we went to the neighborhood pool, and at the end of two weeks, I was swimming. I trusted you."

I took a deep breath. *Be aware of manipulation, Risa.* "Thanks." I raised a finger. "I remember being a high school junior and this jerk of a guy followed me home. Wouldn't leave me alone. You punched him in the nose."

Trenton laughed. "My voice hadn't changed yet, but I wasn't going to let him bother you."

"That's love, Brother." *Oh, Trenton, let this be for keeps. I'm afraid to believe the nightmare is over.*

"And we'll make many more crazy times together. Do you have plans for Saturday morning? I volunteer at a community center for kids at risk. We have a mixed basketball team, and I could use some help with the girls."

I shivered. What a blessing to have my brother back. "All I need is a time and place."

"You never fail me, Sis." He took a long drink of his Dr Pepper. "Are you writing?"

I grinned. "Dabbling here and there."

"I never understood why you left a safe job as a college prof and writer for the dangers of the FBI." He shrugged. "Other than your wild side that you kept more in check than I did."

"Teaching and writing short stories with a few successful publications failed to fill my adventure deficit. Every time I read about a crime, I wanted to be the one working the case. Dad said I couldn't create a crime and solve it—I had to be actively involved."

"Your personality better fits law enforcement. Still married to the FBI?"

I wiggled my shoulders. "Of course. Five years ago, I moved to the violent crime division, specifically crimes against children. It's stressful and emotional, but protecting children suits me."

He frowned. "Because of me?"

I blinked. "A little. My main reason is what happened to the little girl who lived across the street from us."

"Right." He shook his head. "I'm sorry her death still bothers you. Isn't there a special team for finding missing kids?"

"Child Abduction Rapid Deployment or CARD. They're an elite, specialized team, and that's all they do. That's not my role, but we often work together."

"What do you investigate?" Trenton seemed interested in my job, another first.

"My partner and I investigate kidnappings, pedophiles, pornography, online predators, human trafficking, involuntary servitude, parental kidnapping, and any other situation that falls into the 'violent crimes against children' bucket."

"I remember you were the neighborhood babysitter." He gave me his unforgettable impish grin. "And I also remember how much fun you had learning how to handle a car at high speeds."

I couldn't conceal my laughter. "Guess I'm part daredevil. Blame Dad for that. I remember loving to watch him race cars."

"He'd still be at it if Mom hadn't insisted his speed-loving days were over."

"When he taught me to drive, I learned a lot of tricks," I said.

"He already knew I was danger on wheels and asked Mom to teach me." He laughed. "Any potential brothers-in-law?"

I waved off his remark. My thoughts swept to Gage. Maybe I had found him, but that was a future conversation. "Nope. My job scares them off. I had more dates during my stint as a dull college professor."

"You dull? Never. You just haven't found the right guy. Pray about it, and if there's a guy good enough for my sis, he'll appear."

I startled. "Did you say pray?"

"Think about it. Who but God could have turned me around? Helped me walk away from drugs, alcohol, and so-called friends?"

Even in his good days, Trenton had steered away from mentions of faith. Maybe he had changed. "I don't know what to say."

"That's a first." He chuckled. "You always had more words in one day than I had in a week. But honestly, no more jail. No more being tossed out of an apartment because I couldn't pay the rent. No more waking up and not remembering the night before."

Wow. A true miracle. I swiped at happy tears. "I can't wait to tell Mom and Dad."

He leaned over the table as though to tell me a secret. "I'll do the honors very soon."

When our food arrived, he asked to say grace. I was so glad our eyes were closed, or he'd have seen a leaky faucet. We chatted through dinner. Laughed about some of the goofy things we'd done as kids. Time seemingly stopped, and my half-full cup of blessings spilled over with joy.

"Will you tell me about your healing journey?" I said.

"You can hear for yourself when I talk to Mom and Dad." He moistened his lips. "Do you trust me enough to walk you back to your apartment and call them from there? I mean, does your building have a lobby area with a little privacy?"

"It does, but you can call from my apartment. Trenton, they will be incredibly happy."

"I hope so."

I was so focused on our conversation that I didn't think I tasted my favorite dish. We finished and he paid the bill. Outside the restaurant, a few people mingled, and the night sky hosted a half-moon, alerting me to how long Trenton and I had talked. I breathed in thankfulness and expectations for a positive tomorrow. At the crosswalk, we waited for the pedestrian sign to signal our turn.

"How long have you lived in this fancy high-rise?" he said as we ambled across the street.

"Two years. I like the busyness and excitement."

"It must be in your DNA. One day I want a small place in the country where it's quiet."

"Never for me. I'll visit you though." The humid heat mixed with exhaust fumes spiraled around us. "What are you taking in college?"

"Psychology. See if I can't help a few kids understand life and avoid pitfalls."

"Incredible. I'm so pro—"

Trenton grabbed my shoulders and thrust me several feet ahead next to the curb. I landed on my side and rolled over. What—?

A horrible thud.

A woman screamed.

Tires squealed.

Horns blew.

Stinging pain radiated up my leg, side, arm, and head. In agony, I managed to roll over and glance at the street.

My brother's body lay in the intersection, a twisted mass of flesh and blood.

2

I sat on the front pew next to Mom and Dad in a church that had always offered me comfort and peace.

Until now.

I tried to be strong for my parents—Mom's tears and Dad's swiping at his eyes and nose showed me I'd done a lousy job. A nightmarish numbness had taken over my body, except for a horrible churning in the pit of my stomach. I always believed in the power and purity of truth. Then I saw my brother die right in front of me as the driver sped away. My FBI career and my faith were based on ensuring truth stood unwavering.

Until now.

I didn't feel like a trained agent who helped bring down those who muddy their lives by delving into violent crimes against children. Neither did I feel in control, certainly not with my scattered emotions. Stuffing the grief, screaming like a wild animal, and frantic crying were options, but not mine.

Where was God in the poisoning pain that had no antidote?

A young man with a guitar exited the front platform and walked back to his pew. Although I assisted Mom and Dad in selecting the appropriate music and Scripture for the service, I had no concept of the contents. Not even a word from the eulogy spoken by Trenton's sponsor.

Mom and Dad had chosen a gunmetal-gray casket. I'd gone with them to support their efforts, but my bravery collapsed when I was alone. I'd helped Mom go through photos and arrange them in chronological order for the funeral, and we both shed tears. I longed for my sweet brother who loved animals and people.

His death was my fault. I should have seen the car coming. Oh, the guilt and shame. Had I betrayed my own brother?

If I could escape this morbid place, I'd beat the streets to find the madman who ran the red light. He'd left me without a brother and my parents without a son. I vowed not to rest until cuffs were clamped on the driver's wrists. No one else had the passion to solve his death but me.

The service ended, and I took Mom's arm to help her stand. Dad's reddened eyes met mine, wordlessly conveying the sorrow threatening to destroy him. I fought the chill that wound through my body and penetrated my heart. The formalities were over. Dad had made a wise decision by having the graveside service before the memorial commemoration. Now to endure the church's lunch for those who'd come to pay their respects.

How could the three of us handle much more?

Heat poured into my ears and silence like a clock that stopped ticking.

Dad and I ushered Mom to the church's fellowship hall. What a misplaced name for funeral-goers. There among the tables loaded with salad and sandwiches, I walked through the motions of rearranging the sandwiches for a more formal appearance, straightening the paper plates and napkins, and getting Mom and Dad coffee. I knew without tasting, the brew was bitter, and with acid threatening havoc in my stomach, I left it alone.

Gage approached me. His whole body emitted warmth and compassion, his generous height and broad shoulders steadied like an anchor in my torment. I couldn't imagine anyone else supporting me on this miserable day. He gathered me into his arms, and I let him soothe me. Something I seldom let anyone do.

I should have agreed to let him join me with Trenton.

But then Gage might've died.

Others from the FBI trailed him and expressed their condolences, but Gage stayed at my side, my source of understanding, my friend through adversity. So much more, but he could never learn how much I cared until I found Trenton's killer. A relationship threatened our own on-the-job safety and others when personal feelings took precedence over our commitment to protect the innocent.

The line of people continued, while names and faces became a blur.

My head throbbed. Some of them had no thought to inappropriate remarks. If I heard one more "Your brother's in a better place" or "I know how you feel" or the worst one, "All things work together for good . . ."

An agent I didn't know stood before me with his hands at his side. "Sorry for your loss. I see your brother was only thirty. I also saw he had a record, so I'm sure you're relieved."

Relieved? I clenched my fists to keep from punching him.

"That's uncalled for," Gage said.

The man shrugged and walked away.

"I'm sorry," Gage whispered. "His social skills stink."

The last person, a female agent from cybercrimes, took my hand into hers. Her name slipped my mind, but I thought it was Darlene. She peered into my face with dark-blue eyes filled with caring. "Those we love live forever in our hearts."

"Thank you." Her words touched me with sincerity.

Finally Gage and I stood alone, the receiving line empty. Exhaustion rolled over me like I'd been hit by a—

How could I even think in terms of Trenton's demise?

"Risa, where are you?" Gage said.

I dug my fingers into my palms. "Not sure except I'm determined to walk through this fire no matter what that means."

He ran his fingers through thick, rust-brown hair. "We'll find the person responsible for the FSRA—make an arrest together."

Apprehending the driver guilty of failure to stop and render aid was only the beginning. Security cams from the restaurant had captured the crime, and one of the witnesses got the license plate number. But the SUV had been abandoned five blocks away and reported stolen hours before. The FBI and Houston Police Department had formed a task force since a federal agent had been involved. But their sweep revealed no fingerprints.

Nothing but Trenton's blood.

"Risa, are you listening?"

"No. Sorry." My concentration had taken a nosedive. I faced him. "What's wrong with me? I can't even cry today."

"You're grieving, and I'm not leaving your side." Gage's voice softened. "Let me help you get through this. You'd do the same for me."

"I . . . I can't seem to process, make sense of Trenton's death. I'm the logical person, not the one who's lost in a maze." I gazed into his face, and his depth of caring startled me. More like frightened me. "You don't have to keep me company. I need to be near Mom and Dad." We glanced twenty feet away at my parents surrounded by those from their church's small group. Mom referred to them as their 2 a.m. friends.

"Did you or your parents find anything at Trenton's apartment?"

"Nothing but receipts. Dad took his Bible, and Mom packed up a few personal items. Clothes, furniture, food, and kitchen items were donated. That's it."

Gage's hand grasped mine. Normally I'd jerk it back for fear someone might think we're more than friends. I slowly released his hand. Surely the other agents saw he only reached out as my friend and partner.

"The fire won't burn forever," Gage said. "But it may feel like it. Those who care for you will see you through."

Maybe he'd lost someone too. "When did you become so wise?"

He shook his head as though denying my words. "Not sure I fall under that category."

"Yes, you do. Thank you for being here, for supporting me. I wish I could express this emptiness, this nauseating void. Perhaps I'd feel better. Or worse." I peered at him. "Will it ever stop hurting, or am I being selfish?"

"Selfishness is not you. Eventually good memories of Trenton will take over the biting grief. When I was in college, I lost an aunt who was like a mother to me. I still miss her, but I don't want to forget her."

I sighed. "Yesterday, I thought I saw Trenton in the lobby of my apartment building."

"And?"

"He was smiling."

"God must have given you a glimpse of Trenton's new life."

"I want to believe he's free of all torment." My shoulders slumped. "But I'd rather have him alive. We'd just got him back and had the opportunity to redeem the lost years."

"I know it's hard. Call me day or night. I have great listening skills."

"I've seen your skills in action." I wished I could find the words to show how much I valued his friendship . . . and more.

The fellowship hall cleared of those who offered their final words of comfort. I took a peace lily plant from a table, a reminder of today that I could place on the balcony of my apartment. The white, tear-shaped blooms caught my attention as if they longed for care and nurturing. Gage carried the plant and walked me to my car.

No words . . . I had nothing to say. I had everything to say.

The weather hovered in the high nineties, blistering, humid heat.

An envelope beneath my windshield wiper caught my attention. I assumed it was a sympathy card.

I unfolded the paper—*It should have been you. Resign from the FBI immediately or face another funeral. Whose will it be? Yours? One of your parents? Your partner? Tell anyone and watch what happens.*

I gasped and crumpled the note in my hand. Trenton died because someone wanted me dead.

3

Gage asked me to show him the note on my windshield until he was red-faced. I depleted his patience, but what choice did I have? He wanted to take over the situation, and I refused. Never would I take a threat lightly—I'd seen too many instances where recipients ignored potential danger and regretted it.

I thanked him for his concern and drove to the FBI office. The horrendous rush-hour traffic on US Highway 290 reinforced my emotional anguish and stretched my nerves to the max. In the distance, the sound of blaring horns and emergency vehicles speeding to an accident rang in my ears. By the time I arrived at the FBI building, I trembled. Normally my composure accepted city-life hazards, but not on the day of my brother's funeral.

In the privacy of my cubicle, and in the quiet of the late afternoon without the pressure of anyone pressing in on me, my breathing and heart rate found a little rest.

I pulled out the threatening note from my purse and smoothed the crinkled edges and reread it. Moments later, I had my pastor on the phone.

"Sir, this is Special Agent Risa Jacobs. I'd like to thank you for taking care of my brother's funeral today. My parents and I appreciate the care you and your staff demonstrated to all who were there."

"You're welcome, and I'll pass on your appreciation. If you need to talk, we can schedule a counseling session."

"I might need to take you up on that. This call is about another matter. I'd like to see the security-cam footage of the parking lot on the east side during the service. Can you share the video?"

"Was a crime committed?"

"It appears so, and the footage could provide the identity of those involved."

"By all means."

I thanked him again and gave him my Dropbox information. He must have heard my angst, because within ten minutes he sent a link to the security-cam video. The note had to have been placed during the service and luncheon, so I scanned the footage until I observed a woman, medium height, shoulder-length, dark-brown hair, and a thin body walk across the parking lot to my car. She placed the note beneath the windshield wipers with gloved hands, either industrial or medical grade. She kept her face hidden from the cams and walked to the street, taking the sidewalk north until she disappeared into a residential area.

No matter how I pondered the note, the threat gave me no alternative. I relented to what I called a coward's stand and typed out my resignation, saved it to a file, and printed a copy for Special Agent in Charge Dunkin. The woman who'd written the note and destroyed my brother's life just thought she had the upper hand. She'd never dealt with Risa Jacobs before, make it ex–Special Agent Risa Jacobs. No protocol guidelines would hinder me, only the call for justice ripping at my heart.

I texted the SAC and requested a few minutes of his time.

Why aren't you with your family? Go home. In fact, take tomorrow off.

I need to share an important matter.

I can see you in an hour.

I'd studied HPD's report and the four witnesses who'd seen the hit, including the man who'd recorded the license plate of the SUV. To make matters worse, the light at the intersection didn't have a camera recording it, so no chance of facial recognition from a video.

The owner of the SUV, a man in his late thirties who had a clean record, reported it stolen after getting off work late afternoon at Best Buy. I contacted his HR department and learned he had an impeccable reputation and recently had been given a promotion.

The likelihood of Trenton getting mixed up with the wrong people, which he'd done in the past, pierced my heart. Those kinds of people took retribution for whatever reason that suited them. Were my motivations any different? But I shook that question off.

Trenton's criminal record reached back twelve years to age eighteen, and then his charges were underage drinking and DWIs. The problems escalated to possession and dealing. Dad had asked him why he chose to break the law, and Trenton responded with "If there's a law against it, I will break it." Trenton carried a rebellious streak that neither Mom, Dad, nor I understood. Counseling demonstrated a waste of money and energy because he quickly comprehended what to say for the therapist to release him.

I recalled one incident in his midtwenties after he'd been in jail for ten days. He'd stolen a six-pack of beer from a convenience store and struck the cashier when confronted. "Sis, I try to stop," Trenton had said. "I want to quit, but I can't. I'm damaged. No conscience. No concern for the innocent or those I love. Please, don't give up on me."

I'd prayed he'd one day fight his way through his chains of addiction.

Our sweet reunion showed God had answered our prayers. I'd uncover the who and why of the tragedy, whether it lay in Trenton's past or mine.

I noted unsavory characters from his addiction days with the reluctance of not knowing his current friends. Ah, his sponsor might remember details about Trenton that he'd omitted from the FBI interview. If not for the note informing me I was the target, I'd have been investigating those aspects of his life. First I would explore the reality of who I'd upset.

In the minutes remaining before I spoke to SAC Dunkin, I scanned through details of a recently closed child abduction by a noncustodial parent. The child had been found and returned to the mother. The father sat in jail until his court hearing. Nothing out of the ordinary. No threats. Searching through past cases with what I remembered would take lots of time. But not impossible with the upcoming free hours on my hands.

I closed down my computer and took the elevator up to the SAC's office. I'd worked under him for the six years, and while I didn't agree with his every decision, I liked and respected him.

I entered his office, and he frowned, no doubt ready to lecture me on not comforting Mom and Dad. After closing the door behind me, I eased onto a stiff chair in front of his desk. His dark-brown eyes bored into mine, a reminder of Trenton. He folded his massive hands on his desk, a mannerism he used when one-on-one.

"Thanks for seeing me." I handed him my resignation. "My brother's death has caused me to rethink my career. With the overwhelming grief, I'm concerned I might endanger lives."

"Personal time off is appropriate, Risa. Two weeks or thirty days? What seems best to you?"

"Resignation, sir."

He studied the document and seemed to digest my words. "Does this have anything to do with the note left on your windshield?"

My anger meter rose. "Gage told you."

"He's worried about the contents and the sender. He said you were upset and refused to talk further about it."

"I had just buried my brother."

"Understandable. Why don't you tell me what's in the note."

"Impossible."

"A threat?" He held up my resignation. "Since when are you a quitter?"

That pushed my anger needle even higher. "I care about my family and friends."

"We all have family and friends. They are the reason we are committed to our job."

Dare I reveal the demands? I sighed.

"Risa, you are a private person. A perfectionist. Do I need to remind you that threatening a federal officer is a federal offense?"

"Those I care about were threatened, and I was told to resign and tell no one. Now I've told you." I fought to avoid the tears pooling in my eyes.

"Someone shoved you into resigning? The person who wrote it won, and the person looks a whole lot like the one who killed your brother."

The SAC had no right to question my decision. I spoke low. "I was the intended target."

He humphed. "Which means you're still in a killer's sights."

"Possibly. But I'm not giving up on finding him or her."

"Last I checked, playing vigilante is illegal."

"I said nothing about taking the law into my hands."

The SAC sat back. Another of his mannerisms indicating he was in think-mode. Or make me think he accepted my stand. "Working on a case involving a family member is prohibited."

"I resigned, and I'll be investigating who targeted me and . . . missed."

The SAC toyed with a pen on his desk. "You have an outstanding record with the FBI."

"Thank you." What thoughts filled his mind?

"I have an idea, an exception to protocol, and I will need to clear it with DC. Think about this—as far as anyone knows, you've resigned, but you are technically on leave. The status would allow you to view the investigation into your brother's death. I'll request once the threat is resolved and an arrest is made, you'd like to return to your present division." The SAC laid his pen on the desk. "You are forbidden to work in an undercover capacity while our task force with HPD continues their investigation."

I intended to find my brother's killer. "If I do?"

He snorted. "You know the answer to that."

He offered a viable solution. Was it the best? "I'd have security access to databases, online files, and reports?"

"No more than any other agent and only after I've cleared the information and have DC approval. If so, we can set up secure access."

"And no one would know about my status but you and DC?"

"If the higher-ups agree. I have two stipulations—you must keep me informed weekly about your investigation."

I startled. "You just said—"

"I know you, Risa. This is strictly between us. If you go against any of my instructions or if I determine your methods of investigation warrant dismissal, I will bring charges against you and end your career."

"Why are you willing to help me?"

He pressed his lips together. "I chose the FBI when a cousin in high school died in a drive-by shooting. I understand your emotions, the drive to find out who killed your brother. But I don't know if my idea will pass. I'll make the call in the morning and let you know."

Without hesitation, I agreed. "I think it best if I decline a paycheck or benefits because the word would get out. I'll return to teaching." He nodded and I continued. "I plan to break relationships with everyone here and contact you from a burner."

"How much of this will you relay to your parents?"

I had no peace about abandoning them after they'd just lost their only son. "I'll call and let them know they've been threatened unless I resign and keep my distance from them. Can the FBI offer protection?"

"We can do surveillance, but nothing else unless they are threatened again. And Gage?"

"If he knows what we're doing, he'll jump in and play hero." Gage had this must-be-in-control gene. We both did.

SAC Dunkin inhaled deeply. "I must tell him something since his name's mentioned in the note."

"He's not in danger if I resign."

"Wrong. I'll tell him word on the street is to leave the investigation alone or the killer will retaliate."

"You make sense," I said. "I don't want anyone hurt."

"For all practical purposes, you are finished with the FBI. I'm calling security to escort you out with your personal effects. If this arrangement is approved, don't make me regret this."

"Yes, sir. Did you catch the person responsible for your cousin's death?"

"What do you think?"

★ ★ ★

Once home, I phoned Dad on my burner and silently coaxed him to pick up. They despised spam callers. I'd never used it to call him or Mom. Guilt about Trenton's death mounted while I needed to keep my parents safe. Two calls later Dad answered.

"Dad, I need your word that what I'm about to say goes no farther than Mom."

"Sure, baby. What's wrong? Are you in danger? In trouble?" Anxiety rippled through Dad's deep voice.

"I'm fine, but you and Mom are in danger *if* I meet with you. After Trenton's funeral, I found a note on my car demanding I resign from the FBI or expect you, Mom, Gage, or any of my friends at the FBI to be the target of the next funeral. I chose to comply. I'm to tell no one about the threat and walk away from my job, my family, and my friends. The FBI will keep an eye on you and Mom until this is over. If you receive a threat, I'd like for you to move to a secure location."

He broke into a sob, and I kept mine at bay. "Right now your mother and I need you more than ever. I don't care that this sounds selfish. It's the truth. Isn't there another way?"

"Unfortunately not. SAC Dunkin is conducting a full investigation. He'll inform me when an arrest is made. I need you and Mom to let others know I've deserted you. After the funeral, I resigned my job and claimed I needed space to heal from Trenton's death. I will check in with you periodically on this burner phone. It can't be easily traced. I'd like for you to pick up one too. That makes what I'm doing safer. Please, trust no one."

"Can't the FBI help you? Gage?" Anguish continued to smother his words.

It hurt not to tell Dad the truth. But my leave of absence must stay a secret. "They will be, and I expect an arrest will be made soon.

HPD and the FBI have formed a task force—HPD made the request since an FBI agent was involved."

"What if the person makes more demands?"

"Then I'll reach out to those who are trained law enforcement."

"Is this about Trenton's past?"

"I don't know." I couldn't tell him I was the intended victim.

He expelled a sigh of grief that seemed to come from the soles of his feet. "I believe you're working behind the scenes to find out who's responsible for Trenton's death. I have no idea if it's even legal. Be careful, little girl. We just lost one child."

Dad knew me all too well.

4

I dreaded facing my first day of teaching creative writing at Houston Community College's fall session since joining the FBI nearly seven years ago. Back then, my sweet spot focused on writing short stories and teaching writing techniques to my students.

Definitely rewarding, but I'd been bored.

Now pretending to leave the FBI, the career I treasured, and returning to academia kept those I loved safe and assured the killer that I'd complied to his demands. SAC Dunkin received permission from DC to keep my status quiet, but it took convincing on the SAC's part. A blessing if I behaved myself. I'd not received any more threats, and despite the constant searching during the weeks following Trenton's death, I hadn't found any evidence of his killer.

All my leads ended up in the trenches of failure.

Those I'd testified against were in prison or had alibis.

A shorter list of those who hadn't approved of my previous dealings with persons of interest and those charged with crimes were under investigation. From the secure FBI site, I saw Gage primarily worked Trenton's case in addition to crimes against children. Oh, how I missed him.

Trenton's pastor also counseled him and believed my brother stood strong in his faith and convictions. Trenton's sponsor claimed my brother had forsaken his previous life and not indicated any relapse. The sponsor had SAC Dunkin's contact, so I stayed true to my so-called resignation. Trenton's landlord claimed only my brother's sponsor visited him. He'd paid his rent and kept to himself.

Trenton's former employers where he'd worked as waitstaff at upscale restaurants offered excellent recommendations. Friends, past and present, cleared background checks. No one shared a bad report, and those people who'd once been a part of his life during his addiction days hadn't seen or heard from him. Yet I knew there were others from those days who were nameless. My love for Trenton and the raw grief consuming me kept my efforts devoted to justice. If I were pressed hard, I'd confess to an overzealous, near-fanatical drive.

My brother had given his life for me.

Memories of Trenton haunted me and reinforced my determination. For certain until an arrest was made, I'd not find peace or any semblance of healing. I'd play by the killer's rule book until I found the key to unlock the madness. Didn't I believe the murderer just *thought* he walked the streets free?

God, if You can do anything for me at all, please help me find my brother's killer.

The sorrow.

A wasted life. Like a desert that had once flourished with green, flowering plants.

The tears.

Memories.

A stolen future.

A gentle smile.

A quiet voice.

I watched students and faculty swing into the parking lot and exit their vehicles. They waved and smiled at each other. Didn't they know? Didn't they care? These people were strangers, not the agents I'd called friends.

I leaned my head back against the seat, longing to turn back the clock. If only I'd seen the SUV coming.

I wasn't just empty but a semblance of a walking corpse. Weighted nausea gripped me in shades of black and red, hate and anger. Acid rose in my throat. If I died today, how would I explain my rabid thirst for vengeance? How could I pray for justice and admit the dark shadows covering my soul?

My burner phone rang—Gage, the only person besides the SAC who had this number. He'd called on several occasions, but I never answered. Why repeat the lies that kept him safe? As much as I wanted to hear his voice regularly, this would be the last time. After school today, I'd replace this burner and not give him the number. The cell rang twice more before I answered.

"Is this the first day of school for Houston Community?" His deep voice brought back moments I'd taken him for granted.

"How did you know?"

"The SAC told me you planned to head back to your previous role as an English prof, and I assumed today."

"True. I enjoyed teaching in the past, and I will again."

"Do you plan to write?"

I still dabbled in short whodunits, but I needed to keep myself closed to Gage. "Possibly in the future. This is my first day, and I'm here parked in my car ready to meet my class. College students, here I come."

"Which campus?"

"Does it matter?"

He sighed. "Risa, a change in scenery is healthy. And I'm glad you want to be clearheaded before applying to the SAC for reinstatement. But you and I together have the skills to find who's behind your brother's death. Alone, you're in a vulnerable position."

"I haven't changed my mind. I'm fine. I'm thrilled to be teaching again, and I now view my time in the FBI as a learning experience."

"I know you better than that." He chuckled or I'd have hung up. "Investigation is in your blood."

"Wrong, Gage. I'm finished with that life. Contrary to popular opinion, you aren't the commander in this situation."

"You're right. I'm not or things would be different. I'd like to take you to dinner tonight, sort of a way to celebrate your professorship."

How I longed to see him, to lower my guard and enjoy his company. "We aren't working together anymore. No reason for us to have dinner." Silence met me. I hated that life demanded I hurt him. "My life is zipping down a new highway."

"So you've chosen to forget what happened to you and your brother?"

"It's not a choice when I can't do a thing about it."

"I don't believe for a minute you've decided not to find Trenton's killer. What makes you think the driver will surface when he didn't leave anything behind to track him?" Gage's voice rose with certain frustration.

"That's for HPD and whoever's working the case with them to determine."

"Who has your back?"

"I neither need nor want anyone to keep tabs on me." I despised my ugly words.

"Give this craziness up. Drive back to the office. You're a special agent, not an English professor. Why not teach law enforcement classes?"

I regretted telling him about returning to my prior career, and I wasn't jeopardizing lives by teaching law enforcement. No way I'd give the killer a reason to take retribution. I really wanted to tell Gage the truth, but the note made the repercussions clear if I stayed with the FBI. I'd catch the killer my way.

"Risa, you're tuning me out again."

"I'm watching the parking lot fill up."

"When will you be back?"

"Gage, I resigned. My FBI career is over." I spit the words out like pits of remorse.

"I'll continue to search through our past and present cases until I find your brother's killer. The FBI and HPD task force haven't given up."

I gripped the steering wheel with my free hand. "It's been two months."

"You know investigations are seldom done in a matter of days or weeks."

"My point. Someone did a stellar job of covering their tracks. The person, or persons, either followed Trenton when he left to meet with me or hacked into his phone to learn the date and place. I've gone over this until I'm dizzy, and I haven't found a single piece of evidence. That's why I returned to teaching."

"What if someone believed Trenton had given you incriminating info about a crime? What if your brother recognized the SUV?"

I let Gage's questions roll around in my mind a bit longer. "I guess we'll never have an answer. Gage, I'm done with this call. You conduct your job, and I'll educate young minds."

"What about us?"

I stumbled for the right words when I wanted to tell him I cared. More than cared, loved him. Love meant sacrifice, and I refused to lose him too.

"Risa, we've dodged the subject for too long."

"Not until I find my brother's killer."

He sighed. "I'm praying you won't get hurt."

I appreciated Gage's gesture, but I wasn't going there. I noted the time. "I can't be late for class." He wished me luck, and I dropped my phone into my purse.

No sister should lose a younger brother who had his whole life ahead of him. A soul brimming with vitality. All our conversations, laughter, and hope vanished in a vapor. It's not enough that he lived in my heart. I wanted to hug him. Hear his voice and silly puns.

I flew solo without Trenton or Gage. I didn't even have my parents. From now on, memories would have to pacify me. Stiffening my spine, I opened the car door. Grief was a vicious parasite. It had dug and clawed its way into my heart, feeding off the guilt raging through me. But I'd find a way to exterminate it.

"Are you Miss Jacobs?" a young man called out from the sidewalk leading into the building.

I studied him. Habit. Fifteen feet away. Slender. Tousled dark hair. Jeans. Black T-shirt with Jimi Hendrix playing guitar. "Yes, I am."

He approached me and stuck out his hand. "Carson Lowell. I'm in your creative writing class."

Clear blue eyes. Confident. Fresh out of high school. "Great to meet you. I'm excited about the semester. What type of writing appeals to you?"

"Murder mysteries. Suspense. Thrillers. Can't get enough of them."

5

GAGE

My cubicle closed in on me while memories of the cases Risa and I had worked scrolled through my mind. I picked up a framed photo of us from an FBI Citizens Academy fundraiser taken last fall. Three months had passed since she'd returned to teaching college kids. Not one word from her.

I missed her insight into crimes . . . her perspective . . . her sweet face and rare giggle . . . the way she walked or rather sashayed. I should have told her my feelings, but the past tormented me, stopped me, made me feel like half a man. How could I judge her for her silence when I carried my own demons?

A text from Jack, my new partner, diverted my attention. I wanted to ignore him except he deserved more respect than I'd dished out. With a sigh, I read the text.

I'm working out at 5:30. Want to join me?

You and I have too much work to do. I considered my nasty attitude and typed, **Sure. Dinner afterward? On me.**

Something up?

I've been a pain and need to apologize—over a steak.

At the scheduled hour, I entered the fitness room of the FBI building ready to mend my relationship with Jack. The cool and filtered air masked the sweat from agents beating up their bodies to keep them in shape. Some worked out before the day began, but I preferred after hours when the stress level pounded my otherwise semi-good nature.

SAC Dunkin, often referred to as Donut behind his back, talked near the weights with Jack. The SAC's physique had more to do with discipline in the gym than glazed sugar and grease.

Jack reminded me of a bulldog—wrinkled brow, grumpy frown, and large, jowly cheeks, but his mind was like a steel trap. More like brilliant. Once Jack found a piece of evidence, he chewed and drooled until he got to the marrow.

I greeted both men. "Relieving stress?"

SAC Dunkin chuckled. "Between the job and my teenagers, what do you think?"

"Single life has its benefits. I'm sure Jack agrees."

Jack pumped his fist. "Don't think I'll ever settle down. Never met a woman who admired both my handsome face and brains."

"Try registering at a dating service that specializes in desperate women," I said.

Jack grinned, all bulldog of him. "When I do find a woman, she will idolize my many talents."

"I wouldn't hold my breath if I were you."

"I had a date just last week." Jack lifted his chin.

"Where did you take her?" I could only imagine.

"Brazos Bend State Park."

"In the blazing heat?"

He frowned. "I should have taken her to the wolf sanctuary. She had this little dog that got loose."

"Had? An alligator got it?"

"Yeah. She called a friend to come and get her. Not happy with me." Jack brightened. "So I'll wait a week until she gets over losing the dog, then ask her out again."

I couldn't stop laughing. "Jack, you need a dating tutor."

"Wasn't all my fault. She insisted on carrying the dog instead of putting it on a leash. She claimed he was her emotional support."

The SAC added another ten pounds to a barbell. "I agree with Gage. You need help with women. By the way, you two closed a tough case last week. The odds were against finding the little girl alive. Congratulations." He raised the barbell over his head. "Gage, have you heard from Risa?"

Did he have a clue of my misery? I'd moped around like an ego-centered kid. "No, sir. She took her brother's death hard. Destroyed her confidence as an agent."

"She made a wise decision to resign. Her concern of endangering the lives of others spoke highly of her integrity," he said.

"I'm sure she's an asset to the college system." I felt like I'd made a job recommendation.

The SAC's phone rang, and Jack and I moved to the treadmills. "My apologies for my lousy attitude," I said.

Jack started his machine at a fast walk. "No problem. I'm a poor replacement for an ex-partner who breaks communication."

At least he didn't say a woman or mention the rumor about Risa resigning because we were in a relationship. "Appreciate it. Punch me when I'm out of line." I set my speed at eight and incline at seven, ready to sweat off the frustration and get my head in the game.

SAC Dunkin approached us. "I've got an update on the missing Addington baby. Meet me in my office in ten."

In the elevator, Jack and I kept our conversation to choosing a restaurant instead of the questions rolling through our minds about the upcoming briefing. One did not discuss a case outside the boundaries of a secure area.

My mind scrolled through the work done over the past five days on the missing six-week-old baby. CARD had immediately jumped in on the investigation. We all worked with the police, National Center for Missing & Exploited Children, behavioral analysis units, and other agencies and search teams who specialized in missing children. None of us had found a clue—yet. On the evening of the kidnapping, the parents went to dinner, leaving the baby with the maternal grandmother. She put the baby down for the night, and when she checked thirty minutes later, the baby was gone. The kidnapper gained entrance through a first-story window.

As of the day after the kidnapping, the parents, family, and close friends had been interviewed and cleared. Neighbors were questioned and nothing seemed suspicious. No communication from the kidnappers and no ransom note. All who worked crimes against children stayed on task, an emotionally charged commitment. If a child wasn't recovered and pronounced safe, many of us took the loss personally. Risa and I had shared tears more than once over the atrocities done against the helpless. I believed children were our most valuable treasure, and they deserved to be protected. I recalled an FBI director referring to finding missing kids as "holy." I agreed.

In the current case, a noncustodial parent didn't fit the crime. The most barbaric were those who held a child for ransom, and those victims seldom returned to their homes alive. My concern and many of the others in the investigation. Whatever the fate of the Addingtons' baby, the heartache had left scars on the parents, and I knew exactly how they felt. Made this case hard to work.

Behind closed doors in a square office, Jack and I sat across from SAC Dunkin. Floor-to-ceiling bookshelves holding volumes of biographies, history, politics, and various sports showed his eclectic interests. On his credenza perched vacation family pics from deep in the heart of an African jungle to salmon fishing in Alaska.

The SAC folded his hands on his desk and gave us eye contact. "We received a call from the FBI Des Moines office. A hospital there has identified the Addingtons' baby, admitted by a couple who claimed to have adopted him. Yesterday the adoptive parents rushed the baby to a Des Moines hospital for breathing problems. ER doctors suspected CF, ran tests, and administered treatment. The hospital contacted the Cystic Fibrosis Foundation registry, found the baby's records, and discovered the abduction. The kidnappers must not have known about his health issues, or they didn't care."

I digested the update. At birth, when the baby tested positive for cystic fibrosis, the parents underwent DNA testing to find out if they carried the gene. The testing was documented in national medical records. "How is he doing?"

"He's responding to treatment. The Addingtons are on their way to Des Moines now. Once the baby stabilizes and the doctors release him, they'll return to Houston. As we suspected, the kidnapping appears to be the work of an organized adoption-crime ring. One ring is closed down, another pops up."

"Good news. What's the story?" I said.

"The day after the kidnapping, a couple from Des Moines privately adopted the baby through a fraudulent agency there. The so-called director presented the adoptive parents with false medical information and a birth certificate. By the time Des Moines FBI agents arrived at the adoption agency's office building, everything had been cleared out. A security cam from a nearby building caught an unidentified man leaving the office building's parking lot in a Toyota Avalon the day after the couple adopted the baby. The car had been reported stolen."

Jack humphed. "Sophisticated operation. What are the adoptive parents saying?"

"They paid a total of forty-eight thousand dollars to Your Heart for Adoption Agency through a lawyer who specialized in private adoptions. He's the man videoed leaving in the Avalon."

"These people know how to cover their tracks," I said.

"It won't be their last illegal operation until we catch them." The SAC's dark-brown eyes hardened. "I want this baby ring found and prosecuted."

Jack glanced at me. "We have data to gather and work to do."

"I'll heat up my grill for your steak," I said. "Might be an all-nighter."

6

Jack pushed his plate back and patted his belly. "Mighty fine steak. Thank you."

I chuckled. "Not sure that's a compliment considering you like it cooked somewhere between tree bark and leather."

"Yours topped the perfect list." An evening shadow had risen on his face, adding to his bulldog resemblance. "I'm ready to work on the Addingtons' case. CARD's done an outstanding job, as usual. Now I want to find who's behind the operation." Jack carried his plate and utensils to the sink and stuck them in the dishwasher without rinsing, a true bachelor. He took mine and did the same. I liked the guy, a bit odd in his eating habits, especially when he dumped horseradish on his baked potato and ketchup on his bread. But I had my weird moments too.

I reached into my junk drawer and pulled out a pen and one of my many legal pads. "Let's work through what we have."

"I brought my iPad. The only way to travel."

"Until your battery dies. Nothing beats personal notes. You should try it."

Jack held up his iPad and shook his head.

Seated again at the table, we reviewed SAC Dunkin's briefing, investigative findings, and interview information regarding the latest development in locating the Addingtons' baby.

"The best news is the baby's been found," I said. "Michael and Sarah Addington did an interview on Fox, and I have the transcript."

"I have the footage," Jack said. "Seen it three times to ensure we weren't suckers for a scam. Nothing jumped out at me except their vow to not rest until the person or persons who kidnapped their baby is behind bars. We don't need them getting in our way."

"I think either one of them would strangle those responsible." My emotions took a quick dip and I internally shook off the past. "The Addingtons have been married five years. No altercations. Both are elementary school teachers. This is their first child, named after his father. I wasn't aware newborns were given a screening test for cystic fibrosis until the SAC briefed us."

"I did." Jack finished a glass of supersweet iced tea. "Says here the adoptive parents, Alex and Nanette Wade, own a hardware store. Been married fifteen years. Childless. Traditional attempts to adopt were rejected due to Alex Wade's prior conviction of a homicide before the couple were married. They learned about a private adoption agency in Des Moines. After reading the testimonies and contacting two couples who had adopted through the agency and were pleased with their experience, the Wades moved forward.

"Over the course of eight weeks, they handed over forty thousand dollars for a newborn, then eight grand more to assist the woman posing as pregnant with medical costs. Presently the Wades have been cleared of any criminal offense." He leaned back in his chair. "I'd have researched the agency inside and out before I handed over that amount of money."

"Think about it. Seems like the Wades felt like they'd done their due diligence, and they believed in the private adoption agency who claimed to help those who wanted a child. We've seen what people will do to have a child of their own. Check through the mound of parental-abduction cases our division processes."

"Yeah, I have the stats in my head, but it doesn't mean I think the victims used their heads."

I swallowed my anger. "Adopting a child involves emotion. While those seeking adoption believe they are following the law, that's not always the case. We'll interview the Addingtons and the Wades—everyone involved. Add the authorities in Des Moines. HPD initially had the kidnapping case, and we have their records."

Jack wrinkled his nose. "What about the Addingtons' pediatrician and the grandmother?"

"On my list. The grandmother is cleared. The adoption ring obviously falsified information. If this ring's been around awhile, they wouldn't have gambled on not being researched for the short term they were in operation."

Jack held up a finger. "I'm checking to see how long they've been in Des Moines."

While I waited, I made a note for Jack and me to check Houston and Des Moines maternity homes. Often mothers or couples were approached to sell their baby. Kidnapping was cheaper for the baby ring than buying, but less risky. A woman who sells her baby isn't concerned about the legality or reporting the transaction to the authorities.

"I have our answer," Jack said. "Your Heart for Adoption Agency in Des Moines set up an office and closed in twelve weeks. FBI is investigating other potential adoptive parents who received a child or paid for services."

"How many adoptive parents who went through the agency will come forward? And risk losing their child?" The depth of heartache these people must feel tugged at me.

"Although I can't argue with their off-kilter emotions, their silence interferes with justice." Jack shook his head. "We don't have time to waste to find how the agency is paid, the contracts, brochures, references, birth certificate, arrangements made to deliver the child, and medical information used to deceive these innocent people."

"Unless you've been in the victims' shoes, you can't pass judgment."

"I have to find more empathy." Jack stood and paced the floor. "It's integral to unearth their vulnerable areas. Interviews will guide us in the right direction. All those weak points where the perps could slip up."

"Let's send requests to the FIG tonight and a request to the Des Moines FBI for a list of maternity home centers, beginning with those that provided housing, offered adoption assistance, taught life skills and education classes to those women who had no place to go. Many of whom were destitute. Ask if they have agents available to interview those centers. Many of the young mothers plan to give up their babies for adoption, and some would be enticed by money. First thing in the morning, we can scout out a few maternity home centers here in the city," I said.

"High end or low end?"

"The women who live in low-end facilities are destitute, and a higher percentage give up their babies. If approached by a ring, they'd take a smaller amount than those mothers in the high-end centers." I shook my head. "But the Addingtons' baby was taken from their home, which meant no money exchanged hands until the Wades handed over their cash." I paused. "Abortion clinics are another source to find young women willing to give birth for money."

The enormity of what lay ahead meant hours of running down leads and interviewing those who might have insight into the kidnapping. Jack continued to pace. "What's bothering you?" I said.

"I'm back to other people who have been duped by illegal adoption. Most people would want to see justice done. This division is relatively new to me, under two years, so what am I missing? I'm used to violent crime against adults. Why is it so hard to have the scammed people come forward? I know these are kids, but why would anyone want to keep a human being who belonged to someone else?"

The bulldog gnawed on a bone.

"Jack, we're talking about people who ache to have a child of their own. They feel like they've been cursed by nature. This isn't a pet but innocent babies and their parents. The adoptive parents are as much victims as the biological ones. Every second counts to someone who has a kidnapped child or fears their long-awaited adopted baby isn't theirs. Yes, we need to learn the truth, but not everyone is willing to relinquish a child."

"I'm doing my best to see your viewpoint," Jack said. "I don't have kids or any nieces or nephews to understand all the emotions." He paused. "But I remember how my folks protected me and my sister."

Regret twisted in me. "I don't have kids in my life either, but the emotions will hit you hard when you least expect it. We might uncover more than one organized ring and still not find the ones behind the Addingtons' case. Could even be an international crime ring."

"Do you have the physical and mental capacity to see this through to the end?"

My blood pressure rose a few notches. "Why would you ask that?"

"The situation with Risa has you off your game."

"Since when?"

Jack shrugged. "She broke the well-oiled machine and deserted you. Seems to me you'd be better suited for another area or transfer to another office."

I held back the anger threatening to erupt. "I do whatever it takes for *every* situation to ensure the law is followed and people are protected against criminals. I don't have my own agenda. Don't ever ask me again if I'm qualified to do my job. Look. At. My. Track. Record."

Jack stared at me. "My apologies. I engaged my mouth without thinking, one of my many faults."

I calmed down. Hadn't I treated him like scum? "Risa and I were business partners. She chose to return to a previous career and leave the FBI behind, in many ways like your former partner."

Jack held up both hands. "Sorry I screwed up the evening."

"It's okay. We need to figure out our strengths and challenges. How about sealing our partnership with hot apple pie?"

"You bake?"

"Nah. But my microwave thaws out a mean pie."

Jack finally lowered himself into the chair. "I'm not Risa, and I understand your missing her after weeks without her and putting up with the likes of me. But we have brought down a few people who were the subjects of investigations, and we'll bring down this bunch too. Trust me. Whoever is responsible is on a short leash."

7

RISA

Tonight loneliness held me captive in a cell of my own making. My apartment seemed to haunt me with those I loved. I missed the close relationship I'd always shared with my parents. Gage, my best friend, seemed like someone I knew in another lifetime, not five months ago. I envied his new partner, Jack Bradford. When his previous partner had requested a division change, Jack ended up with Gage.

The urge to call and hear his voice tugged at me. The adage of not really missing someone until they were gone was a reality and a heartache. When I finally returned to the FBI—and I fully intended to—maybe I could be honest with Gage. The tenderness in his eyes when we were together told me he kept his feelings on lockdown too. The fear of losing my friend to gain a romantic relationship had stopped me from sharing my heart. The puzzle pieces refused to slide into place. Now regrets pelted me like a stoning.

I swiped the tears from my cheeks and tossed a spinach and chicken salad down the garbage disposal. Another dinnerless day. Were Mom and Dad okay? Oh, I'd hurt them with no face-to-face interactions. Phone calls helped, but those didn't remove the longing. My poor parents had lost a son and now their only remaining child waved from a distance. Dad's birthday had come and gone—a day we always feasted on Greek food. But this year Dad and Mom opted for Tex-Mex.

SAC Dunkin had authorized my continued security access, and I'd used the sites to dig into any potential links to those who might want me dead. I forwarded all info that needed FBI attention to him, and he researched the matter and got back to me. I needed to unravel the motive. That would help unlock the door to finding the killer. The longer my brother's case remained open, the more it faded into the FBI's and HPD's background. Other issues vied for their attention. But not my brother's death. I knew firsthand the situation, but still anger seized me when I least expected it.

I investigated a woman I'd sent to prison for selling child porn online. At sentencing, she'd vowed to kill me. She'd been released six months ago. Since then, she participated in counseling and worked at a fast-food restaurant. Some people rehabilitated but many slipped back into old habits. Their commitment depended on those who positively influenced them balanced with a vow to stay clean. The SAC told me what I already knew—the woman had all the outward appearances of one who'd learned from her mistakes.

The silence in my apartment had a ghostly feel, as though Trenton watched over me. Not a spooky feeling but a presence I'd sensed many times. Even welcomed. I doubted the sensation fit into anything scriptural, but the awareness comforted me. I'd asked God to send me reassurance that Trenton was loved and happy. Perhaps my recurring dream of my smiling brother answered my pleas.

How would I ever come to terms with Trenton dying for me?

Opening my laptop, I sent my students a message through the class portal.

Reminder. Short stories due Friday.

Half of my students' grades came from this final assignment, and I supported their success in finishing the course well. Something in my life needed to be positive. I shook my head. What a self-centered attitude. My grief wouldn't last forever, and if I lost hope in finding

Trenton's killer, the depression would cuff me. My English doctorate and past professorship had gotten me this job, but writing updates in craft and style kept me up late.

I rested my chin on my palm and stared at my laptop screen. My students held a lot of potential, and they worked hard. Watching them grasp techniques and apply them to their writing filled me with . . . satisfaction. I longed to be back at the FBI, yet teaching allowed me to give back to others and fill the longing to inspire and encourage young writers. It probably had a lot to do with the constructive influence of my upbringing.

A response to my class's reminder arrived from Carson Lowell via the portal's chat feature. If I had a teacher's pet, it just might be him. Since my first day, he'd entertained me with his wit and humor, my best student scholastically, and he had the gift of personality. Laughing, I clicked on his name.

> Professor Jacobs, I'd like to turn in my short story tomorrow due to a road trip I'm taking with some friends over the Christmas holidays, starting on Thursday. Is that okay?

> Sure. Enjoy your road trip.

The clock moved toward eleven thirty. I'd try to sleep, but I imagined a repeated restless night.

After little sleep and chastising myself for not seeing what I was missing in Trenton's death, I downed three cups of black coffee and attempted to clear my head for class. Three more days until Christmas break, which meant time alone like the long Labor Day weekend, Thanksgiving, and now Christmas. Holiday decorations were for happy people, not me. My apartment resembled a pagan's.

The next morning, leaving the silence of my home surroundings, I drove to the college campus. I switched the radio to Christmas music, but my heart couldn't handle the season. "Silent Night," "Deck the Halls," and "O Come, All Ye Faithful" had been benchmarks of my faith. Had been. The melodies and words now churned my stomach. I pounded the steering wheel and flipped off the radio.

My lecture today focused on a review of the semester in creative writing and a Q and A. Tomorrow they'd have a written exam. On Friday, I wanted to hear their comments about the class, how it could be improved. What they liked or didn't like and suggestions for additional topics. I'd insisted the students not only complete assignments but submit them for publication. The success of seeing their work in print encouraged them and added to their portfolio of writing accomplishments. I arrived early and scanned my notes before the students arrived. How would I spend my hours during Christmas break? The kids slowly trickled in. They laughed and talked, their enthusiasm for life becoming my inspiration for a brighter tomorrow.

"In our sessions together," I said, "we've covered the fundamentals of writing and publishing with proven techniques. We've talked about the influence of social media in building a platform and developing quality content for followers. We've discussed freelance and magazine writing with an emphasis on research. Your assignments have included practice on every topic covered—query letters, markets for you to submit your work, and submission. Part of your classwork was to submit your work, and some of you are now published. Self-editing tips moved your writing to the next level. We discussed the importance of critique partners and writing groups to improve professional habits and help other writers. We discussed creating a short story, which is 50 percent of your final grade. Questions before we move on?"

"Can I use climate fiction as a setting for my short story?" a female student said. "I wrote it in another genre, but I really like this one."

"Your choice," I said. "Your grade won't be based on genre but on the structure and content of a short story. In your example, setting is crucial, so use it to create a powerful story. You have two more days before the project is due."

A male student shot up his hand. "How much backstory do I need in a fantasy short story?"

"Enough to show character motivations and behavior," I said.

"Can my short story be a chapter from a book?" the same young man said.

"As long as it stands alone and meets the criteria for the assignment."

I'd considered having each student write their own backstory leading up to why they had registered for my class. But I often completed the same assignments as requested of them, and none of these young minds needed to read about my tragedy.

8

Thursday evening, I fought the urge to call Gage . . . just to hear his voice. We'd spent past Christmases as friends, and I'd always taken him for granted. Even then I wanted more. I finished a bowl of Frosted Flakes and milk—my typical evening meal—and closed the blinds to the city's sparkling holiday lights outside my living room window. Balancing a fresh cup of coffee in one hand, I curled up on the sofa with my laptop. A dog would be good company if I wasn't allergic and detested dust. Instead, I used a quilt that my favorite aunt had made for me when I graduated from Quantico. I checked FBI secure sites for any information leading to Trenton's killer—and found the usual nothing. Either deep within my research or hiding in plain sight dangled the evidence.

Other than Carson, my students would be sending me their stories tomorrow, but boredom and curiosity needled at me to read Carson's project tonight. His mind often translated topics with a bit of humor, and he used the technique when writing murder mysteries, even poetry and essays. Although I no longer cared to read about gruesome deaths, his voice added depth to his writing. I opened the file containing Carson's short story "Right Day, Wrong Body." I sighed, much preferring to read a sci-fi or fantasy with a heavy dose of Middle Earth or an alternate universe.

Houston's summers melt the ice in a killer's veins, but the heat just makes him meaner. I know this for a fact. I'm that killer. I crave violence any way I can get it. My favorite color is red, blood red, and I like it best when pooled beside a dead body. Eyes open and staring into nothingness. So while good people are glued to the TV, I get into my car, turn the AC to max, and search for someone to fill my cravings. But tonight I have my target. A woman. I know where she lives and how she fills her hours.

I drive closer to her high-rise apartment building and turn off the obscene rap pounding in my ears. Don't need a distraction. I park and wait. What luck! She's out walking. Now I can eat the pizza beside me instead of using it for a fake delivery.

I have people fooled. They think I'm a good guy 'cause I make sure they see what they want to see and hear what they want to hear. I'm safe, a role model for their kids. But not tonight. I'm on the prowl. She shouldn't have gotten in my way.

My sweet beauty crosses the street a block from her apartment at an intersection and enters the corner restaurant. I swing into the adjacent parking lot and park where I have a direct view through the windows surrounding the dining area. She slips into a booth near a window on the street side. But I have a straight view from my car. She's alone. Deep into her phone. I'd pull the trigger now, but I prefer to see blood up close. I bite into a piece of Canadian bacon and extra cheese pizza, my favorite. Then another. And another. I should have gotten myself a Coke.

Twenty minutes go by, and a tall guy joins her. They hug. She swipes at a tear. They're both in jeans, and she's in a navy-blue tank top. The two sit across from each other. He picks up her hand. Are they together? I haven't seen him before. They order and talk, but she doesn't eat. My gut's growling even after the pizza. Wish I could read lips. Is he FBI too?

I gasped and spilled coffee on my quilt. Heat rushed into my face. I'd worn a blue tank top the night Trenton was killed. I'd tossed it in the trash afterward. How could I continue reading Carson's story, the one that mirrored mine and Trenton's? An eerie tug on my heart drew me back to the screen. I had to read more, find out where it led.

The guy pays the bill, and I pull my car to the one-way street. They leave together. He must be walking her home because they wait at the crosswalk until the signal indicates it's safe to cross the street. I hope he doesn't plan to stay the night. Then I shrug. If he does, then I'll have two for the price of one. I laugh at my own joke. An idea settles on me. I'm brilliant!

I pull my car first into the line of traffic. At eight seconds remaining on the crosswalk, she nears my front hood. I press on the gas pedal. I'm anticipating rich, red blood from her and maybe the guy too.

But he sees me coming and shoves her out of the way! How dare he! I race through the intersection, dragging his body a few feet. He deserves his fate. Blood is blood.

I speed down the street for several blocks and whip around a corner to an area where security cams are non-existent. I park and take off on foot in a state of euphoria, an empty pizza box in my hand. Several blocks later, I start up my own car.

Sweet blood. Until we meet again.

I covered my mouth while a cauldron of horror swirled through me, and I hurried to the bathroom. My stomach revolted against the milk and cereal I'd eaten earlier. How many times had I relived that night? The walls of my apartment closed in on me as though whispering, taunting me that I was to blame for my brother's death. I rinsed my mouth and washed my face, then stared into the mirror.

You were the one supposed to die. Trenton's death is your fault.

Carson's story mocked my sorrow.

How did he know I was that woman?

How did he know about the FBI?

How did he know I wore a navy-blue tank top?

How did he know I waited twenty minutes for Trenton and busied myself on my phone?

How did he detail our dinner?

How did he create the exact scene when Trenton sacrificed his life for me?

Only one way. Carson had driven the SUV that killed my brother. I'd been duped by a nineteen-year-old who thirsted for blood.

9

Walking the floor only tightened the wrench gripping my heart. As an FBI agent, I should process Carson's story as a professional, which meant separating myself from despairing emotions. But the monster called grief took priority over logic, and I hated it.

I completed a background on Carson Lowell, and he was squeaky-clean. By digging deeper into secure sites, I searched for a cover-up crime committed before he turned eighteen. Again clean. For all who read his experiences, Carson played the role of a young man stepping his feet into the waters of college life. The nightmarish question rolled like credits of a bad movie.

Gage and I had worked cases together. Why target me and not him? Not that I wanted anyone to hurt Gage—or worse—I simply wanted to learn the motive and perpetrator.

Had Carson been recruited to commit murder?

Was he a psychopath who'd gone undetected?

Had I unknowingly angered him in the past?

I returned to the sofa and cleaned the coffee stain on my quilt while my mind spun with what-ifs. I searched my laptop and rechecked the few cases I'd worked alone. Minor incidents with little or no evidence of conviction. I recalled a missing child case in which the child had wandered off at a mall and was recovered hours later. I'd testified on several cases, and I had a list of those names and altercations, some with Gage.

I was fishing for answers with an empty hook, and yet I cast farther.

Twice I picked up my burner phone to call Gage, but was I using Carson's story as an excuse to reach out to him? Dare I risk putting him in danger? Or was my discovery destined to end the trauma that had torn us apart? My eyes rested on the phone again. Carson might have killed my brother or witnessed the hit. Perhaps been in the car with the person who committed the unthinkable.

Gage had clarity of thought, and he'd analyze Carson's story and sift through the facts and fiction. How in the world I managed to receive my doctorate in English by age twenty-four was a mystery when I failed to analyze a teen's short story.

Should I contact the SAC with my dilemma or act like a big girl and decide how to proceed? In the past, I'd prayed for direction, but now I was on my own.

I used my new burner phone and pressed in Gage's burner number. Did he still have the same phone? I wrestled with if I wanted him to pick up or let it ring. I needed his wisdom and guidance, even if I had to swallow a little pride. My instincts told me I needed to swallow a whole lot of pride.

He answered, and I nearly lost my nerve and hung up.

"Hello," he repeated.

"Gage, this is Risa."

"Are you okay?" His words jumbled from his mouth.

I braved ahead, squeezing my eyes shut to ward off unprofessional tears. "I have a situation. Can you talk?"

"I'm at home. Jack Bradford is with me."

"Your new partner?" I hoped envy didn't seep through my words while I pretended that I wasn't aware of him and Jack.

"Yes. Hold on, and I'll move to my office."

I'd seen in the FBI files that Jack and Gage had partnered. Oddly enough, I felt betrayed when I'd been the one to take action. When Gage rejoined me, I relayed Carson's story and its uncanny resemblance to the night of Trenton's death.

"A background on this kid goes a long way."

Telling Gage I already had researched him meant confessing to a leave from the FBI instead of a resignation. "Would you pull his record? I'm asking quite a bit, which—"

"No problem. This is necessary. Hang on while I read it."

The moments ticked by. Did I want Gage to find that Carson had a record when I hadn't? My confidence in managing my FBI career had dipped below sea level. Honestly, I wanted answers more than if I'd misjudged one of my students.

"Here's what I have," Gage said. "No traffic violations. No record. He lives with his mother and stepdad—Ethan and Lynn Mercury."

"Sounds like he's a typical nineteen-year-old kid who couldn't have fabricated his story about his English professor's former life."

"Have you asked him to explain it?"

"He left today on a road trip with friends. I don't have his cell number or his parents' phone at home, but I have an address."

"Risa, you recovered more in one night than the FBI and HPD have learned in months. The kid's story isn't a coincidence. I'll be at your apartment in twenty minutes. We'll interview the parents together."

"That's impossible—"

"Risa. I'm a part of this case. Email me the story and anything you've missed or haven't told me."

"What about Jack?"

"He and I will continue working our case in the morning. About to wrap it up for the night anyway."

I didn't believe him. "Are you sure? I can call later."

"No. This is good."

"Take down this number. It's a new burner." I gave him the numbers and hoped I wasn't making a terrible mistake. I wanted to see Gage. Desperately. And I needed his wisdom to figure this out, but fear crawled into my heart. Was anyone still keeping tabs on me?

"I'll email the story and be waiting out front." Had I chosen selfishness?

10

GAGE

Jack sat patiently at my kitchen table while I read Carson Lowell's story, and I felt certain an arrest for Trenton's murder would happen soon. I told Jack that Risa wanted to talk. He stared at me and squinted, a trait I'd noted when he thought through his words.

"You need to see Risa and offer an assist about what's bothering her. We've worked two nights in a row on the Addingtons' case," Jack said. "I'm all for a break to process the evidence or lack thereof. Sometimes my mind needs to let the truth weave in and out of my brain cells. We can prep in the morning for the maternity home interviews."

"Thanks. The Wades and their attorney arrive in Houston tomorrow afternoon. You still okay about meeting them around four at the office?"

Jack snorted. "Armed with more questions than they want to consider. I anticipate those three have concocted a strategy to dismiss us like warm beer."

I smiled at his comparison. "Depends on our questions. I'm suspicious of their offer to meet us on our territory. Might have a lot to do with the forty-eight thousand paid for the Addingtons' baby."

Jack stood. "I sincerely doubt we'll put an end to the malefaction tonight. In the meantime, I'm leaving so you can see Risa." He dipped his hands into his pant pockets. "Does she know you're in love with her?"

I mentally punched his jaw. "What?"

Jack laughed. "If this bachelor detects it, so does half the world."

I held up my hand. "Ridiculous."

"Sure. I'll see you in the morning at seven. We'll start the maternity home interviews early."

On the drive to pick up Risa, I wrestled with Jack's observation about my feelings for her and the truth of his words. Made me feel like a fool. Great. How many others detected my pitiful affections for a woman who'd slammed me out of her life? When I thought about what I wanted to make my life complete—a life with Risa and a family—I refused to give up, but the future didn't hold much optimism.

I determined to do a better job of concealing my emotions and put a stop to the rumors.

My mind swept over Carson Lowell's story mirroring Trenton Jacobs's death. After grabbing my phone on the console, I dictated questions at bullet speed. "Did Risa uncover more than a driver having a joyride in a stolen car? Why did Carson put himself out there as a killer, or could he have deep psychological problems? Did his parents have an idea of his behavior? What about his friends?"

Risa's apartment building—luxury living for the contemporary single woman—seemed like the last place she'd live. The lifestyle didn't fit her. Never had. Why pay the exorbitant rent to live here? She claimed not to enjoy the latest fashion and trends or the nightlife, and she had the early-to-bed, early-to-rise mentality. Unless she'd changed over the past months.

She stood outside the double-glass door front entrance. At least, I thought it was Risa. If I didn't know her so well, I'd be wondering about the woman in the wide-brimmed suede hat and jeans. But the moment she headed my way, I recognized her, the ease of how she placed one foot in front of the other. My pulse escalated. I pulled up next to her, and she slid into the car.

When she placed the legal pad and pen on the console between the front seats, I grinned to break the tension. Seemed like the last five months had vanished. She'd grown out her coffee-brown hair until it lay on her shoulders in soft waves, but little else had changed. She'd lost weight . . . too much, but I remembered her inability to eat when upset. Her cheeks were hollow and her body bone thin.

"Thanks for offering to visit Carson's parents." Her voice trembled yet her green eyes avoided me. "I'm sure you and Jack have a heavy caseload."

"He and I are good." I entered traffic. Risa's nervousness wasn't a characteristic I'd often detected. "You look great. Like the hat and longer hair."

"Thanks." She kept her attention on the street as we crossed the intersection where Trenton had lost his life.

"I miss our times together," I said. "I mean working cases."

"Seems like another person, and that woman no longer exists."

Whoa. Not the way I'd imagined our evening together after all this time. I'd keep this purely business. "I completed a little more background information on Carson. High school records show the kid graduated first in his class, played basketball on the varsity team, a member of a photography club, and active in a Christian club. His stepfather, Ethan Mercury, owns an alarm business with offices in various cities across the US. Highly respected. He coaches basketball on a private league where Carson also played, and his mother, Lynn, volunteers at an elementary school."

"Their activities could be a front." She focused on the street ahead.

"We've seen fronts before. Other than the kid's story, are you enjoying teaching?"

"For the most part. The students' enthusiastic personalities and eagerness for the future give me an optimistic perspective for tomorrow." She frowned. "That sounded straight from academia land. The simple answer is yes."

"I'm sure you give 110 percent like always. Are they all working toward careers in some type of writing?"

"Most are English majors. Some students believed my class would be an easy A. But I challenge them."

"I'm not surprised. Have you learned any information about Trenton?"

"No, why would I?"

"Because you never walk away from anything."

"Haven't discovered a thing until tonight. My involvement in investigation is in the past. I'll leave it to the pros."

Risa had her game on. She wouldn't admit a thing that I might question. Why? Was I reading more into her avoidance of my questions and lack of eye contact? "Just checking."

"Do you think the killer is passing out kudos?" She shook her head. "I'm sorry. None of this is your fault."

"Neither is it yours, but you're not convinced. Before we get to the Mercurys', what's my role?"

"A friend who's accompanying me."

"All right. No need to alert them of my FBI ID. I've recorded questions on my phone." I nodded at my device. "Send them to your burner." Saying "like old times" nearly fell from my mouth.

She handled the transfer. "What are you and Jack working on, or can't you say?"

The kidnapping case had been all over the media. "The Addingtons' baby kidnapping."

"The baby could have died without routine care for CF. When I read about it, I thought the biological parents and the adoptive parents were both victims. Any leads?"

I swung her a grin. "Really, Risa?"

She laughed, the musical delight I'd longed to hear. "It's hard to give up old habits. I'm sure you and Jack will make solid arrests."

I parked in front of the Mercurys' home. The man was worth millions. Lived in an upper-class neighborhood but not elite like I expected. Two-story home, modern architecture, and lots of windows as though the owners had nothing to hide. Caroling angels and a manger scene decorated the front yard, and white lights lined the roof.

While many people encouraged goodwill toward men during the Christmas season, others seized the opportunity to rob and destroy. Somewhere in my Christianity, a bit of cynicism had taken residence about this time of year. Need to shred doubts about God caring for His people, but first I needed to make peace with what happened nineteen years ago on Christmas Eve.

The clock moved toward 8 p.m. when Risa and I approached the

Mercurys' wreathed front door. Risa rang the doorbell, our routine only months ago. A middle-aged man, average height, with fiery-red hair and a matching trimmed beard, answered the door.

"Mr. Mercury?" Risa said. "I'm Professor Risa Jacobs, Carson's creative writing prof."

"Yes." He startled. "Is Carson all right?"

"I believe so. Do you and your wife have a moment to talk?"

"What's wrong that our son's college professor shows up on our doorstep?"

Risa waved away the question. "He requested to turn in his project early due to a road trip. I have questions about it and thought you could answer them. He's not picking up on his phone, and I don't have your numbers. I want to make sure his grade is accurate." She pointed to me. "This is Gage Patterson, a friend."

Ethan Mercury studied us a moment. "Carson is on a road trip in the Colorado Rockies with his buds."

"I'm sure he's enjoying every minute," Risa said.

Mercury shook my hand and gestured us inside. Gorgeous home. High ceilings. Open space. Neutral and gray colors. Huge plants, probably not real. We were seated in a living area with a white-stone fireplace that hit the two-story mark. Four stockings hung from the mantel, and a nine-foot Christmas tree stood in the corner. Welcoming. Homey.

Mrs. Mercury, a blue-eyed blonde, entered the room with a chubby baby and introduced herself as Lynn. "And this is Caleb. He insists bedtime is somewhere in the future." The woman eased onto a sofa beside her husband.

"Lynn, this is Carson's English professor, Risa Jacobs, and her friend Gage Patterson. The professor is trying to locate Carson about his final paper." Ethan swung his attention to Risa. "I'll get him for you." He pulled his phone from his jean pocket and pressed in numbers. After a moment he spoke. "Carson, this is Dad. Give us a call. Your English professor wants to talk to you." He set the phone on his knee. "Who knows what those guys are doing, and they could be out of range."

"Can I have his number?" Risa pulled a notepad from her purse and jotted down Ethan's response. "Thanks. He told me about the road trip."

Lynn patted the baby's back. "It was a last-minute thing. He'll be gone until Christmas Eve, so if you aren't able to talk to him sooner, I'll have him contact you then. When I peeked in his room earlier, I saw he took his laptop, or we'd pull up his assignment."

The Cloud would have his project, but I wouldn't mention it.

Risa handed her a business card from the college. "Appreciate this. Do you expect to hear from him?"

"We're trying to give him space and let him mature. Knowing Carson, he'll call us with all he and the guys are doing." Lynn wound a strand of long blonde hair behind her ear. "And nothing's wrong? He raves about your class."

A smile spread over Risa's face. "Your son is a gifted writer. I see he's an English major."

"He loves words. Always been a huge reader. His dream is to one day teach high school English and write."

"We're extremely proud of our son," Ethan said. "He's part of our church's college class. Has gone on several mission trips. He's never given us an ounce of trouble."

I saw no deceit in the man.

"You have every right to be proud. He's one of my favorite students."

Lynn lifted Caleb to her shoulder and patted his back. "I really want to know why you need to see our son. Your visit is highly irregular, which tells me there's a serious problem."

"Mrs. Mercury," Risa began, "I need to be assured that his short story, which is 50 percent of his grade, is actually his work. I've never had a reason to doubt the validity of Carson's writing assignments or his integrity. That's why I want to verify the project before the semester ends."

Lynn paled. "He could fail the class?"

"Neither you nor I want him to face the consequences of a mis-understanding."

"We assure you he'll be in contact," Ethan said. "Carson is a responsible young man."

"Thank you." Risa glanced at me. "I think we've taken up enough of this family's time."

Moments later we were on the road.

"What am I missing?" She rubbed her temples. "It's late and I need to process what this could mean. For all practical purposes, the Mercurys are the perfect family." She inhaled deeply. "Can I call you tomorrow?"

I tapped the steering wheel. "I'm booked solid and have a possible trip on Saturday." *If you hadn't resigned, we'd be taking the flight together.*

"I understand. Thanks for coming tonight."

"Why have you ignored me . . . and your parents?"

"Gage, I must do this my way. Grieving isn't easy."

"Someone's playing with you. I know it like I know my name. Walking away from the FBI, from me, when we could resolve the crime . . . will make solving his death happen far into the future."

"You have this know-it-all attitude when you don't have the details. I'm grieving the loss of my brother. I've sacrificed my career to protect you from me losing focus in a dangerous situation. How about a 'thank you, you're doing the right thing'?"

"If you'd been concerned about my safety, you could have changed divisions."

"A fogged brain puts everyone in danger."

"Sounds like an excuse to me."

A wall of ice formed between us. "Have you written off Trenton's death since I'm not around?"

"Seriously? Nearly five years of working together, and you ask me if I've swept a case off my desk?"

"Exactly. Have you stamped my brother's case with 'lack of evidence' and moved on to build your résumé?"

Anger hit me hard. "If you want to believe I've neglected my commitments, go right ahead, Professor Jacobs."

We sat side by side, light-years apart, until I dropped her off in front of her apartment building. Not the warm conversation I'd wanted from the woman I loved. Nope. I'd been dumped.

11

RISA

Predators of the heart destroyed more lives than bullets, and Gage had pierced mine with his words.

Anger rushed through my body and left me trembling. I paced the floor of my apartment's living area. Gage had tossed accusations at me like poison darts. How dare he think I didn't have the skills to find Trenton's killer? I'd made sacrifices to protect others . . . and he wasn't aware of the note or the demands.

I sank onto the sofa. Gage, my friend—the man I couldn't share my heart with because I feared no longer being able to work with him. How could I have flung such ugly words?

You owe him an apology.

How long had it been since I'd heard the voice of God whispering to my heart? I needed someone to blame, and God abandoned me. He stepped aside and permitted Trenton's death when He could have prevented it.

I clenched my fist. I pointed the finger at myself as well. I'd committed more than my share of mistakes, and the guilt of causing the accident made me ill. I mean, I knew deep down my sins had nothing to do with Trenton's death, but it felt so much like I was responsible.

Memories scraped the scabs off my heart. Oh, the guilt and the shame. The combination of the two caused incredible depression, and I felt like the poster child. Maybe instead of me making a mistake, I was the mistake? If that were true, then I was of no value to anyone.

Why didn't I ask Trenton to call Mom and Dad from the restaurant? In the quiet atmosphere, he could have talked to them. I didn't think, and now Trenton was a memory. Mom and Dad weren't given an opportunity to hear firsthand about his life change and faith conversion.

Guilt.

Shame.

Blame.

Selfishness.

Gage had pointed out how the FBI was equipped to solve the open case. I'd reacted like a toddler throwing a temper tantrum. He deserved an apology. I picked up my burner phone and texted.

I'm sorry. No excuse for lashing out at you.

Gage's response came within seconds. **I ignored your feelings. I needed a muzzle on my mouth.**

You were right. I was wrong.

I'm in the lobby.

I typed, **You parked?**

Yes, I'd like to talk.

Talk about what? Carson's story? New evidence in the case? Jack? Surely not Gage and me . . . I owed him a chance to say whatever was on his mind without blowing up or telling him how much I loved him. If anyone had seen me leave with him, they'd surely watch him entering my apartment. But why would someone have constant surveillance on an ex-FBI agent? That had to be an idle threat. I placed my fingers on the keyboard.

I'll ok your access. I miss my friend.

I stood and stretched to put optimism and hope back into my battered mind. My gaze captured the coffee maker—our past habit of drinking and talking through investigations. If I brewed coffee, he might stay longer. Did I want Gage inside my apartment when I cared for him far too much? Were the wrong people watching, ready to make good on their threats?

My doorbell rang. My head pounded. Why? Foolish for me to deliberate about my roller-coaster emotions. I started the coffee bean grinder and answered the door.

"Hey." He leaned on one foot. "I hear a woman living here needs help reading between the lines of a story."

Sweet Gage. "She does, and she'll do her best not to throw poison darts at the comments."

He chuckled, and I stepped aside for him to enter. "Come in. What about coffee?"

"Are those beans from the coffee shop around the corner?"

"Your nose is working. Those are the special dark-roast beans from Kenya." I gestured for the towering man to sit. "Let me do a pour-over." I went through the motions of coffee making and shoved aside the nostalgia.

"Okay to sit at the bar?" he said. "In case I spill coffee and stain your sofa."

I smiled and allowed myself the luxury of gazing into the blue-gray eyes that held a hint of sorrow. "I am sorry."

"I apologize too."

"Are you really willing to examine Carson's story together?"

"Absolutely. I'm friends with an English professor."

I relaxed slightly. "I'll print two copies for us to mark up. I know how you prefer hard copy. It won't take but a minute."

A few minutes later I handed him black coffee and Carson's two-page story. I added yellow and pink highlighters to the mix and two pens, then lined them up before I eased onto a barstool.

Gage savored a long sip of his coffee. I'd forgotten his large hands that overlapped around the mug. We both valued good java. "Excellent as always," he said. "How about I read, and you tell me if something's true? If it's a fact Carson found on the police report online, I'll circle it. But if the info is one only an observer would know, then I'll highlight it."

"That leaves speculation to what's left. Pink or yellow high-lighter?" How strange it felt to tease him.

"Do I look like a pink kinda guy?"

"Gage, embrace your feminine side." Seemed like another lifetime since we'd bantered.

Gage picked up the yellow. "I'm being bold. Here we go. 'Houston's summers melt the ice flowing through the killer's veins, but the heat just makes him meaner. I—'"

"The first seven sentences mean nothing to me. Carson doesn't have my address, and my walking to the restaurant isn't in the police report. Highlight that." I swallowed a lump in my throat, the perpetual reminder of my grief. "I took great effort to hide my FBI past from the faculty and students. The dean is aware, and he assured me no one would hear about the FBI from him. How did Carson have a clue that his English professor had been a federal agent?"

"Much is missing, and we won't have answers until we talk to him." Gage continued to read until I stopped him.

"The killer believes he has others fooled, but he claims to follow me and is aware of how I fill my hours." I took a sip of coffee with a shaky hand. "That's creepy, and the statement might or might not be true."

"It reads like the killer planned to gain access to you through a pizza delivery. Since when do you eat pizza?"

An allergy to tomatoes stopped me from enjoying it. "Never, but there are two pizzerias close by."

"You've gotten in the way of something, Risa. It's obscure but a clue." Gage read the fifth paragraph, and I stopped him again.

"The paragraph is accurate as though he followed me inside the restaurant and watched my every move. There's nothing to contradict, and the whole section scares me."

"Did anyone at the restaurant stick out?"

"Not particularly. It wasn't crowded. I arrived early and scanned the few people sitting at tables and booths. Habit, I guess. The killer doesn't state he left his car, so I'm thinking he had a straight view inside the restaurant. Or possibly used binoculars."

We marked our copies before Gage read again.

"Paragraph six and the first two lines of seven are spot-on," I said.

Gage used his highlighter and returned to the story.

Remembering the night held a paralyzing chill. "The hit is exactly how I remember. But I paid no attention to the seconds left on the pedestrian walk. The security cams showed the driver ran the light and abandoned his SUV a few blocks away. Then we learned the vehicle had been stolen." I shoved aside the anguish. "That says premeditated murder to me."

He worried his lip and frowned. "Carson is an eyewitness, or he's the murderer."

"If he killed Trenton, then why write about it in a story? It's too coincidental that he'd take my class and give this to me. Is he a psycho who wants to be arrested?" I paused to analyze conversations with Carson and his interactions with other students. "If it's a game, Carson is dangerous."

"We've got to talk to him. Not sure when because my schedule is booked solid."

"I'd forgotten about the Addingtons' case. Finding who abducted that baby takes priority over any of my problems." I patted his arm. "Always. Life isn't about me or you. It's those who need what we offer."

He placed his other hand over top of mine, strong, warm. "Early in the morning. I'll run Carson's pic through facial recognition and see if the FIG can locate him. I'll let you know what I learn."

The Field Intelligence Group was an elite group of FBI professionals who included special agents, linguists, intelligence analysts, and surveillance specialists. If Carson was hiding anything or trying to avoid detection, they'd find him.

I'd contributed to Gage's stress level by adding to his workload. "Thanks. I'm sorry to have pressured you. I'm hoping he calls me or his parents, but he's not stupid. I really like the kid, and I want to believe there's a logical explanation for his story." I paused, considering remote possibilities. "He could be consumed with guilt and willing to turn himself in, or someone close to him confessed to the crime."

"Do you believe that?"

Gage's gaze nailed me, and I shook my head. "Wishful thinking on my part. Analyzing his behavior in class and the truth of his story equate to him being deranged. But I long to believe he's simply scared."

"Of what? Killing a man or withholding information?"

"Both. Normally I'm confident when reviewing a case. I mean, in the past I could examine evidence and make a viable assessment, but not now. Tomorrow is my last day before Christmas break. I'll have time to work on finding Carson then."

"Risa, update me on every detail that comes to your attention. Anything suspicious or threatening, you call for help."

The intensity in his eyes moved me to agree, at least in theory. "My skills as an agent haven't disappeared. I have my Glock, and I promise I won't do something crazy. You know I won't rest until Trenton's killer is found and justice is served. No point denying it."

Gage stood from the kitchen counter and took his copy of the story. "I'm always here for you, Risa."

My heart sped into overtime.

He stared at me with those incredible blue-gray eyes. "We're still partners in my mind, and I will help you find the killer," Gage said. "Don't forget if he hadn't tossed you aside, you would not be here."

He nodded his goodbye and left my apartment, leaving me wondering what else he had to say.

GAGE

I hated leaving Risa tonight. Not acting on my feelings took all my willpower when I wanted to pull her into my arms. My feelings had deepened, and every time I stared into her face, the intensity grew. We needed a slow approach to our relationship—if we ever were to have one. More than one obstacle stood in our way. I regretted my crammed schedule, but she and I respected the importance of our jobs.

Ignoring the late hour, I ran facial recognition on Carson and emailed the FIG. Tomorrow needed my focus. Carson had been seen midafternoon at a Chevron station on Interstate 20 near Abilene. From what I could tell, he traveled alone. Was he driving to Lubbock and on to Colorado to meet his buds? I forwarded Risa the info.

Friday I climbed out of bed at 5 a.m. after four hours of sleep. Some people only required a few hours to function, but I needed seven. I planned to pick up Jack and head for a six forty-five breakfast at a local café, then visit as many maternity home centers as possible. I'd walked into maternity homes in the past, and each time, my mind ventured back to my inexcusable past.

By 10 a.m., Jack and I had talked to two directors who planned to discuss the baby ring situation with their residents. Now we sat in the director's office of a faith-based facility called Houston Healing and Hope Maternity Care, a residential facility that provided assistance for low-income women. An oval-faced, full-figured woman entered the office and introduced herself.

"I'm Anna Wright, director of Houston Healing and Hope. How can I help you?" She positioned herself behind a desk piled high with books, papers, photos of young women and babies, three cups with various amounts of coffee, and a half-eaten chocolate-sprinkled donut.

We handed her our business cards. She studied Jack and reread his information. "I recognize you, Agent Bradford."

"Yes, ma'am. Two years ago you were influential in the arrest of an unscrupulous Houston doctor who offered unwed mothers the opportunity to sell their babies to him, and he'd find them a proper home. I worked that case with Special Agent Luke Reardon, not Agent Patterson."

Why hadn't Jack told me of his connection to her? He'd asked me to pose the questions so he could observe—unless she showed a preference for him.

Jack offered a rare smile. "I was hoping you'd still be the director here. We appreciated your willingness to help arrest Dr. Zonner."

She startled. "Is there a problem? Your card says violent crime division."

Jack glanced at me . . . my cue.

"No, ma'am," I said. "We are a part of that division, but we work crimes against children. We're investigating the abduction of a baby. Perhaps by an organized ring. We'd like to ask you a few questions."

"Go right ahead." She pushed back the partially eaten donut and sighed. "How horrible to buy and sell babies like a commodity. Agent Bradford, I'll help in whatever way I can."

She preferred Jack, and I'd be an idiot not to notice. "Since you and Ms. Wright have worked together previously, why don't you ask the questions, and I'll write the responses." I had my trusty legal pad and pen.

"Be glad to," he said. "Have any of your residents mentioned a private adoption agency offering money to help them find a suitable home for their baby? I'm not referring to prospective parents who are willing to reimburse medical expenses or legal agencies, but a criminal action."

"You mean approaching my girls to buy their babies like Dr. Zonner, who offered his services free and five grand for their child?" She huffed as though angry at the memory.

"Precisely," Jack said. "Agent Patterson and I want to protect the innocent."

"Nothing has surfaced at our maternity care center since then. But through gossip, although I frown on the practice, I heard a story about one of our previous residents whose baby is missing. The poor girl is afraid to go to the police."

"Why? Does she have a record?"

"No, sir. She's from Vietnam, and I assume she's an undocumented immigrant. She's trying to locate her baby through family and friends." Ms. Wright hesitated. "I have no proof this actually happened or if the baby's been found."

"I'm sure you understand the importance of contacting her. Can you help us?"

Ms. Wright gave her consent. "She works at the same Vietnamese restaurant as her sister. If I'm not mistaken, it's called Saigon Sampler. The sister speaks English but not the young mother who has the presumed missing baby."

"It's imperative we speak to her," Jack said.

I spoke up. "Even if the situation there has nothing to do with our current case, a baby is missing."

Ms. Wright lowered her head. Praying? She lifted her face and pressed numbers on her desk phone. "Suzi, this is Anna Wright. How is your sister and her baby boy?" She listened and closed her eyes. "I'm so sorry. I understand the problems of contacting the authorities, but the FBI can help Hai find the baby. This is a helpless child who could be anywhere or in a dangerous environment. I have no choice but to report the kidnapping, especially since your sister refused to take money for her baby." She ended the call.

Ms. Wright wrote two numbers on a piece of paper and pushed it my way. "I pray I'm not making a mistake here, but the baby is what's important. The first number is the restaurant somewhere in the Vietnamese community on the southwest side of town. Ask for Suzi. Her sister, Hai, is the mother of the missing baby. The second number is Suzi's mobile, and she's the one who told me about the offer to buy Hai's baby. Please let them know I gave you the phone numbers."

"We'll stop at the restaurant late this afternoon before the dinner crowd," I said. "Have any of your residents kept up with Hai?"

"I doubt it. She had an English barrier, which left her isolated. Her sister, Suzi, came to see her often." Ms. Wright stared out a window behind us, but I doubted anything in the parking lot had seized her attention. "This is what I can do. Tonight, during our dinner announcements, I'll share your investigation. Not about Hai's missing baby but related to the buying and selling of children. Ask if any of them have been offered money or have information to pass on. If so, they can see me privately. If they know anything, they'll feel more comfortable coming to me in confidence."

We thanked her and I drove to our next maternity home location while Jack called the Saigon Sampler to confirm the restaurant was open until after dinner. After talking to two more centers and sitting in traffic, an idea rolled into my head. "I'm hungry. Ready to see what we can find out about the Phan sisters? An element of surprise is always a good thing, and I'd hate for those sisters to take off after lunch, thinking they'd miss us."

"You bet. I feel like part of the FBI's hospitality crew, spreading goodwill to all these maternity homes," Jack said. "Social graces are not my expertise. But we never know where evidence lingers."

Jack Bradford had an entertaining streak. "As I said to Ms. Wright, the Phan women may have nothing to do with our current case, but if it's an abduction ring, I want to close it down."

The restaurant had an industrial design except for the landscape paintings of Vietnam on the walls, rustic wooden tables, and rectangular lighting with bamboo coverings.

A middle-aged man eyed Jack and me like we were packing. That part was true. Two women waited tables—an older woman and a teen. A third young woman approached our table with reddened eyes.

Jack and I were the only non-Asians, and our server didn't speak English, so we pointed to the menu.

I ordered *phở*, a soup with beef, rice noodles, and some things I recognized and some I didn't. Jack helped me by pointing out a few of his favorite dishes. "You're sure this is tasty?" I said to Jack.

"It's outstanding." He recommended *bánh xèo*, a type of crepe or pancake stuffed with pork, shrimp, bean sprouts, and other unrecognizable foods.

I always believed that if I didn't know what I was eating, then it didn't reach my mouth. But I gave Jack the benefit of the doubt and ate the two dishes he suggested and a few more. Risa would have been proud since my preference for food were those I could pronounce and a source of her teasing. A few of the customers stared at us—why were two white guys here?

"Follow my lead." I opened the wrapper around the chopsticks. "Would you ask to speak to the owner?"

"About what?" He blew out his exasperation. "For the record, I'd like to occasionally call the shots."

"Noted."

Jack pushed back his empty plate and motioned to our server. She brought the teen girl to our table who spoke English.

"What can I do for you, sir?" The young woman was about sixteen years old, very tiny.

"Our lunch was delicious," I said. "We'd like to congratulate the owner."

She summoned the man who'd been tossing visual darts at us. The owner changed his facade. Now he could find out why Jack and I were patronizing his restaurant.

I jumped right in. "Excellent meal and service. My compliments to the chef."

"Thank you." The owner turned to Jack. "Are you also pleased with your meal, sir?"

"Perfect. Trust me, I'll be back."

I stuck out my hand. "I'm Pastor Pat. My friend and I are planting a church in this area. Do you know who we could talk to about renting space?"

He took my hand for a limp shake. The frown from earlier returned. "I'm Buddhist. No room here for Catholics, Baptists, or Muslim."

I smiled widely. "I understand. We're nondenominational. We want to share the Word of God with residents in the community. A space to start a Sunday service is important, and we can pay."

The man's facial muscles softened. "Ah, I have a friend who could help you. How can he contact you?"

"If you'll give me his name, I can handle the rest."

"My friend is particular. He'll want to check you out first. Good businessman."

"He's a smart man, and we can't be too careful. Do you have pen and paper, and I'll write down my contact information?"

He pulled a cell phone from his pant pocket and glanced up, ready to type. "Name and number please."

"Pastor Patrick." I gave him my spare burner number.

He pointed to Jack. "Your name?"

"Jack Brahms. Same number as Pastor Pat's."

The owner finished and dropped his cell back into his apron pocket. He snapped his fingers at the young woman who'd translated for us. "She will bring your bill."

In other circumstances, I would have laughed. The man was wary of us, but why? Suspicious? Fearful? Rear-deep in illegal activities? "We want to help the community. At the top of our list is a day care to help working parents. Free, of course."

"I'll tell my friend."

"Is it possible to talk to any of your workers to see if they'd be interested in church or day care for their children?"

"No. They're working. Don't bother my people. Thank you for coming."

"A lady in our church knows Phan Suzi, and I understand her

sister has a baby who could use care while she works. Are either of them working today?"

"No one here by that name." The owner left us.

Outside in the afternoon heat, Jack turned to me. "What did that accomplish but a full belly and comic relief?"

"Maybe more. Which one of those women could be Suzi or Hai?"

"The teen wasn't the only one who spoke English. The other young woman listened to what we were saying. She walked closer to us and wiped a clean table while you were evangelizing."

"My goal to talk to either sister fell flat," I said. "I'd appreciate it if you'd keep my impromptu acting to us men."

Jack laughed. "Wrong, Gage. I heard you had an impulsive streak, and this just proved it."

"That was Risa. I usually stick to protocol."

"Right. Consider yourself indebted unless I change my mind."

I surveyed our surroundings. I'd parked across the street from the restaurant. Two men leaned against my car—wearing jeans, T-shirts, and Asian gang tats. We were on their radar. Doubt if I could preach my way out of trouble, but using our weapons lessened our credibility as preachers.

"What do you suppose they want?" Jack said. "Add to their port-folio or raise the status of their gang?"

"Maybe both." I knew he could hold his own in a fight. "I'll do my best to talk us out of whatever they have in mind."

"Noted." He chuckled. "Just point me in the right direction."

I grinned and prayed for wisdom. My Glock holster was concealed under my shirt on the right side. Picking up my pace, I approached the two men with Jack beside me.

"Hi, I'm Pastor Pat." The man on my right pulled a knife. I hated knives. A fight always got messy. "Hey. No need for this."

The man on the left laughed and said something I didn't under-stand. Talking them down kept our cover intact, but neither of us spoke their language.

"How can I help you?" I said.

The man nearest the driver's side of my car pointed to the door. "Get in, and don't ever come back. We don't need your kind here."

"What kind is that?" I said.

"The kind who causes trouble."

"What kind of trouble? We had lunch."

"FBI. Come back here, and you'll bleed out."

"If we're agents, it's a federal offense to threaten one."

"We'll risk it."

Three more men appeared behind the vehicles. From the corner of my eye, I saw guns. I didn't mind a fight, but not with these odds. I sized them up again. No way. "Until next time. We will be back. Count on it."

13

Although an illegal practice, some women got pregnant for the purpose of selling their babies. If a woman stooped that low, she didn't care if her baby went to a loving home or a part of a trafficking ring. That angle made my and Jack's investigation even harder. We interviewed the director of another maternity home who assisted low-income mothers and couples by providing free prenatal care, education, counseling, and job search opportunities. The only thing we accomplished was making sure the director understood the possibility of their residents being scoped out for a baby buy.

The Addingtons' case fell under an organized baby-ring's objective that centered on marketing babies. How they gained possession of the child didn't matter—the cheaper the better. All pregnancy centers understood the prospect of their birth mothers facing an illegal scheme, and like Jack said, we resembled the FBI's welcome wagon. But I still believed face-to-face interviews helped promote our cause and encouraged others to speak up against crime.

Our phones chimed with an alert. Jack read the incoming news report. "Huge fire at Vietnamese restaurant on southwest side of town. Fire department and ambulances at the scene. Fire believed to have started in the kitchen. At least three people dead and five injured." He glanced up. "Hold on while I confirm the address." Jack swore. "Same restaurant we just had lunch—Saigon Sampler. We got too close to our subject's territory."

"Either someone is tailing us or suspected two white guys on the heels of one of their employees having her baby abducted," I said. "I even mentioned Suzi and her sister."

"Ms. Wright told us the women worked there and gave us the restaurant's phone number. The owner lied. Anyway, Ms. Wright will help in any way she can, especially after she helped the FBI previously. But—"

"But what?"

"Someone must have tipped off the subjects about our case while we were in her office. I'm requesting a list of her staff and volunteers, not only the present employees and helpers but also those who were there during the previous case."

"You think one of her staff is rear-deep in this?" I said.

Jack huffed. "Absolutely. How else can you explain the fire?"

"We have a number for Phan Suzi. Let's see if she picks up."

Jack pressed in the numbers and waited. "No answer and no voice mail."

"Get Ms. Wright on the phone now. Ask for the list ASAP while we're en route to the last maternity home for the day."

Jack made the call and placed it on speaker. "Ms. Wright, we have a critical situation. When we were at the Saigon Sampler, the owner denied Suzi and Hai worked there. Now the restaurant is on fire."

She gasped. "Is everyone safe?"

"Initial report is three deaths and two hospitalizations. More may be injured."

"That's terrible. What caused the fire?" she said.

"Not confirmed but it's believed it originated in the kitchen. Suzi doesn't answer her phone. We're concerned one or both Phan sisters were killed or injured."

"Oh no." The woman sobbed.

Jack continued with no comment on Ms. Wright's emotional

reaction. "With the new development, Agent Patterson and I are requiring a list of your staff and volunteers with employment dates going back three years."

"How can you suspect one of my trusted staff? They work for minimum wage because they believe in the ministry." Her tone edged with anger. "Some of these women have been with me forever, and my driver is a man who's like a father to these young women."

Jack glanced at me and shook his head. "Yes, ma'am. Another problem occurred when we left the restaurant. Agent Patterson and I were confronted by Asian men with gang tats who knew we were FBI. Neither of us appreciated the threat, which is a federal offense. With both of those crimes, we need your list ASAP."

"The Christmas season is extremely busy. Can I get the information to you on Monday?"

"No, ma'am. We need the list today. Please expedite the matter."

Jack Bradford didn't have Risa's beauty and unique perspective, but he got the job done.

14

While Jack and I interviewed maternity homes, the Wades and their attorney had booked an earlier flight to Houston and arrived at the FBI office.

Extra time to strategize the Wades' interview would have benefited my comfort level, but conducting the Q and A now made more sense than making us wait hours for answers.

"We're not prepared," Jack said, his face a mass of wrinkles and lines. If I wasn't careful, I'd call him a bulldog. "They've placed us at a disadvantage."

"I doubt they've strategized either. They've faced tremendous losses—an adopted child, thousands of dollars, and possibly implicated due to Alex Wade's former incarceration." I pointed to what we knew about the three waiting in the receptionist area. "The attorney is Alex Wade's cousin, same last name, and he specializes in real estate."

Jack scratched his jaw. "I'd like a background on the guy."

"I'm curious, and I want a ton of answers. Make the request and let's get this done."

Jack and I introduced ourselves and escorted the three to an interview room. I'd take lead on the questions if personalities clicked. Nanette Wade's face blotched red, and her eyes watered. How heartbreaking to believe a baby was hers, only to discover she and her husband had been deceived. Alex's rod-straight spine and stiffened body read anger, nervousness, and a huge dump of wariness. His emotions must be fried. The attorney, about the same age as his cousin, wore an average-priced suit and serious lines across his forehead and the corners of his eyes. Sleep would have benefited the three, but the shock of the crime obviously had worn them raw.

After I covered the preliminaries of name, address, and other pertinent info, I moved forward on the interview. "Mr. and Mrs. Wade, Agent Bradford and I appreciate your willingness to fly to Houston during this tragic time. I have no idea what you must be feeling, but I'm sure shock and anger have tossed you into a nasty arena."

Alex swallowed hard. "We haven't shared the adoption agency's paperwork with our attorney yet because he's been out of town. We met at the Des Moines airport en route here."

Odd their attorney hadn't seen any documentation. "Your attorney didn't read your paperwork before the adoption or on the plane to Houston?"

"Agent Patterson," the attorney said, "I was in first class and slept on the flight. My clients were in economy."

Alex rubbed the back of his neck. Problems there? "Our dream of calling a child our own has been shattered. And while the adoption agency ran off with our money, a baby boy could have died of cystic fibrosis." He glanced at his wife. "As bad as this is for us, we know the biological parents must feel worse. Our emotions are spent, and the biological parents must be filled with relief to have their son back. My wife and I would like to apologize to them. If possible."

The attorney whirled sharply to Alex. "I advise against it. You're asking for trouble and a potential lawsuit for lack of due diligence on your part. Consider your previous conviction, and the high likelihood of you and Nanette being sentenced for neglect."

Alex spoke calmly. "If my child had been abducted, I'd want to meet those who'd cared for him even for a little while."

"Alex, let's focus on exonerating you of any wrongdoing and the missing forty-eight thousand dollars. Get your head on straight.

When restitution is made for your money, you can privately adopt somewhere else. Unless you agree to my terms, I can't represent you."

"Agents—" Nanette's voice trembled—"would you kindly remove our attorney from this discussion?"

"That's Alex's call, not yours." The attorney glared at her. "I am family, and—"

"I agree with my wife," Alex said. "Nanette and I came to Houston to help the FBI arrest those who are responsible for a kidnapping and operating an illegal adoption agency. You claimed to share in our goals, but I haven't seen it. For the record, recovering our money is last on the list. We believe other couples have faced the same scam, and any information we can provide to stop the scammers benefits good people. No other agenda."

The attorney jabbed a finger at Alex. "You're an idiot. I shouldn't have jeopardized my reputation for the likes of you."

"Sir," I said, "your clients have requested you to leave the interview. Agent Bradford will escort you."

"When I'm ready!"

Jack stood, all five-foot-ten inches of bulldog tenacity. "Sir, either leave with me now, or you will face arrest."

The attorney slowly stood. "You're a bigger fool than I thought, Alex. I'll take a taxi back to the airport. You could have invested that money into something valuable instead of getting taken by a fraudulent adoption agency."

"You mean invest in some of your real estate?" Alex maintained a calm demeanor. "Agent Bradford, the receptionist has a manila folder with paperwork and receipts regarding the adoption. Can you retrieve those for us?"

"Of course." When Jack and the attorney left the room, Alex took his wife's hand. "Agent Patterson, I apologize for that scene. We needed an attorney fast, and my cousin fit the bill. Or so we thought."

"Not a problem." I'd heard worse. I hoped the couple had documentation that pushed ahead the investigation. The more we uncovered, the more I questioned if the fraud stretched across other states besides Texas and Iowa. "As soon as Agent Bradford returns, we'll resume."

Jack opened the door and laid the manila envelope on the table before he took his seat. I grabbed my legal pad and pen. "Mr. Wade, we'd like to begin with you relaying your adoption story. Every detail matters."

Alex continued to hold Nanette's hand. "My wife and I are unable to have children. I'm sure you learned about my previous conviction from the FBI in Des Moines. My conviction was my fault. I lost my temper, got into a fight, and the man died. I paid my debt to society."

Nanette gave her husband a reassuring smile. "It's all right, honey. What happened with the baby is not your fault or mine."

Alex closed his eyes, as though refocusing. "My wife saw an ad on social media about a private adoption center opening in Des Moines—Your Heart for Adoption Agency. We thought we'd try once more to see if a private agency could find us a baby. The man we met, by the name of Harvey Sinclair, said if we were up-front to the biological parents about my past and showed financial and community responsibility, we could adopt. My record since prison is spotless, eliminating any discrepancies in our reputation. The agency asked for ten thousand dollars to start the proceedings. A second ten thousand was due when the agency found a potential child for us, and a third installment when we met the birth mother. A fourth and final payment was due when we took possession legally of the baby at the agency's office. At that time, we'd be presented with medical papers, the child's Social Security card, and a birth certificate. Mr. Sinclair gave us a brochure with a history of the agency. It also contained testimonials and state phone numbers for us to check on their legality. I compared their brochure to Iowa's online private adoption guidelines and laws and believed the agency was within the recommended parameters of our state."

"What guidelines specifically?" I said.

"They displayed their state licensing for starters. I requested and read their documents and references. Mr. Sinclair said there were no shortcuts in adopting a child. Every letter of the law must be upheld. He asked if we wanted to hire our own social worker to interview the birth mother, but we chose to use theirs, which was Mr. Sinclair. I should have suspected something then, but we were so excited to have a child."

"Did Harvey Sinclair or anyone you met have an accent or appear not to be a US citizen?"

"No, sir."

"Did you follow through in verifying the agency?" I said.

"Yes. I talked to two women, one who is the state licensing specialist and the second who represented the state attorney general's office for any complaints."

Suspicions rose in my mind. "You used the numbers on their brochure?"

"Yes, sir. The brochure is in the packet of information."

"Good. You and Mrs. Wade met the birth mother. When and where did this happen?"

"Five weeks ago. We met a very pregnant young woman at the adoption agency's office. She had questions and was concerned about us caring properly for her baby. Her name is Emily Lock, but now I question if it's her real name. But she might not have been aware of the fraud. We saw a sonogram with her name on it. It didn't show the sex, but we were fine with that."

"Did she mention where she lived or any personal information?"

"She claimed to live north of Des Moines. She refused visitation rights but needed approximately eight thousand dollars reimbursement for medical bills. Mr. Sinclair said he'd add the extra reimbursement to our bill. A week ago, Sinclair informed us that Emily had gone into labor. But she claimed to have second thoughts about giving up her baby. Mr. Sinclair told us he could refund half of the money if she chose to keep her child, but the remaining twenty thousand covered adoption fees and her medical expenses. Then last week we received a call from him that Emily had signed off on parental rights. We could pick up our baby boy at his office and take him home. Our official adoption proceedings would be in front of a judge in approximately three to four months. A few hours after we had the baby home, Nanette and I noted he was very fussy, so we placed his crib in our bedroom. We blamed the new surroundings on his inability to get comfortable. Nanette held him all night and the whole next day. The second night, his condition seemed worse. The next day he showed signs of breathing difficulties. We rushed him to the hospital. The rest you know."

"You believed the child was days old instead of six weeks," I said.

Alex and Nanette nodded. "According to Des Moines FBI, the birth date on our paperwork is false," Alex said.

"What was your method of payment?"

"Credit card. I checked with my bank yesterday and found out the money had been taken from our account for a total of forty-eight thousand dollars."

A nightmare for sure. "So a minimum of two people were involved in the deception—Harvey Sinclair and Emily Lock, the pregnant young woman?"

"Yes. He had the legal papers ready for us to sign, and he said he'd take care of filing them." Alex pointed to the manila folder in Jack's possession. "I kept every bit of correspondence, even phone call conversations and dates. Emails were printed out as well as copies of documents."

"And you have an extra copy of everything?"

"Yes, sir."

"Did the agency conduct a home study?"

"Mr. Sinclair handled it," Nanette said. "He toured our home, requested our business records, copies of tax returns for the past seven years, our home mortgage, retirement provisions, and the name and address of the pediatrician we'd chosen."

"Bank accounts too?"

She startled and turned to her husband.

"I took care of canceling our credit cards and alerted the bank as soon as the FBI told us of the scam," Alex said.

She relaxed slightly. "Harvey Sinclair was a guest in our home for dinner. How could we have been so stupid?"

"Mrs. Wade," I said. "He's a professional. He knows how to secure your confidence and play into tender emotions."

Nanette swallowed hard. "Could Emily have faked her pregnancy? I think the correct term is a putative mother."

"Right. A putative mother means the biological relationship to a child hasn't been established." No matter how many times I interviewed heartbroken parents, it never got easier. "Or she might be a victim too. Her baby could have gone to another home."

Alex spoke up. "Originally, I made two copies of the original documents from our first meeting when Nan and I decided to move forward with the adoption application. I had all three copies in the car while we were at Sinclair's office. But someone broke into our car and stole them. The theft seemed odd, random, until now. Those papers were valuable only to us." He paused. "Actually they were more valuable to Sinclair."

"Did you file a police report?"

"Yes, sir," Alex said. "Mr. Sinclair phoned the police, and I have the officer's report in the manila envelope. While at Sinclair's office I insisted on him making a copy of all the documents that he had there. I checked to ensure the important ones were included. I also added his business card and brochure. Those I have with me."

Jack slid the envelope to Alex. "I think we should see what's inside. Mr. Sinclair made a dangerous error by not counting on you keeping copies of the paperwork and documents."

"I assume you'll want a copy of the contents." He opened the metal fastener and pulled out a stack of paper.

All the pages were blank.

15

Alex stiffened and shuffled through the blank pages. Twice. The interview room grew icy. "Where are all the papers I copied?" He fumbled through them again. "Those were the evidence needed to show we'd been scammed."

"Mr. Wade," I said as gently as possible. "Could your documents be in another place? Has someone switched them?"

He released a ragged breath. "I don't have any explanation."

When the devastation of the stolen documents calmed around the Wades, I asked if they could answer additional questions.

"Yes, sir." Alex gave his wife a nod. "We're committed to helping you."

"When did you last review the envelope's documents?" I said to him.

He rubbed his face. "The morning we picked up our . . . the Addingtons' baby, Nanette and I wanted to make sure the papers had been signed and were in order along with the copies for our records. We determined nothing was left for us to do but gain possession of our baby. The envelope was intact. My instinct told me to bring the envelope, but we were excited."

"Alex, we have an alarm system," Nanette said. "Why didn't anyone call us about an entry? No other explanation is out there but the documents were swapped with blank pages."

Alex startled. "Oh, my—"

"What is it?" Nanette said.

"I told Sinclair the night he came to dinner that I'd made a second copy of the paperwork he'd given to us after the theft."

I held up a finger for a question. "You made a copy of the copy Sinclair made for you to replace the stolen documents."

"Yes. I then had two copies of our agreement. He knew about our precautions. He also insisted I keep the copies together until we had our child, then place both in a safe." He massaged neck muscles. "What have I done?"

"Won't the alarm company have the entry in their reports?" she said.

"When we're finished here, I'll call them for a moment-by-moment report. Or check online."

Jack caught my attention. We must have been on the same wavelength. "We are flexible, and this interview is yours. Why not check with your alarm company now?" Jack handed Alex his cell phone since the Wades' mobile devices were at the front desk.

"What's the name of your service?" I positioned my hand on the legal pad and clicked my pen.

"It's local—CitySafe."

I pulled up the Des Moines alarm system for the website, phone number, and physical address of the company.

Alex navigated the phone and pressed in a number. Someone must have answered because he gave his name and password along with the date his home was burglarized, the same day the Addingtons' baby was placed in Nanette's arms. He jutted his jaw. "You have nothing on your records other than the times we alarmed and disarmed our system?" He studied his wife. "I see. How do you explain a break-in while my wife and I were away from our home?" He listened. "We have discovered missing valuables, and no, we haven't alerted the police department or home insurance company. We called you first." He stiffened. "Filing a report doesn't return our property or give us clarification about how thieves gained entrance into our home—our home that we paid for an alarm system and ongoing monitoring. I will be in touch after I contact the police." He huffed, then ended the call and glanced at me, then Jack. "That went well." He was seething, and I'd feel the same way in his situation.

Jack picked up the conversation. "While you were at Your Heart for Adoption Agency meeting with the perspective birth mother, someone broke into your car. They took the original and copies of your dealings. Right?" Alex nodded, and Jack continued.

Jack verified the date. "For clarification, were other valuables taken from your vehicle?"

"No, sir. The Des Moines police department has the crime report in their records."

"I'll check now." Jack tapped his thumbs at lightning speed on his phone. "I need the officer's name?"

"I don't remember." Alex took his wife's hand. "We were eager to meet Emily." He clenched his fist and pounded on the desk. "We were taken for fools."

Nanette's lips quivered. "By professionals, those who make a living by capitalizing on people's dreams. We—" She stopped to pull a tissue from her purse and dabbed her nose. "How do these people prey on so many innocent people?"

I took over while Jack verified the Des Moines police report. "Fraudulent adoption agencies operate around the world under the guise of caring individuals. They arrange placement of kidnapped babies to those who are not only unsuspecting of an illegal operation but are also often unable to adopt through normal channels or don't want to wait years for a child. Sometimes the agency will take the money paid and leave the area without following through on their end of the contract. Sometimes people, like you, meet the supposed birth mother who fakes her pregnancy and longs for her baby to be adopted into a good home. Hundreds of thousands of dollars exchange hands. If knowledge of the crime surfaces, the child and the biological and adoptive parents suffer." I paused while tears streamed down Nanette's face. "I promise you, various organizations are working to stop these horrendous crimes."

Alex pulled his wife close to him. "Thank you."

"When you met Emily Lock the first time and on the placement day, was anyone else in the office besides Harvey Sinclair?"

"No, sir. The office was small. Nanette and I signed the final papers. Harvey said he'd have them notarized and delivered by certified mail." Alex studied me. "It's a wonder my wife and I are still alive. If Sinclair and his cohorts are so ruthless to kidnap a baby who has a life-threatening illness, they will do anything to cover up their crime."

I placed my pen beside the legal pad. Alex had nailed the truth. "You're right. My guess is you two would probably be dead if Sinclair hadn't arranged for two burglaries."

Jack checked his phone. "We have our answer from the Des Moines police department. On the date your car was burglarized, the police weren't notified."

Alex blinked and paled. "An officer in full uniform met us at Sinclair's office. Are you saying the cop was fake?"

"I imagine so," I said.

"How many people are involved in this scam? My mother used to sing a song about the devil had blue eyes." Alex scowled. "Makes me think of Sinclair."

A small clue. "He had blue eyes?"

"Yes. What about Emily Lock?"

"Sea-green eyes. Long auburn hair," Alex said. "We had dreams of a beautiful baby with some of her features." He paused. "Harvey might have been wearing contacts."

"They both could have been wearing contacts or other disguises," I said.

Empathy for the Wades and other victims caused a sense of anger and justice to roll through me. "The FBI, other agencies who advocate for missing children, and our team from CARD, which stands for Child Abduction Rapid Deployment, are investigating what happened to you and the Addingtons' baby."

"You know our case." Alex's voice trembled. "It also looks like we could have been a part of the abduction."

Nanette turned to her husband. "Alex, no reason to put yourself through this. We are victims."

My phone buzzed—a background of the Wades' attorney met my scrutiny. Initially the attorney had a clean record.

"Yes, you are victims," I said. "If the Addingtons' baby hadn't been ill, no one would have ever learned the truth. While this is heartbreaking, by sharing your experience, we're one step closer to bringing justice to so many other innocent people."

Alex paused for a moment. "Sinclair could have taken our money and not given us a child, and that is despicable. But what he's done is much worse. How can we offer anything of value to your investigation? Our paperwork is gone, and the names given to us are probably phony."

"We'd like for you and Nanette to meet with our artist. Through your descriptions, we can use facial-recognition software to help further the investigation."

"I have something to contribute," Nanette said. "I used my phone to snap a picture of Emily when she wasn't aware. At the time I thought as our baby grew, I might find a resemblance."

I showed her a pic of the man from the security cam in the adoption agency's parking lot. "Can either of you identify this man?"

Both confirmed the man was Harvey Sinclair.

"Mrs. Wade," Jack said, "would you come with me, and we'll check your phone for the birth mother's photo. I also want your husband's phone to check both for any hidden tracking devices."

Jack and Nanette left the interview room to retrieve the phones at the receptionist's desk. I took advantage of the few moments alone with Alex. "Are you certain meeting with the Addingtons is in your best interest?"

"My wife and I believe it's best. I'd be a fool not to realize they hurt more than we do, and I don't want them to think we've been part of a crime."

"I understand. I'd want to do the same. Alex, are you keeping information from your wife or the FBI?"

He rubbed his temples. "Ninety thousand dollars is missing from our business account. I discovered it before we boarded the plane. Nanette deserves to know the truth, but she's already devastated, and the missing money might push her over the edge." He leaned back in his chair. "I talk too much when I'm nervous, upset."

"No problem. In turning this inside out, valuable information may surface."

"We wanted a child, and this offered the perfect solution. With my criminal record, Nanette will never be fulfilled as a mother, and we've tried every way possible. She wanted so much to help you." He paused. "Maybe to find out there'd been a mistake. But I told her the FBI and police rarely make errors."

"Thank you for the confidence. You and your wife have provided useful information to help us find those involved in the fraudulent adoption agency."

"Yes, sir, but any mention of trying to adopt again is impossible."

"Why? This isn't your fault."

"I don't think my wife or I will ever recover."

16

RISA

While most of the world shared in the excitement of the Christmas season, I shoved the merriment aside. "Just get through the holidays" was my mantra. Talking to Mom and Dad rather than seeing them face-to-face meant no physical touch from them or for them. I sounded like a disappointed child, and the title fit. No delicious smells and tastes of Mom's celebratory recipes or Dad's deep baritone voice singing traditional songs.

Frustration wrenched at my being. What was wrong with the world that no one saw the pain and heartache so many of us felt during this time of year? Labor Day and Thanksgiving were hard, but Christmas without Mom, Dad, and Trenton seemed grossly unfair. I wanted to feel joyous, but nausea churned 24-7. Ginger ale had replaced Dr Pepper in my food group.

I despised my grief and wallowing in self-pity. How long would it last?

Ethan Mercury phoned me on my drive home after classes on Friday. I listened through my Bluetooth. "How are you, Mr. Mercury?"

"Lynn and I have been better. We haven't heard from Carson. His mother and I are worried he's hurt or in trouble. He's no longer on our phone plan, so that idea to find him didn't work. He wanted independence, more opportunities to make his own decisions, and we thought it was a good idea. I've checked law enforcement for accidents and hospitals along the road to the Rockies, and nothing has been reported. I wanted to update you on his status."

Why was I not surprised? Carson witnessed or confessed to killing my brother on his writing project and then left town. My head pounded at his treachery, but I must keep my emotions intact. But . . . if he had driven the car that killed Trenton, then why write a short story and turn it in to me? Had guilt driven him to a strange type of confession? Or like the story indicated, did he have deep psychological issues?

"I don't think you've received bad news, sir. He hasn't been in an accident or in the hospital."

"It's not like my son to be irresponsible."

"Did you offer authorities Carson's driver's license and license plate numbers?"

Ethan exhaled. "Yes, and his Jeep's description. Our concern was an accident. Now too many things are stalking us."

Were they aware of his story contents? Suspected psychological issues? "I know a few people in law enforcement. My friend Gage Patterson could help. I can't promise anything, but I can try."

"Sure. Appreciate your help." Ethan gave me Carson's info, but I already had it from prior research.

"Have you contacted any of his friends or a girlfriend? Most kids talk to their peers more than their parents."

"I was young once and did stupid things. Thought I was mature and didn't need to tell my parents everything. To the best of our knowledge, he no longer has a girlfriend. We'll contact all those we can think of and let you know. We're close to some of the parents, and they could have asked for more information before their sons left. A mistake his mother and I will never make again."

"I'm sure he's fine. He's probably hiking or camping where there's no connectivity."

"Hope so, Professor Jacobs. He's young and susceptible to pressure.

We expect experiments of drinking and even drugs, but he hasn't ever shown us that kind of behavior."

Once home, I deliberated about the Mercurys and Carson. They'd made a critical error in not asking for their son's travel plans or the names of those traveling with him. Would they live to regret their decision of giving him space, and in the process, my brother's killer went free?

Life ticked by like a metronome, marking the beats of each breath. When our song finished and we breathed our last, our lives slipped into eternity.

My mind flowed back over all those weeks I walked from my apartment to the restaurant where Trenton and I ate his last meal, trying to remember a bit of evidence. I refused to step inside. Much too painful. Two days after his death, I'd gone back to his apartment and searched for anything Mom and Dad, HPD, or the FBI might have missed. All roads led nowhere.

I frequented those places where Trenton spent his hours before and after his decision to turn his life over to God. I questioned many people about him, some more than once. I showed his pic to everyone and told all who'd listen that he was my brother. His sponsor invited me to Trenton's AA meetings. There I met his new friends and welcomed their sweet compliments about him. I'd taken to attending his church and the same small group, but God had failed me. Hearing about how he'd given back to others, I believed in Trenton's healing from alcohol and drugs. He could have done so much for others if he'd lived.

I didn't have my brother or the person who'd killed him. My misery led me to blame someone, and I inched toward God. Why hadn't He helped stop a tragic death?

Then I read Carson's story. Could the killer have been right in front of me for months, and I let him slip right through my fingers?

17

GAGE

Neither Jack nor I expected the Addingtons to video-call us from the Des Moines hospital. The FBI assistant special agent in charge there explained the couple wanted to talk to us as soon as possible, and she'd arranged it. I wish we'd interviewed them before Fox News and taken the opportunity to coach their responses. Words spoken in despair were often misunderstood. Often information could be relayed that should have been kept private until arrests were made. In the case of the Addingtons, they'd expressed their gratitude to the FBI and the hospital for finding their baby—and told the kidnappers their freedom was short-lived.

Jack and I logged on to the secure site and greeted the couple. Michael Addington had a few days' beard growth, and his shirt showed a coffee stain. The circles under Sarah's eyes reminded me of my sister when she slept without removing mascara.

"Thank you for all your hard work on our behalf and our son's," Michael said. "We're grateful to you, the FBI here in Des Moines, and the hospital for saving our son's life and taking the initiative to identify him." He wrapped his arm around his wife's waist. Exhausted mildly described them.

"How is your baby?" I said.

"Doing well. He's receiving the best care, and we plan to bring him home by the end of the weekend."

Sarah spoke up. "I'm adopted, and we had no idea I carried the genetic disorder. And Michael didn't know he carried it either. Seems like one hurdle after another." She glanced at her husband, and he sighed.

The moment she said "adopted," I flinched inside. Must be the time of year . . . My son or daughter would have been nineteen in November, stepping into life with hopes and dreams. Never knowing the years I spent searching for him or her.

"I have a cousin with cystic fibrosis," Jack said. "The Cystic Fibrosis Foundation has made great strides in moving forward with research."

"Yes," Michael said. "Another reason we're grateful. Researchers have identified the gene and protein responsible. Those discoveries have led to new treatments."

Jack continued. "Sounds like a cure is on the horizon in our lifetime. Mr. and Mrs. Addington, Agent Patterson and I appreciate your call. We have our questions too."

I respected Jack's support and encouragement for the Addingtons, a side of him foreign to me. He was trying. If Risa were here, she'd say, "Jack did have a humane side."

Sarah reached for a tissue before Michael began. "Right before this call, we met the Wades briefly here at the hospital. Although the introductions were extremely uncomfortable and short, they were devastated to have been victimized with such a horrific scheme. Sarah and I empathized with them just as they did with us. Neither Sarah nor I believe they willfully consented to an illegal adoption. We realize the FBI will continue investigating them and their testimony to ensure their innocence, but that is where we stand. The second matter is determining how the kidnapping occurred. To us, the crime must be one of many. We were told the Wades paid forty-eight thousand dollars to the illegal adoption agency. While the sum is large, it couldn't have gone far with the people involved. Are we looking at organized crime and other couples presented with abducted children?"

Jack turned for me to answer. Alex Wade had shared the disappearance of ninety thousand dollars from his and Nanette's business account. "When a fraudulent adoption agency does a background check, that includes financial information, which makes it easy access for more money. It appears the operation may have been in business for a while. CARD, the FBI's Child Abduction Rapid Deployment Division, has two goals—the safe return of abducted children and apprehending the person or persons responsible."

"Is there more than one CARD team in the US? We don't know much about them except they were working our case right after we learned our son was missing. We were told they have around a 90 percent success rate in finding missing children."

"The FBI has five CARD teams in the US, and each one has a dozen or so agents," I said. "These special agents are experts. They are in communication with each other, organizations that are committed to finding kidnapped children, law enforcement, and other agents to apprehend the abductors." I hated what they'd been through. The nightmare would haunt them for years. Probably forever. "We celebrate when a child is recovered and mourn when they aren't. I promise that I will not rest until the kidnappers are under arrest."

"You aren't God." Sarah huffed. "I'm sorry. I'm still upset."

I forged ahead. "We'd like to ask you a few questions beyond your original interview."

"Go ahead," Michael said. "I can't imagine what more we could share."

"At the hospital, did you note anyone lurking around who seemed suspicious?"

When the Addingtons shook their heads, I continued. "Before the abduction, did you notice anyone parked near your home or following you?"

"No. Why would we?" Michael said.

"What about a repairman or someone offering services?"

"We had our seasonal heating inspection, but we've used the same technician for years." Michael turned to his wife. "Am I missing anything?"

"A tree service was in the area, and one of them asked if we needed limbs cut. They weren't in the house, and I have the company's card. It's at home in case we needed them."

"We'd like the information," I said. "Have you been threatened professionally or personally?"

"Not at all. We're teachers in an elementary school," Michael said. "I teach math and science, and Sarah works with special-needs children. I'm sure you already knew that since several of our peers were questioned."

"Yes, sir," I said. "They all cleared including the parents of the students you teach. However, we are revisiting many of them. What is the response from your alarm company?"

Michael lifted his chin. "A source of irritation. We'd sue but what purpose would that serve? The company claimed their equipment was not at fault, and our alarm hadn't been set. I disagree because I set it myself. Someone hacked into our security system. No other explanation."

"We've talked to Mercury Alarms too, and their reporting shows the alarm wasn't enabled."

"We're ending the service as soon as we find a new company. The night of the abduction, my mother-in-law checked it right after we left to ensure the house was locked and alarmed."

I couldn't blame them, although the alarm company operated nationwide and was highly rated for home and commercial customers. When Jack and I called them, they displayed cooperation and were investigating what had gone wrong in the equipment at the Addingtons' home. For that matter, I'd just been at the owner's home. "Agent Bradford, would you follow up with the alarm company?"

Jack nodded and typed into his iPad.

"One more question," I said. "We've done a thorough background on your ob-gyn, and she has an impeccable record. Do you have reason to doubt her integrity?"

"No, sir," Sarah said. "She's been supportive since the beginning of the pregnancy. I've been her patient for over ten years."

"Your pediatrician?"

"Highly recommended by my ob-gyn."

The background on her pediatrician was spotless. I leaned back in my chair. The Addingtons needed rest, and other questions could wait. "We'll stay in touch. Do either of you have additional comments or questions?"

Sarah raised her finger. "If I find who abducted our baby before you do, trust me I will blow a hole right through their black hearts."

"You don't want to take the law into your own hands, Mrs. Addington." I understood her anger all too much but trusted it was her emotions talking.

"It wasn't your child who was abducted and nearly died."

18

RISA

Ethan Mercury called me again shortly after 9 p.m. From the sound of his voice, he still hadn't been successful in finding Carson. I expected him to be more professional, and I filed the peculiarity away for later.

"None of Carson's friends went with him," Ethan said. "Neither did he mention the hiking trip to them. According to his friends, he claimed to be spending a boring Christmas at home with the family. I contacted his old girlfriend, and she hasn't heard from him either. She'll call if he contacts her. Nice girl. Pretty. Smart. We thought Carson cared for her, and although they're young, she could have been the right one. Not sure the reason for the breakup."

"Maybe he'll reach out to her."

"Doubtful. They broke up the end of July."

About the time of Trenton's death. "Maybe he needed space to think about his future and felt uncomfortable about letting you and his mother know. Have you noticed a change in Carson's behavior?"

"Unusual question from his professor, unless his schoolwork is a problem. Am I missing something here? Are you interested in my son other than his schoolwork?" His tone flattened, and I didn't appreciate the implication.

If my goal didn't center on finding Carson, I'd have given Ethan

Mercury a piece of my mind. Then again, could I blame him for suspecting something malign? "That remark is totally inappropriate. Mr. Mercury, I'm being your friend by posing questions that could help you locate your son. I'm his college professor, and I have a question about Carson's final paper. It's to his advantage to reach me before the semester ends."

I waited long moments before he responded, which gave me time to curtail my anger.

"I apologize," he said. "He's been preoccupied, and his mother believes his silence, or rather broodiness, comes from leaving his teenage years and entering his twenties. I view it differently. The breakup with his girlfriend has him depressed. He spends hours alone in his room, and he says he's not playing online games or listening to music. His mother and I aren't the type of parents to pry, but it appears we should have. When he informed us about taking a creative writing class, we supported a form of expression to help him work through his emotions. We didn't object or question why he originally intended to major in engineering, then did a complete change to study English. What kind of writing have you seen from Carson?"

I carefully formed my words. "Mystery mostly."

"Maybe the breakup affected him like a mystery. I don't know. He prefers fantasy and futuristic movies. In any event, we have no concept of our son's whereabouts."

"Thank you for letting me know what you've learned. I'm sure he has a solid reason for his behavior." I ended the call before I spouted out a huge lie that my concerns weren't important, but they were. Carson had the answer to what happened to my brother.

The truth would seep through the fabric of their world soon enough. I hoped they had support from family and friends because they'd need it to handle the inevitable.

Gage wanted me to keep him informed, and the two conversations with Ethan Mercury warranted a call. I snatched my burner and pressed in his number, longing for the call to go to his voice mail. That way I wouldn't have to talk to him in case he detected my whirlpool of emotions. But he answered.

"This is Risa. I'm using a different burner phone."

"Normal precautions?"

"Always. Do you have a minute to talk?" When he assured me to go ahead, I told him about the two phone calls from Ethan Mercury regarding Carson's disappearance.

"He sends you the story about Trenton, lies about his trip, then disappears?" Gage expelled a breath. "All three are indicators to his involvement. I'm not easily persuaded about someone's guilt, but this kid has blood on his hands. It would take a lot for me not to charge him. I'll run his plates, see if we can find his exact location."

"With the holiday break, my days are free to chase him down."

"Not without me."

"I forgot this time of year depresses you, and here I am unloading my woes."

"This is my job, remember?" Gage yawned.

"Late nights? I'm sure you have your hands full, by your own admission."

"We've been busy," Gage said.

"Is your and Jack's case coming together?"

"Not by a long shot. You know the drill—following a million trails until something connects."

Yes, I remembered all too well. The ticking clock, the river-rapid adrenaline, and the weighing of evidence. "I'll let you go. Sounds like an early-to-bed night. Is this a work weekend?"

"For sure. I'll get back to you about Carson."

I could put in the request to trace Carson's plates from SAC Dunkin, but this was the weekend, and he had family obligations. If I had to wait until Monday, I'd be ready for mega doses of muscle relaxers and antidepressants. And if I conducted the trace, my presence in the system would give me away.

I thanked Gage and bid him good night. I'd read on the secure FBI site more about the Addingtons' baby abduction to get my mind off my own problems. Organized crime had covered their bases on this one.

Gage, Jack, and CARD were knee-deep in a potential national

or international kidnapping ring. I read what they'd uncovered and questioned if the explosion at the Vietnamese restaurant, taking the lives of three people, mingled with the current case . . . Of course it did. Why else would Gage and Jack include this in their investigation? The restaurant had to be connected, but how?

Curiosity, and a longing to help rid this world of those who committed crimes against children, led me to research deeper into the case.

Interviewing directors of maternity homes allowed the agents to speak to the directors and residents candidly about organized-crime rings who offered high dollars for babies.

Pulling together the interviews of the biological and adoptive parents for any discrepancies in their testimonies or body language—imperative.

I wanted to get back in the game, to doggedly pursue a case again. To laugh at my own fears of danger and challenge the subjects of investigations. But that was impossible until Trenton's killer stared back at me behind bars. *When, Lord? Will I ever understand?*

GAGE

At midnight, I learned the Phan sisters, Suzi and Hai, had died in the restaurant fire. An empty gasoline can was found in the rubble and debris. Both women had bullet holes in their foreheads. Close range with a .22—execution style. The third death was a male waiter who died of smoke inhalation, the result of a locked door. HPD found no witnesses to the fire, and security cams in the area neglected to video an hour prior to the explosion and thirty minutes afterward.

Had the killers locked the kitchen door after igniting the explosion? Investigating the three deaths was a matter for HPD and the FBI task force. My concern focused on the coincidence of why two women were murdered, the women who were part of Jack's and my investigation.

Jack and I labored over the fire and death reports until the early hours of the morning, drinking one pot of coffee after another until our guts burned.

I stood to stretch my aching back and ease the acid in my belly. I had a prescription for moments when staying awake on a caffeine binge warred with good sense. But the meds put me to sleep, and that's a luxury I'd take another day. I set my empty cup in the sink.

"I don't think I'm off base here, but this isn't a local kidnapping ring. Not with the Asian community involved," I said. "Granted, I'm tired and attempting to make sense of this. But could we be dealing with national or international fingerprints?"

"Appears so. But at this point, the subjects of our case speak English without an accent." Jack waved his hand. "While Harvey Sinclair and Emily Lock might be the kingpins, dollars buy what organized crime needs. I'm thinking three countries where the ring might originate—Russia, China, and Colombia."

"You covered three continents," I said.

"Four if you count the US. As I was saying, while the Phan sisters were Vietnamese, a fourth country, our reports point to Colombia. There's easier access in and out of the country, and criminals using the same route deal in drugs, running weapons, and human trafficking."

Jack needed rest and was pulling at straws. "It's nearing 3 a.m. Let's get a few hours' sleep to recoup and start back up around ten this morning."

"You're right. I'm not thinking logically." He stood from where his rear must have stuck to the chair with the hours we'd put in. "Where do we meet?"

"I'll pick you up at your apartment and drive to the explosion site. I want to see who's hanging out there, talk to anyone who knew the Phan sisters. Sift through a few ashes around the kitchen. It's still inconclusive why the male victim couldn't get out. Did he have a phone?"

"I'm too tired to suggest any other agenda." Jack said his goodbye and held up a finger. "Add tracing the ballistics of a .22 that killed those women. Probably goes nowhere, but it could go somewhere."

Like a drunk, I stumbled through the house to set the alarm, snapped off lights, and made it to my bedroom before remembering to check the FIG to see if they'd located Carson Lowell's car. I pulled my phone from my jean pocket and checked for an update from the Field Investigative Group. Carson's car was parked at a small motel near Santa Fe, New Mexico—a long way from Estes Park and the Colorado Rockies. According to the motel records, he traveled alone, and he'd signed the register as Andy Sloan. Good news for a change.

The kid was on the run, but he needed a few lessons on how to outsmart the FBI.

I wrestled with giving Risa what I'd learned about Carson's location, but she deserved to know. My call wouldn't be the first time I'd wakened her with an FBI matter. I pressed in her new burner number and envisioned her wrapping her fingers around her phone. She claimed to sleep with it and her Glock. Her sleepy voice on the first ring reminded me of how often I'd taken her for granted. Now I wanted to hold her and never let go, get lost in those green eyes.

"Hey, I know where Carson's hiding out."

"Where?" She sounded more awake.

"Canyon Rock Motel, near Santa Fe, New Mexico." I gave her his alias.

"Hold on, Gage. I need to write this down."

"I'll send it in a text to this number."

"Thank you so much. I owe you. I'll be on the first flight out there."

"Not without me. It's too dangerous for you to walk into a potential danger zone alone."

"Have you forgotten my training?"

"Nope. Have you forgotten the reason for working in pairs? I'll make the flight arrangements for both of us."

"But you have a huge case with Jack. Don't tell me you're not on it this weekend because I know you."

He chuckled. "You nailed me."

"Have you even been to bed yet?"

"About to."

"Gage, you need a keeper."

He remembered a mug he'd given her for her birthday—Gage's Zookeeper. "This animal is heading to bed. Remember I'm flying to Santa Fe with you."

She sighed. "Impossible. The wrong people might find out we're traveling together."

"Who cares? But if you're worried about us being seen together, you book your flight, and I'll book mine. We can leave in the afternoon after Jack and I check out a crime scene. Once we're in Santa Fe, we'll team up, and I'll rent a car."

"Gage, I appreciate you but—"

"No buts. I'll wear a disguise."

"I don't know what to say, but this is crazy."

"Then say yes and pack your things for tomorrow. I'll text you with the flight number and time."

After the call, I made my reservations for Santa Fe to arrive midafternoon and texted her the info. Had I lost my mind? How could I keep my hands off her?

If I didn't make a break in the Addingtons' case before the flight, maybe I'd make progress in who killed Trenton Jacobs and targeted Risa. Monday morning, I'd be back on the Addingtons' kidnapping and investigating who'd killed the Phan sisters and set fire to the restaurant. Add the man who died of smoke inhalation and if the gang were responsible.

The gang was a stubborn puzzle piece. Neither the Wades nor the Addingtons had mentioned a gang member. But someone tipped off the gang and tried to prod Jack and me into an outnumbered fight.

But before I solved the world's problems and attempted to cuff the bad guys, I needed a few hours of sleep.

I believed in sleeping until the last minute, but my phone rang at 7 a.m.—Jack. Why call when we were meeting in three hours?

"You're . . . on your own today." Jack sounded strained, weak.

"What's up? Are you sick?"

"I wish. The truth's humiliating. You'll find out soon enough. I was attacked in the parking area of my apartment complex. I'm at the ER . . . waiting for the doctor to stitch me up."

The reality of Jack's attack jolted me awake. "What hospital?"

"Houston Methodist . . . medical center."

"Don't you live in a gated community?"

"Supposedly. Always a way around security."

"True. What happened and how badly are you hurt?"

"Hold on." He paused, waited while I assumed he wrestled with pain. "I . . . I parked my car outside my apartment and walked to the stairway. Someone jumped me from behind, stabbed me a little too close to my heart." Jack drew in a ragged breath—not in any shape to talk.

"Hey, I'm sorry. Why don't you get some rest? I'm on my way to the hospital. You need a ride home?"

"No need for either." His labored breathing alarmed me. "The doc's keeping me overnight to monitor Superman's body. I'm no good to you until at least Tuesday. Keep talking. It fills my brain before the pain and sleep drip starts to work."

"Do you have any idea who did this?"

"None . . . or many. Go figure. He left a note, tucked it into my shirt." Jack gasped. "Sorry. Said the world was a better place with one less FBI agent."

"He thought you were dead." The attacker must have watched Jack fall to leave a note. "Can I call anyone or do anything?"

"No thanks. My brother lives on the north side of town, and he's on his way . . . Intends to camp out here." Jack took another strained breath. "Be careful, Gage."

✯　✯　✯

I called SAC Dunkin while driving to the restaurant bomb site and told him about Jack.

"I'll arrange immediate protection, and I'm heading to the hospital in a few minutes. Don't take any bets on his being in the office on Tuesday," the SAC said. "Unless he plans to catch up on paperwork."

I hated that job, but Jack was odd enough not to mind. "I've requested the security cam from his apartment complex. Another thing . . . a situation has arisen, and I need to leave town until Monday morning. I'll have my devices with me."

"We want the abduction case wrapped up, but it's the weekend and your partner is incapacitated. You haven't taken time off in months. Go for it."

What would I walk into with Carson? "The truth is, I have a lead on an open case. I'm dealing with critical timing."

"Which one?"

"Trenton Jacobs. A witness to the FSRA came forth, then disappeared. I've tracked him to a motel near Santa Fe."

"And you're heading there alone?"

"I just want to talk. Make sure his testimony is legit and offer protection if needed."

"Did this man approach you?"

"No. Risa."

"I see. Is she going with you?"

"Yes, sir. We leave at noon. First, I'm driving to the Saigon Sampler bombing site to see if anyone there can help detail the reason for the Phan sisters' murders. Jack and I planned to interview any potential witnesses there before his attack."

"Gage, I want your word that you'll update me every step of the way on both of these cases."

"I will."

"Watch what you're doing. I can put another team on the Trenton murder case."

"No thanks. Risa would shoot me."

"I imagine she'd unload several rounds."

★　★　★

The once-thriving restaurant lay in smoking rubble. I recognized the state fire marshal sorting through the debris, a friend for several years. Although the fire department believed the explosion occurred due to gas tossed around the kitchen, the fire marshal investigated the scene to exemplify due diligence. I shook his hand. He and I ran track together in high school, and back then he went by the nickname "Smoke." Still fit him, considering.

"Gage, let's walk the area, and I'll point out what I've uncovered." We skirted the perimeter of what had been the kitchen. Smoke bent to examine ashes, and I joined him. "Over there—" he pointed—"is where firefighters found the women's bodies. Apparently the killers shot them, then set fire to the kitchen as a deterrent. The male, overcome by smoke, collapsed on the opposite side of the kitchen by the door."

"He might have seen the shooters but couldn't get out the locked door."

"The door makes me question if the man was an intended victim too." Smoke used a pen to sift through more ashes. "I'll leave my report open until we hear from the three autopsies."

"Have you seen anyone digging through this?" I said.

"Some. Those Vietnamese over there have been here the longest."

He gestured to a woman and two men huddled together about fifty feet away.

"I wonder if they speak English."

"They don't, but I speak Vietnamese. Need a hand with the language?" When I nodded, Smoke walked with me to the three people. "They're very cautious," he said. "I had difficulty getting them to talk to me. They're grieving the fire victims. My guess is they're family, but they refused to give their names."

"Anything I should know beforehand?" I said.

"Vietnamese culture is reflected in respect for the dead."

"Fear and grief are tough to process. I'll do my best." Without showing the deceased persons proper reverence, I'd lose any trust. "We believe one of the sisters recently had her baby abducted."

"And you're thinking their deaths are linked to it?" Smoke said flatly. "I doubt you'll get anything from them, but we can try. They will want to know why you're here."

"Tell them the truth."

Smoke spoke in their native language and introduced me as an old friend who worked for the FBI. I wanted to find out what happened to three innocent people and help bring justice to their memories. I shared my condolences and gave my word to find out the source of the fire and who'd killed the women. I learned one man lost his brother in the fire, and the couple were cousins to the Phan sisters. Smoke's soft tone and facial expressions showed his concern. I maintained a solemn stance.

"Do any of them know why the sisters were killed?" I waited while Smoke translated.

The men responded negatively. The woman paled. Fear etched deep into her face, and her eyes were rimmed in red.

I took a gamble and asked Smoke to translate. "Their deaths were an execution. Any information leading to the killer's identity and arrest honors the lives of your loved ones."

The three still claimed they had no idea of who or why. "Where is Hai's baby?" I said.

Again no one had information. The woman swiped beneath her eyes with a shaky hand, and the man with her stiffened.

"Ma'am," I said, "Hai told a friend her baby had been kidnapped." After Smoke translated, the woman blinked, and I continued. "Did the person who shot Hai and Suzi also take Hai's baby?"

Smoke interpreted and faced me. "If they haven't responded to your other questions, they won't now either."

And they didn't. "My work is to find out why the sisters were murdered and if the deaths are connected to the missing baby."

Zero response. But I read the apprehension in their body language.

I gave each of them a business card to call me if they learned anything.

Hai's missing baby could have roots in a Vietnamese gang, a separate crime, or the same kidnappers as the Addingtons' baby. I'd not find any answers today. I sent a prayer upward, a rarity, but Risa's situation, Jack's stabbing, missing babies, and the days creeping closer to Christmas told me I needed supernatural help.

21

RISA

Gage's and my flight left Houston for Santa Fe at 2 p.m. and not soon enough to suit me. Checking baggage for one or two nights stay made no sense, but I couldn't pack an unloaded Glock and ammunition in a carry-on, only a checked, locked container according to TSA regulations. If we were detained at the Santa Fe Regional Airport for luggage, Gage would know in an instant I'd brought my firearm.

Investigating a crime meant an uncertain future, which always held surprises, and in the FBI, that meant danger. Still, I had little choice but to leave my Glock behind. If I ran into trouble on this trip, then I knew how to get my hands on a gun. I tossed together a few belongings and toiletries for two days.

A taxi would pick me up in an hour, and it sounded like a week. I tried to wait and be productive on my phone, but patience wasn't a class I excelled in at college or Quantico. I rechecked my memorized questions for Carson with the anticipation of asking them by nightfall. And anticipating answers. The typical who, what, where, when, and why held importance. But the motive for targeting me and not Gage or another agent bubbled to the surface.

Gage and I were partners. Or had been. Nothing emerged in the way of interviews or searching for evidence without the other's knowledge. Once I had moved beyond the awkwardness of being with Gage again, I could set the stage for open communication, like before.

Visions of the real Carson Lowell nudged me. When had my judge of character fallen to ground zero? I questioned if Carson sold or used drugs, but I hadn't seen any indication of that in class or in his writing. Here I thought returning to academia would help me heal. Teaching on a college level, especially creative writing, had given me an opportunity to positively influence the future leaders on a small scale.

As a much younger woman, I entered the world of publication with short mysteries. Then I veered off to a doctorate in English and on to the FBI. My education and experience had helped me understand myself, others, and the ever-changing world. My brain absorbed the sciences, and I'd done well, but the concept of studying people was much more fascinating. While in the FBI, I'd written a few short stories, some completed, some that needed editing, and some would never see the light of day. A passion I never intended to let go. Writing helped me process the good and the ugly.

I longed to be back with the bureau, and one day it might happen. A professor much more dedicated and competent than I could take these kids to the next level in their careers. While I reveled in the satisfaction of urging them to grow their skills, I failed to see teaching as my lifelong career.

I glanced at the time. The taxi would pick me up in fifteen minutes, and my excitement meter to step into an investigation soared. I grabbed my carry-on and purse before heading to the elevator. The idea of finding Carson and establishing the truth both motivated and frightened me.

On board the flight to Santa Fe, I fastened my seat belt for the two-hour flight, more than furious with Gage. He'd arranged for us to sit side by side on the plane. So much for keeping him safe, although he didn't know the truth behind my actions. Gage wore nerd glasses and a bright-red sweatshirt with a moose on the front. He showed me how to press the moose's nose that activated battery-operated lights around the antlers. He softened my fury and had me laughing.

"Your control side is showing," I said.

His blue-gray eyes widened, drowning me in their depths. Would I be able to focus on him and not crave his lips on mine? "You mean booking a seat beside you with my moose?"

"Exactly." If I admitted the truth, I relished the idea of spending two hours with him beside me, our shoulders touching, basking in his voice, and the scent of him filling my nostrils. I sounded like a character in a romance novel. The saying was true—absence makes the heart grow fonder.

"We're going to spend a lot of hours together over the next two days," he said. "How do you feel about it?"

Had he been reading my mind? "Thinking I'd like to punch you."

"You'll get over it." He smirked, drawing on my previous irritation.

"Do you ever get rattled, lose your temper?"

A shadow passed over his face and quickly fled. I'd seen a glimpse of an off-limits topic in the past, but I hadn't pursued it. Always happened around the holidays.

"I'm the typical cool, calm, and collected guy. You haven't answered my question. You know the one, the one you're avoiding. Like, Gage, really great to see you."

I read more in what he didn't say. "Crazy for answers. Honestly, I've missed you—the conversation, laughter, late nights, bad fast food, lousy coffee, and the satisfaction of cuffing the subject of an investigation."

"Anything else?" he said, his tone wistful.

My heart thumped like a puppy's tail on steroids. "I'm sure there is. All selfishness on my part."

"This weekend might cause you to reverse your resignation. We're a better team than Frodo and Sam."

"I'm not a hobbit. When I showered this morning, my feet weren't hairy, and my ears hadn't grown. I'm sure Jack will be a welcome sight on Monday."

"Doubtful. He was attacked in the early hours of the morning. I've been thinking about how to tell you." Gage shared Jack's injuries and his brother staying with him. "The attacker left him for dead, and if the security guard hadn't found him, he'd have bled out. The knife wound came within inches of his heart." He reached for my hand, and I let him.

The horror of Jack's assault brought back reminders of Trenton. "Oh, my goodness, Gage. Any idea who did it?"

"No and yes." He blew out the frustration of suspecting one of many.

"I know what you mean." Was this about their current case or vengeance from a previous one? "I'm glad his brother will be with him. Any evidence?"

"He received a note stating, 'The world was a better place with one less FBI agent.' All bad guys claim the same thing, except not all write love notes."

First me and now Jack received a threat. Were they connected? "Have you had an opportunity to run the handwriting?"

"Requested it. But I haven't seen the report."

The writer of my note wasn't in the handwriting database. I thought back through any crossover cases that I'd worked in conjunction with Jack and Luke or even the four of us. Jack's previous partner needed a break from violent crime against children and now worked the Civil Rights division. Not a single idea surfaced. Who were these people? Who would be targeted next? "What's going on, Gage? Have you been threatened and not told me?"

He stiffened. "How could I have told you anything when you blocked me from your life?"

I heard the disappointment . . . and more. "I'm sorry. I never meant to hurt you. I have no idea who or why Jack was attacked, and I wish I could offer something solid. Grief has altered my emotions, my thinking . . . everything."

"Risa, I need you back in my life." He reached over and kissed my cheek, then held my hand in a firm grip.

I blinked and dug deep into my being to pull away my hand. "Possibly when this is over," I whispered. "I can give you an explanation for deserting you. At the time, my actions were intended to help me work through the loss." I wanted to tell him the real reason I'd avoided him and my parents, but I was afraid. "I'm running in too many directions. Right now, I'm wondering if Carson might be working for a crime syndicate."

I could almost see the wheels turning in Gage's mind. "One of our many questions for the kid is, who else is involved? That will help put the right perspective on Trenton's case."

"I can't think of a single reason for him to target me that night." I fidgeted in the seat. "I just want answers. Jack's attack is another matter. Is there anything you can tell me that would help talk it through?"

"I wish. Jack and I are investigating a kidnapping with the strong likelihood of national or international fingers. But his attack could have been a separate issue, which means a case you and I handled or Jack and his partner worked. No one's been released from prison who is currently under suspicion, and I've ordered surveillance on any who are borderline cases that involved us. CARD is working with us as always. You and I have experienced every angle of violent crimes against children. We've shut down online predators and porn. Returned kids in parental kidnappings and discovered bad situations that made us shed tears. Pick one of those, and we might find answers."

"Were any of Jack and Luke's cases linked to ours?"

"I'll dig deeper. But you and I know crimes drip into more than one division. It's possible you, me, Jack, and his former partner worked parts of the same crime. And we won't have more info until Jack's stable and we're able to talk to Luke."

"Hey," I said. "Working two cases simultaneously is unfair. I'm so sorry to have dragged you into this."

He gave me a smile that wiggled into my heart. "I volunteered, remember?"

★ ★ ★

In Santa Fe, Gage leased a Ford Explorer and drove straight to the motel housing Carson. Inside the vehicle and in the middle of driving, Gage removed the nerd glasses and shrugged out of his red sweatshirt to a plain black one under it. Neither of us had eaten, but neither of us were hungry. Our appetites were for answers. How I longed to move forward with an arrest and put my life back together. Whatever that might be, and I longed for Gage to be part of it.

At the hotel, we learned Carson, alias Andy Sloan, had checked out about the same time we'd boarded the plane in Houston for Santa Fe. The manager identified his photo. I feared my favorite college student had eyes on us.

"Can we see his room?" Gage showed him his creds.

"Sure, but the room might have been cleaned." From what I saw of the hotel, I doubted the rooms were ever cleaned. We followed the manager to the room Carson had used, all the while I prayed for something to give us a clear path forward.

Gage and I entered a room that smelled like sewer overflow. A wrinkled bed and a thin, bare, off-white towel pooled on the floor. He and I searched a plastic container with drawers, behind a cracked mirror, an open closet, under the bed, and flipped the mattress. Plenty of dirt and cobwebs, but no signs of Carson.

22

Carson Lowell had fooled Risa, and she'd not taken it well. The ruse of taking her college class, posing as an eager student, taunting her with his short story, escaping Houston under the guise of a road trip, and outwitting their pursuit of him added up to a dangerous criminal. I'd met kids who were geniuses, and instead of using their high IQs to make the world a positive place, they chose illegal ways to fill their pockets.

"We need rest, and I need to contact the FIG to track down Carson," I said outside the motel. The setting sun streaked across the sky's canvas in magnificent shades of yellow, copper, fiery red, and purple. I paused to thank the Creator for His handiwork.

"A desolate kind of beauty," she said. "Like the area's been forgotten for thousands of years."

"Eight thousand of them to experience the same magnificent sunset. I suggest we get rooms and head out first thing in the morning. Or sooner if I'm notified of Carson's location."

Risa frowned. "I suppose we have no choice if we're dependent on the FBI to locate Carson again, and I hope he hasn't changed vehicles or license plates and added another name to his résumé. He must know a few shady characters to have a forged driver's license." She humphed. "Of course, that's not hard."

I took inventory of the few battered cars and trucks in the partially lit parking lot and the shabbiness surrounding us. "Two rooms shouldn't be difficult." I studied her troubled face. "Want to try another motel?"

"No, this is okay. I don't have my Glock to rid the room of varmints, but the front desk might have a can of Raid."

Loved her sense of humor. "Okay. I promise you can have the room with the least mold and fungus."

She laughed. "Gage, I'm aggravated, but I miss us. I'm sure Jack is wonderful, and he's certainly a brainiac."

While I understood she meant our work, I wanted it to mean so much more. In moments like these, my vulnerability hit the transparent zone. The airplane kiss on the cheek made me want more, to feel her lips on mine. "Yeah. Jack is a smart guy, but a shade between odd and weird."

"What FBI agent isn't? Who in their right mind puts their life on the line to protect others? Do you mean his chicken noodle soup every day for lunch with a mix of coffee and Sprite?"

I shared his dating experience at Brazos State Park, and we both laughed.

"Poor girl and her little dog." She sobered. "He needs to recover soon, so you aren't stuck getting used to another partner."

I had the only partner I ever wanted beside me. "I'll check on him after we've settled."

"Please do. I'm worried about him." She turned to view the lobby behind us. "Carson could have us in his sights now."

"If he's involved with a crime ring, he's hiding out . . . or dead. Stupid move on his part to write a story about his crime."

"I think arrogance took over," Risa said. "I was set up from the start. The first day of class, he approached me in the parking lot, introduced himself, and told me he was taking my class." She captured my attention. "His favorite genres are murder mysteries, suspense, and thrillers. I am such a fool, Gage. I let a kid manipulate me, and I've been trained to know the signs. The smartest move I ever made was resigning from the FBI."

"Don't go there. No point. You're a great agent, and the bureau has lost a strong woman who gave 110 percent to a tough division. We regroup and move forward, just like we've always done." When we investigated together, her optimism kept us from the half-empty syndrome.

But that was before Trenton's death.

We registered for adjacent rooms on the second floor. I requested a trace of Carson's license plates and prayed he hadn't gone off the grid. We found a small Mexican restaurant that served the best fajitas and guacamole.

"Oh, my," she said, gazing around us. "The decor is red and yellow."

"Most Mexican restaurants are."

"Both colors incite people to eat more."

I chuckled and took a generous bite of a beef fajita smothered in pico. "That's right. I should have remembered how much you like to weave color into personalities. What color am I?"

Risa had relaxed, and the tiny lines fanning her eyes softened. "Green."

"Gotta think a little. I either make you sick or remind you of weeds or I'm an alien."

She grinned, then quickly stiffened. "Remember Carson's story? He talks about the driver of the car longing for blood red."

I despised how she'd been betrayed.

☆ ☆ ☆

Nearing 3 a.m. on Monday, the FIG located Carson in Marathon, Texas. He'd paid for gas with a credit card and a room for the night near the Big Bend National Park along the Texas-Mexico border. Why there? Running or was someone directing him? Another less-than-smart move for a kid on the run who should know there were always ways to find people. I phoned Risa, and within twenty minutes, we were driving southeast for the nine-hour trip of nearly six hundred miles.

Once the sun rose, I gave Carson credit for choosing a beautiful but desolate part of Texas, and if it wasn't for chasing him down, I'd have enjoyed the scenery.

Risa's nearness distracted me, though not necessarily unwelcome. In the past, I pushed aside my feelings with the consolation that we were together and talked seven days a week. I searched for the right words to talk about our relationship. We were alone, and the road ahead was deserted of traffic. I found it a whole lot easier pulling information from a lawyered-up bad guy. Or telling her about the tragedy that walked with me since high school.

"Everything okay with your parents?" she said.

"Yes. They're putting together a Christmas party for a children's home."

"Will you see them on Christmas?"

"I usually do. Why?"

"This time of year seems to bring you down."

I glanced away. "Let me think about it."

She nodded.

"Did you know the Big Bend National Park covers over eight hundred thousand acres?" I said.

"Huh?"

"The park where Carson is hiding out."

"With that much rock and land, I hope he doesn't take off again. Gage, I've been there, and he could walk across the Rio Grande into Mexico."

"Which is why we must find him first. He might have been recruited by a cartel who has assured him safety once he's across the border. I'm yanking on straws," I said. "A part of me thinks he's randomly running with no plan, while another part questions if he's pulling us away from Houston into a trap."

Risa swallowed hard. "I think the latter. He's not an idiot, but he didn't change his license plates."

I pointed out the windshield. "Wow, the scenery and desert are gorgeous, especially the layers of colored rock."

"Today isn't one to enjoy the view."

"I understand. Just trying to break into a tough subject."

She tilted her head at me. "You've never had a problem speaking your mind to me before."

"This is different. Risa, I have so many things to say, and I don't know where to begin."

I sensed her gaze settling on me, but I had my eyes fixed on the road. She smelled of freshness and gunpowder, sweetness and fire.

"I'm listening. That's the least I can do with your helping me find Carson."

"Not exactly, but the status of—"

My phone rang—SAC Dunkin—and I snatched it.

"Gage, are you in a position to talk?"

"Yes, sir. What's up?"

"I got a phone call from Methodist Hospital. Jack suffered a heart attack related to the knife injury. He's been rushed into surgery."

I gripped the steering wheel, my knuckles white. "Not Jack. But he didn't indicate a serious problem when he called me."

"He lied. The knife pierced close to his heart, and he wasn't aware of a previous heart condition. I'll keep you posted."

I placed my phone in the console and whirled to Risa.

"What's wrong with Jack?" Her frantic words mirrored my troubled mind.

I repeated SAC Dunkin's words.

"I'd suggest driving back to—"

"No, Risa. We need answers. The best way to help Jack is to find Carson."

23

Gage used the Explorer's Bluetooth to phone the hospital. Jack was still in surgery—and listed in critical condition. I knew the man, superintelligent, standoffish, and a protocol-rooted agent. He analyzed evidence and interviews like a mathematician, which meant following his thinking paralleled with quantum physics. Jack needed prayer, but God and I weren't on the best of speaking terms, and usually I doubted He was listening. I bit back my pride and asked Him to bring healing. My prayers hadn't saved Trenton, but God might help Jack.

Hours later, we found Carson's Jeep at another motel, one in sore need of renovation with a half-lit vacancy sign. Shutters on the outside of the office hung from one hinge, and the potholed parking lot could have buried a car. The marquee light might have read *Merry Christmas* before I was born, but now lit up was *Mer y hri mas*. The trash bin spilled over onto the cracked concrete, and the outside reeked of cigarette smoke. A crooked candy cane yard ornament leaned precariously against the motel's door. The establishment must have been built in the fifties.

Inside, Gage flashed his FBI ID to the hotel manager. "This is the third and last time I'm asking you—in what room is the owner of the

Jeep parked outside and owned by Carson Lowell? I know he gave you his driver's license number, but here it is to refresh your mind."

The young woman with more hair colors than Christmas lights swallowed hard as though the effort hurt. "I'd like to take a pic of your ID for my boss. I can't afford to get fired just before Christmas."

Gage pulled his ID from his pant pocket again. Miss Christmas Hair studied his credentials, snapped a pic with her phone, and handed Gage's items back to him. She aimed what was probably her best glare at me. "And you?"

"I'm FBI too."

"ID, please."

I reached into my purse and gave her my creds. Gage bored his gaze into me, but I ignored him. One day soon I'd tell him about my leave of absence. Until then, he could think I had the same lying habits as many of those we investigated.

"Room 85," Christmas Hair said. "Take the outside walkway to the left."

"Thank you." Gage followed me into the chilly air. "Impersonating a federal agent is against the law."

"I'll take my chances."

"Risa, if I live to be a hundred, I'll never understand you."

"Don't try." I forced a laugh. "It's impossible."

He growled and I hid my mirth. At room 85, Gage knocked. No answer. He knocked again. Still no answer. I held my hand up and he smiled. Wow, I loved working with him again.

I knocked and raised the tone of my voice. "Housekeeping."

The door opened, and Carson stood in the doorway. No shirt, messed-up hair, barefoot, and . . . surprised. More like frightened out of his mind, like a deer in the headlights.

He started to slam the door, but Gage stuck his foot inside. "Not so fast. We've come a long way to ask you questions."

"I have nothing to say."

"But we do." Gage grabbed the door and held it wide for me to enter. Fury raced at breakneck speed from my toes to my hair and back again.

Carson glanced around him as though he might bolt. He gulped. "Professor Jacobs," he choked out the words.

"Right and you're Andy Sloan?" I walked into the dank room with Gage on my heels. "Close the door, Carson. It's cold. You're either shivering because of the wind or scared to death." I scowled at him. "You're pale too."

He obeyed.

Gage flipped on a lamp light and pulled out drawers.

"What are you looking for?" Carson's voice shook.

"A weapon," Gage said.

"What makes you think I have one?" He stared at Gage and back at me.

"Where is it?" I said.

"In my backpack."

Gage unzipped it and pulled out a Sig Sauer P320. "How does an underage kid get his hands on a handgun?"

"Belongs to my stepdad."

"He gave it to you?"

"No, sir."

"You stole it?"

"Borrowed it." Carson trembled.

I'd not seen a killer so terrified. What were we dealing with here? A psychopath like I originally considered?

"Do you know how to use the gun?" Gage pressed in, his voice an even tone while Carson's tone shrilled with his answers.

"Yes, sir. Dad showed me."

"I'll be keeping it." Gage examined the Sig. "At least the safety is on." He stuck the weapon in the back of his waistband.

"How did you find me?" Carson said. "I didn't tell anyone where I was going."

I frowned. "Shouldn't have used your credit card for gas and the motels. My friend here is FBI Special Agent Gage Patterson. We have a few questions."

"FBI?"

I pointed to the ripped vinyl chair in a hideous shade of orange.

"Take a seat, and let's talk about my creative writing class, the one you were excited to take. Why am I not surprised you prefer blood and gore? I'll be sure to add horror fiction to my next class."

He gulped. "I can explain."

"Wonderful. Mind if Agent Patterson and I sit on your bed?"

"Suit yourself."

We eased onto the unmade bed. Probably had bugs like the other one.

"This is nice and cozy." I peered at him. "Are you getting sick?"

"No, ma'am."

"Good." I took a breath to calm my nerves. "Carson, your parents are worried about you. You lied to them about your road trip."

"How I spend my vacation is my business." He lifted his chin like a ten-year-old. "What do you care?"

"Oh, I have my reasons." All I could think of was Trenton's twisted and bloody body lying in the middle of the street. "Why the change of plans? Change of name?"

"As I said, my business."

"For the record, I don't mind a road trip when it's fun. Trailing after you has put a bitter taste in my mouth. Who or what are you running from?"

Nothing. His body shook . . .

"Carson, I asked you a question."

"You're not FBI, so he's not taking orders from you. Besides, I haven't broken any laws." His gaze flung daggers at me.

Gage clasped his knees as though he intended to leave. "I can cuff you and drive to the nearest office. Or you can cooperate."

"Agent Patterson," I said. "I like the idea of pressing charges against him for a murder attempt on a federal officer and the murder of Trenton Jacobs. Both occurred on July 29." Reciting the date fanned the flames of my anger.

"Hey, I told you I haven't done anything wrong," Carson shouted.

My anger rose higher. "That's not true. Let's chat about your short story. Shall I say it's original? Where did you come up with the idea?"

Nothing.

"The details sounded like a firsthand account. How could that be? Or did you mistake the assignment for nonfiction?"

He clenched his hands together.

I stood slowly and walked to Carson's chair. Heat swirled through my body, the rise of fury and revenge taking over logic, emotion. My senses were locked in malicious intent.

Not this way, Risa.

I dug my fingers into Carson's arms. "Why did you kill my brother?"

Carson tried to pull away, but I gripped him hard. "It wasn't me."

"Why mock me with his murder?" I bent over the kid, nose to nose.

I wanted to wrap my fingers around Carson's throat and destroy him like he'd destroyed my brother. My sweet brother who wanted to live with purpose, who wanted to help kids stay away from drugs and alcohol. I pierced my fingernails deeper into his flesh.

Don't give in. You aren't a killer.

"Shut up," I said to Gage.

"I haven't said a word. Risa, stand down. Let's hear what Carson has to say."

"I want him to answer my questions."

"He will." His voice floated soft as though I were another person. "Give him room to breathe. This isn't you."

Listen to Gage.

The heat rushed through me. I shivered and released him. Blood seeped from where I'd dug my nails into his shoulder. He flinched, and my unrestrained emotions slammed into my chest.

I'd lost control, something I'd never done in the past, even with the jerks who harmed or killed children. My reasoning was for my actions never to discount testimony in court.

I wrapped my arms across my chest. Stepping back, I peered into Carson's terrified face, then to Gage standing beside the bed. Both stared at me as if I'd morphed into something vile.

Had I turned into a monster, a detestable killer? A psychopath like Carson?

"I need air." I rushed to the door and flung it open. Outside, the cool night air bathed my face, and in the next moment I smelled the telltale odors of unwashed bodies and sordid behavior, reminding me of how I'd tainted my vow to always act with integrity.

I walked to the front of the hotel office. Carson's parents would be appalled at the conditions where their son took refuge, and yes, he was hiding—peeling paint, weeds for landscaping, a broken light, and a cracked window. More reminders of what a thriving and well-maintained property had once been, respected and valued. Too much like me. The woman in my mental mirror displayed another woman's face. How far had I fallen?

Guilt slithered through me like a poisonous snake. I despised myself and who I'd become. The SAC's warning swirled through me. *"If I determine your methods of investigation warrant dismissal, I will bring charges against you and end your career."*

I blamed God for Trenton's death, and I blamed myself for not reaching out to Mom and Dad at the restaurant. My eyes pooled with liquid regret. Had I slipped into the depths of no return? I hated this stranger, this unfeeling, decrepit excuse for a human being.

God didn't cause evil. Those actions weren't in His character. God used the free will of another man to take Trenton home. To a home where my brother no longer had to wrestle with addictions or unscrupulous friends, where unconditional love bathed him in the light of our Savior. If I forced myself to dwell on Trenton struggling with life's challenges for years, then he truly lived in a better place. Why couldn't I believe and accept he was in a better place?

Dare . . . I . . . Give. In. To. Pure. Truth? The thought warmed my cold body. Slightly.

Missing Trenton would never fade, and I didn't want to put him in some remote part of my heart. That kind of wish came from a selfish, insensitive soul. For if I lost my ability to feel, then I lost what I'd once treasured. No matter how much I ached. No matter how hard the grief. No matter how difficult to face the truth.

Memories of our childhood offered snapshots of our special relationship, my little brother who'd let me paint his toenails, curl his hair, and apply makeup—much to our father's horror. I remembered when Mom had brought him home from the hospital and placed him in my arms. I wanted to play dolls with him, dress him in dozens of outfits. When he cried, I cried too.

The bitterness of his death placed a wall between me and God. I needed to accept the impossibility of bringing my brother back. At his funeral, I despised those who'd repeated clichés as comfort or recited the all-things-work-together-for-good phrase, but now they soothed me. I now understood others' need to help me deal with the tragedy.

How had I lost my focus with Carson?

I'm sorry, Father. Please forgive me. You took Trenton home so he wouldn't have to battle with addictions. You took him home because he'd struggled long enough.

The eeriness of the supernatural wove with reality . . . The voice inside me belonged to Gage, the one urging me to stop and listen to reason . . . that voice belonged to God. How could I quarrel with a God who showed more love in His holy breath than I'd ever encounter in my lifetime?

I walked slowly back to the entrance of Carson's room and grabbed support from a post holding up the motel. All I could do was cry over my own miserable condition.

24

No one should ever separate themselves from God. Nothing good comes from stepping away from the only source of life and healing. Standing outside the less-than-stellar motel where Gage and I finally tracked down Carson Lowell, I faced the ugliness of my vengeance. Instead of trusting God to guide me, I'd chosen my way of justice—and confessed I'd followed that crooked path since Trenton's funeral. But why did my brother have to die?

Carson needed to hear my sincere apology, no matter if he was guilty or innocent. Truth would unfold and justice would be served—righteous justice, not my definition. Someone once said truth was often an opinion, but no one could argue with facts. I needed facts to see the real truth. But I needed truth to show me the way.

Gage deserved to hear what I'd done since Trenton's death. He'd spoken of his caring, and I couldn't ignore it, especially when my heart ached for him. Alone in the gathering darkness, I forced myself to journey through my scattered feelings for him . . . Scattered might not have been the best term but definitely confusion. With Gage, I felt at ease. No pretense or facade. Right from the first day of our partnership, we had a strange connection as though we'd known each other for years. He brought out the best in me, and he claimed I did the same for him.

I smiled and leaned against the pole outside of Carson's room. Sometimes Gage and I brought out the worst in each other and learned from our errors, and when we disagreed, the resolution brought us closer together. Our respect for each other kept us friends. But I sensed more, an unexplainable bond, as if . . . I was home. No point in denying my feelings.

I loved Gage. I needed to tell him.

The color green represented him. He stood for nurturing, growth, and renewal. Odd, but true.

The door behind me creaked open, and I felt Gage's presence. The scent of strength and warmth emitted from him, so difficult to describe but easy to embrace, to treasure. I wanted to face him, but I feared I'd cry more. God had wrung me dry, and rightfully so.

I reached deep inside for courage, yet I still couldn't give him eye contact. "I'm sorry for what I did to Carson. I'll apologize to him."

"Are you okay?"

How should I answer? "Trying to be. I made the mistake of judging Carson without even hearing him out, wanting him to pay for Trenton's death. Placed myself in a role that warred against all I believed right and holy. His guilt or innocence is not my decision but for a court of law and God."

I breathed in slowly to calm my trembling body. "Gage, I've been incredibly wrong about too many things. I failed you as a friend. Not just failed but acted as though I didn't care about all the bits of life we'd experienced together."

"You've never failed me." In the dark shadows, his presence calmed me.

I forced myself to turn and gaze into his face, the face of a man brimming with integrity. The faint light highlighted his rust-colored hair. "I've hurt you, and I'm sorry."

His kind smile told me I had cut deep with my selfishness. "Are you convinced Carson drove the killer's car?"

I shook my head. "Not sure, except he knows something. He's scared and running. You and I have seen enough frightened people to know the two are not a good mix. Is he brilliant and manipulating us so we think he's innocent? Is he running from something too big for him to handle? And the hugest suspicion is that he suffers from severe mental issues."

"Let's talk to him. Get some answers and try to figure this out."

"As in calmly without me stumbling off the insanity cliff?"

He chuckled. "An excellent starting point."

"I'll not let my emotions take over this time."

"Would you lead out?" Gage said. "Carson may open up quicker to a friend."

"This friend wanted to kill him."

"He got the message."

I bit back the regret threatening to seize my emotions. "If he wasn't afraid of me as his prof, I'm sure he has a new taste of my potential. Before we go in, I have a confession. Only SAC Dunkin knows this and DC." I struggled to keep from bursting into tears again. "I'm on leave, not resigned from the FBI. I should have told you right from the start. And when this mess with Carson is talked through, I'll tell you the whole story."

Relief spread over him, and his shoulders relaxed. "Wonderful news. Worth a moose sweatshirt and black-framed glasses. We'll see what Carson has to say."

I needed God's help to restrain my emotions. But I was afraid of myself.

25

Gage opened the door to Carson's room, and the kid stood as though expecting me to level him. Who could blame him? His professor had morphed into a horned demon. I studied him in the faint light and detected, even smelled, fear—the sickening inability to perceive what I might do to him.

I longed to build back the trust I'd fractured. "Carson, I apologize for losing my temper. You experienced a cruel, insensitive, unprofessional—"

"Listen, I messed up big-time." He ran his fingers through dark hair. "I ran because I was scared. I know things . . . things I wish I didn't. I . . . don't know what to do. I'm sorry."

I forced gentleness into my tone. "Agent Patterson and I can help."

He blinked. "Maybe. But first I need to tell you the truth. About my story."

Why couldn't I have initiated this conversation without dumping rage? "Yes, please. We need to know what happened and why. I'm incredibly confused."

"We both are," Gage said. "I've worked this case since last July, and your story is the first solid piece of information we've had. Part of the content offers an explanation to why Risa's brother faced a killer." His voice offered logic amid highly charged emotions.

How often had I shoved a friendly tone into suspects to relax them and urge them to talk? I gave both guys a mental thumbs-up.

"Shall we try again?" My stomach growled audibly. My fault because I refused to stop for food on the drive here.

"I have a Snickers in my backpack if Agent Patterson could get it."

Gage retrieved the candy bar and handed it to me.

"My favorite. We're off to a good start." I ripped the paper off one end and sank my teeth into deliciously sweet chocolate and peanuts. Normally I'd relish every bite. Now I worried it might make me nauseated.

"Carson, your parents are worried sick." Not the best choice of words considering my whirling stomach. "I'd like your phone to text them. If you agree with the wordage, you can send it."

He reached for his phone on a beat-up particleboard nightstand and gave it to me. I typed: **Mom, Dad, I'm sure I've upset you. Sorry. I'm ok. I'll be home soon.** Carson read the message and sent it to his parents. He replaced his phone on the nightstand.

"I saw no reason to tell them you're with an FBI agent and me," I said. "When we're back in Houston, you can tell them, or we'll tell them together. Whatever works best."

We took the same seats as before, but my attitude had taken a refresh. Professionalism in the conversation was imperative or I'd lose him for good. I really wanted to record the conversation, but I also risked Carson refusing to speak up. "I imagine you and Agent Patterson talked a little."

He nodded, his lips quivering. "He said you were hurting about your brother's death, and my story made me look like the bad guy. I didn't drive the car . . . but I saw who did. The whole thing."

Then who killed Trenton? I reined in my questions to keep Carson comfortable. "Losing my brother has been extremely difficult. After his passing, I resigned from the FBI and returned to teaching. Your story and taking my class weren't a coincidence, right?"

"No, ma'am." Carson scrubbed his hand over his cheek. "Listen, I gotta have your and Agent Patterson's word about something. Just telling you what I saw puts my mom and baby brother in danger. I'm not a fool, and I know you have to report this stuff, but I'm begging you to please wait until you arrest the guy. Promise you can keep my mom and brother safe."

What kind of trouble had he gotten himself into? I dipped my chin at Gage.

"I assure you," Gage said. "If what you are about to tell us places them in danger, the FBI can protect them. What about your dad?"

"Stepdad. Everyone thinks he's my real dad. My father died a long time ago. Don't remember him. Mom remarried when I was seven." Bitterness laced Carson's tone.

"You and your stepdad have problems?" I said.

He shrugged. "My end anyway. We got along great until about a year ago." He drummed his fingers on his ripped, jean-clad knee. "I'll start there. And you promise my mom and brother will be safe?"

"Yes," I said. "Agent Patterson gave you his word, and I'll do whatever it takes on my end."

Carson took a long drink from a water bottle on the nightstand. "Dad, Ethan—I don't know what to call him."

"Whatever makes you feel comfortable."

He hesitated before continuing. "He used to be my dad. Still is no matter what he's done, no matter how much I want to hate him." He bit into his lip. "I must sound like a kid."

"You sound like a young man who's afraid his dad is mixed up in a horrible crime."

"Yeah," he whispered. "Dad started to change after my high school graduation. At first, I thought Mom being pregnant had him paranoid 'cause he had to know where we were every minute of the day. When Caleb was born, he nagged my mom about leaving the house with the baby."

Carson snorted. "He even tried to change my curfew. I'm nineteen and a half years old. No reason for me to have a curfew of midnight, but he wouldn't budge. I asked why, and he claimed Houston had become too 'crime infested.' Things at home got worse. I mean, he'd fly off the handle for no reason. Surprised Mom and me. She made excuses for him, said work pressures must be stressing him out.

I saw him leave the house a few times, late, like two in the morning. Made me wonder if he was cheating on my mom. Once he left in his SUV, and twice some guy picked him up in a car."

"What kind of vehicle?" I said.

"A black Lexus."

"You're sure it was a man?"

"Yes, ma'am. The guy got out of the car once, and I saw his broad shoulders and bald head. Kinda tall, taller than Dad. And he could have met with this guy during the day or while we slept. I decided not to tell Mom unless he took off again, then I'd follow him. No reason to upset her. The guy could have something to do with the alarm business."

"I have a question," Gage said. "Have you ever seen the man up close?"

"No, sir. Just what I told you."

"License plate number?"

"No, sir. Didn't think of it. Sorry."

"Thanks, go on with your story," Gage said.

"One night, in July, Dad said he had a work meeting and a customer wanted to have dinner with him. The same guy in the black Lexus picked Dad up. I'd had enough and followed him in my Jeep, staying far enough behind not to be seen. They drove to a shopping area at Town and Country, left the Lexus, and got into an SUV. They drove to a high-rise apartment building and parked in front of it. I waited far enough behind and parked."

"My apartment building?" I said.

Carson leveled his gaze at me. "Yes, ma'am. You came out the front and walked down the street. Dad and the guy tailed you in the SUV, and I walked far enough behind not to let Dad suspect anything. That's what I thought anyway. In one block you crossed the intersection to the restaurant on the opposite side. The guy in the SUV pulled into the restaurant's parking lot. I watched you from a bus bench across the street. I wore an Astros cap pulled down over my eyes and pretended to read on my phone. The short story shows what I saw. The fictitious part is the crazy driver and the pizza. Like in the story, I later saw the SUV with my dad in the passenger side pull to the street from the parking lot and go through the intersection while you and your brother crossed. Because they followed you from your apartment building, I assumed you were the target."

I drew in a sharp breath, unable to disguise my emotional tremors.

"Professor Jacobs?" he whispered.

"I'm okay. Your stepfather sat on the passenger side?"

"Yes, ma'am. I witnessed the whole thing, and the hit wasn't an accident. But I don't know why. The SUV headed for you first, but the guy, your brother, shoved you out of the way." Carson bit his lip. "I made up things in the story because I don't know what my dad and the other guy said or where the SUV went afterward. I saw in the media that the cops found it."

I struggled not to relive the horror again. I excused myself for a moment and stepped outside for fresh air. I forgot the stench, and my break didn't last long. I'd craved truth, and now I had many of the answers to what plagued me—if Carson told the truth. The *if* lingered like the churning in my stomach. Unanswered questions needled me, and I rejoined Carson and Gage. "Then you walked back to your Jeep and drove home?"

"Yes. I couldn't sleep, like who could've? About an hour later, Dad came into my room. He sat by my bed in the dark and said, and these are his words, 'If you want your mom and unborn baby brother to stay alive, you'd better keep your mouth shut about what you saw tonight.'

"I was mad and scared. I remember whispering, 'Why did the guy try to hit the woman?' He told me to mind my own business. I started to ask more questions, but he stopped me. Said, 'Enough, just forget about it.' I obeyed, not telling anyone until now." Carson drew in a sharp breath. "Dad could have jerked the steering wheel or done something. I don't want to believe he's a killer or knew the guy wanted to run you down. What am I supposed to think?" He buried his face in his hands, while his knee bounced.

I stayed silent for him to think.

Carson slowly faced me. "Has my dad always been like this? 'Course you don't have answers. This all is making me crazy. My girlfriend accused me of using drugs and broke up with me. Couldn't tell her anything either."

"Why didn't you call HPD or the FBI with an anonymous tip?" I said.

Carson covered his mouth, then dropped his hand to his lap. "I saw the reports online, and no one came forward as a witness. Yeah, a couple of people got the license plates, but it happened fast. Anyway I'd be the first to blame, and I couldn't risk Mom and the baby."

I glanced at Gage, and he gave me a thin-lipped smile, encouraging me in his special way.

"Why did you take my class?"

"Sounds so lame now. I searched the Internet and found your name and your brother's name. I'm a Christian, Professor Jacobs, and I'd seen real evil. I couldn't ignore any of it, but why had my dad taken part in a murder? I prayed for a way to help and keep my mom and brother safe. When I saw you were FBI, I went through page after page on their website.

"At first, I assumed the cops or you would find my dad and the other guy and arrest them. I checked online, sorta OCD with it. While doing a Google search, I read you'd left the FBI. I dug deeper on social media and found your mom's page. She used your full name and told her followers that you'd resigned from the FBI. The next thing that happened is weird, and I have to think God pointed me to you. Mom and Dad were after me to register for fall college classes. No way would I move away and leave Mom and Caleb alone. There's a Houston Community College campus near me, and I recognized your name as faculty for teaching creative writing. I really like English and took the class to find a way for me to tell you the truth. But every time I thought about staying after class, I couldn't put the words together."

Tears streamed down his face. "No matter what I did, my mom and baby brother were in danger. The junk in my head wouldn't leave me alone."

My head pounded as though it swelled with information—or a pack of lies. "Then you wrote the short story?"

"Yes, ma'am." He swiped at his eyes. "It seemed like the best way. You said fiction allowed writers to tell truth in a nonthreatening environment."

Not sure I'd ever use that defense of fiction again. "Why run after you turned in the assignment? That makes no sense to me. If you were afraid for your family, why not go to your mother with what you'd witnessed and convince her to accompany you to the authorities?"

He paused as though thinking. "I told you—I didn't know what to do. So I wrote the story and believed if I took off, then Ethan would come after me. I'd find a way to contact Mom and have her hide somewhere. I thought we could get to Mexico and head to South America. That's really lame. Too many holes."

My heart threatened to leap from my chest. I'd been trained to handle interviews, although my internal reactions made me feel like a rookie. I wanted to believe Carson, but he sounded like a psychopath who had no idea of his actions. I'd play along to garner his trust and maybe he'd slip.

"Why did the driver target me?"

"I wish I knew."

"Have you seen the man with your stepdad since then?"

"A few. Always at night. I've never followed them since the one time."

I stood on wobbly legs and took two steps to Carson. "I will never forget what you've done for me. You are the bravest young man I've ever met."

"But will the truth get my mom and brother or us killed?"

I nodded at Gage and for the third time took refuge in the cool night air. I kicked the tires of a pickup parked close by. What should I believe?

26

GAGE

Carson phoned his parents and told them he'd been out of cell phone range and had decided to take the road trip by himself. He told them the breakup with his girlfriend had messed up his head. And he'd call Professor Jacobs right after talking to them. His fabrication about a change of plans sounded somewhat believable. Did he have a habit of lying?

Shortly before nine that night, the three of us went for burgers and fries, and Carson checked out of the motel with the flickering *Mer y hri mas* sign. I drove the Jeep, and Risa drove the Explorer to another motel with cleaner accommodations. She had Carson's Sig under the driver's seat just in case. I wanted Risa to have every opportunity to pry info out of him, yet I wanted her safe if he turned on her. His story was still out with the jury as far as I was concerned. After eating, we found an upgraded property that had adjoining rooms where I'd room with Carson. No way would he leave my sight.

We were all exhausted, but I had more work to do, not only with Carson's claims about his stepdad but also the Addingtons' kidnapping. My life reminded me of pancake syrup—spread too thin I accomplished nothing.

But I had Risa on the other side of the door. I almost told her about my inability to handle this time of year. I should, and if she and I moved ahead with our relationship, then I must.

Risa kept Carson company while I stepped outside to phone SAC Dunkin with the updates. "I'm driving Carson's Jeep back to Houston in the morning, and Risa will drive the rental. That way, he may open up more or retract his story."

"Do you think he's responsible for the murder?"

"I don't know. If we can find proof for his claims, we might need a safe house for his mom and brother."

"I'll arrange protection and accommodations if the kid's testimony rings true, although his story sounds sketchy. Does he appear mentally competent?"

"Hard to tell. If Carson's lying, he's got it down to a science. What bothers me is he didn't get the license plates of the Lexus. He alleged to have seen the car more than once, so why didn't he get the numbers? On the other hand, what reason does he have to target Risa other than a paid hit, gang initiation, or he's a psychopath?"

"We'll evaluate him for psychoanalysis when you're here."

"For sure I'll be in the office Tuesday morning. I'd also like to have Ethan Mercury brought in as a person of interest for questioning."

"I'll make sure he's served."

I thanked the SAC. "How is Jack?"

"Still in critical condition. The surgeon repaired the problem to his heart, found clogged arteries, and inserted two stents. His recovery depends on lots of rest. Currently we have guards posted 24-7 outside his room. I met his brother. They are a lot alike, and I thought there could only be one Jack Bradford."

We shared a chuckle. "Any arrests made?" I said.

"A security cam captured a hooded person walking away from Jack's apartment building. Slight build. I'll send you the video."

"Are you thinking one of the gang members or a woman?" I said.

"Both are in the running. Let me know what you think after viewing the video. The consensus here is the person doesn't walk like a woman. However, that could be on purpose. We ran the handwriting on Jack's note through the database and came up with zero. You'd recognize Carson Lowell's handwriting. Any similarities?"

"Not that I recall."

"We'll examine his and Ethan Mercury's for comparison."

"Yes, sir. Risa told me about her leave from the FBI. I assume she'll be in contact with you."

"She already has and requested to continue working in the same supposed resignation mode. However, she understands you will need another partner. Once her brother's death is resolved, she'd like to return. I told her I couldn't guarantee the two of you would be partners. Her fall semester is finished, and she's completed her obligations except for final grades. Unless the crime is solved in the next few weeks, she may choose to continue teaching for the next semester. Gage, if you detect a problem with her ability to resume her FBI career, I need to be aware, whether it's personal or emotional."

"I believe she's working through issues."

"Good to hear. Now that you know her status, I compared the handwriting to a note she received the day of her brother's funeral, and while it isn't in the database, it matched the one Jack received. I'll tell you what I told Risa—don't put me in a position to regret this."

I had gone back to the church after Risa had refused to show me the note and viewed the security cam. "Of course. Do you mind if I bring Risa up-to-date on the Addington case and what Jack and I learned about the killings at Saigon Sampler?"

"Go ahead. My guess is she's read the case notes online."

After the call, I requested a complete background on Ethan and Lynn Mercury. Not a coincidence the Addingtons used Mercury Alarms. My search revealed no more than the previous one. The Mercurys appeared to be good citizens. Ethan's nationwide alarm business thrived in several states, mostly homeowners and a few small commercial customers. Mercury Alarms Inc. was the parent company, but many of the businesses in other locations were called by different names to maintain a local feel. The ease with the customer using online tools to manage individual systems and extensive advertising had made the company extremely popular across the nation.

My attention turned to the Saigon Sampler, where the Phan sisters and the worker were employed. The restaurant used a different service. But the Wades' alarm system in Des Moines had Mercury Alarms as the parent company.

I researched the FBI's secure files for a connection between home invasions, kidnappings, and Mercury Alarms, a task I should have done sooner. Before I could process what all this meant, my phone indicated the search I'd made earlier had downloaded. I read what I needed to know and sent it to Risa's burner. While the information populated, I checked on Carson, asleep and snoring.

I texted Risa and asked if I could join her to discuss Ethan Mercury and the kidnapping cases. Switching to FaceTime, I muted my phone and positioned the camera with a view of Carson sleeping.

I knocked on the door of Risa's adjoining room. She unlocked it and greeted me with reddened eyes, a sure sign she'd been crying. Had she heard grim news? Grief? Lack of sleep and unanswered questions? I closed the door behind me and studied her.

"You're definitely not okay. How can I help?"

"If I could lasso my ups and downs, I'd do so and maybe put a stop to the predator called grief." She smiled through quivering lips. "Trenton's not coming back. He's gone, forever gone. In one breath I'm glad his fight with addictions is over, and God has him safe and loved. Then my emotions send an unexpected surge of nausea, anger at myself and the situation, and a perpetual lump in my throat. Why did God have to take my brother? Am I drowning in a swirling pit of hopelessness?" She swiped beneath her eyes. "I'm sorry. I've said all that before, but I despise my weakness. You have enough on your mind without my self-pity."

"A strong woman faces the enemy and walks through the fire. Just like you're doing. A coward stuffs her grief and attempts to will it away. Six months have gone by. You were in shock at the beginning, but now your heart's defenses have crumbled. Reality has set in."

"His birthday is tomorrow. He was Mom and Dad's early Christmas present that year."

I groaned, and my own past stabbed me. "Milestones are the

worst, especially the first ones. You're dealing with Trenton's birthday, Christmas, and a horrible loss."

"You've lost someone close to you, beyond the evil we've seen committed against children."

I nodded. "It's a topic for another time."

"All right. I'm ready when you are."

I couldn't stop myself. "Risa, I'm in love with you." I held up my hand. "Please don't say anything. We have so much going on right now, but I had to tell you."

She lifted her pale face. "How I've longed to hear those words. I love you too." She imitated my raised hand. "Later. We've waited this long, and as hard as it is, we can wait a little longer."

We stared at each other, and the tension, the heat, between us escalated. I reached for a bottle of water and finished it, then took a deep breath.

I felt her eyes on me. My resolve disappeared.

I crossed the room and took her face in my hands. Her green eyes glowed like soft candlelight. I bent and lightly kissed her, then deepened. She tasted sweeter than I'd ever anticipated. Not sure I could or even wanted to stop.

She pulled back, trembling. "Gage, we can't—"

I kissed the tip of her nose and stepped back before I regretted my next move. "We should be working." My hoarse voice caused a nervous giggle from her.

"Should we try to concentrate on this case instead of the obvious?" she said.

"Right. We have a murderer on the streets and a frightened kid who may or may not be telling the truth."

"Don't forget your and Jack's case."

I moved back to a chair. *Distance, Gage. Keep your distance.* I paused to change the atmosphere, pretending to increase my attention on Risa's phone screen that still showed Carson asleep. She needed a clear head to digest the seriousness of what we faced, and I needed a moment to process her words. "In the morning, I plan to leave an hour earlier than you and Carson. If the wrong people have me in their sights, I'd rather deal with them alone in Carson's Jeep."

Risa gestured for me to sit onto a blue upholstered chair with an ottoman, and she curled up on a matching sofa. "I don't have a firearm unless it's okay to keep Carson's Sig."

"Keep it."

"Before we dissect this case, how's Jack?" she said.

I told her what SAC Dunkin had reported as well as the entire conversation. "Once we're back in Houston, I'll pay Jack a visit."

She rubbed her palms together. "I didn't want to have this discussion in front of Carson, but what are your initial thoughts about his story? What links me and Ethan Mercury plus the killer who drove the stolen SUV? What's the common denominator?" She leaned her head back on the sofa. "Here's what I think. Since you haven't been harmed, I'd say Jack and I have worked the same case or suspect." She stared at the wall beyond me. "He and I never worked together, so it's something else. Something woven into the fabric of a colossal crime. I question the wisdom of the killers trying to eliminate us because the deaths of two federal agents would attract more attention than the subject wants or needs. The intensity of a mass investigation to find out who's killing agents could lead to the crime ring and expose other illegal activities."

"True. Or they're devising a way to eliminate all three of us. And any others on their list."

She closed her eyes. "We've got to sort this out. You wanted to talk, and I haven't closed my mouth since you walked in. What else have you learned?"

"What's your impression of Ethan Mercury?"

"Hmm. Am I being interrogated? Answering a question with a question?" She paused. "Initially, he appears to be a caring man, worried about Carson, devoted to his family. Yet Carson painted another picture. He had to recognize me when you and I visited them that night, but I didn't see anything to indicate it. What if Ethan Mercury expressed concern over Carson's noncommunication because he feared Carson might inform law enforcement what he saw that night? That ups the reality of Mercury's so-called threat to his wife and child. Why target them instead of his stepson? I'd think he'd be quicker to eliminate his stepson than his wife and baby. The bottom line? If Carson is the one person who can testify against Mercury, why isn't he dead?"

"That brings me to another bit of info I just learned. The kidnapping cases link back to Mercury Alarms and their subsidiaries. Each victim was a client, including the Wades."

She pinned her gaze on me. "Trenton's death and the Addingtons' abducted baby are connected?"

27

Sleep evaded me with the memory of Gage's kiss and his words, our words. I wanted a solid relationship, but how?

The unveiling of Ethan Mercury's connection to Trenton's death, intended for me, and the kidnappings told me the crime had many players. My pondering seemed redundant, but my mind refused to offer new data. Why had Jack and I been targeted? What did someone fear we knew that could expose them? The answer to Jack's or my information threatening Ethan Mercury dwelled in a past or open investigation, but which one? Targeting me and Jack but not Gage should narrow the possibilities. If only I could find a case or an interview I'd conducted without Gage. I searched through FBI files for an indication of crossover cases involving only Jack and me with zero chance of Gage's or even Luke Reardon's involvement.

Then what about the buying and selling of babies for profit in which a mother or couple willingly made the exchange? How wide and deep did that scenario stretch? Was it even a factor in this case? If so, the ring had already proved they'd take whatever measures necessary to protect their investment.

I forced the whirling thoughts in my mind to stop and rebooted my focus. Breathe in. Breathe out. Empty my brain of nonsense and inapplicable info.

Nearing one in the morning, I contemplated the perfectly made bed, where I should be sleeping. The notion dissipated while my mind whirled with confusion. When Gage and I worked a case and a suspect proved hostile, the other took over. Sometimes the passive agent stayed quiet during the Q and A, and sometimes that agent left the room to observe the interview through a one-way mirror, though the whole proceedings were captured on video.

I recalled the last case before I took my leave . . . Typical, and the transcript didn't provide anything unusual. I did the same with three other cases. When nothing jumped out at me, I chose to wait until Gage and I talked through them in detail.

Was he awake? If I tapped on his door, would he think I wanted another kiss? I tiptoed to the adjoining door and slowly turned the knob. It made a slight click, and I peeked inside. The sound of a soft snoring duet met my ears. The room smelled manly—not bad—a mix of leftover fragrances and soap. No more brainstorming tonight. I'd spend my awake hours thinking what I might have done to offend Ethan Mercury and whoever he worked with.

I slid into the comfy chair that Gage had taken earlier and closed my eyes. A prayer for guidance soared upward. Most of Gage's and my cases were the noncustodial-parent type, but the few hideous ones had resulted in arrests. Those violent deaths and human trafficking weren't as prevalent. Many of our tragic cases resulted in a prison sentence that kept the criminal behind bars. Were any of those cases open-ended?

Those who kidnapped children were motivated by different scenarios, but too many were driven to buying and selling children to lace their pockets.

Gage discovered Mercury Alarms as potentially the way of gaining access into a home, but how were the babies chosen? Did the adoptive parents complete a profile and the crime ring matched them up? Perhaps that made sense in some cases, but not all. They merely wanted a healthy child. In the case of the Addingtons' baby, were the abductors aware of the child's health problems and didn't care? I shuddered at the thought.

I glanced again at the FBI secure reports. Gage and Jack had talked to maternity homes, which was how they stumbled on to the abducted Vietnamese baby and the subsequent murders. Jack's attack wasn't a coincidence or a random assault.

Where did I fit?

I heard a knock on the adjoining door and answered it.

"Professor Jacobs?" A sleepy-eyed Carson stood in the doorway. "You haven't been to bed?"

"No," I whispered. "Can't sleep. Trying to make sense of what we know slamming against the many unanswered questions."

"Are you angry with me? I know I made a mess of things."

I'd keep my convictions to myself. "No reason for me to be upset when you used your best conceivable way to tell me the truth. My concern is ensuring justice is served and to ease your mind about your mother and baby brother's safety."

I pointed to the sofa. The Sig lay in my purse. "Have a seat." When he did, I forced a smile I didn't feel. I didn't trust him, but I refused to let it show. I retrieved my purse across the room under the pretense of a pen to take notes on the hotel's scratch pad. "Take a deep breath. For the record, your short story gave you an A for the class."

"At whose expense?"

I heard the remorse. "Are you blaming yourself for my brother's death?"

He turned away, tapped the chair arm, then back to me. "Kind of. Maybe I could have shouted at you or come inside the restaurant and warned you the guy and my stepdad were following you."

"Please, don't beat yourself up for a crime not of your doing. It's not your fault—I should know since I've done it enough."

"You? But you were nearly killed."

"I was the intended target, remember? I'm working hard to forgive myself, and honestly, the blame isn't for you or me to carry."

"I understand what you're saying, but it's hard to accept. The 'If' poem by Rudyard Kipling keeps rolling through my head, about what it takes to be a moral and ethical man. I had to memorize it my junior year of high school, and it's stuck with me about how to live my life." He shook his head. "My dad memorized it with me. Another reason why this whole thing is hard."

"I'd like to hear it."

"Seriously? It's nearing two in the morning."

"Can't think of a better time."

Carson took a deep breath and recited the poem. His eyes pooled.

Could he be the real thing? If only I had transparent vision to discern between the lies and truth. "What does Kipling's poem say to you?"

He blinked. "If I'm to be a man of truth and take a stand on what I feel is right, then I must be ready to stand alone, to choose the positive instead of the negative. But I also need to seek humility and accept my faults. Not complain but learn from my mistakes."

I crossed my arms over my chest. "How do those things apply to what you're facing now?"

"I wanted to protect those I love. Still do. I've made stupid mistakes. Lots of them. The man-thing to do is face what I've done and accept the consequences no matter what they are. I'd like to be wrong about my dad, but I hope not. I will tell the truth as I know it."

A deep-thinking young man who carried far too much weight on his shoulders. "One day you'll see the heartache today has made you stronger, and you'll be able to help someone who is struggling."

"I hope so. My girlfriend understood me until I weirded out on her."

"If she's the right one for you, you'll get back together. Carson, it takes time for all of us to evaluate our life experiences and grow into commendable people. But we won't ever get it right in this life. When we fall, we get back up. And sometimes God puts the right people in our lives to help us walk on the hot coals."

He blew out emotion. "I think that's you, my prof with an attitude."

I waved my hand in front of my face. "Don't get me all emotional. Let's talk about something else before we're both bawling and squalling. Did you receive a text from your parents?"

"Yes. I answered like you and Gage suggested."

"Tell me about your baby brother."

"Miss Jacobs, he's so cute." Carson's face beamed. "Three months old, and he's growing so fast. He laughs and likes for me to talk to him." He reached out with his right hand. "When he reaches out and grabs on to my finger, I keep thinking one day I'll have a kid of my own." He shook his head. "Sorta dumb, right?"

"Not at all. You'll be a great dad, I'm sure."

"Gotta get an education and find the right girl first."

Was this a charade, the means to blame his stepdad for a murder? "Sounds like before all this happened, you and your stepdad were close."

"Dad's always been amazing. He took me fishing and hunting. Told me how proud he was of me. Taught me how to play basketball and how to use what he taught me in real life. We read books together. He treats my mom like she was the most important person in the world. When Mom and Dad told me about the baby, he cried, said I was his number one son no matter if Mom had a dozen more kids." Carson frowned. "Then everything changed. It was all an act to cover up whatever he's doing."

"Are you sure? With what you've told me, he sounds like a good man."

"Bad guys can treat their families okay."

"Gage and other law enforcement will figure this out and learn the truth."

"They have to. And soon."

"How does your dad treat the baby?"

"Great. Changes diapers and gets up in the night with him. Mom really loves Dad. All this will hurt her."

"Like you're hurting now?"

Carson swiped beneath his eyes. "I'd give anything for the nightmare to go away. I feel so da—" He trembled. "I don't need to be swearing. Where is God in the middle of murders and threats?"

I wished I had a solid answer for him when I questioned that very thing. "I question God too. He's not a genie we can summon when we want Him to grant our wishes. The Bible tells us He's near the brokenhearted. In my grief, I built a wall between God and me. That never works."

"Is trusting God harder when you're in law enforcement? I mean, you had training and carry a gun."

"We're also in dangerous situations, walk into firefights to protect others, and stop crimes. I trust Him to have my back. Gage feels the same way."

"Bad things happen to good people," Carson said with far too much cynicism.

"True, and it will continue. Let me ask you this . . . Who is best suited to model a relationship with Jesus, a believer or an unbeliever?"

"I get it. Ever shoot a bad guy?"

"Yes. And I remember every one and wish there'd been another way."

"How many agents are believers?"

I studied the young man before me. He had so much of life ahead of him. "Carson, everyone believes in something, but we may not have a name for it."

He pushed to his feet. "I'm confused. Everything around me is broken. See you in a few hours."

The door closed behind Carson, and my words to him about God being near the brokenhearted whispered around me.

I've been with you all along.

I shuddered. Had God not left me alone? He'd directed me to protect my loved ones, to teach again, to find Carson. I'd been so blinded by grief and anger at God to see He walked with me all along.

God, forgive me for doubting You. The liturgy of proper words failed to surface. Yet God never asked for fancy prayers and ceremony, neither did He expect perfection. God wanted my heart wholly devoted to Him—not most of it that I parceled out in scraps.

My step toward reconciliation with God hadn't stopped the raging fear for those I treasured.

28

Carson and I left the hotel at five thirty in the morning before the sun chose to usher in a new day. Gage drove the Jeep and left earlier. If anyone had been following Carson, they'd deal with Gage. I assumed my charge would sleep until he was ready to face what lay ahead in Houston.

Carson and I would have plenty of miles to talk, but I'd avoid bringing up the case too soon. Last night, we'd bonded as friends who had questions about life and where our faith fit amid chaos and tragedy. I wanted to believe in his testimony and hoped he'd reacted to witnessing a murder like a confused kid. But I'd seen plenty of professional liars who'd manipulated others. I'd try to keep our conversation pleasant. But I'd be tracking down evidence that proved his innocence one way or the other.

The majestic copper-and-gray cliffs of the Big Bend were in our rearview mirror, and ahead lay the flatlands of Texas. Even with stops along the way, it would be dark before we arrived in Houston. Carson and I rode in silence, which gave me miles to process what Gage and I had gathered. The huge question plaguing me was my connection to Ethan Mercury . . . like a broken record, pushing the listener into a frustrated zone.

"Christmas sucks this year," Carson finally said.

"We've both had more memorable holidays. Did you register for next semester's classes?"

"Yours for starters. Ethan wanted me to be an engineer, except I'm not interested. Especially now since that's what he is. I want a major in English. I'm also taking calculus, Spanish V, and another semester of history."

A full load. "After your basics, what college or university interests you?"

"Not sure." He paused, and I questioned if it was to draw sympathy from me. "Depends on where I'm living. At the rate I'm going, I'll be in witness protection."

I refused to probe deeper into his remark. If the case led to an operation nationwide or internationally, Witness Security Program might be a viable option. All that meant if he told the truth. "So English is your career choice?"

"Something there. I like to write, but I need to make money too. Maybe teaching high school. Your classes are fun, challenged me. I like learning how people communicate and the history of language." He shifted in his seat. "I sound like a nerd."

"Not at all. Have you written on your own?"

"The typical poetry and dabbled in fantasy. I'm working on a novel. I told you I liked thrillers and mysteries, and I do. But fantasy and sci-fi are my favorites."

"Have your reading habits changed since the issues with your stepdad?"

He huffed. "Yes. Can't concentrate. Keep trying to figure out a reason for what I saw."

"I understand you want an explanation that exonerates him."

"Yes, ma'am."

"You were successful in publishing some of your work in my class and earning a few dollars. That's a good beginning for your résumé."

"If I live long enough. Sorry. My mind keeps going to dark places."

"Trained people are working to bring back the light." I sighed. "Carson, you're an adult, and what you're experiencing isn't for the weak or cowards." I shot him a sideways glance. "You've already proven neither one fits you." I cast aside my thoughts to keep conversation low-key until later in the trip. I suspected Carson might try something stupid to protect his mom and brother—or escape. "I'd like to ask you a question, but first I want to confirm you won't lie to me."

"I've been lying to you since the first day of classes. What makes you think anything has changed? Except what I witnessed that night?"

"Because I want to believe you told Gage and me the truth. Because I believe you're a man of integrity. Because you're more concerned about your family than yourself."

"Glad you think so, Professor. Not sure you have the right guy. But go ahead."

"Where were you going when we caught up to you?"

"To think about the best way to protect Mom and Caleb from Dad and that strange guy. And to figure out if I told you what really happened, would you believe my story. But I kept driving. I don't make sense even to myself."

"Why did you retrace your steps? Big Bend is closer to Houston than Santa Fe."

He stared out the passenger-side window. "I love my mom and Caleb. Running didn't keep them safe. But fear took over. Still am."

So was I. "Thanks for telling me. Are you up to one more question?"

"Depends." He wrung his hands, a trait I'd seen before. "A lot of junk is going through my head."

"I understand."

"I think you believe me, but I'm not sure about Agent Patterson."

"I'm sure you've been told that trust has to be earned," I said.

"Oh . . . yes. When do I get the gun back?"

"Never. I have it for multiple reasons."

He raised his hand. "Okay. I have a question for you." When I nodded, he continued. "What led you to join the FBI?"

Gage knew the story. "When I was fifteen, I became the neighborhood babysitter. Kids were special to me, and sometimes I refused to take money for watching them. The problem came when I repeatedly saw bruises on a little girl. Her parents said she had the clumsy syndrome, and she would outgrow it. Then one day I was staring out my second-story bedroom window and witnessed the mother in their backyard beating the little girl. She left the child lying in the yard. I immediately told my parents, and Dad called the police. The little girl died of internal injuries, and the mother went to prison. The father said he had no idea his wife abused their little girl. I didn't believe him. What about his daughter's bruises? No one was that stupid. From then on, I wanted to help innocent children."

"But your degree is in teaching?"

"Right. In the beginning, I believed education provided the solution to the mounting cases of child abuse, but I craved more involvement. The FBI offered me an opportunity to ensure justice was served, and that sealed my commitment."

"Makes sense," Carson said. "Mind if I turn on the radio? I lost my earbuds somewhere."

Carson had hit the end of conversation mode. "Go ahead." Lecturing would alienate him, and all I wanted to know was where he saw his future.

He found a pop station, and his body relaxed. Did I pity him for his stress and pressure or keep my boxing gloves on? He'd stolen a handgun. Underage, potentially dangerous.

My burner phone sounded with a call from Gage, and I answered. "I have a safe house for Carson, at least for tonight," he said. "He'll be under surveillance in case he tries to run. Don't tell him. When you get closer to Houston, let me know so we can make a transfer."

"All right. He'll ask me about what's next."

"He wants to know, or you do?"

"Very funny. But true." I forced a smile at Carson, who'd roused from his near-sleep mode. He turned off the radio, most likely guessing the caller.

"Would you like to join him?" Gage said.

"No. Not even an option."

"If what we've uncovered is fact, you're in danger."

"So are you by association. I'm self-sufficient and I'm trained for trouble just like you are. I've covered your rear more than once."

"That you have. For the record, I'm not convinced of his testimony."

"Me either." Someday I'd tell Gage about how he rooted me in reality.

"SAC Dunkin wants to talk to Carson and me first thing in the morning. Ethan Mercury is scheduled for a 10 a.m. interview."

I longed to be there. "How are the interviews scheduled?"

"They're separate. I'll tell you after I'm sure how it plays out. Should be interesting. By the way, have you slept recently?"

"I will tonight." With one hand wrapped around my Glock under my pillow.

"Okay, talk to you later."

I slid my phone into the Explorer's console that fit my phone perfectly. "Get some rest, Carson. We have several hours left before reaching Houston, and that's without stops."

"How are you going to stay awake?"

I laughed. "You sound like Gage. I'm pulling over at the first place that offers coffee."

He glanced around us at the empty stretch of highway and the desolate landscape on both sides. "Miss Jacobs, from what I see, any coffee out here will be nasty. But I need some too, so I can keep you awake."

"I'm a big girl, Carson."

"Nope. I'm selfish, doing all I can to stay alive. Wanna hear the plotline for my novel?"

"Mystery or thriller?"

"Postapocalyptic fiction."

I groaned. "Why not? Reading about chaos, breakdowns in society, and massive deaths can't be any different than today."

He chuckled. "No zombies, medical pandemics, or aliens destroying the world. But the earth has collapsed, and people are struggling to survive."

"*Hunger Games*?"

"Kinda, and yes, I am."

"Me too. Do you have another Snickers?"

"One left. I'll split it with you—if you'll listen to my story idea."

I rolled my eyes. "Deal. But you drive a hard bargain."

He reached into his backpack for the candy bar, broke it in half, and gave me the biggest piece. "When I'm finished with my story, I'd like honesty. I mean, if it's any good."

"More of the hard bargain?"

"Yep. What's the plan once we're in Houston?"

"Gage will let us know."

"I can lie better than that."

My fears exactly.

★   ★   ★

At 130 miles out of Marathon on US Highway 90, I called Gage for the transfer location. Still hadn't told Carson. The more I chatted with him, the more I liked him. He'd gotten tired and decided to share the rest of his novel later. When I considered my lack of sleep, I wanted to pull over. We were still a long way from San Antonio and farther to Houston.

I saw Carson staring at the road. "Gage is meeting us at a McDonald's on I-10 outside of Houston."

He cocked his head. "And?"

"He's taking you to a safe house." I swung him my best reassuring smile to ease the worried lines across his forehead. "He'll fill you in on the details."

"Okay. Will my mom and brother be at the same place?"

"I have no clue. Ask him. I'm the college prof, remember?"

"Thanks, Miss Jacobs." Carson's tone turned somber. "I appreciate your confidence in me, for listening when it seems like I'd hit your brother. I want to do the right thing as long as Mom and Caleb are okay. I pray I'm wrong about Dad. The thought makes me sick."

"When this is over, you'll get a handle on your future and your life."

He shook his head. "Like make the best of a bad situation? Normal is always in the past."

I checked my rearview mirror. A white Dodge Ram pickup had been following us for the last twenty or so miles. Now it sped closer to my bumper. My pulse raced and caution threaded through me. "Carson, we have company." I kept calmness in my voice. "Are you expecting anyone?"

"No, ma'am."

"I'd like for you to lean down in the seat as far as you can. Don't move or give me any grief."

"Why?"

I reached under my seat for the Sig and released the safety.

My side mirror shattered with a crack.

29

A second shot whistled past my left ear. I sensed a sting, and it fired up my fight-or-flee attitude, and in this case—both.

"Who is shooting at us?" Carson shouted. "You're bleeding!"

"Get down."

He ducked while I readied the Sig. I pressed the window button to lower the driver's-side window and did a U-turn. I aimed at the pickup's windshield. Squeezed the trigger. My shot hit spot-on, spider-webbing the glass. But it didn't deter the driver. I whirled back onto the road and pressed the gas.

"I'm a good shot," Carson said with his cheek kissing the car's console.

"I'm better." Another shot pierced the Explorer's rear glass and exited the windshield on Carson's side. He twitched. No need to comment.

I fired, aiming at the pickup's engine and hoped the gas vapors would escape and ignite, but the vehicle swung a vicious right, then left as I pulled the trigger. My bullet hit the front bumper, but I couldn't tell if it penetrated the engine. Obviously not. I saw the driver was a man, and he kept on approaching my bumper.

"Who is it?" Carson said.

"He didn't send a calling card. A friend of yours?" Another quick glance in the rearview mirror showed no passengers to double the firing power of the shooter. The driver veered left to come around me. "No way, jerk." I swung to the middle of the road. A semitruck approached about a half mile away. Good thing Carson had his face to the console.

The pickup swerved right.

I slid in ahead of him.

"If I find out you've lied and this guy is your doing, I'll make sure you're put away for a long time."

"Why would I have a bad guy shoot you and risk me getting killed?"

"Because you'd outlived your worth."

The pickup yanked left again. I whipped in front of him. One of us faced the hood of the semi, and I had no intentions of being the loser in this game of chicken.

Carson bolted upright. Idiot kid. "I can shoot while you drive."

"Get down! I have enough to worry about without you bleeding out."

Another bullet whistled by my right ear and exited the windshield. Carson hit the console. I fired again.

"Hold on tight." I stomped the gas and headed straight for the semi. The left and right shoulders of the road were stone and flipping the Explorer could happen to the best drivers.

The pickup raced within inches of my bumper.

The semi shifted to the center of the road and laid on the horn.

I drove into the center.

The pickup moved with me.

I calculated the seconds needed to get out of the semi's way and concentrated on the road—five, four, three, two, one.

I jerked the steering wheel left out of the semi's path and sped around it, hitting unfriendly stones. The Explorer bounced and bucked like a wild horse.

The semi lunged right. The pickup's tires screamed. The driver lost control and slammed into the front of the massive semi. The pickup lifted from the road. Flipped twice. The engine exploded and burst into flames.

Adrenaline raced from the top of my head to the tips of my toes. I laughed, certain I must be insane. But being alive exhilarated my spirit.

I slowed and stopped. Carson whipped around to see the flames leaping from the explosion. Gripping the Sig, I narrowed a gaze that would frighten the dead. "Stay here. Call Gage from my phone."

I raced toward the scene. The driver hadn't crawled from the pickup, but if he had escaped, he might still blow a hole through me. The driver of the semi left his rig and rushed to the pickup.

"Stay back! He's armed!"

The driver stared at me in disbelief, and I repeated myself. Within seconds he hightailed it back to his rig. With the Sig held at chest level and my arms extended, I scanned the scene and walked slowly toward the hot flames. Burning to death wasn't a way anyone should die. Neither did I want to get caught in the inferno. Yet the idea of the driver enduring immense pain got the best of me.

"Toss out your gun, and I'll help you out of there."

Crackling sparks met my ears.

I crept to the pickup, leaning precariously on the driver's side. He still had a gun in his right hand. I shrugged out of my sweatshirt, then wound it around my hand three times and yanked open the driver's door. The man inside stared back at me with vacant eyes, a mix of blood and open flesh. Nothing more I could do for him. Death at my own hand never set well, although some would argue the driver had chosen his own actions. They'd be right, but I would have risked my own life to pull him from the burning car. I stepped back several feet.

The driver and Carson rushed toward me.

"Don't you two listen?" I said. "You could have been hurt."

"Is he alive?" the truck driver said, a man in his midfifties, faded ball cap, and scraggly salt-and-pepper beard.

"No." I shielded my eyes from the fiery furnace. "Are you okay?"

"Yes, ma'am. Your ear is bleeding."

I'd forgotten. I turned to Carson. "Were you shot?" When he affirmed he was fine, I asked, "Did you call Gage?"

"I told him what happened, all of it. He's calling for help, and he needs to talk to you." Carson's pale face and trembling body showed he'd had enough excitement. "Has someone been following us?"

"It appears so. Thanks for calling Gage."

Carson shook his head. "I've never seen shooting or driving like that."

"Me either. If I hadn't been scared, I'd have been gawkin'," the semitruck driver said. "Hold on, miss. I have a first aid kit in my rig." He trotted to his truck.

"Carson, do you recognize the pickup?"

"No. Wish I knew if he was after you or me."

"As I said before, both of us. You know too much, and the driver assumed you'd told me the whole story." The shock had started to wear off, and my ear stung. "I will find out his name."

"How? You're not with the FBI anymore."

The semitruck driver returned with a small metal box hosting a red cross painted on top. His presence gave me freedom not to answer Carson's question. The man flipped open the first aid kit and peered at me. "Hydrogen peroxide work for you?"

I nodded and he tore open a package containing a soaked pad of the antiseptic. I placed it over my earlobe, then examined it. Guess I wouldn't be wearing earrings for a while. "It's nothing. The ear bleeds easily."

"I thought we were dead." Carson stared into the fire.

"The idea crossed my mind," I said. "Training helps."

"Lady, what do you do for a living?" the driver said.

"I'm a college professor. Creative writing."

30

GAGE

Risa's brush with death made me crazy worried. She could handle herself, and I'd seen her squeeze out impossible shots and drive like a maniac. Except I hadn't been with her in the Explorer. The incident happened on a deserted stretch of highway. Fortunately the state highway patrol was nearby, and I confirmed she and Carson were a part of an FBI case. She still made it to the transfer spot only two hours late—after stopping to eat in San Antonio. Did I even want to know how fast she drove?

Now with Carson beside me, I needed to garner the kid's trust.

"Ready to ride with Risa again?" I added lightness to my voice to slow his heart rate.

"Not sure." Carson laughed but it failed to sound natural. "Depends on who's chasing us. Or how fast I want to get somewhere. I mean, I like math, but I never saw any calculations like she made at the last minute turning in front of that semi. Did Quantico teach her how to drive like a stuntman?"

"I think her dad has those honors. He'd been a race car driver in his younger years. The first time I experienced Risa in action behind the wheel, I about lost my lunch." I glanced at him.

"Don't stop now. What happened? Did anyone get hurt?"

159

Carson asked more questions than the psychologist who analyzed me after debriefing a difficult case. Probably the same shrink who'd evaluate Carson.

"We were after a man who'd abducted his two young daughters from their mother. He didn't have custody. The older of the two girls took her sister to a gas station's bathroom and told a woman inside that the man outside the door had kidnapped them and hurt their mother. The woman went to get help, but the man overheard her tell the manager. The father took off, but Risa and I were able to pick up his plates from a security cam."

"Like you did with me?"

"Yes. She took the driver's seat and told me to buckle up. She raced west out of the city on I-10. Weaving in and around traffic like we were on the Indy 500. When we turned on a side road, I thought she'd slow down. No way. She kept up the craziness—doing a darn good job, and we caught up with him." I chuckled. "She rode his bumper. Tapped it a few times, then pulled up alongside him on our right. I lowered the window and ordered him to pull over."

"Wow. Miss Jacobs never came across like an FBI agent or anything close in class."

Now curiosity bit me. "What's she like as a professor?"

"Oh, one of the best teachers I've ever had. Firm. Clear. Not afraid to laugh. Oh, her desk always had to be in order, from smallest item to the largest." Carson paused. "I wondered once how she knew what was going on in the back of the room when her back was turned. I mean, I knew about the FBI. But it seemed to give her superpowers."

I envisioned Risa letting a class full of kids know who was in charge. "What did you like the least about her class?"

"She refused to curve the grades."

I smiled. "No slack?"

"Right, and an odd thing is whatever assignment she gave us, she did it too." Carson stretched his neck muscles. "Agent Patterson, who was the guy in the pickup?"

"No idea at this point."

"I hate that my stepdad might be behind it . . . to have her killed and me too. Seems like a different guy."

He quieted and I let silence settle between us. "Tell me about the handgun. This will be a factor in your briefing, and I want to be on your side. How did you intend to use it?"

"What else? To protect myself."

I didn't care if I made Carson mad. I wanted the truth and catch any discrepancies that fell out of his mouth. "From the man you still call Dad? The man your mom loves?"

"What do you want me to say? Do ya think I'm all happy about this?"

"I'm saying if you need to change any part of your testimony, now is your chance to do it."

"Are you calling me a liar?"

Typical answer coming from a kid in trouble. "I'm the FBI agent and you're an underage runaway. Here's the first lesson in Gun Use 101. Never take ownership of a weapon and aim it unless you can take the responsibility of shooting someone. Not threatening them but using it. If you hesitate, the person will take the gun and unload it in you."

"Big deal." Carson shrugged. "Like does it matter? Who witnessed a murder and had his mom and baby brother threatened?"

We drove the rest of the way in silence. Before putting him up in an extended-stay hotel, I drove through Sonic and filled his gut with a cheeseburger and fries. Inside the hotel room, I closed the drapes.

"Take this burner phone." I reached inside my pocket and handed him the extra device I carried for situations like this. "It's activated. I need your word you won't contact anyone except me."

He ran his hands through his dark hair. "Yes, sir. I'm going to shower and go to bed. How will I get my Jeep back?"

"I want it checked for a tracker at the FBI office, then I'll arrange for agents to return it."

"Okay. You said you'd pick me up at 8 a.m.?"

"On the dot. Keep the door locked. Stay inside, and if someone knocks, ignore it. If the knocking persists, call me. I'll call you when

I pull into the hotel parking lot in the morning. Then again when I'm outside your door and convinced no one's lurking."

He eyed me. "Are you sure all that stuff is necessary?"

"It is if you're telling the truth. Agents are in the parking lot 24-7 to ensure you stay put."

"Guess I'm glad for the protection. I got weirded out back there. Sorry. I don't know how to make you believe me, but I told the truth."

I bid him good night and waited in the hallway until I heard the door lock click. Hard to tell if he was exhausted or scared or both.

On the way home, I stopped at the hospital to check on Jack. Visiting hours were long over, but the nurses might give me an update, especially if I flashed my FBI creds and informed them Jack and I were partners.

I learned, which I expected, that Jack's name had been omitted from the hospital's patient list. SAC Dunkin had given me the floor number. As soon as I stepped off the elevator, a nurse twice my size stopped me and asked who I wanted to see.

"I'm checking on Jack Bradford." I pulled out my FBI ID. "He's a good friend, and I'd like to see him if possible."

She eyed me like I carried the latest virus. "You can flash your fancy badge until you're blue in the face, but you aren't seeing my patient. Besides, we don't have anyone here by that name."

The police officers outside Jack's room weren't familiar. "I understand, ma'am. The precautions and police protection are to keep him safe. He's my partner, and all I want to know is how he's recovering."

"Your stormy eyes might work on another nurse, but not me."

I'd met the hospital's guard-nurse. "Would you confirm my ID?" I held it out to her again, and she moved behind the desk, my ID in hand. With her back to me, she made a call. The woman must be six feet three inches tall. Muscles bulged from her uniform's shoulders. She'd make a great bouncer.

She faced me and handed me my creds. "You checked out. The patient is in critical condition, and even if it were visiting hours, the guards have been told no one enters his room without my approval. We all have instructions that any visitor must have security clearance, which you have. Even the doctors and nurses must be cleared. Currently the patient is sedated."

"Is he improving?"

"I'll tell you the same thing I told the other man who asked to see Mr. Bradford. Absolutely—"

"What other man? Did he have an ID? Jack has a brother."

"Anxious, aren't you? The patient's brother left around five thirty to go home and shower, then this other man requested to see a friend—Jack Bradford. I had to call hospital guards to escort him out of here."

"When was this?" The man knew Jack by name.

"After the patient's brother left. About six thirty."

"Can you describe him?"

Her frown deepened, and I thought she might call hospital security on me. "Bald head. Medium height, like you. White skin. Expensive suit. Probably spent every day in the gym. Midforties. I suggest having the FBI view the security cam."

Sounded like the description Carson gave of the man who hit Trenton. "I will before I leave here. Do you remember anything else about the man? Or did he give a reason to see Jack?"

She shook her head. "He said they were neighbors. Shared a common fence."

I huffed. "Doubt that. Jack lives in an apartment. Thank you, ma'am. I'm heading to check the hospital cameras." I nodded my goodbye.

Midway to the elevator, she called to me. "Agent Patterson, your partner is in life-threatening shape. I'm sorry." Compassion filled her eyes.

"Thank you. I appreciate your tenacity to keep him safe."

"You mean my charming personality?"

"Worked on me." I smiled. "I'm going to find out who's behind his attack."

While I waited for the hospital's security to approve my viewing of the video and audio footage, my phone alerted me to a text. The .22 used to kill the Phan sisters belonged to Duong Tuan, one of the men who'd met us outside the Saigon Sampler. I checked on his known affiliations and recognized a man by the name of Vinh Bui, another gang member. A text to SAC Dunkin started the proceedings for their arrest.

The hospital's security had my information from the guard-nurse and cleared me, so I could view the video and audio footage. I studied the well-dressed man who'd attempted to see Jack. Could have passed for a doctor. He entered the hospital and walked onto the elevator without checking in at the visitor desk. He obviously had Jack's floor number beforehand. How did he get it?

The encounter with the guard-nurse played out just as she'd relayed to me. I sent the footage to the office for the techs to evaluate.

Every muscle in my body felt like I'd been beaten and left for dead. My head had a jackhammer pushing against both temples. Sleep called to sleep. Nothing more I could do at the hospital anyway.

No surprise to find a note under the driver's-side windshield wiper of Carson's Jeep. I presumed a love note from the killer. I opened it.

You'll always be a step behind us.

Us. They had me in their sights too.

Now we had a third handwriting to compare, and confirmation on more than one player always gave an advantage. I suspected the bad guys would track Carson's Jeep, but instead they tailed Risa. I texted her on my burner reserved just for her to see if she'd received a note.

Risa texted. **I was spared. You're the lucky one.**

I retraced my steps back to the hospital to check out the parking lot security cam. I expected the man from the interior security cam. This time, the person, dressed in jeans, tennis shoes, and a hoodie, could very well be a woman. The note deliverer resembled the size and walk of the person who'd left a note on Risa's car back in July. The person kept their face away from the camera. Jack's note and Risa's were a match. But now mine was in the mix.

I hadn't told Risa about checking the funeral homes' security cam after Trenton's funeral, but I was sure she suspected it. No reason to put off bringing her up to speed. I texted her before leaving the hospital.

Someone left a note on my windshield. Could be the same who left one on your car.

At the funeral?

Yes. I viewed the church's security cam months ago.

I would have been disappointed if you hadn't.

Need to compare all three handwritings.

Is tonight's hospital video in FBI files yet?

Should be by now. Be careful. Don't open the door to anyone. Want me to come over?

LOL, Gage. I'm fine. Get some sleep.

I dropped off Carson's Jeep at the FBI office and drove my SUV home. Once there, I did a sweep of my small one-story house and found nothing out of order. I had a Mercury home alarm like the victims, and I had no desire to be the next one. The irony made me laugh. Only an idiot hacked into a federal agent's house unless the idiot wasn't aware of his person-of-interest status. Or the idiot had jumped into the overconfident arena.

Would Risa be okay? The idea of her being targeted again meant a sleepless night for me. Should I show up at her door? What did Jack know that an unknown man and woman would be at the hospital?

No point in fooling myself. No one knew who'd be targeted next.

31

My phone alarm sounded much too early in my opinion, but I didn't have a say over the sunrise. Three hours' sleep, and already my head ached. I'd become a wimp. The surveillance team watching Carson assured me he'd stayed put. After I picked up Carson, who'd followed my morning instructions to the letter, I drove through Starbucks for coffee and hoped it cleared my mind and his.

"Nervous?" I said to him while we waited for our coffee.

"Kinda. Well . . . yes, a lot."

"You look more rested than last night."

"I slept hard," he said. "Makes me feel a little guilty with all the junk going on. Did you find out who drove the pickup yesterday? I was hoping it might have been the guy I'd seen with Dad."

"Not yet. He doesn't have the build of any bad guy on my radar. Did you recognize him?"

"No. Miss Jacobs got real upset when I didn't stay down in the seat. Afterward, she wouldn't let me get near him . . . with half his head gone."

Risa had sheltered Carson, even if he'd killed her brother. "She can be insistent."

"Are you in love with her?"

What? First Jack and now this kid? "We're good friends. Worked together for five years."

"You don't stare at her like she's your coworker."

That didn't deserve a comment.

"I get it," Carson said. "She doesn't know, and you haven't the guts to tell her."

He had it wrong. "Really? You're talking through your rear. Enough."

Carson snickered. "How long will I be at the FBI office?"

"As long as it takes to give your statement, answer questions, and whatever else I add to the list. The man who picked up your stepdad, what did he wear?"

"I think jeans. Nothing stood out. Am I under arrest?"

The anxiety of a kid who had a lot to lose with his testimony. "If there's evidence to charge you, yes. Your stepdad may have an alibi for your claims."

"He'll be there?"

"Like you, he's a person of interest."

Carson breathed in deeply. "The 'innocent until proven guilty' thing." He faced his day of reckoning.

At the office, I escorted Carson to an interview room with ASAC Kendall of our division, who'd been briefed on the investigation. He was about to retire after serving thirty years. Gray hair cut in a buzz from his military days. Just divorced his fourth wife. All business. Any humor was only if he initiated it. After introductions, Carson retold his story, and I found no inconsistencies.

"We're processing your request for your mother and brother's safety," the ASAC said. "Am I to understand you'd like to join them?"

"I guess so. When will you talk to my stepdad?"

The ASAC didn't miss a beat. "In about thirty minutes."

"I'd like to watch it."

ASAC Kendall squinted. "Why?"

"From what I said, doesn't it make sense?"

"Impossible."

"But—"

"Impossible. Think about it. Do you want your stepfather privy to our discussion?"

"No, sir. Will what I say and what he says be released later?"

Turn it off, Carson. The ASAC isn't as congenial as I am. I shot the kid a glare.

"Sorry, sir," Carson said to ASAC Kendall. "Do I sit here until you've finished questioning him?" His knee danced under the table.

"Yes. We need a sample of your handwriting and an appointment made for a psychological interview."

"Why? Do you think I'm crazy?"

"We simply need to make sure you're not fabricating anything."

Carson's emotions had to be off the charts. I left him with another agent, a female who could talk the legs off a wooden horse.

The receptionist texted the ASAC and me when Ethan Mercury arrived for his scheduled interview—twenty minutes early. Odd. Perhaps he was only anxious. I stood with the ASAC outside the interview room, with my legal pad and pen in hand, and observed Ethan Mercury through the one-way glass. He would remember me from the night Risa and I had stopped by his home. Although I hadn't deceived the Mercurys, I hadn't been up-front either. The interview could go south quickly.

Mercury trembled, and perspiration beaded on his brow. Why? Fear? Curiosity? Remorse?

We entered the interview room, and I immediately saw recognition in Mercury's eyes. ASAC Kendall made the introductions, and I took the lead.

"We've met before, Mr. Mercury."

"You were with Professor Jacobs the night she was digging for information about Carson." His voice rose. "You lied to me and my wife under the guise of locating our son. Is that how the FBI operates? Lie to innocent people?" Mercury stood, his face red and his eyes wild.

"Sit down," I said, firmly. "Mr. Mercury, your son had disappeared. Professor Jacobs had questions about his term paper that affected his grade, and I had reason to believe he was a person of interest in a murder case."

"My son is not a murderer!"

"Then prove it by cooperating." I'd taken a gamble—one I might live to regret.

"Is Professor Jacobs in this with you?"

"Professor Jacobs is not available. She retired after her brother was killed on July 29 in a failure to stop and render aid while crossing the street with his sister."

Mercury's face paled. He eased back onto the chair. "What have I done?"

32

Mercury's breathing slowed. The flush of blood in his face faded. "Why am I here?" he said, his tone flat. "Is this about Carson? Has he been hurt? Is he in trouble?"

"We assure you Carson is all right," I said. "We also would appreciate your cooperation in answering a few questions."

"What kind of questions? Do I need my attorney?"

"Legal counsel is your right," I said. "If you'd feel more comfortable with your attorney present, we can wait here until that person arrives."

"Not necessary." A sigh seemed to be dredged up from his toes. "All right, I'll do my best to answer your questions. But first I need to call my wife. The more I think about it, I'm concerned she and our infant son may be in danger."

"What kind of danger, Mr. Mercury?"

"If the wrong people find out I'm here, they might—no, they will . . . kill her."

I let silence increase his stress. "They're safe."

"What do you mean?"

"Agents are with them at your home. They are providing protection as a precautionary measure. May I call you Ethan?"

"Yes, of course." He gripped the side of the chair. "You know about that night?" he whispered as if the wrong people might hear. "Carson must have told you."

"We talked to him after tracking him down. He's afraid for his mother and brother."

Mercury swallowed hard. "I don't care what he told you. I mean, it doesn't matter, and it's better this way. But please, I must know for sure my wife and baby are safe."

"They are. Talk to us, Ethan. What's the issue here? Would those who'd hurt your wife also abduct your infant son?"

He clenched his fist on the tabletop. "Either sell or kill him. Don't you understand? I'm afraid for my family."

"We want to help you, but we need answers to find a killer."

"Professor Jacobs's brother." He shook his head. "If I tell you what I know, will the FBI make sure my family is in a safe place?"

"If we determine it's necessary, yes."

"And Carson is included?"

"Yes. Tell us about the night Trenton Jacobs died in a failure to stop and render aid meant for his sister."

Ethan rubbed his pale face. "What I'm about to say stays here?"

"Depends. Understand if you have evidence against someone, you'll be asked to testify in a court of law."

"All right. And we are currently being videoed?" When I confirmed the video, he continued. "The problems began last fall. I was contacted by a man who wanted to discuss a business opportunity. I met him for lunch. He introduced himself as John Smith and claimed he was a broker. He represented an investor who offered me ten million dollars for a partnership in Mercury Alarms. I refused, told him I didn't want a partner and planned to one day turn the business over to my children. He said a refusal wasn't in my best interests. I left the meeting angry and with plans to go to the police. He called me before I reached my car. He said if I valued the lives of my wife, son, and unborn child, then I'd better turn around and hear him out." Ethan paused.

I gave him a moment to compose himself.

"How did he know we were pregnant?" Ethan said. "Believe me, the threat got my attention. I walked back inside, told him I had no interest in his money, and asked him why my business appealed to his investor. He said if I had no use for the money, then we'd take a different approach on a partnership. Before I could form the words about what he meant, he left the table. I paid the bill, so there's no way to trace him through payment."

I stopped Ethan. "Most restaurants have security cams in place. What's the name and date?"

"Morton's steak house on Westheimer. January, I think. I'll confirm with my calendar later."

"Thanks. Please, continue."

"A week went by without hearing from the so-called Smith character, and I assumed the threat had been someone's idea of a bad joke. But I didn't tell anyone. The man had information about me and my family, and it scared me when I didn't know how or where he'd gotten it. My wife and I do our best to keep our private life off social media. The man had given me a business card, but the website didn't exist, and the phone number went nowhere." Ethan breathed steady, held firm eye contact, and was upset.

"He contacted you again?"

"Yes, sir. He showed up at my office and insisted we talk outside. I wanted to know why, and he said our conversation must be private, and it was being recorded for security purposes. That sounded like a line of garbage to me, but his tone and my past dealings with him caused me to comply. I hadn't forgotten his threats. We talked in the courtyard of my office building or rather I listened. He told me the partnership offer had been retracted. At first I was relieved, then he claimed to have a new deal. The person he represented demanded information about those whom my company serviced, or my family faced extinction." Ethan shuddered. "The man showed no emotion, as though he'd been programmed like a machine."

"I'm sorry, Ethan. Extortion is a serious offense," I said. "What kind of information did he want?"

"Security codes to override alarm systems . . . across several states. His ultimatums were criminal offenses, and I told him I'd had enough." Ethan lowered his head and pressed his fingers into his temples. "He pulled a gun on me and said the negotiations were over. I'd do what he said, when he said, or face the consequences. I called his bluff. Told him I'd already gone to the police. He pulled up a photo of my wife sitting on our patio by the outdoor firepit and Carson shooting baskets at a friend's house. That's all I needed. He handed me a phone and said it couldn't be traced and he'd be calling. After that, he'd phone me for a meetup somewhere, or he'd pick me up at my house. Whenever we met in person, he took both my phones, searched me, and kept my devices until we were finished. He entered the accounts his boss requested on my phone and instructed me to text the related codes to a specific number. Never the same. I assumed his methods eliminated me having a tracker of some sort installed on me or my phones."

"Right." I showed him a pic of the man who attempted to gain access to Jack's room. "Is this the man?"

Ethan gripped his fist. "Yes. Who is he?"

"Our techs are working on his ID. Did Smith ever give you his boss's name?"

"No," Ethan said. "I've heard him take calls from someone he called sir. I assumed the boss must be a man."

"Maybe. Depends on the chain of command. When was the last time Smith contacted you?"

"A week ago. I expect a call any day."

"How many accounts have you provided?" I said.

"Thirty-seven. Across many states."

"Residences or businesses?"

"Thirty were homes and seven small businesses."

"What kind of small businesses?" I said.

"Drugstores, pharmacies."

"Michael and Sarah Addington's home?"

"Yes. I read their baby was recovered."

"They were extremely lucky. We need the list of clients before you leave." When Ethan opened his mouth to speak, I held up my palm. "You're an accessory to several violent crimes where innocent babies have been kidnapped. A former agent lost her brother when she was the target. Two women were found executed in a restaurant fire, and a man died from smoke inhalation. An attack on an FBI special agent has him listed in critical condition. You're facing those charges and about a dozen more. Answering our questions is the prudent response here. You have yet to tell us what happened the night of Trenton Jacobs's death."

"Carson is innocent of any wrongdoing," Ethan sputtered. "I swear, he's done nothing wrong."

"Then let's hear your side of the story."

"I'll do whatever you ask. I already despise myself for all those people who've been hurt and killed. And sometime, I'd like to share the truth with my wife and son. But in answer to your question, to protect Carson, I made it sound like I'd been a part of the pedestrian murder."

"How?"

"Carson followed me and Smith the night the man was hit. Smith picked me up in his Lexus, then we changed vehicles to an SUV. We waited outside a high-rise apartment building until a woman left on foot. He followed her until she went into a restaurant a block later."

My face heated and I lifted a finger. "Do you know the woman's identity?"

"FBI Special Agent Risa Jacobs." He startled. "Professor Jacobs?"

"The same."

"But how—?"

"Continue with your story, Ethan."

"Smith drove into a parking area belonging to the restaurant and parked where he watched her. Nothing was said between us. I saw Carson sitting at a bus stop across from the restaurant bench but didn't let on. I knew Smith would hurt him. After he hit the man, Smith told me he'd killed the wrong target, but this might work for the best. He also said anyone who got in his boss's way was killed. We drove a few blocks, abandoned the SUV, and took a Dodge pickup truck that had the keys in it." Ethan paused. "It was an older model, Dodge Ram."

"What color?" I said.

"White. After I returned home, I told Carson if he wanted to keep his mom and unborn baby brother alive, he'd better keep his mouth shut."

Almost word for word of Carson's statement. "Carson is here."

"Can I talk to him when we're finished?"

"If he's willing."

Ethan's shoulders relaxed. "Thank you. I hope he'll forgive me. I'm glad he told you, but I'm worried Smith will follow through on his threats."

"Carson is under our protection."

"Against Smith or me?"

"Depends," I said.

"That seems to be your common answer to my questions," Ethan said. "Look, I'm a businessman, not a con man, a family man, not a killer."

"Point made." I tapped the table with my pen. "Have you kept any info from us?"

"Only I didn't know what to do. I was trapped." He paused and stared at me. "What do I say to my son?"

"The truth. Carson can handle it."

"The truth?" Ethan scowled. "Then I need advice on what to tell Smith because he'll want an explanation of why I'm here. I'm sure Smith and his goons followed me this morning. He claims to have eyes everywhere."

I'd been thinking about that very thing. "Where is the burner that Smith gave you?"

"At your front desk."

"And your personal cell phone?"

"There too."

"I'm sure he's tracking you through one or both phones. When we're finished here, I'll have a tech examine them for bugs. Tell Smith that Mercury Alarms is under investigation for installing faulty equipment on several alarm systems, not only in Houston but nationwide."

"Would an FBI investigation cause Smith to back off?"

"Doubtful," I said. "He's after the security information from your clients. Don't be surprised if he offers an attorney to represent your case. If that happens, you and I will talk."

"I've long since concluded Smith's boss isn't local and this is an organized-crime ring operating in several states," Ethan said. "I'm not a professional investigator by a long stretch, but it makes sense to me." He stared at me. "When they're finished with me, I'm a dead man."

"Not if we close them down first. For now, we'll issue you a burner phone to contact us. No one else is to have or use the number. Neither are you to call anyone but me or ASAC Kendall using the numbers programmed. And never use the phone I'm giving you within twenty feet of your personal or Smith's burner. If my suspicions are correct, he's not only geo-tracking your location but also recording conversations."

"Recording as when I'm making calls?"

"No. I mean every word you speak. Do not say anything when those phones are nearby that you wouldn't want Smith to hear. Got it?"

"Yes, sir."

"As soon as Smith gives you an assignment, walk outside your office or home and call me immediately with the requested names and security information. The extra precaution is imperative."

"What about my family's disappearance?"

"Tell him they left you. You'd changed over the past several months, short-tempered, disagreeable. You have no idea where they are. Understand?"

"Got it." He held his forehead in his hands. "Will I be under surveillance?"

"Count on it. If we sense you're in danger, we'll pull you out of the situation. Also, we need a handwriting sample from you."

He nodded. "I'll give it to you now."

I lifted my notepad to a clean sheet and slid it to him. He wrote and pushed it back to me. I read: *This is Ethan A. Mercury, owner and CEO of Mercury Alarms Inc. I have never killed anyone, but I have been blackmailed by John Smith.*

"If he's to pick me up, do I wear a wire?" Ethan said.

"Not a good idea for an untrained man. If detected, you're dead."

"Might be worth the risk to end these crimes. I'm caught in a trap by organized crime, and I have no idea who's involved. Agent Patterson, I'll do whatever it takes."

"Don't play rogue or hero. Understand?"

"Yes, sir. I'll take a polygraph."

"Ethan, in Texas polygraph tests are not admissible in a court of law. You are innocent until proven guilty. We'll find the evidence to make arrests. That's our job."

"You are all I have left." His eyes watered. "I must talk to Carson. Is it possible to see him now?"

33

I weighed Ethan's statement, and unless he and Carson had collaborated, they'd told the truth. After listening and observing Carson and Ethan, I leaned toward the innocent side for both men. But it wasn't my job to pronounce innocence or guilt. My job was to protect the innocent and find the facts.

I studied Ethan, who sobbed.

The Mercury family needed each other, whether the men were lying or telling the truth. I contacted the agent with Carson and learned the kid had reservations about talking to his stepdad, then reconsidered. I asked to have him escorted to the interview room with ASAC Kendall. I believed Ethan and Carson experienced terror and desperation to protect the ones they loved. Both had used futile methods that brought them to the FBI's attention. If I'd misjudged their character, I needed to resign. My gut instincts hadn't failed me in the past. But there was always a first time.

Carson entered, red-rimmed eyes and trembling lips. He stepped back at the sight of his stepdad and stiffened.

Neither Ethan's nor Carson's body language revealed deceit, but fear . . . an emotional apocalypse.

"Carson, I'd like to talk." Ethan stood and kept his distance. "Will you hear me out?"

"Why?"

"Please, Son, I need to explain my actions, the threats, and danger."

Carson glanced at me. "If I listen, will you stay?"

"If that's what you want. You and Ethan have expressed concern about your mother and baby. They are with agents now."

Wordlessly, ASAC Kendall and the agent who'd escorted Carson into the room exited. No doubt, the ASAC would view what transpired.

"Carson, why don't you sit on the other side of the table, and I'll join you?" I said. The tension in the room could have been sliced with a hunting knife. He obliged and I gestured for Ethan to begin.

He retold the story about John Smith with accuracy of what he'd relayed in the interview. When he finished, Carson faced me. "Do you believe him?"

"Do you?"

"It happened exactly like Dad said. What I don't understand is why he didn't try to stop the guy. But I didn't do anything either."

"Son, are you blaming yourself?" Ethan said.

"Maybe. Dad, do you remember the color and make of the pickup truck you switched to?"

"Agent Patterson asked me the same thing. White. Dodge Ram. Why?"

I took over the conversation and gave the short version of Risa and Carson's encounter with someone who had tried to run them off the road while on the way back to Houston.

Ethan sank into his chair. His face seared with trauma. "This tragedy is worse than any nightmare."

I took the lead on the conversation. "Security cams should confirm much of the testimony. Carson, your dad has offered to help the FBI bring in John Smith. In the meantime, your mother, brother, and you will be escorted to a safe house until arrests are made. Ethan, you will not be able to contact them or know their location."

"That's fine. Peace of mind means everything to me." Ethan peered at Carson, obviously searching for a reaction. "I'm sorry I lied to you. I honestly felt like I had no recourse but to follow orders."

Carson stared back. Emotions swirled silently around the small room. "I wouldn't be here if it wasn't for Professor Jacobs and Agent Patterson. They saved my life. I'll tell you everything one day." He gulped. "Dad, I wish you would have told me the truth. I didn't want to believe you were part of what I saw. I . . . I—"

Ethan moved from the table to the other side and embraced his son. Both shed tears. "No matter how this ends, I love you, Son. My family is my life. Whenever I think of what those people have done to others, what they forced me to do, I'm ready to help no matter the cost."

I turned away. Too private a moment to gawk. The reunion of father and son gave me one more reason to show up to work every day, why I vowed to keep people safe from predators. Not all of life was shadowed by dark corners. My phone buzzed with a call from SAC Dunkin, and I stepped outside to talk privately.

34

RISA

After drinking a full pot of coffee, I managed to shower and find a clean pair of jeans, for what I had no clue, but the effort gave me think time about Gage. Had I made a mistake in telling him I loved him? Kissing him back? When normal life returned, we'd talk and figure things out.

Where did I fit in the obscurity of Trenton's death and the kidnapping case? Because somewhere I did. I sensed a mockery of all I believed in, like a nightmare where the world flipped upside down—bad was good and good was bad. I needed a ticket out of that world—before others were hurt.

I turned to reason, logic. Investigative mode picked at me to learn about what happened with Ethan Mercury's and Carson's interviews.

After digesting FBI updates—minus the morning's interviews—I phoned the hospital to check on Jack. Good news. His condition had improved with a medical upgrade status of serious. No visitors were permitted without proper identification and then only five minutes on the half hour. I'd take those precious few minutes, and if whoever had threatened me last July disapproved, then so be it.

I grabbed my purse and ID, then evaluated my actions. My family and friends were in danger whenever I chased a suspect. Anyone with an ounce of sense could track down those whom I cared about. That had always been the reality of my FBI career. The blow of Trenton's death and his incredible sacrifice had shaken the very foundation of my commitment to protect the innocent.

I texted SAC Dunkin.

I'm tired of hiding out. I'll request my parents take a vacation.

Immediately he texted me back. **That's the spirit.**

Thanks. I'm not cowering from bullies.

I called Dad and explained my change of plans. He'd need to talk to Mom. "How soon should we leave on this vacation?"

"ASAP," I said. "Lots of good places to visit during the holiday season."

"Who has your back, honey?"

"God."

"I can't argue with Him. Guess we could drive to South Carolina. Your mom loves Charleston at Christmas."

Had she convinced him?

Fifteen minutes later, he called with confirmation of their road trip. "We're prepared to do our part in ending the search for whoever has tried to destroy our family. Your mom's making hotel reservations at this very minute. We'll pack and leave in less than two hours. I'll text you once we're on the road."

"Don't tell anyone where you're going," I said.

"Sure. Friends can find out later."

"Sorry to spoil your Christmas."

"We didn't even put up a tree this year. We're fine with a different way of celebrating our Savior's birth. Plenty of churches in Charleston."

"Love you. Pray all the people working this case are successful. It would be my Christmas gift to you."

"Stay safe, Risa. We love you. We can't lose you too."

After Dad texted that they were on I-10E for a road trip, I snatched my keys. First stop was the Methodist Hospital in the medical center to see Jack. A nurse stopped me at the nurses' station, and two police officers met me outside Jack's room. I appreciated their diligence and told them, yet neither officer budged until my creds were approved.

"Has Agent Bradford received visitors today?" I said to a female officer, about my height, highlighted hair, and earth-brown eyes.

"A brother to the patient who stated he'd return tonight and a woman whom we refused entry. Claimed to be a niece. She wasn't on the list the brother provided us. The patient was asleep, and we refused to wake him for clarification or entry."

Her photo would be on the security cams. "Do you remember her name?"

"Yes, and the front desk would have it too. Mary Smith."

Right. "Thank you." I texted her name to the office techs and gained permission to view the security cams. I sent her image to SAC Dunkin, ASAC Kendall, and Gage.

The female officer approached me. "Agent Jacobs, the patient is awake. You have five minutes."

I entered Jack's private room to the sound of life support equipment, vital monitors, and the drip of two IV bags offering healing fluids to his battered body. I stood over his bed. "Hey, Jack. It's Risa."

He opened his eyes to reveal slits of recognition. I expected a pale face but not the gray gathering darkness of death and the craters beneath his eyes. I inwardly shuddered and forced a smile to shake off my concerns. I leaned closer so he wouldn't need to move. He opened his mouth but nothing audible met my ears.

"No need to talk," I said. "Just checking on you."

He wet his cracked lips. "Ice," he whispered.

A paper cup of chipped ice and a spoon sat on his nightstand. I spoon-fed a small amount, and he nodded his appreciation.

"We will find who attacked you," I said.

He blinked and mustered strength to whisper. "How?"

"I've been on leave. Only the SAC was aware of my true status. I had great difficulty sorting out my life and career after my brother's death. I'll explain when you're feeling better. Now I'm back to work. What can I do besides spoon you ice?"

He shook his head slightly. "Nothing." He closed his eyes. "Brother . . . takin' care of things."

"I'll be back to see you. I'm sure Gage will too. We're praying for a speedy recovery. Get some rest."

"Luke?"

"Luke Reardon?" When he mouthed a yes, I understood. "You want me to contact him?"

"Yes . . . I . . . suspect."

"Who?"

His eyelids struggled to stay open. "Worried . . . Gage . . . I know link." Jack drifted off to sleep.

"Jack. What's the link? Do you have a name?" But I couldn't rouse him. The female police officer informed me that my five minutes were up.

I thanked her and waited at the nurses' station for the nurse who'd talked to me earlier. "Excuse me, I just visited Jack Bradford, and he fell asleep. Can you tell me with his meds when he'll waken? I'm with the FBI and would like to ask him a few questions."

The nurse pulled up Jack's file on his computer. "The doctor prescribed sleeping medication, and those were administered about ten minutes ago. He may be out for hours."

I handed the nurse my business card. "When he's alert, would you call me?"

"Yes, ma'am. But I encourage you to check back on your own. We often get busy."

Before leaving the hospital, I called Gage. He didn't pick up, so I left a nonurgent voice mail to get back to me. I told him what Jack had alluded to before falling asleep. I drove back to my apartment, where I'd rewrite my sloppy notes from this morning.

I'd contact Luke Reardon next to possibly fill me in on what Jack couldn't say. He and his wife had been married about three years. I'd gone to their wedding, a spring event with dozens of yellow, pink, and white tulips. No children yet, and they lived in a small bungalow in the Heights. Before I could contact him, an email landed from SAC Dunkin.

Mary Smith is Emily Lock, a fugitive wanted in Columbus,
Ohio, for representing a fraudulent adoption agency. She
has been ID'd by the Wades as part of the illegal private
adoption scheme in Des Moines. She posed as single and
pregnant. You can be sure this ring is working beyond the
three states already identified.

By Emily Lock showing up in Houston, she'd made a mistake, an
opportunity for law enforcement to arrest her. Why attempt access
to Jack except to kill him? Perhaps finish what she or someone had
started? I texted the SAC. **I'll be in the office tomorrow. Thank you
for all you've done for me and my career.**

The SAC's response arrived moments later. **Just help bring in
those behind the adoption fraud. I'll forward our texts to the ASAC
and Gage. Good to have you back.**

I'm trying to locate Luke Reardon. Just to talk.

He hasn't been in the office this week.

Had my logic been hijacked? Trenton used to say I overthought
too many scenarios, and my IQ often stood in the way of common
sense. His rationale also said my logic got in the way of emotions.
We were so opposite. A brother was supposed to be wired for logic,
and a sister had the drama personality. Not Trenton and me. *My sweet
brother. How I miss you.*

If enduring a tragedy made a person stronger, then I had achieved
an emotional phoenix. Maybe. I hadn't talked to God about repairing
our relationship fully. I'd started but much needed to be done.

The best way for me to remember Trenton was to find his killer.
Did Jack suspect his former partner's involvement?

A shiver at my nape disturbed me, an intuition that wouldn't
leave me alone. If Luke didn't respond soon, I'd drive to his house.
Jack seemed insistent I talk to him, and the motive stayed fixed in
my mind.

35

I entered an empty interview room to talk to SAC Dunkin, but my mind weighed down with what bad news he might report. "I'm alone," I said.

"Did Ethan Mercury confess?"

I updated the SAC on Ethan's interview and the likeness to Carson's story of the night Trenton Jacobs was killed. The video and transcript would be further evidence the two had given an identical testimony. "I'll retrieve his phones and ensure a tech checks them for tracking and recording."

"You have free rein on this, Gage. Whatever expedites the investigation, go for it. Mrs. Mercury is aware of a threat to her and her sons, but nothing else," the SAC said. "Agents have given her one hour to pack, except she refuses to leave her home without talking to her husband first. Ethan needs to be coached on what to tell her, a reasonable explanation but omit Carson's involvement and the attempt to eliminate him and Risa. She can find that out later, but not today."

"Mrs. Mercury must be upset," I said.

He groaned. "Extremely."

No one wanted to deal with a person in distress mode. "I met her

186

recently, but with her agitation, I won't mention it unless needed. I'll give Ethan and Carson your instructions."

"At this point, we address the bare facts until we have evidence to make arrests."

"I'll handle it, sir. Last night I drove Carson's Jeep to the hospital on the chance I might talk to Jack. I learned from the charge nurse that he's not doing well. His room is heavily guarded, but a man tried to get by the nurses' desk a couple of hours before I got there. They called hospital security, but he left before they arrived. I viewed the security cams, and his build resembles the man Carson described as John Smith."

"Stay on it. Check to see if Ethan can identify him," SAC Dunkin said.

"Will do. Someone stuck a note on the Jeep window informing me, 'You'll always be a step behind us.' I've got it with me and will have it analyzed. The hospital security cam caught a slight figure that could be a man or a woman."

"Put a rush on the handwriting analysis. The one in your possession may be a different person or someone attempting to disguise their handwriting."

"We might get lucky."

"Good thought. To bring you up to speed, as of this morning Jack's been upgraded to serious condition, and he's able to have visitors five minutes on the half hour. We have a positive ID on the man who attempted to run Risa and Carson off the road. His name is Norman Peilman from New Brunswick, Canada. Although his plates were from New Mexico. No employment listed or prior convictions. No connection to Mercury Alarms or any of its companies. Peilman might have been a thug hired for grunt jobs with no idea of who's paying him. Or he used an alias and possibly altered his appearance. We've found nothing connecting him to the Phan sisters or Trenton Jacobs. I'm sending Peilman's info to your phone."

"Anna Wright at Houston Healing and Hope Maternity Care supplied us with a list of past and present employee information. I haven't dug deeper into the findings other than one of the present employees by the name of Clyde Washington said he'd only talk to Jack Bradford or his partner, meaning Luke Reardon. He might change his mind knowing Jack's in the hospital."

"What's Washington's job there?" the SAC said.

"Little bit of everything. He shuttles the residents to doctor and other professional appointments. Does repairs and odd jobs. He's been there nine years and remembered Phan Hai. Seeing Jack is on my list for later today."

"I saw where you and Jack identified two of the gang members. Both are in custody until you interview them today. After Mercury's interview, the two lawyered up. Your charm might change their testimony. Offer a plea bargain."

"The connection to our case is there if they'll talk," I said. "I'll arrange an interview at two today. Charging them with first-degree murder and arson puts them away for a long time."

"Word on the street is the gang was paid to eliminate the Phan sisters and set fire to the restaurant."

"They must have counted on Jack and me taking in the restaurant later on in the day after they murdered the sisters." I blew out my exasperation. "Seeing us threw off their schedule. Surprising we walked away with just a warning, but the executions and setting the explosion must have been the bigger agenda. Keep me posted. I'll report in with new info."

"Hold on, Gage. I have a call coming in from an agent with Mrs. Mercury."

I waited until the SAC returned. "I told the agent to tell Mrs. Mercury that Ethan would call her in approximately fifteen minutes. Then she was to load her car in plain view and leave with the baby."

"Yes, sir."

"Agents will follow Mrs. Mercury to a previously arranged hotel. She'll check in, and they'll transport her and the baby out the rear of the building. An agent will alert me when they are at the safe house. We'll escort Carson once we're finished here."

When the SAC concluded the call, I made my way back to Ethan and Carson to brief them. I wasn't in the mood to play referee. Not a fight I wanted to stop with more to-do items than hours in the day.

The two inside the interview room talked quietly, and no blood or bruises surfaced. I greeted them, sensing a lot less tension but a whole lot of intensity.

"I have new information and instructions," I said to Ethan and Carson. "Mrs. Mercury is with agents, and she's packed and waiting to load the car. She refuses to leave your home until she talks to Ethan. But before the call, we need to be on the same page."

"I don't want Lynn to know the whole story until it's over," Ethan said. "What I've done and what Carson's experienced needs to be presented in an environment where there's victory over evil."

"Dad, you can say Mom's dramatic, it's okay."

Ethan shook his head. "We love her, but she worries over us too much. Agent Patterson, what do I tell my wife?"

"I recommend telling her a man is angry with you about business practices and made threats to your family. You came to us, and we conducted a background on the person and chose a safe house."

"Am I going to a safe house?" Carson said. "I'd rather—"

"You're going," Ethan said. "No questions asked."

"Right," I said. "The problem is what Carson can tell Mrs. Mercury that will ease her mind and provide a solid reason why you aren't joining her."

Ethan peered at me, yet not seeing. "I'll provide enough of the truth to satisfy my conscience but not enough to drive her over the top. I won't lie to Lynn. Here are my thoughts—the FBI can't charge and arrest their suspect until I identify him. I volunteered to aid in the investigation by meeting with the man at a public place."

"Mom's going to freak out with the danger," Carson said.

Ethan frowned. "If she has a meltdown, I'll assure her the FBI will be with me every step of the way."

I handed Ethan my cell. "Do it now. And sound convincing."

Carson pointed to my device in his dad's hands. "What's your plan if she doesn't buy it?"

"Option B," Ethan said. "Agent Patterson will talk to her."

36

RISA

Where was Luke Reardon? Pacing my apartment living area, I phoned his office at the FBI building twice with no answer, then twice more on his cell phone and left messages at both places. I should have gone into the office and conducted business there, but my appearance without the SAC first having ample time to tell others of my reinstatement wasn't appropriate. Luke held the respect of many agents, known for his integrity and professionalism. He'd return my calls at his earliest convenience.

Working again without threat of the wrong people moving in on my parents was an answered prayer. Satisfaction filled me on multiple levels. Trenton had been right. Sometimes my IQ shoved me into wrong conclusions. The road trip had ushered me back into God's arms, even if I admitted to fear still taking over my concern for others.

I brewed a fresh pot of coffee and searched for more data on Emily Lock. The woman, age twenty-five, had mastered disguises. Her real identity showed long blonde hair and blue eyes. The Wades knew Emily Lock with long auburn hair and green eyes. Another pic showed her in spiked blonde hair and blue eyes, and still another with dark-brown hair worn in a shoulder-length style and huge glasses. Curiosity got the best of me, and I pulled up the security-cam footage from the church where Trenton's service was held. Emily Lock had placed the threatening note on my car.

Gage's report named more players in Des Moines. I placed the name of Harvey Sinclair into software that used technology more advanced than any human brain to connect and link names and places. How many were on the payroll here in Houston? Did those involved move from city to city? Possibly. I jotted down Norman Peilman, the man from Canada who'd attempted to run Carson and me off the road. I clicked the app and waited.

An operation as large as what I suspected we were dealing with meant well-paid attorneys who ensured employees had their rears covered. *Their rears covered.* I sounded like Gage. He had rubbed off on me in a very good way. Loved that man to the moon and back, as my grandma used to say. I leaned my head back against the chair and massaged neck muscles. Stress never brought an investigation to a close.

I needed to unpack my carry-on. The idea of leaving dirty clothes in a piece of luggage disgusted me. I walked to my bedroom and unzipped my bag. I gathered up my clothes and deposited them in the laundry room. Next came my toiletries. I carried them into my bathroom. The shower curtain stood partially open. A towel lay on the floor, evidence I wasn't alone. In my bedroom, the closet door was ajar an inch. My apartment lock hadn't been tampered with or I'd have noted it when I returned home.

I viewed the mirror for someone who might be behind me. Sweat beaded my forehead, and my heart ached with the incessant pounding. My home had been violated.

Sickening dread washed over me. They could be viewing me through the scope of a gun, waiting for the opportune moment to strike.

Dumping my toiletries in the sink, I slowly returned to the living room and lifted my Glock from my purse. I chambered a round and aimed my firearm into the closet.

"FBI. Come out with your hands up."

Quiet met me. I kicked the door open and flipped up the closet

light. Empty except for my belongings. I strode into the second bedroom, stood to the side of the closet door, and repeated my warning.
Empty there too.

I returned to the bathroom and swept aside the shower curtain.

Luke Reardon's severed head lay in the bathtub sitting on a blue
baby blanket.

37

GAGE

Lynn Mercury demanded my attention on the phone before she'd leave her home with agents to a safe house. I repeated what Ethan had told her with reassurance that we'd protect him from harm. Finally she agreed.

The initial comps of Carson's and Ethan's handwriting showed no likeness to the previous notes. The only match continued to be the notes left on Risa's car and Jack's wounded body. At this point, Carson's psych eval would be handled at the safe house. For certain, the family would need counseling when this ended. Poisoned thoughts could destroy the strongest person.

I introduced Carson to the agents who'd been assigned to escort him to a safe house where his mother and brother awaited him. I wanted the kid to feel secure with the agents.

After Ethan compiled the list of his clients' security information that he'd given to Smith, I downloaded the list to research who had already been victimized and the type of crime. While I had a huge list of tasks penciled into my day, acting swiftly on those victims exposed to crimes was critical.

Thirty-seven names of people and businesses, addresses, phone numbers, and security codes opened the door to multiple felonious activities. John Smith's demands spread across twenty states.

In the privacy of my cubicle, I waited for my laptop to refresh with the crimes previously committed from Ethan's list and if any had resulted in arrests or convictions. I sat back and studied the screen. How did the scammers know where to find the homes of babies? They must have inside people watching social media for birth announcements. Most people didn't realize the danger of geo-location on their posts.

Twelve baby abductions. Only the Addingtons' baby recovered.

Seven drugstores robbed of opioids.

Seven couples who were scammed by a fraudulent adoption agency. Each taken for forty thousand dollars plus the birth mother's additional expenses.

Eleven crimes were yet to happen. Or were happening. Or had happened, and those victimized hadn't come forward.

I walked back to the interview room and assured Ethan he wouldn't be detained much longer. "Remember all we've talked about. If John Smith contacts you, I want you to get back to me ASAP. In the morning, another agent and I will discuss how to handle any meetups with Smith. I want the passwords changed for every client you've given to Smith before you leave here. Text me when it's done."

"Yes, sir." Ethan's worn features showed he'd spent a lot of sleepless nights. An agent escorted him to the reception area while he retrieved his phones, cautioning him to be careful of what he said to anyone.

My phone alerted me to a call from Risa. She'd phoned about an hour ago, but I couldn't talk then. Interviewing the two gang members in custody might have to wait until three o'clock. I answered Risa's call.

"Hey, I've meant to call you all day."

"Gage, the police are here." She sounded strange . . . off.

"What's going on?"

"I visited Jack. He's heavily sedated and couldn't stay awake. He alluded to a suspect and that I should talk to Luke. I didn't know what he meant."

"But now you do?"

"I . . . I found Luke's head in my bathtub on a blue baby blanket."

My face grew hot. My stomach rolled. The crime ring had sent a powerful message—bold, gruesome. "Risa, are you okay? Of course you're not. I'll let the SAC and ASAC know immediately."

"SAC is aware." The distant tone of her voice said she needed someone with her. We were trained for macabre situations, and we'd seen plenty of those in investigating kidnappings. Hard things. Horrible things done to children and adults. But nothing prepared us for the gruesome sight of one of our own brutally murdered.

A baby blanket? As though mocking the victims and those investigating the crimes.

"I'll finish up what I'm doing and be right there." The rest of the afternoon could take a hike into nowhere.

"I'm all right. You have responsibilities there," she said weakly. "Gage, where is the rest of Luke's body?"

"It will turn up. Those responsible will make sure we receive the whole message."

I called the SAC. Normally everything we did went through the ASAC to minimize the workload for SAC Dunkin. But Risa's recent status negated protocol.

"I don't think she should be alone," I said. "Have agents been sent to her address?"

"Yes. They should be there shortly. We've formed a task force with HPD for the investigation. ASAC Kendall and I are leaving within the hour to inform Luke's wife."

"As soon as I'm finished here with Ethan Mercury, I'd like to see Risa."

"I need you to conduct the interview with the two gang members first and get a statement. I want this crime ring stopped."

I swallowed. I had a job to do. "I'm on it. A request here—would you send agents to my house? It's a Mercury alarm but not on Ethan's list. In the meantime, I'll go online and change my account's password and forward that to you. I've requested Ethan change all the password information on the accounts in the hands of John Smith before he leaves the building."

"Smith will be after Mercury with both barrels. Make sure he's on 24-7 protection detail."

I stood in the empty interview room and digested the repulsive news about Luke. His poor wife. I prayed she had family and friends to comfort her.

Risa was one of the strongest women I'd ever met, one of the many things about her I respected. This all led back to the night her brother had given his life for her. Jack and Luke must have been on the hit list too. What had the two discovered? Why not me? How soon before Smith and his thugs came after Risa again?

38

RISA

I fought the urge to scream at the brutal savagery in my home. Standing in my living room and gazing out the window to the street below decorated in festive Christmas decorations nearly sent me crumpling to my knees. *Why, God?*

I'd learned in dealing with tragic cases how to compartmentalize my emotions until I had privacy to process rage and grief. Horrific images of what a victim suffered at the hands of a brutal killer were not unfamiliar. Yet blood, the pinnacle of violence, never got easier to face. Blood . . . liquid life. When necessary, I sought counseling to rid my mind of terrible images and often blame.

Trenton's and Luke's deaths shouted as one of those times I'd need professional and spiritual help. And always prayer. Forgiveness of myself came hard for me, especially when my personality thrived on perfectionism, and I held myself responsible for not finding a way to end a crime sooner.

While God and I were on much better terms, He refused to answer why. Was it just last week that I poured out my heart to God? And now I needed Him even more.

"Agent Jacobs," a male voice called.

I turned to a police officer who'd arrived first on the scene with his partner. "Two FBI agents are here asking for you."

I hadn't heard a knock or the doorbell. My muddled mental state held me in emotional shock. I longed to see Gage. His words about my strength were almost laughable—more like cry-able.

Help me. I can't help others without You.

Two agents approached me, Darlene, a dear woman who'd mailed thoughtful cards to my apartment ever since Trenton's funeral, and a young male agent I didn't recognize. The same numbness threatened to take over now. With seemingly every breath, I saw Luke's head and Trenton's battered body. Each superimposing the other. Further contemplation—possibly overthinking—that guilt had nested in my head and my heart. I shuddered at how low I'd sunk in the past, when placing one foot in front of the other took monumental effort. Would I ever be the woman from the past . . . Special Agent Risa Jacobs? I wanted to believe I could move on, but Luke's severed head in my bathtub—

My stomach revolted. I rushed into the kitchen and vomited in the sink. Impossible to venture into the bathroom with Luke . . . I hated my inability to master my body's responses.

Trenton died in my place.

Jack's attack could be woven into it.

Luke's murder was to deter me from the investigation.

How many other lives had been destroyed because of something I'd done or knew?

God, help me. I'm afraid.

I wiped my mouth with a wet paper towel, rinsed my mouth, and flipped on the disposal. The rumbling sound increased the pounding in my head.

"Risa," Darlene said. "What can I do?"

I turned to the woman who'd offered compassion and friendship. I'd never forget the depths of caring in her dark-blue eyes. "Darlene, please, I'd like the box of baking soda in the refrigerator." I refused to look at her with the disgust and contempt that must be written in her features.

She handed me the box, and I dumped half of it down the drain.

"When I learned about what happened to Luke," Darlene said, "I asked SAC Dunkin if I could accompany Agent Kendall." The sound of her sweet voice was like a gentle breeze.

"Thank you. Glad you're here."

"Of course. If your stomach has settled, we can sit in the living room. The ASAC is waiting there." She reached out for my hand, and I grasped it.

"Where is my strength?" I whispered.

"It's there. Take a deep breath. I'm not leaving you."

Thank You for bringing the right people into my life. "Thank you for being here today and for saying the right words at Trenton's service."

"Risa, I'm sorry for all you've been through. But you will get through this. You are the strongest woman I know."

Darlene's words, an echo from Gage, reassured me that God had my back. He had all of me—my weakness and my fumbling. I closed my eyes to clear my swimming head, then opened them and nodded at her, finally able to face the woman who'd seen my reaction to such horror. "Yes, I will, and I'll help find Luke's killer." I moistened my foul-tasting lips. "You need info from me. We'll sit, like you suggested, and I'll go over the details leading up to finding Luke." I straightened and let her walk me to the sofa. ASAC Kendall greeted me and asked Darlene to handle the interview.

So often I comforted and encouraged people in anguish, but being on the receiving end seemed wrong . . . just like at Trenton's funeral.

"I saw ginger ale in the fridge," Darlene said. "Would that settle your stomach?"

"Maybe later. When we're finished, I'll try a little."

"Ever independent. That's one of your most admirable traits."

"Tell Gage. He'll love it since I just broke down on the phone with him."

"He misses you," Darlene said. "With Jack in the hospital, Gage wanders through the office as though you might suddenly appear."

"I didn't resign but took a personal leave. I'd hoped to find my brother's killer, but nothing surfaced." I pointed to her phone.

"Record our conversation so you will have it word for word. The idea of repeating any of this makes me ill all over again."

Darlene pressed Record, and I began. "I left my apartment around ten thirty this morning after learning Jack could have a five-minute visitor. The doctor had prescribed medication to make him sleep, and rest is what he needs. Jack barely spoke until he drifted off, and my five minutes reached its limit. I talked to the SAC and drove home. It was eleven forty-five when I walked in. Everything appeared in order, and the lock on my door hadn't been tampered with. I made a pot of coffee and worked for a little over an hour on my laptop. I took a break to unpack my overnight bag . . ." I finished the story. Odd, my head seemed to clear but I still trembled. "I called 911, the SAC, and Gage."

"Have you spoken to Luke since last July?"

"No. I learned he returned to civil rights, and Jack needed a partner, which turned out to be Gage."

Darlene paused. "I have a tough question."

I lifted my chin. "Yes, I believe . . . I know why Luke was murdered and why . . . he's here."

"Does the SAC know your thoughts?"

"Yes, and Gage too."

"Okay. An FBI team is on its way for a sweep."

"Has Luke's body been located?" I said.

"Not yet." Darlene smiled at Agent Richey, who'd been listening intently. "Do you have any questions?"

"No. My sympathies, Agent Jacobs. I know the past several months have been difficult. I'm new to violent crime, but I will do whatever is needed to arrest whoever is responsible."

Darlene pressed Stop on her cell phone. "Where are you staying tonight?"

A place for the night hadn't entered my mind. The atrocity in my bathroom . . . No, I couldn't stay here for a multitude of reasons. "I can go to my parents' home." I wouldn't go there, not with photos and memories of Trenton in every corner. A hotel suited me better.

"If your parents' home doesn't work out, give me a call and you can use my guest room."

Her generosity touched me. Could she tell my emotions were off the chart? I took another breath. "Thanks. I appreciate you more than you could ever imagine."

"Wouldn't you do the same for me?"

"Without a doubt," I said.

"I suggest you tell me what you need from your bedroom and bath, and I'll pack them."

Another act of caring. "My overnight bag is on my bed, and my toiletries are dumped in the sink. If it's not too much of an imposition, I'd like my toothbrush and toothpaste now to rid the taste in my mouth."

"No problem at all. Sit tight. I'll get them and then your other things. I'll walk you to your car."

"Not yet. I prefer staying until the investigators are finished. I'm okay, really."

"Okay." But the skepticism in her eyes revealed her disbelief. I understood. While I fought my way upstream, I'd take it one stroke at a time.

Lord, be with Luke's widow. Love her through the horrible news of how he died.

39

I should be with Risa. No one else. She knew my feelings, and I knew hers. Every moment away from her hurt, and now she faced walking through a gruesome murder alone. So much to talk through. Right now, I wanted to protect her from the evil. But the SAC was right—I needed to do my job. The best way to help Risa was to have confessions and leads. But how did I convince my aching heart who wanted to comfort the woman I loved?

A tech examined Ethan's burner and personal phones under secure conditions that prevented Smith's knowledge. Smith had installed a bug on both to alert all usages, geo-tracking, and enable recording. We chose to keep those in place. Awareness was all we needed. I arranged for surveillance and released Ethan to go home once he changed the passwords. Granted, his willingness put him in the line of fire, and my conscience nudged me about permitting it.

ASAC Kendall and I met outside the door of an interview room. He introduced me to a female agent who spoke Vietnamese and would interpret the conversation. Through the one-way mirror, we scrutinized the three men awaiting questioning, one in a suit. I held the gang members' files, and both had been in jail for misdemeanors, but this was their first felony. Tuan Duong and Vinh Bui had shaved heads. Tuan had a jagged scar alongside the left side of his neck. Jack and I had ID'd both young men from previous charges. They'd been two of the five gang members who'd threatened us. He and Duong were caught on video pulling up to the Saigon Sampler shortly before the fire broke out, and Duong's .22 had executed the Phan sisters.

Their attorney, Giang Lam, represented influential Asian clients—not the respectable ones but the kind the FBI wanted off the streets. Most likely, Giang collected his fee from the crime ring that had kidnapped the Addingtons' baby. Made sense the two under arrest would be represented by one who understood the culture and the game organized crime played with the judicial system. Giang representing the gang members also distanced the fraudulent adoption agencies from the murders and arson at the restaurant. Legal representation would argue the cases weren't remotely connected. Another angle for me to twist around in my brain.

We entered the room where the two cuffed gang members and their attorney had waited for over an hour while I finished with Ethan. The room nearly exploded in frustration.

I shook hands with the attorney, a man who wore a silk suit and tie more expensive than I'd ever own. The two men in dirty jeans and T-shirts didn't have the high dollars to pay him, just puppets used to broaden the crime ring's agenda.

I introduced myself and ASAC Kendall. "I apologize for the delay, Mr. Giang. Your clients, Tuan Duong and Vinh Bui, are charged with first-degree murder in the deaths of Phan Suzi and Phan Hai. Your clients are also charged with a first-degree felony, arson and a death resulting from the fire. The third is a federal change for threatening FBI agents. How do your clients plead?"

"Not guilty," the attorney said.

No surprise there. "Mr. Giang, I was at the Saigon Sampler restaurant, and your clients accosted me and my partner. Within an hour of leaving the area, the mentioned crimes occurred."

"Who is your partner? Where is he?" Giang had his poker face down pat.

"Special Agent Jack Bradford. He's in the hospital."

Bui smirked. At least one of them spoke English.

"I'm sorry to hear that," Giang said. "Is he ill?"

"I'm fairly certain your clients can fill you in on Agent Bradford's attack."

"Highly unlikely," Giang said. "Did you arrest anyone?"

Now my frustration level threatened to explode. "You and your clients are here for me to ask the questions. Not the other way around. Sir, I repeat, your clients are facing first-degree murder and arson charges."

"Mr. Tuan and Mr. Vinh are innocent."

"Doesn't negate the charges and evidence proving otherwise."

"We'll let a judge and jury decide," Giang said.

I studied the two cuffed men—young and hard. I shared the video footage of the two arriving at the restaurant and the proof of Duong's gun used for the murders. "In Texas, the sentence for first-degree murder can be life imprisonment or the death penalty. Think about it, gentlemen. A cell for the rest of your life or a coffin? Are you two willing to take that risk? Because if you're not, we can discuss a plea bargain."

The three exchanged words in Vietnamese, but they weren't aware of an agent interpreting their conversation. I didn't know what they said, but the prisoners' body language demonstrated neither a life sentence nor the death penalty set well.

"Will my clients have all charges dismissed if they cooperate?" the attorney said.

"I will inform the judge of their cooperation and request the charges be reduced."

"What do you want from us?" Vinh Bui said.

"You told me you're innocent." Giang glared at him.

"Doesn't hurt to hear the man out," Vinh said.

"All right." Giang pulled a small notebook and pen from inside his jacket. "We talked about a plea bargain before and decided it wasn't in your best interests and instead to plead not guilty, which you claim is the truth. What has changed your mind?"

Vinh spoke up. "I'll listen. Duong, what about you?"

Tuan Duong nodded. Both spoke English when convenient.

I allowed a moment of silence to wrestle with their future. "Word on the street is you were paid to execute the Phan sisters and set fire to the restaurant known as the Saigon Sampler. Who paid you?"

The attorney jotted down my question. "That assumes they are guilty of the charges."

"If your clients weren't guilty, we wouldn't be having a plea bargain discussion."

The attorney huffed. "Any other questions?"

"Have you committed crimes for this person or persons in the past?" I gave the attorney time to write the question while the prisoners stared back at me. "What were those crimes and how much were you paid?" I paused. "I want the name of the person who attacked Special Agent Bradford. I saw five of you in the parking lot the day of the two murders and fire. I want the names of the other three men and any others who were involved."

"For what purpose?" the attorney said.

"Questioning." I concentrated on the two men in cuffs. "Your attorney will get his money whether you answer my questions or maintain a not-guilty plea. From the designer of his suit, his bank account is stuffed by someone other than the likes of you two. He doesn't care if you walk the streets or face a deadly injection. All he wants is his fee." I leaned back in my chair and gave a smug smile to the weasel of an attorney. "I suggest you and your clients reach a decision in the next ten minutes."

The attorney eyed his clients. "I advise you not to comply." The silk suit might not receive as much of his retainer if the two talked.

I stood and the ASAC joined me. "We will leave you three alone to make a decision."

Again we watched the three from outside the interview room. They carried on a heated conversation in Vietnamese.

"Don't think our guys want to cooperate, but Giang doesn't agree," ASAC Kendall said. "We don't need an interpreter to figure that out."

"But I have the exact translation," the female interpreter said. "Giang told them they are dead men if they budge from their not-guilty plea."

I nodded. "If they give up names, it could come back to haunt Giang."

We waited the full ten minutes and made our way back to the three men. ASAC Kendall and I took our previous seats. I stared at the three. I believed silence sucks out the truth.

"Are you ready to hear my clients' decision?" Giang said.

I motioned for him to proceed.

"Mr. Tuan and Mr. Vinh would like to plea-bargain, to assist the FBI in solving the murders and arson, but they don't have the answers to all of your questions."

"Which ones do they have answers?" I said. "Without clear information, I can't talk to the judge."

"If they gave you a name of who supposedly paid them to commit the felonies, that jeopardizes their not-guilty plea. Mr. Tuan and Mr. Vinh aren't willing to provide you with a fictitious name."

"You're telling me they don't know who paid them?"

"They are innocent. They are aware of accosting you and Special Agent Bradford on the day of the alleged crimes. But have no idea who attacked Agent Bradford, committed the murders, or set the fire."

"What about Mr. Tuan's .22?"

"He claims it was stolen."

I pressed my lips into a tight smile. "Gentlemen, we're finished here. I will see you in court." I paused again, all for effect. "Mr. Tuan and Mr. Vinh, you lose either way. If you stand before a judge and jury with the evidence we have against you, my guess the judge will pronounce the death penalty. Sleep well tonight."

40

RISA

Evening shadows rippled through the slats of my living room blinds, reminding me of how faint signs of light could give insight to a tragedy. The FBI and two HPD detectives still processed the crime scene—where killers had left a reminder of how Luke had been murdered. I'd forgotten how long it took to conduct a thorough sweep. During an investigation I often became so absorbed in finding evidence that I lost track of time.

So here I sat in my ever-darkening living room and sipped on warm ginger ale, willing someone to shed light on the nightmare crimes that stalked me.

The doorbell interrupted my self-centered musings, and I answered it without checking to see who stood outside. Gage . . . I flung open the door and wrapped my arms around his neck. No sobs, just clinging to him for support. Forget the nonsense about me being strong. I was too weary to construct a facade.

"Hey, I got here as soon as I could." His voice quieted me. He kissed my cheek, and he rubbed my back.

"I'm okay, really." Hadn't I repeated the same thing to Darlene, who'd left fifteen minutes ago with a promise to check back later?

"You will be."

I stepped back and allowed him to enter. Lines etched around his eyes, stress reminders. The past few days had aged both of us. "The team is still here, finishing up." I gestured to my bedroom.

"Give me a moment with them."

I nodded with a poor attempt of having my emotions intact, and he disappeared down the hall. I should have walked that mile with him, but instead the image of Luke's head scrolled through my mind interspersed with his wedding . . . and how happy he and his wife had been. My comfort lay in recalling his commitment to the FBI and professionalism, like I'd chosen happy moments with Trenton. Sweet memories and Jesus kept me sane.

I leaned against the back of the door with my arms wrapped around me. Who was with Luke's wife? For certain, the SAC had broken the news and remained with her until family or friends arrived. Determination spiraled through me to focus on finding the evidence to stop these senseless killings. Glancing at my laptop on the coffee table, I pondered the distraction of entering people and data into a spreadsheet . . . More like busywork when software would do the task more efficiently.

Unfortunately, the fog in my mind more closely resembled an impossible maze. The tasks I couldn't finish today would be there tomorrow.

Gage appeared in the hallway. He won the gold medal for strength, stamina, and wisdom, traits I had once thought I possessed. "I appreciate your being here when I know you're exhausted."

"No place I'd rather be." For a brief millisecond, his blue-gray eyes flashed his love, the love I so desperately wanted. He glanced away. "The team is preparing to leave."

"They'll expedite the fingerprint check, but will it provide answers?" I shook my head. "Ignore me. I'm angry and justice is elusive. Are Carson and his family in a safe house?"

"Yes, but not Ethan." Gage explained what had transpired at the office. "We need a name, solid evidence to move forward. Ethan's willingness to force John Smith's hand could shove puzzle pieces into place. Before Ethan left, he changed the passwords on the accounts in Smith's possession. His choice, knowing once the bad guys know what he's done, they will spare no bullets."

"Courage is one thing but setting himself up to be killed is another. Whatever happened to meliorism?" I said.

"We grew up and saw the world for what it is. For now," he said, "we deal with what we have. I haven't checked for updates yet today."

We took our usual places at the kitchen counter while he pulled up info on his phone. "What a relief." He took my hand. "Two things here. One is Luke's body has been found."

"Where?" I whispered.

"In his car on a back road near Kingwood. My guess is it's not a random location. The car's being searched as we speak."

I could only imagine the blood. Not going there. "That's relief for his wife. I hate this for her. Every victim we've encountered has nightmares to live with, and I remember them all."

"We both do. A bit of good news—we have a positive on John Smith."

"Who is he?"

"Peter Florakis, last known address in New York City. Person of interest in a car bombing and murder. The victim worked for a crime syndicate. Florakis is wanted for questioning in two additional murders in that city. He's an expert in avoiding arrest and disguise, but we can get a BOLO on him."

"Details on the other crimes?"

"I'll send you his file, and I need to call Ethan. Inform him of what we've learned." He reached into his pocket for his burner phone and placed the call. Gage shared the update about Peter Florakis. "He's a professional and knows that we'd ID him. Would you like to join your family?" Gage caught my attention. "You've made a dangerous decision. If you change your mind, give me a call."

"Ethan is playing the hero?" I said.

"He believes Florakis will be calling him any day for client info. My concern is Ethan living through the repercussion when Florakis discovers the previous data is worthless. We have a team with eyes on the Mercury home, but Florakis is slippery, or he'd be cuffed by now." Gage deposited his burner into his pocket and pulled out his work phone. "I'm texting the FIG to find us everything on Florakis."

My need-to-be-in-control hero. I longed for a little osmosis to seep into my reasoning. My head whirled with how to find Florakis. "We need family info. Last known address. Files on past charges. Anyone we can interview. And what about a handwriting comparison?"

"No match to what we have." Gage lifted his gaze from his phone's screen. "Risa, even superheroes need to recharge."

I tilted my head. "I'm not running or flying. But I want to put on my superhero cape and handle my job like a professional."

"You will, Risa. I know you. Let me take care of you."

I remembered what I was doing before . . . finding Luke. I eased onto the sofa and lifted my laptop lid. "None of those in our database resemble Harvey Sinclair, the man who posed as a lawyer who handled private adoptions." I studied the screen. Nothing had surfaced.

Gage eased beside me. "Try the artist's sketch of Sinclair with Norman Peilman and Peter Florakis."

I pointed. "Florakis's brown eyes, square jaw, and bald head by no means resemble Peilman or Sinclair. Their body builds are different too. Have the Wades seen Peilman's and Florakis's pics?"

"Good one." Gage sent Alex and Nanette Wade in Des Moines the pics.

Within minutes the couple responded. Both recognized Peilman as the man who'd impersonated a police officer.

After the FBI and police left the scene with what remained of a friend, I took a deep breath and stared down the hall.

"Don't go back there," Gage said. "There's no reason."

"Darlene repacked my overnight bag from the weekend, but I need clothes to wear to work tomorrow."

"Okay, I agree going to the office will keep your mind off gruesome reminders."

I raised a brow. "You're now my keeper?"

"I wear that label every day. I'm trying to help. Honey, I don't think it's a good idea to visit that area, not with the blood in the bathroom. Besides they said they might return tomorrow. Tell me what to pull from the closet and bathroom, and I'll get it."

He sounded like Darlene, and I understood his protectiveness. His personality pushed him to fix me. Honestly, I'd do the same for him. The nausea had passed, yet my skin felt clammy, and I was drained mentally and physically. Dizziness had replaced my inner sickness. I recognized definite symptoms of shock, and I'd monitor it.

"Thanks. I'd argue with you but not today. In my closet on the right-hand side is a black jacket and pants. On the opposite side are four or five long-sleeved white blouses. Just pick one. My black pumps are on the floor." I shook my head. "I need underthings too, and they're in the two upper drawers of my dresser."

"Okay. If I run into problems, I'll holler." He started toward my bedroom and turned. "Shouldn't you have more than one outfit?"

"I suppose so. Beside the black jacket is a navy-blue one, and beside the black pants are navy pants. Oh, navy pumps. Add an extra blouse and underthings. I already have pajamas and jeans packed."

I assembled my laptop, cords, and papers strewn across the coffee table.

"Where are you going for the next few nights?" he called.

Darlene had offered her home, but I wouldn't drag anyone else into this. "A hotel."

"Where?"

"I haven't decided."

"What about my house?"

As tempting as his offer sounded, I couldn't accept. In my emotional state, I might do something totally inappropriate . . . and regret it. "It's impossible for me to stay with you, Gage. Not with how we feel about each other. But I appreciate the offer."

He appeared with his arms full. I took the underthings from him and stuffed them in my overnight bag. "Why refuse my invite?"

"People will talk."

He startled. "We took a trip last weekend together."

"Carson was with us, and we had separate rooms in a hotel."

"Technically adjoining. Pretend he's there, and you'll be fine."

I wanted to say yes. "Agent Patterson, I'm vulnerable right now."

"And you think I'd take advantage of you?"

I shook my head sadly. "Quite the opposite."

Gage chuckled. "Doesn't sound like a bad idea."

I longed to crawl inside his embrace forever, let the warmth in his dark eyes keep me safe and loved. "And if I stayed with you, I'd agree."

With his hands full of my clothes, he leaned over and kissed me. "Make your reservations, and I'll follow you there to ensure you're okay. In the morning, I'll pick you up for breakfast—"

"Aren't we meeting with Clyde Washington early?"

"You're right. And I'm sure he has information to keep us busy all day. He's skittish, so I'd like you to lead out."

"Are you sure since he asked for Jack?"

"You're prettier. Give it a whirl. See where it goes."

"Thank you," I said, "for believing in me and not giving up."

"I'd never give up on you. Now let's get you to a hotel where you can rest up."

"You still believe in us?" I said.

"Absolutely. But I need to tell you something about me." He glanced away. "You might change your mind about us."

41

Was Clyde Washington afraid of meeting Gage and me at the FBI office? Or did he prefer a bakery and coffee shop at 6 a.m. near his home for convenience's sake? After the horror of finding Luke yesterday, my cautionary perception slammed into overdrive. I'd heard every moan and groan of the heating unit in the hotel room, and when I did manage to fall asleep, the images repeated. But prayer and determination had a strong grip on me, and without either one, I'd fail . . . again.

The bakery had five café-size tables along a wall opposite the display counter. From the people already lined up, takeout was their specialty. Gage pulled up a third chair to the table farthest from the door where he could see all who entered and left. We introduced ourselves, and Gage made sure we had coffee.

Most people were nervous when in the presence of FBI agents and the focus of questions. I would be too. Clyde Washington was no exception.

"Mr. Washington, this bakery smells wonderful, but why meet here and not at our office?" I said.

He dragged his tongue across his lower lip. "Seemed like the best place and not far from work. I hate traffic. You can call me Clyde."

"Thanks. I'm Risa and this is Gage." I glanced around the busy bakery, glad we sat apart from the line of customers. "A popular spot for commuters." I subconsciously urged him to relax. His tense shoulders indicated he carried a lot of weight. "Do you want a donut or pastry?"

"No, but thanks. The coffee's enough."

I took a sip of my own. Definitely strong. "How long have you been at Houston Healing and Hope Maternity Care?"

He dug his left fingers into his palm while holding his coffee in his right. "Going on nine years. I do odd jobs—repairs, painting, heavy lifting, and drive the residents to their appointments. Most of them don't have cars, and we have a courtesy shuttle." He dropped his napkin on the floor and reached to pick it up while muttering something unintelligible.

"Did you ask me something?" I shepherded kindness into every word.

He flushed. "No, ma'am."

"Do you enjoy your work there?" I smiled.

He moistened his lips. "To me, it's a ministry. Those women who come to the care center have nowhere else to go. Most of them have been deserted by the men who got them pregnant." He held up his palm. "I know the woman is responsible too. But she's the one usually faced with the financial responsibility and often raising the child without help." Clyde's words indicated a man committed to his job.

"I know the maternity home has helped a lot of women, and I'm proud to say my church is one of the sponsors," I said.

"Then we have a connection." He peered at me, then Gage. "Why do you want to talk to me? Have I broken a law?"

"No, sir," I said. "You have an outstanding work record. Not even a traffic violation. Your uneasiness tells me you might already be aware of our concern, especially since you preferred speaking to Special Agent Jack Bradford. He is recovering from a heart attack."

"At home or in the hospital?"

"Hospital. He's in serious condition."

Clyde paled. "Is the attacker in jail?"

"Not yet. As soon as we're permitted to talk to him, we'll find out what he remembers."

He shook his head. "I hate it when good people are hurt, especially law enforcement who risk their lives to protect us."

Gage and I needed to find answers. "Clyde, in my experience, I've found we're either afraid of the unknown or fearful of what we do know, especially when we're confused about a situation. Not sure about you, but the unexplainable always raises questions in my mind."

"Yes, ma'am." Sweat beaded on his brow.

"This is a safe place, Clyde. Your words stay right here with Agent Patterson and me. You have our word. Is there anything going on at the center that alarms you?"

Clyde took a gulp of coffee. "Ms. Risa and Gage, I have a wife and two teenage daughters. If anything happened to me, they'd be okay financially . . . except . . ."

I lowered my voice. "Are you worried about someone taking revenge on them because of what you might say?"

He drew in a heavy breath. "I've seen things not right. Very wrong."

"Like Hai and her baby?"

He paused. "Yes. Is she why you wanted to talk to me?"

"Agent Patterson and I want to make sure justice is served," I said. "An investigation is in progress to determine why the sisters were killed. Do you have any idea who might have taken her baby or why someone wanted them dead?"

Lines fanned from his eyes. "She was a sweet girl, always smiling." He paused again. "I've overheard conversations that made me wish I couldn't hear. I speculate Hai wasn't the only resident caught up in illegal dealings. But she didn't speak English, so I can only repeat gossip about her."

"What have you seen or heard?"

He scanned the area before speaking. "If I heard right, some of the women were offered money to give up their babies, a few obliged. Birth mothers disappeared, which to me seemed strange."

"How horrible. Do you mean one day they were at the maternity home and the next day they vanished?"

"No, ma'am. I need to explain. Over the course of nine years, I transported hundreds, maybe thousands, of women to the free clinic for doctor's appointments. The missing women I'm talking about are the few I dropped off while I waited in the van. But the women never came out of the clinic. When I searched inside for them, they hadn't checked in for their appointments. I assumed they'd left through another door. That happened ten, maybe a dozen times. They were never seen again."

"What did Ms. Wright say when you reported it?"

"She always reacted frantically. Ma'am, she loves those residents. Later she reported some of the young women went back to their boyfriends or husbands. The others who contacted her said they'd returned to family. What I never figured out was how they could have left the center without stringing me along. There aren't any rules saying they have to stay or bars on the windows and doors."

"Were their personal belongings picked up?"

"Yes. People would show up at the home, ask to see Ms. Wright, and together they packed up the residents' things. It could mean nothing." He rubbed the leg of his jeans. "But leaving me in the parking lot with no word of their plans didn't make sense. Those women always seemed grateful for whatever they received, and the home is free to help them. Guess I shouldn't have taken it personally."

"I'd have been upset too," I said. "Do you have any names and dates?"

"No, ma'am. I don't have an online calendar like most people. I use the paper kind, and when the year's up, I toss it."

No help there. "I see. The other unusual occurrences bother me, like the women offered money for their babies. Do you suspect any of the workers or volunteers?"

"I wish I could give you a name, but blaming an innocent person is wrong."

"What if your suspicions are right? The birth mothers trust everyone at the care center. Clyde, we need whatever you can give us. Your conclusions by no means pronounce guilt."

"I don't have firsthand information."

"I understand. Who spends the most time with the residents?"

"I suppose the woman who handles intake. She spends hours counseling the young women about the clinic, medical needs, potential adoption, counseling, employment for after their babies are born, and affordable housing."

"What is her name?"

"Myra Cummings."

"Anyone else?"

He blew out a ragged breath. "I've wondered about different people, but they're all good and kind. So is Myra."

"Like who?" I said.

"The cook, she gives cooking lessons. The nurse who comes by three days a week and teaches them prenatal care. And a woman from a church who does Bible study. She's from a church that supports the center." He startled. "That's your church. My apologies."

"No problem." The idea of a criminal in disguise as a Christian wasn't a new concept. I made a mental note to talk to my pastor and reexamine the backgrounds of the women employed and volunteers at the center. Jack and Gage had requested the information, but I hadn't been diligent about studying it. I swung to Gage. "What have I missed?"

"Clyde," Gage said. "I'm a friend of Jack's. He's a good man. What is your connection to him?"

"Two years ago, he and his partner arrested a doctor who was in the business of buying and selling babies. Ms. Wright helped with the case."

Gage nodded. "I remember."

"I don't think Agent Bradford got the full story back then. I remember overhearing him and his partner argue about the case not being over just because they'd arrested the doctor. That's all I heard or remember."

"Did things calm down after the doctor's arrest?" Gage said.

"For about six months," Clyde said. "I mean, questionable things could have occurred, but I didn't see or hear anything. Then it started again about six months later."

Gage thanked him. "What went on then?"

"I heard talk again." He worried his lip. "The residents live at the maternity home for around five or so months, so unless something is unusual about them, they slip my mind. After Dr. Zonner's arrest, new birth mothers arrived. After six months, I overheard a young woman say she'd met with prospective parents and their lawyer. They offered her five thousand dollars for her baby and to pay her medical bills."

"Who was the birth mother?"

"I don't remember. I'd hoped whatever had been going on had ended."

Gage pulled out his phone and scrolled to a photo of Norman Peilman, the man who attempted to run Risa and Carson off the road. "Have you seen this man before?" Clyde responded negatively, and Gage displayed the one of Peter Florakis.

Clyde studied Florakis's pic longer. "No, sir. Never seen him before either."

I pulled up the photos of Emily Lock and her three disguises on my phone. I handed my device to Clyde and asked him to scroll through the photos. "Have you seen any of these women?"

"Are they wanted?"

"Yes, sir."

Clyde pointed to the disguise of dark-brown, shoulder-length hair and huge glasses. "This woman was at the center about three years ago. She arrived shortly before the doctor scandal."

"Do you recall her name?" I said.

He appeared to think for a moment, then shook his head. "I'm sorry. Nothing stands out, so she must have delivered her baby, then left. Ms. Wright could tell you."

"Thanks. You're a big help." I sent the one pic to Ms. Wright and asked her to call me.

"I remember the other agent's name who worked with Agent Bradford. Luke Reardon. He showed up a couple of times alone. Have you talked to him?"

I faced Gage for him to answer.

"We can't," Gage said. "Agent Reardon is dead."

Clyde leaned back in his chair, his face a wash of white. "Sick? Accident?"

"Murdered."

"How?" Clyde whispered.

"It's too gruesome for me to explain. I'm sure the media will have a report today. We believe it's linked to a crime ring that buys and sells babies."

"At the second visit, he lost his temper when Ms. Wright told him she didn't have time to talk to him."

"What were Agent Reardon's words?"

"That he'd be back and ignoring a crime didn't make it disappear." Clyde slowly stood. "I . . . I need to get to work. Appreciate y'all meeting me here." He left the bakery, the bell above the door ringing in his wake.

Turn around and come back. Tell us what we need to make an arrest.

42

GAGE

"Do you think Clyde recognized Peter Florakis?" I said. "He might have posed as a doctor. Or been at the center under the guise of a Good Samaritan."

Risa eyed the bakery door as though Clyde might walk back through. When she faced me, her pale face showed the stress. "I think he shared more than he intended. I also think he witnessed more than he admitted. My guess is he's seen too much and chose to end the meeting after hearing about Jack and Luke on the heels of Hai's murder."

I sighed. "Yes, he's afraid. Did you hear what he said when he dropped his napkin?"

"Something about the napkin was his cue to leave."

The noise in the bakery played havoc with what Risa and I needed to discuss. We grabbed our coffee and headed to the parking lot. I inspected my SUV for anything suspicious attached to my car—wouldn't be the first time a triggered bomb destroyed investigators. Risa explored the usual places right along with me. We silently completed our search and slid into my SUV.

"Do you believe Clyde?" I said.

"Enough to follow up on what he said but not enough to discount an inflection of truth. I've read the backgrounds on every employee and volunteer at Houston Healing and Hope, and no one raised any doubts." She held up a finger. "But I plan to review them all again. Do you think Luke could have been involved?"

"I hope not, Risa. The intake woman has access to personal and financial info. If she's guilty, she has all a scammer would need to approach a resident," I said. "It doesn't match the Addingtons' case, but we have no idea of the enormity of the crime ring."

"We're creeping closer, Gage. My intuition says we have more pieces than we think." Her stomach growled, and she apologized. Her phone buzzed with an incoming call. "It's from Anna Wright." She pressed Speaker and answered. "Thanks for returning my call. Did you recognize the photo of the young woman?"

"Yes, I remember her."

"What's her name?"

"Um . . . Elizabeth. I'd need to verify her last name in the files. Why? Has she been hurt? Is she okay?"

"We'd like to talk to her. I'll hold on while you find her last name and address." Several moments passed before Ms. Wright returned to the phone. "I can't find her file. I'm sorry." She sobbed. "I'm always so fastidious about my documents. No one is allowed in the locked cabinet but me. I'll go through each one after we're finished."

"I appreciate your willingness to help us." Risa ended the call.

"Shall we get breakfast and map out our next move?" I said. "My brain doesn't need a sugar kick, or we'd head back inside for donuts."

We agreed on a First Watch location, Risa's favorite breakfast spot. We drove to the restaurant with little conversation, which was how we normally worked together. She'd have her mind engaged with one angle, and I'd focus on another. Would this always be our way of settling in to our lives? I wanted kids, a dog, and a backyard. For sure when we talked or rather debated, reasoning rolled into place. We were both headstrong, but that only meant we needed proof to agree to the other's viewpoint. The big difference rested in our relationship. I reached for her hand and wished I held her in my arms. Soon.

★ ★ ★

We'd been on the road about fifteen minutes when my phone buzzed with an unrecognizable number.

"Gage Patterson."

"Sir, you gave me your card after Saigon Sampler fire." Her thick accent perked my attention, and I enabled Bluetooth so Risa could hear. "You said to call if I knew anything about Phan Suzi and her sister, Hai."

An image formed in my mind of the woman at the fire scene on the afternoon after Saigon Sampler burned to the ground. She'd been very upset about the Phan sisters' deaths. I'd been led to believe none of the three Vietnamese people spoke English—they'd used Smoke as an interpreter. Just like the gang members I'd interviewed yesterday— English must be the language of convenience. I pointed to my legal pad, and Risa grabbed it with a pen. She jotted down something. I assumed the topic of the woman's call.

"Do you have information to help the FBI solve those murders?" I said.

"Yes, sir. I have a little."

"Can you give me your name?"

"No. Too dangerous."

"I understand." I refused to push the request for fear she'd hang up. I could research the number later. "Thank you for your courage to call me. I'm listening, so go ahead with what you can share."

"Hai had a two-week-old baby boy who was taken from her."

"Kidnapped?"

"Yes."

"Do you know who did this?"

"No name. Hai was offered money for him and refused. Then he was stolen."

"Was Suzi trying to help her locate the baby?"

"Yes. The man who died in the fire was baby's father. He wanted her to take money. Boy babies get higher price."

"Hai wanted to raise her son."

"Yes, sir."

"If she no longer had her baby, why were she and her sister killed?"

"They were going to police because father helped the bad people take the baby."

"I have the father's name in the restaurant fire report—Ly Nien. Did he have family here?"

She hesitated. "Maybe."

"Are you his family?"

Soft sobs met Gage's ears. "My brother. I have nothing left in this country."

"I'm sorry for your loss. Those who took the baby, were they part of a gang?"

"No, sir. Gang do killings and set fire to restaurant but not take the baby. The bad people who have Hai's baby not Vietnamese."

"Who killed Hai and Suzi?"

"Tuan Duong and Vinh Bui."

"How do you know this?"

"They come by my house after fire. Drunk. Say they did it, and my husband and I next if we tell anyone."

"You're telling me now."

"For you to keep them in jail. But I can't testify."

I understood, although I didn't agree. "Thank you for coming forward. You're a brave woman. The FBI, police, and others will find the killers and learn what happened to Hai's baby. How can I let you know when the baby is found? Are you the only living family?"

"I am. But no use. Maybe you find me through Phật Quang Vietnamese Buddhist Pagoda." The phone clicked.

I shook my head. "I'll investigate the pagoda and put a trace on the phone number once I'm back at the office. Makes me wonder if the Vietnamese community has experienced other child abductions."

"I'm wondering too," Risa said. "It's barely eight o'clock in the morning, and we have two huge pieces to analyze. We should eliminate breakfast and drive to the office."

"When did you last eat?"

She moaned. "Yesterday morning."

"My point. Remember, I'm the handler." I tried to make her smile, but she stared out at the street ahead.

"Gage, sometimes the right people are placed in our lives at the right moment for the right purpose. This will help the case against Duong and Bui."

"Doubtful, but it's a lead."

43

Risa and I sat at a secluded corner booth at First Watch where we could talk privately. After we ordered, she opened her laptop while I relied on my legal pad notes. "Don't you think the maternity home would take photos since they advocate a family environment?"

"Not sure," I said. "Privacy issues might stop them. Think about angry baby daddies." I inwardly grimaced.

"You're right. Not safe. I'd like to establish a summary overview," Risa said. "Viewing the progression of the investigation up to what we learned this morning. It's old-school, but since you're the legal pad guy, I think it's the best way for us to operate. I've worked on a partial list but with only a few names."

I grinned. "We're both old-school types. Nothing's changed." I pointed to her laptop. "Go for it. First let me give you this number. See if it can be traced."

She typed the email to the techs while I admired the way the light above our table highlighted her brown hair.

"Sent," she said. "I'll start the chronological list. Trenton's death occurred on July 29, which per a note after his funeral, stated the victim should have been me."

Had I heard right? "Is that what the note said?"

She met my gaze.

"Risa, before we go a step further, tell me the rest of the story."

She tapped her finger on the tabletop. "Okay. Whoever wrote the note threatened my parents, you, and friends if I didn't resign from the FBI. I tried to resign, but SAC Dunkin offered another solution, and that was a leave of absence. The arrangement would be confidential. I had access to secure sites, and if my research would reveal my status, then he retrieved the information for me. I'm very appreciative of how he's helped since some of the higher-ups probably didn't approve." She took a sip of water. "The combination of grief, guilt, and threats to others affected me physically, mentally, and spiritually."

"I'd have done the same thing." I needed to come clean with her too. "I know how you operate and how others' welfare comes before yours."

"Taking a leave to protect others and allowing them to believe I resigned served multiple purposes—for me to find healing, pacify the killer, and investigate on my own meant I could track down the killer. Vengeance played a huge motivator. It didn't help matters when I had no clue who was responsible, and as each day passed with no evidence or leads, I sank deeper into depression. My parents were the only ones besides the SAC who knew the truth. We've kept in contact through burner phones. They supported me, but I despise that they've had to grieve alone. Right now they are in Charleston for an extended stay until this is over."

"I wish you'd have told me the contents a whole lot sooner. I had no clue about it except the grief."

"Note, I haven't done well in figuring out who's behind my brother's death."

"We can figure this out together. I hate what you've been through alone." I squeezed her hand. "I'm here now. You have all of me. Remember I love you."

Her lips lifted in a smile. "Those three words mean more to me than you'll ever know, the best three words in the English language."

"Absolutely. Where are your thoughts since you've decided to return to the FBI?"

"Teaching hasn't been a bad experience, and most of the time, the kids are great. Honestly, Gage, I missed the challenges . . . and working right beside you." She shrugged. "I took seeing you every day for granted. I know we'll need to figure this—"

"Not today, honey. One step at a time. During those months, I felt like I'd lost an arm or a leg. Good will come of this."

"It already has. We're together now." She glanced at the keyboard. "Gage, if I hadn't made those choices, I wouldn't have met Carson, and we wouldn't be together. Or closer to finding the killer and who's behind the Addingtons' case."

"God has your back."

"And yours. I think our prayers to find who's responsible for crimes are dangerous, but dangerous prayers are the ones that bring truth."

"When Jack and I teamed up and I continued investigating your brother's death, the evidence seemed to swallow up. Nothing made sense until now."

"The Addingtons' baby abduction and the unraveling of an operation that appears to make money through illegal private adoptions and murder show us a ruthless ring," she said. "I can't help but hope—and pray—we are able to find justice."

"Add to what we've learned, and you've seen the files—we'd be nowhere if not for the hospital in Des Moines contacting the FBI."

Risa typed. "I read the interview transcript from the Wades. The illegal private adoption agency disappeared, and you've uncovered several players in that operation."

"Right. The Wades gave us their—"

"Give me their names and roles slowly," she said. "Everyone and everything. I'll place my findings in chronological order."

I pulled up my phone to make sure I didn't leave anyone out. "Ethan Mercury was blackmailed to hand over client information. Before I forget it, I'm giving him your new burner number." I sent the info to Ethan on the private burner and glanced back to Risa. "How many others have been victimized?"

"Far too many."

We stopped for our omelets. As soon as she finished, Risa turned her laptop for us to view the screen together. Call it luck or a blessing, we still sat secluded in our corner booth.

"Whoever targeted me believed I had incriminating information that was worth killing me to keep quiet," she said. "Brain fog stalks me, but if I interviewed anyone regarding a crime or went to a crime scene alone, the data would be there. I'm lost, Gage."

I pushed aside my plate. "With all we have, I feel downright stupid that something doesn't jump out at us. Three threatening notes and right now we know two of the three handwriting matches. And I'm the first to admit not all handwriting is identifiable. Risa, you're the one with the higher IQ. What do you see other than the security breach with Mercury Alarms?"

She rolled her eyes. "I only wish I had the intellect to give you the right answer."

A text landed in my inbox, and I pulled it up to read before turning my attention back to Risa. "Norman Peilman's pistol, a Beretta semiautomatic, was used in the murder of a crime-syndicate victim in New York City three years ago. It was believed Peter Florakis had done the hit."

"Looks like Peilman and Florakis had been working together for a while," she said. "We have connections in Houston, Des Moines, New York City, and possibly Columbus, Ohio, where Emily Lock is wanted for questioning." Risa rested her chin in her palm. "The adoptive parents of these children believe those little ones are theirs. Even if they suspect or know their child came by illegal means, they won't come forward and risk losing a child they call their own."

"Jack and I talked about that very thing, and you and I have experienced the same scenario. The FBI in Des Moines has reached out publicly not only to those who adopted through Your Heart for Adoption Agency but to those who were scammed and denied a child."

"Results? Where is that in the file?" Risa said. "I've read through it repeatedly."

"Good question." I glanced at the time before making the call to the Des Moines ASAC. "Give me a moment while I find out, then we probably should hit the road."

The female Des Moines ASAC answered. "I'm assembling a

report to send you by close of day. Two couples lost thirty-five and forty thousand dollars respectively. I have their receipts. One paid by credit card and the other by a cashier's check. Neither of those couples received a child. A man phoned the FBI anonymously and claimed his nephew and wife adopted a baby through the agency, but he refused a name."

"I've noted other cities with adoption scams," I said to the Des Moines ASAC. "None used the same name or names linked to the Addingtons' baby. Unless similar aliases or pics of the same people are found, we have no way of knowing how widespread the crime ring is." I thanked the ASAC and relayed the conversation to Risa.

A text landed on my phone about the origin of the Vietnamese woman. **Caller used a burner phone in a southeast Houston location.**

Risa closed her laptop. "One brick wall after another. I have a theory. Is it possible separate teams work specific cities, and no one comprehends who's in charge at the top except for a few elite? If my theory is true, a team could be apprehended and face charges, but the rest of the teams under the umbrella wouldn't be obstructed from continuing business. No plea bargains if the accused has no concept of what's occurring and who's the kingpin."

She made sense. "Do you have any idea how hard it would be to bring down an organization like that?"

"The magnitude would require a huge nationwide task force," she said. "Or possibly worldwide. What about the buyer for Hai's baby? Where is her baby now? The US or international? The woman who called you earlier understood correctly—boy babies in some cultures bring a huge price. Can we close our minds to other victims and simply find who and how the Addingtons' baby ended up in Des Moines?"

"I can't close my eyes to a crime," I said. "It nails why I work this division."

"Impossible for me too. Must be another reason why we love each other." She took a deep breath. "Do you want children?"

I did, but how could I tell her the truth? "Yes, but it scares me."

"Me too." She studied me. "Gage, why do you work this division?"

"Short version or the long? If the long, I'll tell you on the way to your hotel."

Risa stood with her shoulder bag intact. I picked up her laptop and took her hand. Easier to talk while I drove. That way I could concentrate on the street while I opened the door to my demons.

44

The drive to the extended-stay hotel from the restaurant was about twenty minutes—twenty gruesome minutes to dig up my shame. I sensed Risa's attention on me, not wanting to prod but wordlessly encouraging me. She reached across the seat and touched my arm.

"This is me, the woman who loves you. Your friend through thick and thin."

"I'm thinking about the best way to say this," I said. "You told me you wanted to work our division after you'd experienced a neighbor woman beating her child, and the little girl died."

"Why did you choose our division?"

"The source happened when I was a teen."

"When I told you about Trenton's birthday, you said milestones were hard. That comes only from experience. Once you talked about the evil of losing someone close to you."

"Right. This is a sad story. Nothing I'm proud of."

"You've seen me at my worst, Gage. Think about my malicious response to Carson. You witnessed my humiliating fall."

"And how you got right back up." I wanted to say my worst fear was losing her. Not yet. My confession came first. "You wanted my motivation for protecting children, and I should have told you before now." My heart pounded like I'd walked into a firefight without a weapon. "I was sixteen years old and a junior in high school. I fell in love with a girl my own age. She claimed she loved me too, when neither of us had a clue about real love. Both of us hit sexual overload and gave in to the pressure. Several times. To this day I don't know why I ignored the possibility of her getting pregnant. But I did and it happened. I wanted to marry her, finish high school, and go on to college. My parents were disappointed, and her dad, a widower, blew. He wouldn't let me see her and whisked her off to a home for unwed mothers." I paused. "Every time I walk into one, I look for the youngest girl."

"I've seen misery on your face," she said. "But never asked about it. I'm so sorry."

"She wrote me, told me she loved me, and intended to keep our baby. Her dad insisted she give up the child, but she refused. Nothing would keep the three of us apart. We were wrong. She never saw the baby or learned the sex. Her dad arranged for the baby's adoption, and the new parents took the baby home from the hospital. When my girlfriend returned home, depression hit her hard, and her dad refused her counseling, said she'd be fine. He hired a tutor to help her finish high school and keep us apart.

"I tried to see her, but he obtained a peace warrant to keep me away. On Christmas Eve she cleaned out his medicine cabinet and took everything she could swallow—died in her sleep from the overdose. Two reasons why this time of year is hard. Her dad cremated her too. I learned later he attempted to file charges that I'd corrupted her, but my parents stopped it. I have a son or daughter somewhere. Nineteen years old. Birthday of November 1."

Risa gasped. "Gage, how did you survive?"

"Oddly enough, I don't know. The demons are still there. My parents are good people, and they never turned their back on me. When she died, they took me to a Christian psychologist, and I saw him every day for weeks. I remember my anger, needing to blame someone. Wanting to kill myself like some kind of Romeo and Juliet syndrome. After all, I should have been more responsible.

"I told my parents that I was all right and thanked them. Did everything I could to find my child. Went on to college. Mastered in law enforcement with the idea of joining the FBI. I vowed back then to one day work in a field where kids of all ages were protected. But I've never found a trace of my child. Many times I questioned if her dad simply gave the baby to someone." I shrugged. "I dated several girls for a while. Nothing lasted. All I could see was her face and question what happened to our child. I've never been able to shake off the guilt and blame." I shook my head to dispel the humiliation.

"Gage, what was her name?"

I hadn't spoken it aloud since she died. "Kara. Why?"

"When I say Trenton's name, it confirms that he lives on in my heart. You don't want to forget her, so don't shy away from speaking her name."

"Kara," I whispered. "The mother of my child, who is out there somewhere."

"Do you believe your child is in a good home?"

I studied Risa. She'd asked a tough question. "I don't think I could survive if I didn't believe two people love my child."

"Is that a source of comfort?"

"Possibly, or is the comfort a way to cover up my guilt?"

"Only God can help you through that."

"Risa, I might never be able to forgive myself. But I do want to be a father. When you asked me if I wanted children, it hit me that I'd waited too long to tell you the truth."

She squeezed my arm. "Honesty brings us one step closer to healing and giving the tragedy to God."

I remembered at Trenton's funeral when she asked me when I'd gotten so wise. "Can we table the forgiveness and God-thing for now? I'm wrestling with it. Have been for years."

"Of course. I have my own problems with forgiveness."

"We'll work through our issues together. The Bible says something about a strand of three cannot be broken," I said.

She'd not let go of my arm since I started my story. "We're a team. I'm in awe of the man you are today. Gage, as dreadful as your experience must have been, still is, you are incredible. I've seen you mentor new agents and encourage others. Every case we've investigated, you've shown caring and empathy. Forgiving ourselves for tragedies is hard, real hard. Thank you for trusting me with your secret."

"Thank you for listening."

I loved this woman. Wanted to protect her and make her mine until God called us home.

45

RISA

Gage insisted upon walking me to my room at the hotel and checking inside, although I had the skills to do a sweep and use cuffs. But he'd shared a personal story with me that had stalked him for years, and I wanted him to understand his past made no difference to me.

Once we finished a sweep of the small room, he turned to me. "Thanks again for listening about my past."

"Love should be unconditional." I ran my fingers through his thick, rust-brown hair. "We've seen each other broken, and we're still moving ahead." I took an inward breath of courage. "I'll always be here for you."

He placed his arm around my waist, and I leaned onto his shoulder. "Where are you now?" he said.

"No longer lost to God. He knew my misery all along, and He's made it plain I haven't been forgotten. My problem is I blame myself and God for Trenton's death."

"We could go to counseling together."

I nodded. Lifted my gaze to meet his. His lips touched mine, a feather, a gentle deepening of the moment. I wrapped my arms around his neck and begged for the moment to last forever—my best friend and the man I loved.

"I'm scared," I said.

He stroked my cheek. "Running down international killers without a firearm is easier than facing my feelings for you."

I smiled. Sweet man. "Fear comes in all shapes and sizes."

"This one is about five feet six, green eyes, and coffee-brown hair."

"She's harmless," I said.

He laughed. "Not in my book. And if I don't leave now, I might be here awhile."

He kissed me again and reached for the doorknob, then slowly turned back. "You and I have seen the problems when partners get involved, the late hours contribute to a high divorce rate. Each cares so much for the other that they forget their commitment to others." He kissed me one more time. "We will figure this out. Us out. Make it work." He left without another word.

Did I prefer my feelings for him to be a dream and keep them there? Somewhere along the line of career, obligation, and responsibility, I'd neglected my longing for a family. Did I deserve such happiness? And with Gage?

★　★　★

I had several reasons to work from the extended-stay hotel, other than a good scolding for allowing my emotions to soar a bit wild. But I ached to be with Gage every minute of the day.

I read an update on Peilman and learned his ex-wife lived in New York City. The FBI had interviewed her, and she claimed not to have seen him in three years.

Gage had requested the FIG do a background on Peter Florakis, who'd given Ethan Mercury the name of John Smith. In contrast, the person who'd attacked Jack had a slighter build. Perhaps one of the gang members? Or Emily Lock?

My next inquiry dealt with the attorney, Giang Lam, who'd represented Tuan Duong and Vinh Bui. If a link existed between Florakis and Giang, we were headed in the right direction.

I had no idea how long my request would take, but the longer it took, the more lives were at risk.

Earlier over breakfast, Gage and I put together an overview of the events since Trenton's death, and I needed silence to process them.

I also needed to work under the assumption that our subjects kept tabs on our every move. Not necessarily impossible, depending on how far advanced their technology and who held control.

- July 29: Trenton's death. Threatening note left on my car. I was the intended target.
- Michael and Sarah Addington's baby kidnapped.
- Alex and Nanette Wade adopt a baby unknowingly through a fraudulent private adoption.
- Addingtons' baby found in Des Moines.
- Wades arrive at Houston FBI for interview. Taken for forty-eight thousand dollars. Offer names of Harvey Sinclair, attorney and director of fraud agency, and Emily Lock, supposed birth mother. Both disappeared. Other fraud players—the man who posed as Des Moines police officer, the woman as the Iowa state licensing specialist for private adoption agencies, the woman at the Iowa state's attorney general's office, and two couples who recommended the adoption agency. All phone numbers disconnected.
- Michael and Sarah Addington interview. Unclear how kidnappers entered home.
- I receive Carson's short story indicating his eyewitness of Trenton's death.
- Gage and I interview Ethan and Lynn Mercury for Carson's whereabouts.
- Gage and Jack interview maternity home centers. Houston Healing and Hope provide names of Phan Suzi and Phan Hai. Hai is a birth mother whose baby was abducted. Gage and Jack visit the restaurant where the Vietnamese sisters work. Not there. Warned by gang members to stay away. Phan sisters executed and fire set to restaurant.
- Jack attacked. Left for dead and note left by assailant.

- Gage and I find Carson in West Texas. Learn his stepfather, Ethan Mercury, was passenger in car that hit Trenton.
- I drive Carson back to Houston in rental. Norman Peilman killed while trying to run us off the road.
- Gage drives Carson's Jeep. He checks on Jack at hospital. Threatening note left on Jeep window.
- Carson confesses at FBI office to what he viewed. Requests protection for his mother and brother. Ethan Mercury confesses at FBI office of turning over security info to John Smith, including the Addingtons'. Requests protection for whole family. Lynn Mercury and sons in safe house. Ethan wants to help FBI.
- John Smith identified as Peter Florakis.
- I decide to return to FBI and visit Jack in hospital. Woman identified as Emily Lock tried to gain access to Jack. He attempts to tell me something about Luke, his former partner. At my apartment, I find Luke's severed head in my bathtub.
- Gage interviews two men identified as part of the gang who threatened him and Jack. The two men in custody plead not guilty and refuse plea bargain. Their attorney known to represent gang members.

I stopped and checked the records on the status of the two men in custody. The judge had set bail, and someone paid it. The two were free to roam the streets. Wonderful.

- Gage and I interview Clyde Washington, who works for Houston Healing and Hope Maternity Care as driver and handyman. Believes the buying and selling of babies continues from previous case.
- Vietnamese woman calls Gage. Third person killed in fire was the father of Hai's abducted baby. A gang committed the execution and set the fire, but not responsible for kidnapping.
- Norman Peilman and Peter Florakis connected via New York City crimes. Peilman's gun used in murder.

• Three samples of handwriting. Two match but nothing is in the database.

I scanned the list. In addition to the maternity home centers, abortion clinics had been notified of potential fraudulent means of convincing young women to give birth for money. Nothing had surfaced there. I read the list backward.

Then I had an idea.

46

Not telling Gage about my plan to expose Peter Florakis made sense, especially when I knew Gage wouldn't approve. The excuse "Easier to ask forgiveness than permission" fit perfectly. Except our admittance of love meant trust. But if my idea brought the case to a close, he'd thank me later.

I phoned Ethan Mercury on the burner Gage had given him. "This is Risa Jacobs. Are you free to talk?"

"Give me a moment." I heard footsteps, and he greeted me. "I'm at the office. Professor Jacobs or Agent Jacobs?"

I smiled into the phone. "Presently both. Have you heard from Florakis?"

"Not yet."

"I'd like to speed things up. Mr. Mercury, what I'm about to propose has a high level of risk involved."

"Can't be any worse than what I've lived with for the past several months. I told Agent Patterson this, but I'll do whatever it takes to help make arrests."

"Okay." I explained what I had in mind. "I'll call you on your personal cell that we know is bugged. I'll arrange for us to meet and state it's urgent."

"Got it. Will Agent Patterson be with you?"

"Not sure yet." *If he doesn't wring my neck.*

I made the arrangements with Ethan, and we planned to meet at a Starbucks not far from the FBI office. The coward in me texted Gage.

Meeting Ethan in two hours to draw Florakis out from under his rock. Want to join me? Or do I go solo?

What have you done now? Hold on, I'm calling you.

I laughed. Not sure why, except it felt incredibly good to be my free self.

★ ★ ★

Right on schedule Gage and I pulled into Starbucks. Gage had picked me up to represent an official FBI interview, and he wore a scowl.

Ethan had parked his car in an isolated area beside a trash dumpster on one side and the curb on the other. While Gage and I walked into Starbucks, a mobile pet-grooming van blocked our view for about twenty seconds. I didn't trust Florakis, and while we hadn't seen anyone tampering with Ethan's vehicle, Gage dashed out after it, but the woman driver had only tossed trash into the dumpster. Still Gage jotted down the plates.

Inside, the heavenly scent of coffee met my nose as I cased out a potential John Smith/Peter Florakis. But no one captured my attention. Our subject didn't need to show up or send a hit man until he overheard our conversation.

We sat at a table with Ethan where Gage and I had our attention on the door. Now on with my idea. "Thanks for meeting with us, Mr. Mercury."

"I'm not sure this is a good idea. You're investigating me for using faulty equipment in my alarms, then you want to meet here. What's the deal?"

"We have a connection to you and a man who's wanted in New York as a person of interest in a murder case."

He snorted. "Agent Jacobs, I don't run a background check on my clients. You're wasting your time."

Gage stepped in. "Mr. Mercury, in view of your business practices investigation and the link to a man we want to apprehend, we have a few questions."

Ethan huffed. "I'm here, so ask away."

"You know a man by the name of John Smith," Gage said. "His real name is Peter Florakis. We'd like his contact info."

"I have never met a John Smith or Peter Florakis. Try asking Pocahontas."

I studied Ethan. His snarky attitude gave him a few extra points. "We have video footage of you two together."

"How? Where?"

I scrolled through my phone and showed him a pic of Florakis. "Sir, do you know this man?"

He peered and frowned. "Absolutely not. Are we finished here?"

I scrolled and pretended I had a pic of him with Florakis. "Here is one with you two together. Are you in the habit of keeping company with strangers?"

He pointed to my phone. "You photoshopped those. I'm no fool."

I sat back and nodded. "You've been on our radar for months. We'd like to work out a deal."

Ethan startled. "What kind of deal? I haven't done anything."

Gage cleared his throat. "We need Florakis's contact information, and we'll work out a deal with the alarm business investigation."

"You've got to be kidding." Ethan crossed his arms over his chest. "That means I admit to installing faulty equipment, which I haven't done. What makes you think I have a way to get hold of a man I've never met?"

"All right, Mr. Mercury," Gage said. "Your choice. We have the evidence to charge you with withholding information in a federal murder case unless you choose to cooperate."

Ethan shook his finger at us. "I'm wondering if you two are running a scheme on the side. I might be better off to talk to those higher up than the likes of you." He stood. "I came here in good faith, thinking you'd exonerated me of false charges. Instead you fabricate photos of me and a stranger. Trust me, the FBI will hear about this." He headed for the door with Gage and me staring after him.

I watched Ethan leave. "He might earn an Oscar after that performance."

Now as Ethan made his way to his Jaguar, I prayed for success. He touched the handle of his vehicle, then retraced his steps to the Starbucks entrance. Anger ripped across his face, as though ready to level both of us. He swung open the door and headed straight for our table.

I gambled on what would happen next. Ethan wore a bug . . . *Come on, Florakis, call Ethan.*

The Jaguar burst into a fiery inferno.

My plan had drawn out our subject, but not in a way that resulted in his arrest. Now I had to face Gage. My foolishness could have killed Ethan.

47

GAGE

In the distance, the whine of fire trucks and police cars drew closer. I'd reported the explosion but not the particulars. Fortunately, no one had been injured. We waited for the ER vehicles, and I fumed. I stared at Risa and Ethan seated across from me in Starbucks.

Ethan could have been killed.

Risa could have been killed.

Innocent people could have been killed.

Risa's idea would get her a reprimand if not worse.

For sure my head would spin on a platter.

To think I'd allowed her irresponsible game to take place. Her determination to find who'd killed her brother and the source of the fraudulent adoption agency had put others in danger.

Trembling, Ethan pulled the burner phone from Florakis from his pant pocket and stared at it as though willing it to ring. "My family could have been in there. Have you set me up?"

I dove into our acting mode. "Mr. Mercury, your family has left you."

"How did you know? You—"

Ethan's burner rang, and he answered. He walked outside, and we listened through the listening devices in our ears. Thankful the FBI's tech team had successfully installed a monitoring app.

"Hello." Ethan's tone lifted with agitation. "What do you want? I'm in the middle of something."

I picked up a man's voice. "Calm down, Ethan. You knew I'd call. I hear sirens. Is that the fire department? Doubtful they can put the pieces of your Jaguar back together, and I liked the shiny red."

"You blew it up! I've done everything you've asked."

"And you handled those agents nicely too. I wanted you to understand nothing gets by me. Do yourself a favor and behave yourself."

"Apparently not. What now?" Ethan said.

"I'm sending you a list of clients. You know the drill. I want them by the close of the day or I might have to take further action."

"All right. I'll get what you need. Do you have my family?"

"Oh, they're alive for now. Cooperation is all I ask. I suggest you pay attention to today's news. There's an interesting report on the demise of Special Agent Luke Reardon."

The call ended, and Ethan left us to join HPD and the fire department. Florakis's implications made me shudder. I texted the agents assigned to Ethan's family and learned they were safe.

Risa and I walked outside to the burning site, the heat and smell of melting metal and gasoline fueling my frustration with all that had happened and kept happening. I spoke to HPD and told them I'd be escorting Ethan to the FBI building for questioning.

Inside my vehicle, I wrote Ethan a note to give me his personal cell phone and the phone Florakis used to call him. Already a list of client names filled a text in the burner. I removed the rogue bugging apps from both devices and handed the phones back to him. "For your own safety, no more games with Florakis. You're done."

"These guys play for keeps." Ethan's voice rattled with fear. "What happened to Agent Reardon?"

I licked my lower lip. I hadn't given myself time to process his death. Anger pounded through me. Grief tore at the memory of a good man. "Ethan, it's gruesome. He was beheaded."

He gasped.

For a moment, I feared Ethan would be sick. "Do you want me to pull over?"

He shook his head. "What kind of barbarians are these people?"

"They're serious. We know they are involved with kidnapping and fraudulent adoptions. Possibly drugs too. Are you ready to join your family? We now have information to help us locate Florakis."

Ethan nodded. His whole body trembled. "Like an idiot, I thought I was immune because he needed what I provided. Yes, I'm ready for a safe house, but not with my family. Put me somewhere far away from them. The idea Florakis might try the same thing with Lynn, Carson, or the baby—" He vomited into his lap.

Risa handed him tissues and rolled down her window.

After a few minutes, Ethan regained his composure. "I'm sorry. I'll pay to have your car cleaned."

"No worries. I'll handle it," I said. "Now you understand these guys play for keeps. At the office, I'll arrange for a safe house." I glanced at Risa in the back seat. She hadn't spoken, and it was probably in her best interests to stay that way. I hadn't been this angry with her in all the years we'd worked together. But she'd risked the lives of innocent people. Her red-rimmed eyes showed me that reality had settled. I loved this woman, but she'd been reckless. Maybe her stepping back into the FBI had been premature.

My phone alerted me to a call from SAC Dunkin. Ignoring him would only make the situation worse.

"Yes, sir."

"Gage, what the—"

I listened to Risa's and my deplorable representation of the FBI.

"I want you two in my office before the day's over."

"Yes, sir." I slid my phone back onto the console and glared at Risa in the rearview mirror. "The SAC. Before the day's over."

Her face etched with what we'd witnessed. "I take full responsibility. I'm sorry. I made a reckless move. I planned for the worst but didn't expect it."

"I'm glad no one was hurt," Ethan said.

"Me too." She avoided my image in the mirror.

In the parking lot, Risa exited and faced me. I could read her like a book, and she oozed with remorse. She stepped beyond

Ethan's hearing. "Gage, I've gotten out of hand. My actions can't be repeated."

"You're right, but I'm at fault too. I should have called off the whole thing before we even got started, especially after Luke's brutal death." I rubbed a day's beard growth on my chin. "At the moment, all I have is the mobile pet-grooming van's plates."

"A woman drove it, right?"

"Yes, older."

"Emily Lock in disguise?"

"Could be."

Risa stared at the door leading into the building. "I'll request the SAC replace me with another partner for at least this case."

I had no words to comfort her. All the complimentary things she'd said about my patience and encouragement just went up in flames. Literally. My greatest fear of losing her had almost happened.

"We need to get inside and face the SAC." I guided Ethan to the entrance. I'd used poor judgment . . . because I loved her. Like a fool, I'd let my emotions ignore what should have smacked me in the face.

Yep. Agents involved in a relationship shouldn't work together.

48

The debriefing with the SAC dissolved Risa's and my confidence as human beings. Not that we didn't deserve a good rear chewing. His face and tone matched the inferno we'd left behind near Starbucks.

"Agent Jacobs, didn't I tell you not to make me regret my concessions to you?"

"Yes, sir." Risa maintained the formality and respect I'd come to appreciate from her, but my frustration didn't lessen.

"Then why set up Ethan Mercury to be hurt or murdered? Did I miss your call for backup? Putting innocent people in danger? Resulting in blowing up a perfectly good Jaguar?" He leaned over his desk, his Adam's apple bouncing in overtime.

If not for the circumstances, I would have laughed with the ribbing about the Jaguar. Not today.

Risa stiffened. "I didn't think Florakis would react so violently. I thought he'd merely call Mercury after hearing our conversation and demand another list of client info."

"And?"

"Florakis texted Mercury with a client list after the explosion."

"Do you think jeopardizing others' welfare made it all worth it?" The SAC's voice thundered around the room.

"I'm not sure, sir."

He leveled his finger at her. "Do you want to keep your job?"

"Yes, sir."

"I want an appointment made today with one of these psychologists." He handed her a piece of paper. "Until I see the report of your mental stability to return to work, you keep your rear in the office."

"Yes, sir."

"Now get out of my office. Before you leave today, I want the paperwork completed in detail regarding today and sent to my inbox. I don't care if it takes you all night. Understand?"

"Yes, sir."

"One more thing, tomorrow afternoon, your apartment will be free for you to move back in. I received notice that the cleaning crew will be finished by then."

"Thank you. Is someone with Luke's widow?"

The SAC's face softened. "Her parents, and she's under a doctor's care. A memorial service is scheduled for Friday at ten. You're dismissed."

She stood and left without another word. The door closed behind her.

My turn.

SAC Dunkin glared at me. Silence thickened like cement. He drummed his finger on the desktop. "She's not to do anything until I have her psych eval." His tone was flat, low.

I refused to relax.

"There's more on the line here than me raking you two over the coals." He leaned across his desk. *Here it comes.* "Get to the source of the crime ring. Now. The monitoring bug on Mercury's phone gave us a downtown location in a bank lobby. The back of a man, who appears to be Florakis, is to the camera. Agents are combing the area and setting up surveillance, but for now he's still on the loose."

"Yes, sir."

"Who planted the bomb in Ethan Mercury's car?"

"I have only a suspicion. I have the license number of a Happy Feet Pet Grooming van, a legit business. The female driver confirmed dropping trash at the Starbucks location and the time. She remembered seeing Mercury's Jaguar but didn't see anyone."

The SAC's scowl stayed intact while he uttered a few expletives. "Follow up on the list of Mercury's clients. Do your job, Agent Patterson. Do it right. Do it now." He pointed to the door.

I didn't need a written invitation.

★ ★ ★

I arranged for Ethan's safe house. The isolation protected him from those who meant business, but unless he was the type of personality who opened to strangers, the agents assigned to him wouldn't be much company. Too much think time increased the worry over his family.

"Ethan, you have a few minutes before agents arrive. They'll escort you to your home to pack a few things. Until then, I'd like for you to join me in a conference room."

"Are you sure? I smell rank."

"We're good. Don't worry about it."

Wordlessly he followed me back to my cubicle. I grabbed a chair for him.

"Any questions for me?" I said.

He pressed his lips tight and shook his head. "Just want this over."

"We all do."

"I forgot you have an agent in the hospital and another one dead. My apologies. When this is over, how long will I be sentenced to prison?"

"You were blackmailed with threats to your family, and you've helped the FBI by risking your life. It's not for me to say, but I believe a judge may look favorably on your case."

"Thanks. A judge's favor goes a long way. Not sure if the guilt for those who've been hurt or killed will ever leave me."

"Counseling would help."

"Have you read the names on Florakis's list yet?"

"About to handle that now." I pulled up the list of requested Mercury clients on my phone. "Tracking down these people will show why Florakis needs access to their security systems."

"Usually they are located in different states."

I scrolled for any recognizable name. I snorted . . . Midway down I saw my name. Glad I'd changed my security info since I'd made the hit list. Of the fifteen names, three were pharmacies. I texted the FIG to find out what kind of drugs had been stolen in past break-ins. While I waited, I contacted one of the agents with Ethan's family. After speaking to him and explaining the next steps forward, I gave Ethan the phone.

"You might want to tell your wife about your new status. I'm sure she'll be relieved. Carson too."

He sighed and took the phone. "Hey, honey. I have good news . . ." His voice sounded happier for her benefit.

While they chatted, the info on previous crimes and what had been taken from the pharmacies connected to Mercury Alarms Inc. dropped into my inbox. As I suspected, oxycodone, codeine, and basically opioids. Illegal adoptions weren't the only way Florakis and his buds made money. I forwarded the reports on to ASAC Kendall and SAC Dunkin.

Agents arrived for Ethan, and I made introductions. But I had a change of mind. "I recommend driving straight to the safe house. I don't want to take any chances."

Ethan startled. "I need clean clothes. I smell horrible. And work items like my laptop."

"Make a list of personal items for one of these agents to pick up at a Walmart. No devices. Nothing for Florakis to trace you."

"That's absurd. I have a business to run. What do I tell my employees?"

"With the FBI investigation into Mercury Alarms, your attorney recommends you leave for a vacation over the holidays and let your board run the business."

"I'm a hands-on owner."

I glared at Ethan. "Think about Special Agent Luke Reardon."

49

RISA

SAC Dunkin instructed me to keep my rear in the chair until I completed the paperwork for today. He also said I couldn't join Gage for any case until I had an all-clear, mentally balanced report. When I received a call from one of the approved psychologists that she had a cancellation for today, I agreed and drove to her office.

Now I waited for a woman who had the power to make or break my career. My mind swept across mental health disorders like anxiety, depression, insomnia, PTSD, and schizophrenia. The longer I sat, the more I formed an accurate diagnosis for me. Anxiety fit. Depression fit. Insomnia had become a fact of life. I hadn't considered PTSD, but that was a viable possibility.

The door opened, and a tall woman with shoulder-length white hair and a pleasant demeanor gestured for me to enter. "Risa, I'm Dr. Looney, welcome to my office."

I'd forgotten the psychologist's name. In my eagerness to comply to the SAC's demands, I'd simply called the numbers he'd provided. If not for the reason I'd been sentenced here, I'd find humor in her name.

I followed her down a short hallway, past a receptionist who had her red head buried in her phone. Inside the small office, Dr. Looney invited me to sit. "First of all, I want you to know that I married into the Looney family."

That broke the ice. We laughed, and I relaxed.

Dr. Looney glanced at her notes on a legal pad like what Gage used. "I see you have experienced a tragic death. You took a leave from the FBI and recently returned to work."

"Yes, last July my brother was killed in a failure to stop and render aid, and I was with him. The driver remains at large."

"Were you off duty?"

"Yes."

"SAC Dunkin is requesting assurance of your mental astuteness to resume work. Would you tell me what happened then and to date?"

Her open body language told me this wasn't her first rodeo. I needed to slash my internal sarcasm. "Only a few people know the story. SAC Dunkin, my parents, and Agent Gage Patterson, my partner." I paused. "Not sure if we will continue to be partners, but we worked together when my brother was killed."

"As a private person, telling me about the incident and leading up to now will be difficult."

"To say the least."

"How have you handled the grief to this point?"

My heart rate sped. "I studied the twelve-step recovery program for grief. I expected not to follow the textbook definition and soon gave up."

"Each person's response is rarely in order. I assume you struggle with depression, denial, sadness, anxiety, and anger. From your file, I'd say you try to move through each one far too quickly." She leaned in. "Risa, we don't have to understand every emotion. Simply accept those feelings as they come. Fighting razor-sharp emotions instead of allowing them to heal only makes the grief longer and more painful."

"I know talking things through is best." I paused to swallow hard. "How long are you willing to listen?"

"We can send out for Chinese food." She scooted a box of tissues across the coffee table separating us.

I didn't want to need them. Weepy women made me uncomfortable, although I'd cried my eyes out with Gage. "Dr. Looney, I understand why I'm here, and my brother's death is raw. Finding an agent's head in my bathtub hasn't helped. My question is, are you a Christian?"

"I'm Roman Catholic. Faithful." Her genuine smile settled my doubts. "How I counsel is always based on my core beliefs about God. However, my method with those who are believers reflects a Christian worldview. Would you prefer a Christ-centered approach?"

God, I hope this is from You because the guilt of Trenton's death is affecting my judgment.

"Yes. I need a faith-filled perspective." I breathed in deeply. "My brother had a rebellious streak." I paused. "I guess I do too. He turned to alcohol and drugs. Lots of problems. He broke contact years ago. In July, he called . . ." I finished the lengthy story and relayed finding Luke's severed head. "Thank you for listening."

Dr. Looney leaned forward. "Risa, you're carrying a huge burden, one that would destroy most people. I commend you for your courage to turn back to God, to honestly admit your inability to forgive yourself, God, the person who ended Trenton's life, and to move forward in finding who's behind the crimes of late."

"Why do I sense a *but*?"

I saw the concern in her eyes. "What do you think?"

I blinked back the embarrassing tears. My mind wandered to those dark corners that shouted "killer" and "your fault." The memories flooded like the humiliating tears. My head throbbed in time to Trenton's heartbeat—not mine. I no longer felt mine—oh, I loved Gage. Or had my emotions dissipated to the point I really had no concept of love?

Trenton . . . Maybe if I'd tried harder when he was gone those years. I monitored his criminal charges, but I didn't reach out. Why? How could I represent Jesus if I couldn't communicate as a sister to my own brother? Why hadn't I called Mom and Dad about the dinner with Trenton? If they'd been there, the walk across the street might not have taken place.

Blame game.

Guilt game.

Shame game.

I'd attempted to return to my career, but who else would die because of me?

Time didn't heal. That was a lie from the pits of hell. I'd tried to make sense of life, even determined to shove my pain into something creative by showing students how to fashion words into something beautiful, meaningful, and bursting with purpose.

God knew I needed all three to heal . . . and maybe forgive myself.

I lifted my chin and wadded the wet tissue in my fist. "How do I forgive?"

50

GAGE

I intended to work until I dropped, and the service cleaning my car wouldn't be finished until after six today. I checked security cams near the traffic lights and Starbucks where Risa and I had met Ethan, focusing until I saw enough of the female driver of the mobile pet-grooming business to determine her height and build. The woman was taller, older, and she wore tennis shoes. I zoomed in and studied the screen.

A second person hunched low from behind the dumpster. He or she placed something underneath the front carriage of Ethan's car, then disappeared. I couldn't get a clear picture if the jean-clad person was a slight man or a woman with hair tucked under a ball cap.

I forwarded the findings to Risa and texted her, but she didn't respond.

My phone alerted me to a call—Ms. Wright from Houston Healing and Hope Maternity Care. Curiosity rose in me. We all could use solid evidence.

"Good afternoon, Ms. Wright. How can I help you?"

"Clyde Washington, my right-hand man, told me about meeting with you. He's more than an employee, he's a good friend, a confidant during trials, and we've done our best to parent our birth mothers.

Agent Patterson, I'm eaten up with guilt about a matter. I . . . I can't hide it any longer. I wanted to talk to Jack Bradford or Luke Reardon, but the receptionist said neither man was there. She asked if I'd like to speak to you."

"Jack is in the hospital."

She gasped. "Why?"

"Assaulted and suffered a heart attack."

"How terrible. I hope he has a full recovery. Is Agent Reardon out of the office?"

"No, ma'am. Someone killed him." Silence met me for several moments.

"What is wrong with our world?" Ms. Wright whispered. "Good people hurt and killed while protecting the rest of us. I'm glad I found the courage to call you. I think I have information about Hai and Suzi Phan. I . . . I suspect one of my staff."

"Who?"

"I hate to say this, but my intake person, Myra Cummings. She's been with me for nine years, and I love her dearly, but I overheard her having a conversation with one of our mothers. Myra was in the middle of a counseling session and providing resources in the way of medical assistance. The mother asked how to give up her baby other than taking a newborn to a fire department or police department location. Myra suggested a private adoption where the birth mother would be reimbursed for expenses and more to help her get back on her feet. She'd be willing to find a lawyer to arrange it. Agent Patterson, her offer frightened me, and I've kept it bottled up inside."

"How long ago did you overhear this conversation?"

"Six or so months ago."

"Is she there now?"

"No, sir. She works Monday through Friday, seven to seven, except Wednesday and weekends. She'll be here tomorrow morning."

"I'll be there."

"Agent Patterson, I have a meeting in the morning and won't be here until around ten. If you insist Myra be questioned here or at your office, no one will be available to answer the phone."

"I'm sure you can make arrangements."

"Guess I don't have a choice."

Ms. Wright huffed, but I ignored her subtle complaint and thanked her. "What do you remember about Elizabeth, the young woman you identified from the photo?"

"She made a few friends. A dear soul. She and Myra formed a bond during her stay with us. She stayed with us but for a few months of her pregnancy. A family member offered her a home."

"Has she contacted you since?"

"No. Sometimes the birth mothers stop by for me to see their babies but not Elizabeth."

"I see. Do you remember any of the women she befriended?"

"No, sir."

"But she and Myra were close?"

"Yes. Extremely. Like mother and daughter."

51

I'd asked the psychologist how I could forgive myself, God, and Trenton's killer. "Too often I feel like I drove the car ending his life."

"But that's not how it happened." Dr. Looney leaned in. "Risa, you didn't ask your brother to push you out of the car's path. He chose his actions."

My head pounded with desperation for her to understand my emotions. "Haven't you heard me explain what happened?" I'd shared with her my list of what I could have done differently to change the outcome. While I trembled, I longed to show professionalism.

"You said you're a Christian." Dr. Looney's words wafted softly around the room. "You believe in a God who is omniscient, omnipresent, and omnipotent. Which of those three attributes do you possess?"

I stared into her kind face. "None."

"Then why blame yourself for actions and behavior out of your control?"

I saw where she was leading me, but I couldn't accept it. "I need to blame someone."

"God?"

"Logic says holding Him responsible is wrong. But I'm angry that God let Trenton die."

"Does judging yourself and God bring Trenton back? Are you taking over God's role?" Dr. Looney's voice lowered. "Accepting the choice Trenton made to save you shows how much he loved you. Accepting God's plan to free Trenton from the chains of addiction doesn't mean you aren't to mourn his death or question why. Forgiving the driver of the car will give you peace." She stopped. "Risa, let's begin with your guilt. You are not responsible for Trenton's death. Can you say those words?"

I hesitated. She was right, and the blame game didn't come from God. I moistened my lips. "I am not responsible for Trenton's death."

"Good. Can you add this? I forgive myself for anything I could have done differently."

I repeated those words.

Dr. Looney tilted her head. "I'm very proud of you. Let's move a step further. Do you blame yourself for Special Agent Jack Bradford's attack?"

How did she know? "Yes. I have no idea who or what is behind this case, and that's my job to uncover it."

"And what about Special Agent Luke Reardon's murder?"

I gasped. "Yes." Finding him in my bathtub with the unspoken message of a blue baby blanket might haunt me forever.

"Do you blame yourself for every unsolved crime?"

I closed my eyes. I hadn't ever focused on the other . . . missing children . . . hurting parents . . . trafficked youth. "Maybe. I don't know."

"I think you do."

Face the truth, Risa. "As a perfectionist, my answer may be closer to yes."

"Repeat these words aloud—I have no power over other peoples' actions or choices."

I closed my eyes again and said the words.

"Do you believe them?"

"I want to."

"For you to be perfect, you must be faultless, ideal, and exempt of flaws. Do you have those qualities?"

"No."

"Do you believe God's love is conditional?"

"No." The tears flowed, and I couldn't stop them.

"Too often we have more difficulty forgiving ourselves than for-giving what others do to us. If we are unwilling to forgive ourselves, we are in effect telling God His Son's sacrifice didn't do the job. His death wasn't enough. Do you want to carry that burden?" When I responded no, she continued. "There is no reason for you to bear the load of unforgiveness of yourself in any past or present events. You are a beloved child of God. If you agree, simply nod."

For the first time, I accepted the truth.

For the first time, I felt free of my own condemnation.

For the first time, I sensed God's love with no stipulations.

"Does God work for good or evil?" Dr. Looney said.

"Good," I whispered. "I believe Trenton is with Him. I prayed for Jack, and he's recovering."

"Is God to blame for doing good?"

I shook my head.

"The driver of the car had his own agenda. Does he care if you hate him?"

"No. He probably enjoys the idea."

"Refusing to forgive him will only keep peace at a distance. Do you have the courage to forgive?"

I sensed the walls I'd built start to crumble. "Not yet. I want to, but I can't."

Dr. Looney allowed me to sit in silence for a few moments longer. "Risa, healing takes time. You've come a long way today, and I know the rest will come. I can give you the green light for active duty based on seeing you every other day for the next ten business days. At the end of our five sessions, I'll determine if more are needed."

52

GAGE

Nearing 6 p.m., Risa appeared in the doorway of my cubicle. At the sight of her, my earlier anger dropped into the trash. The tiny lines around her eyes showed she needed sleep. I stood and drew her into my arms, a place I wanted her forever.

"You must have completed your paperwork," I said.

"I have. And a report from an approved psychologist delivered to the SAC. I agreed to a minimum of five more sessions, every other day."

I rested my head atop hers. "Impressive. Who did you see?"

"Dr. Looney."

I laughed. But I'd heard good reports about the psychologist. "Sorry. The name just doesn't fit the title."

Risa stepped back and crossed her arms over her chest. "She's excellent, and I really liked her. Gage, I understand you're furious with me, and I'm ashamed and embarrassed. My idea resembled a rookie agent's, and I put far too many people in danger. I'm sorry, and I meant what I said about your needing another partner for this case. The SAC may have cleared me, but I lost your trust today. Who knows? Jack could make a speedy recovery and join you soon."

I took her hands into mine. "I don't want another partner unless we decide it's best for our relationship. I'm as much to blame today for not having backup in place or not informing the ASAC or SAC. We made a mistake, which we can't afford to happen again. Right now, we're both exhausted and stressed. But it's not all about us ending these crimes. The law enforcement agencies working alongside us aren't giving up either." I stopped. "But I'm not telling you anything you don't already know."

"Reminders never hurt."

"We'll get through this and be stronger for it," I said.

"Right. Maybe we could see Dr. Looney . . . as a couple."

"Sounds good to me. She'll need a crowbar to pry out my past."

Her lips touched mine, and warmth spread through me. I didn't want to think of another day without Risa. "I . . . made progress in forgiving myself and God. But I couldn't bring myself to forgive his killer. Would you keep me accountable?"

"That works both ways. Really glad she helped you." I glanced around us at the empty cubicles. "We couldn't get by with this during the day."

She stepped back into my arms. "I'm taking advantage of it."

"Me too."

"Any new developments while I had my session?"

Risa had said all she intended for now. Dr. Looney had helped and would continue to help her work through the trauma. I brought her up-to-date on the afternoon.

"Do you think the person who hid behind the dumpster was possibly Emily Lock?" she said.

"I'm digging up everything we can find on her, including pics taken with Florakis, Peilman, and Harvey Sinclair. Locate her and she just might lead us to an arrest."

"I want to study the security cams later on tonight," Risa said.

I led her to the chair in my cubicle and remembered Ms. Wright's call. I updated Risa. "I'd like for you to join me in the morning to interview the intake woman. I'm requesting agents pick her up for an eight o'clock meeting. Are you okay to be here early to go over info? Or should I pull in ASAC Kendall?"

"Give me a time, and I'll be ready."

"Around seven and I'll have coffee and breakfast burritos."

"Perfect." Weariness crept deeper into her lovely face. "I'm going to call it a day."

"I'll walk you out. My car should be sweet-smelling by now. Want to grab a bite to eat somewhere?"

"Two stipulations," she said. "Someplace fast and I buy."

"Deal. Tomorrow's got to have a positive spin somewhere." But the moment the words fell out of my mouth, a chill skittered up my spine. A prickly sensation told me this case would get worse before it got better.

53

Myra Cummings didn't protest to having agents bringing her in for questioning. Risa and I studied her through the mirror before engaging in the interview. Age forty-five, light-olive skin, dark hair minus any gray, but she could color it. Nothing on her record indicated any problem. Married with a son and daughter in college. No nervousness. No touching her face or hair. I almost wished I could see a trace of guilt.

"I don't read any discomfort." Risa tilted her head. "Maybe she wanted a few hours away from the center."

"Let's find out. Are you okay with me leading out?" I said.

Risa, who appeared more rested than the previous night, gestured to the door. "Fine with me."

Inside the interview room, I introduced myself and Risa, although I'd met Myra the day Jack and I first interviewed Anna Wright. Risa hadn't met Myra due to her church's volunteer work taking place on the weekends.

"Is this about the FBI's investigation of the Phan sisters' deaths?" Myra clasped her hands on the table.

"Yes," I said, and we went through the preliminaries. "How well did you know Hai?"

"Not well. She was trying to learn English, but the task seemed so hard. I felt sorry for her, and she had a difficult pregnancy. Sick nearly every day and almost lost her baby. But she helped around the home and always had a sunny disposition." Myra swiped at a tear. "She lived at the maternity home for nearly four months. I'm surprised since family is important to Vietnamese culture. According to her sister, Suzi, the baby's father abused her. Hai needed a safe place."

"Do you know in what way? Physically or mentally?"

"Suzi said he wanted her to abort, and she refused. He beat her. My guess is he wanted Hai but not the responsibility of a child."

"But she returned to the same environment."

"I asked Suzi about that, and she said family and friends had told the baby's father to leave her alone." Myra paused. "The question in my mind has to do with why he was in the kitchen with the sisters when they were killed."

"I thought he worked there."

Myra shook her head. "According to Suzi, he'd been fired for stealing."

"Any theories?" I said.

"No, sir. I hesitate repeating what Suzi told me when it may or may not be true."

So far, I believed Myra had given an accurate statement. I framed the questions she might not want to answer. "Ms. Wright shared with us that someone approached Hai about selling her baby, and she refused."

"Anna shared the same with me after Suzi confided in her. According to Anna, via Suzi, so I can't verify this, the baby's father wanted her to follow through."

"Do you have any idea why he was in the restaurant's kitchen when the sisters were killed?"

"None other than now that someone had taken the baby, he wanted her back."

"It's odd he'd be there when the sisters were killed. Unless he arranged it, and the killers didn't trust him."

Myra glanced away, then back to him. "Anna and I have cried a lot of tears for our birth mothers, but with those two sweet ladies, we are grieving for their senseless deaths."

"Have you heard of other situations in which a birth mother was offered money for her baby?"

Myra closed her eyes, then opened them, not dramatically, but more of her facing reality. "Unfortunately, yes. A young woman lives at Healing and Hope because she has nowhere to go and no money. We offer classes and present them with skills and job opportunities, but the responsibility of not only taking care of themselves but also a baby is often overwhelming."

"How many of these cases have you seen?"

Myra swallowed hard. "Too many. Anna and I do our best to shut down those situations, but unfortunately the choice of giving up a baby to a licensed adoption agency or giving up a baby for a price is tempting."

"How do those seeking to victimize the woman learn about your birth mothers?" I had my own conclusions and data, yet I wanted to hear hers.

"I'd say predominantly the waiting rooms of medical clinics. The predators form a relationship with the birth mothers to gain their trust. We use just one clinic, but other patients and doctor's offices are housed there too. That is how a doctor worked a few years ago until he was arrested and sent to prison."

"It seems like someone could access your intake records and select the resident who appeared most vulnerable."

Myra startled. "Are you accusing me? Or one of the other employees or volunteers?"

"No, ma'am. I'm simply stating a fact."

She lifted her chin. "Then take your investigation somewhere else. My role at the care center is to show love, help, and healing to the birth mothers. Anything of the magnitude you're implying is morally and legally wrong. No one here remotely fits such a vile description."

Risa reached across the table within inches of touching Myra's clasped hands. "You're obviously upset."

"I am. I resent being implicated in these crimes."

"We are not in the least implicating you. Agent Patterson just noted the ease someone could obtain the birth mothers' records." Her tone softened Myra's stiffened body. "Are your records under lock and key?"

"Yes, for paper copies. And related information is password protected on my computer. Often the files have personal information, especially if the young woman fears for her safety." Myra glanced at Risa and then to me. "I don't suspect anyone. Those of us who've been at the center for years aren't there because of the money but to ensure the young women have every opportunity to give birth in a safe and healthy environment. Also to provide tools so they can be successful in caring for their children."

Risa gave her a warm smile and withdrew her extended hand on the table. "Agent Patterson, do you have additional questions for Mrs. Cummings?"

"Not at this time. Thank you for allowing us to inconvenience your day. If you hear of anything that might help us, would you notify us immediately?"

"Yes, sir. It's appalling the depths some people will go to make money."

More like the depths some people would go to *keep* making money.

One of my pocketed phones buzzed—Ethan's burner from Florakis. Only one person had the number.

I glanced at Risa. "Would you escort Mrs. Cummings to the reception area? I need to take this call."

★   ★   ★

In the hallway, I touched Answer on the burner phone. "Mr. Smith, how can I help you?"

"Where's Ethan?"

"No idea. He gave me his phone. Said he had no use for it."

"Who's this?"

"Special Agent Gage Patterson." Any call could be traced, but Florakis no doubt had his rear covered.

"The FBI hasn't learned its lesson."

"Let's meet and talk about this. Name the time and place."

He laughed. "Reardon wanted to meet up. I obliged and he lost his head in the deal. Are you volunteering for the same arrangement?"

"You sound sure of yourself."

"Mercury's a dead man. So is his family."

"You tried really hard with Agent Jacobs."

"Her life's on a short leash. Just like yours. She should have listened."

"Do you plan to take out the whole FBI?"

"Depends on what my boss wants." The call ended.

Florakis admitted to a few crimes, but he denied being the boss. Threats seemed to be his specialty—and murder. Risa and I needed to talk to Luke's widow.

54

RISA

I met Gage at his car with hundreds of thoughts swirling in my mind. Peter Florakis didn't scare me, but he should. He'd leaned into the arena of arrogance, and he'd make a mistake and find himself staring down a life term or the death penalty.

"What did he say?"

When Gage repeated the brief conversation, I silently confirmed Florakis's arrogance again.

He ran his fingers through his rust-brown hair. "Moving back to your apartment today isn't a good decision."

"If Florakis wants to find me, he will. But I have an idea."

"Your last idea nearly got innocent people hurt and both of us fired." He palmed the steering wheel. "I'm sorry. You didn't deserve that. What are you thinking?"

"This is more like a sting, and we'll clear it with the SAC. Hear me out first. I'll move back in and let Florakis think I'm settled. You could pose as an electrician and install an alarm and camera. Once you leave and it's dark, you return through a back entrance, and we wait for him. Florakis, or someone he hired, found his way into my apartment before, and he will again."

"It's so old-school, Risa. Still, it has merit. How many nights will it take?" He winked at me. "I'm beginning to like this plan."

I blew out feigned exasperation. "Shouldn't take long. Every day that passes increases the chances of us finding evidence. For sure we won't get much sleep. We could request surveillance while I'm at work and ensure they see and hear everything. Since you're on his list too, you could add equipment to your house."

"Already handled my place after I realized Mercury Alarms is my service." He chuckled. "My name was on the last list. Why is it you refused to stay at my house but now you're requesting I stay at yours? Have I become irresistible?"

She couldn't stop the laugh. "The listening devices will be our chaperones."

"You can be so unpredictable," he said. "But lovable."

"I'm trying to be serious." I focused on putting myself in our subject's shoes. Florakis served as a gofer for someone desperate to keep the money flow going. Someone who had fingerprints nationally or internationally. "Remember when I posited a theory about our bad guy having teams who knew nothing about what the others were doing?" When he nodded, I continued. "Those teams could separately specialize in kidnappings, fraud adoptions, drugs, human trafficking, and whatever else. While the ring's headquarters might be anywhere, Houston has their attention. None of the agents were killed in Des Moines, New York, Columbus, or the other cities where we've seen activity. Unless deaths occurred that haven't been linked or solved."

"We're too close to identifying and locating them." Gage's words mirrored my conclusion. "It reverts to Jack, Luke, and you stumbling onto the evidence to break the ring."

"Can we talk to Luke's widow, then stop at the hospital to visit Jack?" I said. "I checked, and his condition still isn't good, but we can see him for five minutes. Unfortunately, he had a setback due to an allergic reaction to a drug."

Gage made the arrangement with Mrs. Reardon and pocketed his phone. "I'd appreciate it if you'd take the lead with Mrs. Reardon.

She's expecting us, and I thought talking to another woman might be easier for her."

"Sure. Luke referred to her as his lovely bride. They were so happy together." My mind leveled at ground zero. "Were the agents assigned to Luke's murder able to learn anything?"

"His phone hasn't been recovered, but his last call came from a burner and located in the downtown area. He received the call, told his wife he'd be back in an hour, but never returned. She's in bad shape, but her sister is with her."

Gage's suggestion ushered in compassion for Mrs. Reardon. I'd lost Trenton, and she'd lost Luke. Not a club anyone willingly joined.

★   ★   ★

Gage pulled next to the curb in front of the Reardon home. A small one-story brick, decorated for Christmas with a waving Santa in the front yard and three elves at a workbench. Lights framed the sidewalk and roofline. No sign of the tragedy, which almost made it worse. I understood so well the void, loneliness, never-ending grief, and one day of darkness rolling into the next. And now I knew the reason why the season competed with Gage's emotions. Yet I could feel God's healing, and He'd heal Gage and Mrs. Reardon too. If she let Him.

Gage rang the doorbell, and she answered. I'd seen Mrs. Reardon at an FBI event, but that had been months ago. Then she wore her jet-black hair below her shoulders, makeup artistically applied, accenting huge sky-blue eyes and long lashes. Not so this morning. Her hair hung in strings, swollen red eyes, and ragged pajamas. I'd resembled her not so long ago, and the pain still cut through me sharp . . . ragged.

She opened the door wide enough to see us, clinging to it as though she'd changed her mind about agreeing to an interview. If so, I couldn't blame her.

"Hi, Mrs. Reardon. I'm Agent Risa Jacobs and this is Agent Patterson."

"You came to our wedding."

"Who's there?" a woman's voice called in the distance.

"FBI. I've been expecting them," Mrs. Reardon said.

"I'll be right with you."

Mrs. Reardon opened the door and showed us into a modest living area where Gage and I sat on a cream-colored sofa. Photos of the young couple mingled among the Christmas decorations.

The other woman joined us and introduced herself. No need to say she and Mrs. Reardon were sisters. Same angular face and sky-blue eyes. The sister sat in an adjacent chair next to Mrs. Reardon and took her hand.

I peered into the widow's drawn face. "Thank you for seeing us during this tragic time. We are so very sorry about your loss. We plan to attend the memorial service."

She bit her lip and whispered thanks. "You found Luke's—?"

"Yes," I said.

"Your brother was killed last summer, right?"

I gave her a slight nod and filled my tone with sincere compassion. "The driver intended to hit me, and we believe Luke and my brother were killed by the same man."

Mrs. Reardon's mouth quivered, and she visibly fought to maintain composure. "Then you understand how I won't rest until the murderer is found. I . . . I told the other agents all I know."

"Agent Patterson and I have your testimony. We're here for two reasons, to express our condolences in person and to ask you a few questions of our own."

"Thank you. I'll do my best." She closed her eyes and touched her stomach.

"Nauseous?" I said.

"Yes. It never stops." She captured my gaze. "I think I'll hurt forever."

"It feels that way. A doctor gave me a prescription for nausea, but the memories haunt me of how my brother died . . . identifying his body and the horror of it all. I'll tell you the same thing a good friend told me." I took a quick glimpse at Gage, and he gave me a slight nod. "'The fire won't burn forever, but it may feel like it. Those who care for you will see you through.'" I had no idea why I never forgot his words until now. "I encourage you to seek counseling."

"My sister recommended I visit with the pastor who married us."

"Excellent." I reached into my shoulder bag and gave her my card. "You can call me anytime."

Mrs. Reardon clutched the card and thanked me. "Excuse me if I close my eyes while I talk. It helps me focus." She reached for a tissue on the coffee table. "Monday morning at breakfast, Luke received a call and went outside to talk. He was gone no more than five minutes. When he returned, he covered his plate of half-eaten pancakes with plastic wrap and set it in the fridge. I asked him if something was wrong, and he said an informer needed to meet with him right away." She paused. "Now I wonder if he lied to protect me, but that's what he claimed. He kissed me and left. On his way, he called. He said he loved me and would call later from the office." She dabbed her eyes. "I never heard from Luke again. I remember him saying he was glad he didn't work violent crimes against children any longer."

Gage spoke. "We know this is extremely difficult. Luke's current case in the civil rights division doesn't seem tied to a violent crime."

"No, sir. He wanted a break from violent crimes against children because too many of the cases gave him nightmares. The horrific situations affected him too much. Though he liked working with Agent Bradford."

"Did he mention any of the nightmares' contents?" Gage said.

She sighed. "One in particular rattled him repeatedly. I don't know if it involved a case or all of them. He said babies were crying for their mothers, but their mothers were dead. In the nightmare, Luke couldn't get to the babies or the mothers in time to save them." She bit her lower lip. "Sometimes he'd cry out and shout, 'Stop.' My Luke would wake up in a cold sweat unable to go back to sleep."

Were Luke's nightmares a sign of deep emotional involvement? Or had he gotten in too deep with the wrong people? If only Jack could give us information.

"I'm really sorry," Gage said. "Did he ever mention any of the cases in particular?"

"As a rule, no. Except . . ."

"You can tell us," Gage said. "Nothing's being recorded. Agent Jacobs and I simply want to learn the truth and bring justice to these crimes."

Gage spoke with the grieving woman in his familiar soothing tone. Such a dear man.

Mrs. Reardon swiped beneath her eyes with a tissue. "Luke and his partner arrested a doctor who persuaded pregnant women to sell their babies. The doctor was found guilty, but Luke also believed someone higher up ran the operation. He couldn't find the evidence, and his partner didn't support him. They argued, and I don't think Luke ever got past it. He said the case had more moving parts. Combined with his nightmares, he resigned from working crimes against children."

"Had he talked to Dr. Zonner since his sentencing?"

"I have no idea. Do you think the case is related to how he died?" Mrs. Reardon said.

"I wish I knew." Gage turned to me. "Agent Jacobs, do you have any more questions?"

"Just one. The agents investigating Luke's death mirrored his work and personal devices. Nothing there appeared to indicate danger or suspicions. However, he had two dates highlighted on his calendar, and we confirmed these were dates he and Jack interviewed Anna Wright at Houston Healing and Hope and the second involved the arrest of Dr. Zonner. Have you located anything else?"

She shook her head. "If he had notes, I'm not aware of any, and I've searched through everything here in the house. Yesterday I went to our safe-deposit box. Nothing existed there to help you."

I thanked Mrs. Reardon and gave her a hug. "If something comes to mind, please contact one of us."

"I'm sorry I'm not more help. I should have pressed Luke to talk about his work. Maybe things would have been different."

I ached for her. "I'm sure he did his best to protect you. I do encourage you to move forward with counseling."

If Luke Reardon had been a part of the baby ring, he took his guilt to the grave. But with his stellar record and the recurring nightmares, he might have been on the right track. Maybe if he had shared with his wife where he'd gone last Monday, he'd be alive today.

55

Risa and I drove to Huntsville's state prison, a minimum-security facility north of Houston. Dr. Alfred Zonner had been sentenced to a maximum of ten years for the buying and selling of babies. He'd pleaded not guilty. The FBI hadn't met his approved visitor list, but he might be curiously tempted.

Having Risa beside me rattled my thoughts. *Focus, Gage.*

She scanned the closed case notes for the third time. "Jack and Luke worked this case, and we weren't involved. Apparently Dr. Zonner managed his side business without the aid of others, which is ludicrous." She tossed me an aggravated frown. "To sell a baby, he needed a buyer."

"Buyers play for keeps. Most likely if Zonner survives his prison mates, he will be released early on good behavior, and he's a free man."

"His ex-wife and two young boys left him and now live in Arizona. Nothing to return to around here." Risa stared at the highway. "He can't practice medicine, but several thousands of dollars are stashed away somewhere. Getting caught educated him for his next big scheme, and who knows what he's learned in prison. I can't come up with strong enough motivation for him to help us. Sounds like Luke never gave up on Zonner concealing information." She bounced her thumb on her leg. "If Zonner is aware of Luke's murder, he won't tell us a thing."

I had an idea. "This might work to our advantage. If he offers credible info about who killed Luke, we could offer a deal to shorten his sentence."

Risa peered at my speedometer. "We'd get there a lot faster if you'd let me drive."

I laughed. "It's not even noon. What's left for the day except running by the hospital and spending five minutes with Jack before getting you back into your apartment?" I knew she liked to drive, so I'd tease a little. "Riding with you means adding blood pressure meds to my pill regimen."

"Good one, Gage. How long did it take you to come up with that? Since Carson and I dodged a semi?"

"Okay, you got me." Now for the big serious question. "What about dinner Friday night?"

"What's the occasion?"

"The shrink gave you a conditional report, and we're together?"

"Reminds me of Kermit and Miss Piggy together again," she said.

"I like green."

A smile played on her lips. "Where?"

"Churrascos? Seven o'clock?"

"Oh, my favorite. I suppose you're driving," she said.

"Yep. I might even get a car wash."

★ ★ ★

At the prison, Risa and I showed our credentials and requested to see Dr. Zonner. I pulled out the stops. "Tell him evidence has surfaced with the bureau about his not-guilty plea, and we'd like to ask him a few questions."

We waited forty-five minutes before a guard escorted us to the interview area where Dr. Zonner sat at a small table. We took chairs opposite him, and I introduced myself and Risa.

Zonner's salt-and-pepper hair hung past his ears, and he sported a bald spot on his crown. He swung a stoic glance at Risa, then me.

"What could you have possibly discovered to support my not-guilty plea? I'll give you five minutes."

I took the lead. "We have an opportunity for you to get out of here sooner."

"I'm listening." Not a muscle moved on his stoic expression.

I showed him a pic of Peter Florakis. "Who is this man?"

Zonner's eyes trailed to the man. "No one I know." His index fingers rose slightly.

I scrolled to one of Emily Lock. "This woman?"

"No idea."

I found Norman Peilman's pic. "What about him?"

"Not anyone I've met or seen before." Again his index fingers rose slightly.

I showed him one of Jack. "This man?"

"Agent Jack Bradford. He worked my case."

I found Luke's photo. "And this man?"

"Agent Luke Reardon. Worked with Bradford. Both testified against me."

"None of those other people hit your radar?" I said. "Because info about any of them is your ticket to seeing if the judge would shorten your sentence."

"Guess we're done." Zonner leaned back against the metal chair.

I folded my hands on the table. "Not yet. Who are you covering for? Someone arranged for the illegal adoptions after you purchased the babies."

Zonner glanced away, his face still without emotion. I waited, employing silence to tempt him to talk.

"Your time's up." He scooted back his chair.

"Dr. Zonner, you'd rather waste years here than take an early release, start your life over without the confines of a cell?"

He shrugged. "I know the status of Bradford and Reardon. I'm no fool."

"The Witness Security Program is an option. I saw the reaction to Peilman and Florakis. You've had dealings with both men. By the way Peilman is dead."

He exhaled. "The way I look at my conviction is I offered those women a win-win situation. Their babies went to good homes, to people who wanted children. The mothers received money to get on their feet. That's a service, Agents. How odd is our system of justice when I'm in prison for doing good, and I could have agreed to abort their babies and not broken any laws? Go figure. I'll take my chances. A few more years here is safer than facing a beheading." Zonner stood and walked to the guard in the back of the room.

He knew exactly his demise if he opened his mouth.

56

RISA

Gage's eyes showed his frustration with the morning's interviews, first with Mrs. Reardon, then Dr. Zonner. I offered to drive from the prison, but he refused. But I believed we'd moved closer to drawing Florakis out of the cobwebs.

"Florakis knows who we're interviewing," I said. "He's grown bolder by bragging about past crimes and threatening others." I focused on what we knew about him. "He or his boss obviously has enough money to pay gang members to murder and set fire to a restaurant. Houston is a hub of diversity, which means they could transport any child internationally by air, through Port Houston, or via land into Mexico."

"CARD is researching those possibilities." Discouragement frosted his words.

My mind spun with how broad the crimes might extend. "We've discussed the likelihood of the operation also dealing in drugs, and I know TSA, south border patrol, and the Coast Guard and Department of Homeland Security police the ship channel for contraband. The reality of smuggling illegal goods takes different strategy than transporting babies or human trafficking."

"If we spread ourselves too thin with the what-ifs, we'll never find Florakis and his people."

I agreed with Gage. "I tend to get carried away with suppositions. We've already proven the magnitude of the illegal adoptions, and I think this is larger than what we've ever imagined."

He gave me a slight nod. "We bring down one bad guy at a time with the resources available to us."

"Well stated."

"Have you changed your mind about moving into your apartment?"

"No. We have a plan and the SAC's approval."

★　★　★

At the hospital, we were granted no more than five minutes visitation with Jack, providing we didn't exhaust him. I appreciated any coherency.

Gage and I entered his guarded room to find Jack's eyes closed and the steady beat of machines monitoring his vitals. We stood together at his bedside.

"Jack," I whispered. "It's Risa and Gage."

He opened his eyes at half-mast and his lips turned up slightly. "My favorite people."

"How are you feeling?"

"Better than yesterday."

I touched his shoulder. "Your color is better."

"Yay." He closed his eyes. "Cartwheels next."

"I still owe you a real steak dinner," Gage said. "I'm sure it beats IV juice."

He forced a chuckle. "At the moment, broth sounds good."

Jack needed rest, and I doubted he could stay awake for the full five minutes. "Do you remember when I visited before?" I said.

He sighed. "Vaguely."

"You tried to tell me something about Luke."

"Talk to him." Jack paused, and his weakened body alarmed me. "He . . . has a theory about the Zonner case . . . Thought he might visit me."

I wasn't about to tell him about Luke. Glancing at Gage, he shook his head. "Luke's been busy," I said. "Did you two talk about his theory?"

Jack's eyes slowly opened. "I don't remember, but I'll work on it. We argued."

I patted his shoulder. "Sounds good. We'll be back tomorrow. Can we get you anything?"

"Only thing I'm good for is sleep." Jack closed his eyes, and we said goodbye.

In the hallway, we stopped at the nurses' station. Gage recognized a head nurse, a woman who could have played defense for the Dallas Cowboys.

"We just came from Jack Bradford's room, and he's very weak. Can you give us an update on his condition?"

The woman paused and picked up a chart before responding. "We nearly lost him twice yesterday, but he rallied this morning. Agent Patterson, your friend is a fighter, or he wouldn't be here."

"Agent Jacobs and I have been praying for him."

"Something is keeping him alive. I'm not much of a religious person but keep it up because he's still with us."

In the elevator, Gage massaged his neck. "Do you feel like everywhere we turn a barricade stops us?"

"Which tells me we're getting closer to a breakthrough." I didn't feel so optimistic and yet I wanted to think we were narrowing the investigation.

Too many suspects.

Too little information.

Too many bodies.

No wonder Gage faced discouragement.

57

I took my car to the extended-stay hotel and packed my belongings. Although I wanted to return to my home, the memories soured my stomach. Gage's presence would keep my mind occupied, and with the surveillance team listening to our every word, I didn't feel like I'd break a moral code. SAC Dunkin approved the arrangement. He wanted this ended too.

At my apartment, I set my overnight bag in the living area and walked back to the bathroom. Not a trace of blood anywhere, only the telltale odors of disinfectant and the haunting memories. Those were the worst. I hadn't slept at the hotel, and I wouldn't now either. What kind of pain had Luke suffered before his death? How many more would die at the hands of the killer before they made an arrest?

Two hours later, while poring over reports, the front desk requested permission for an electrician to check out the heating in my apartment. Gage followed up with a text. When my doorbell rang, I confirmed Gage through the peephole before I opened the door. He was barely recognizable.

"So glad you're here," I said. "The heat won't come on, and the building's repairman couldn't fix it." I let him in, closed the door, received a soft kiss, then studied his appearance.

He wore nerdy glasses, probably the same ones he'd worn on the plane to Santa Fe. Baggy jeans, an Astros ball cap, and a shirt with an emblem of Houston Lighting & Power completed his rather disheveled appearance.

"You will never make the hot electrician calendar."

"Got any music?" He whipped off his glasses as though he'd break into a dance.

"Classic, Gage. Simply classic." I pointed to the coffeepot and poured him a fresh cup of our favorite brand.

"Do you realize the interviews today?" he said after a sip. "Myra Cummings, Mrs. Reardon, Dr. Zonner, and Jack. The only thing we established is Luke most likely went to his death possibly with evidence to stop Florakis and his bunch."

"Jack may still come through. We'll find the evidence." Gage had supported me from afar while I grieved for Trenton and experienced emotional paralysis. Now I could reciprocate.

"But not today." He waved his hand. "I need to find my never-give-up attitude."

"Think about the Addingtons, the Wades, the Reardons, and the many other victims."

He gave me a dip of his chin. "Could be tonight."

Forty-five minutes later, Gage finished the installation of the equipment for the surveillance team and received confirmation that both worked. He'd return in the same disguise at 8 p.m.

★   ★   ★

My body must have known the surveillance team had my back because I slept for three hours sprawled across my bed. Probably snored. The temptation to crawl under the covers nibbled at me until I forced myself up. I caught up on email, checked in with Mom and Dad, and before I realized it, Gage texted of his arrival through a rear entrance of the apartment building. This time the jeans and T-shirt were Gage.

"I understand your heating unit has kicked off again." He grinned. "I'm your man."

I swallowed my laughter until the door closed behind him. If not for the camera and audio, we'd be in each other's arms. We chatted and drank more coffee. Both of us admitted the day had been exhausting. I found *It's a Wonderful Life* on my laptop and kept the volume low. The computer screen was the only light visible, although the drapes were closed.

Shortly after midnight, and the close of George Bailey's reunion with family and friends, Gage turned to me. "What are you doing for Christmas?"

I gestured around my apartment. "This is it unless things change." Oops. I didn't want to be a downer. "But—" I lightened my tone—"if I can, I'll Zoom or FaceTime Mom and Dad."

"I don't see a tree or any of the Christmas decorations from the past."

"Too hard this year. What about you?"

"Christmas Day with my parents in San Antonio. My partner used to help me trim my tree, but not this year. Maybe next."

I stared at my empty coffee cup. "I hope so." For a moment I'd forgotten about the audio and visual live streaming to a couple of agents outside. "Have you bought pre—?"

A male voice alerted us through our earbuds. "We've called for backup. Watching two men in black hoodies and masks trying to pick the rear entrance lock. They're in."

"We're ready," Gage said while I closed my laptop.

We grabbed our guns and took positions on either side of the door. A slight rustling from the outer door told me these guys were pros. In the dark, I stared at the doorknob.

It turned ever so slowly.

A faint click.

The door opened and two figures entered the room.

"Drop your weapons!" I said. "Hands up."

"FBI!" Gage thundered.

The two whirled to exit, but Gage kicked the door closed. "Toss those guns on the floor, or I'll blow your hands off." I snapped on the light.

The two crouched low and laid their firearms in front of them and slowly stood.

"Stay down."

One man lunged at me and the other at Gage. The man grabbed my right wrist and wrestled for my gun.

I pulled the trigger into his shoulder, sending him to the floor. I flipped him onto his stomach and flex-cuffed his hands. A glance at Gage showed his man now cuffed. Adrenaline flew through my veins with the hand-to-hand combat—I couldn't do this in the classroom.

Gage ripped off the mask on his man. I did the same.

"Mr. Duong and Mr. Bui," Gage said. "How good of you to visit."

58

GAGE

My two friends Mr. Duong and Mr. Bui were taken into FBI custody, photographed, and fingerprinted—again. They were charged with a first-degree felony for breaking and entering with the intent to kill a federal officer. Risa and I, now wide-awake, studied them outside an interview room.

"Duong Tuan has a jagged scar on the left side of his neck, and Bui Vinh is three years younger," I said.

"I had a bad feeling about those two when they were released on bail," she said. "But when I saw Old Judge Lenient's name, I wasn't surprised."

"I'll be leading the campaign against him at the next election." I blew out my frustration. "So here they are again. I'm ready to hear their story without their attorney."

"They didn't lawyer up?" Risa said.

"Sure. But he's not here yet. Ready?" We walked into the interview room, and I dug right into my agenda. "We meet again, gentlemen. Only strengthens my case against you." Risa and I took our seats across from them. "It's late or rather early, so we might as well get started. Who hired you to eliminate Special Agent Risa Jacobs?"

Both men stared at the table. Duong, the one Risa shot, wore a bandage on his right shoulder where an EMT had packed his wound. His face etched in pain.

Risa slowly stood and walked around to the back of the men's chairs. She bent to Duong's ear. "You're not very comfortable. I suggest you answer Agent Patterson, or my fingers might find that bullet hole."

Risa would never in a million years abuse a prisoner but . . . she had gone after Carson. I didn't want to risk anything. "I'm losing my patience. Who hired you to eliminate Agent Jacobs?"

Nothing.

"Who hired you to kill Agent Jack Bradford?"

Nothing.

"Don't they speak English?" Risa said. "I can find an interpreter."

"Oh, they speak English just fine. Those two know they are facing life or a lethal injection for the Phan sisters. I'm thinking they beheaded Agent Luke Reardon. Is that so?"

Duong shook his head wildly. "That was not us."

"The Phan sisters or Luke Reardon?"

Bui spoke up. "We didn't kill Reardon."

"So you killed Suzi and Hai Phan?"

Bui's shoulders arched. "No. We already pleaded not guilty to Phan sisters' deaths."

"All right," I said. "Who killed Luke Reardon?"

Duong scowled at Bui. "We don't know. We want to keep our heads. Where's our attorney?"

"He's on his way. We woke him, and he's not in a good mood."

Risa walked back around the table and sat. Calm. In control. I breathed inward relief. "Was Agent Reardon's killer the same person who paid you to come after me?" she said.

When neither man responded, I took the lead. "With the murder charges filed against you, there is no way I can recommend life."

Bui stiffened. "Either way, we're dead men."

I nodded. "I get it, guys. You give us a name, and you're dead. You head to prison and wait for the injection, you're dead. Add to that, you failed tonight. I bet your attorney doesn't show because Florakis won't foot the bill."

Both men shifted in their seats.

"Life sure sounds better than a needle." I studied them. "In my opinion, Florakis took advantage of two young guys who only wanted a few extra dollars in their pockets."

Duong and Bui exchanged glances. Bui took a deep breath. "We don't know who pays us. We get a phone call with instructions. We do the job and then another call tells us where to pick up the money."

"Neither of you had a phone. Where are they?"

"Crushed," Bui said. "The pieces are in different places."

"Your no-name boss provides a phone for each time he needs you to run an errand?"

"Yes," Bui said.

I pressed my lips together and stared at them. "Bui, you're twenty-one, and, Duong, you're twenty-four. Is protecting this guy worth it?"

Duong swore. "We don't have a name, or we'd tell you."

"All right," I said. "Any of the other guys I saw you with a part of this deal?"

"No. We are the only two."

These two guys were scared and in over their heads.

★　★　★

I viewed the interview video for the fourth time in my office. Duong and Bui played the tough-guy role, but their fear of spilling their guts or facing a judge and jury was real. They were dead men no matter what the future held. Lam Giang, their attorney, never showed. Upon Duong and Bui's request, I asked for a court-appointed attorney. If the two weren't involved in multiple murders, I'd feel sorry for them. In my mind, a plea bargain for life in solitary confinement kept them alive. I'd wait until Monday to arrange another interview. Let them sweat the weekend to see if their stories changed.

Risa stayed fixed in my mind. We were wading knee-deep in the mud of unsolved murders and chasing down a fraudulent adoption agency, and I wanted to take her to dinner. A date. Made little sense even to me.

Should I have waited? Spending time with Risa without the case seemed selfish. But I didn't care.

59

RISA

At 4 a.m., SAC Dunkin told Gage and me to go home and not show up until Monday morning, the week before Christmas. While these orders sounded good in theory, Gage and I planned to attend Luke's memorial and work the case over the weekend. I drove home, craving sleep and expecting to be pulled over for driving like a drunk.

I woke at 8:30 and grabbed my phone to text Gage.

You're picking me up at 9:30 for the memorial?

Yes.

I hurried to the shower and dressed on time. Standing room only filled the church—many of them agents like at Trenton's service. Luke's brutal death had hit everyone hard. Senseless. Mrs. Reardon endured the memorial in tears with her sister right beside her.

In the receiving line, I took the widow's hand, remembering the two times Darlene had comforted me. "I'm here for you. Call me anytime. You can shout or rant at the unfairness, or we don't need to talk at all. Is anyone staying with you during the holidays?"

"My sister will be with me until January 1."

"I'll check on you January 2."

She nodded and bit into her lower lip.

Afterward in Gage's car back to my apartment, I questioned him about the evening's plans. We could go to dinner when we weren't exhausted.

"It's the closest to a Christmas celebration that we'll probably get," he said.

"All right. But I don't feel much like wearing a red bow in my hair."

He took my hand. "Maybe we need to forget the tragedies for a while and remember the season. But the decision is yours."

His compassion stopped any protest. "I'll be ready. With all we've been through, you are my gift."

✶   ✶   ✶

Close to five, after a two-hour nap, I received a call from the doorman about a flower delivery. He offered to have the desk clerk bring them up. Ever cautious, I didn't open the door until I saw him. Living the life of an FBI agent kept me in continuous caution mode.

The portly desk clerk handed me a dozen red roses with baby's breath, greenery, and arranged in a crystal vase. "Enjoy. Merry Christmas."

I responded with the same words. Glad he hadn't opted for *Season's greetings*. I closed the door and set the bouquet on my kitchen table. The flowers' intoxicating fragrance filled the apartment. I opened a small, white envelope and pulled out a card.

Risa, looking forward to our dinner. You are my Christmas blessing.

I trembled and tears filled my eyes. Amid one tragedy after another, had we found what I'd always dreamed? How like God to shine His light when I least expected.

Or maybe I anticipated too much, and Gage understood this Christmas marked another first and he wanted to make it special. I texted him because I feared I might cry like a sixteen-year-old.

The roses are beautiful. Thank you so much. See you soon.

Within moments his response sailed into my phone. A smiley face emoticon.

All the while I got ready, I lingered on tonight being our first real date. I chose an off-the-shoulder red dress, not my usual black or navy blue. A little short but we weren't going to the office.

My heels were a little tall, but we weren't going to the office.

My makeup a little extra on the eyes and lips, but we weren't going to the office.

At seven, he called from the lobby, and I gave permission for his access. Waiting for him to arrive, I paced the floor. This was Gage, the man who'd seen me at my worst . . . many times. The man who'd cried with me when a child didn't survive abduction. The man who'd laughed with me at stupid things. The man who loved me, and I loved him.

The doorbell rang, and I jumped.

Pull yourself together, Risa, before you make a fool of yourself over roses.

I opened the door. Gage's mouth stood agape.

I touched my throat. "Is something wrong? Should I change? Is this a bit much?"

He laughed. "You are stunning. Beautiful. You said no to a red bow, but this is soooo much better."

"Great." I tugged on his navy-blue sports coat, urging him to enter my apartment.

I loved his smile, the one he only gave to me. "I feel like a kid at Christmas."

"You are a kid. And it is Christmas."

★ ★ ★

Seated at the restaurant, I gazed into those blue-gray eyes that held me captive. Gage would call me cuffed, and I fit the description.

"Thank you again for tonight." I gestured around the South American restaurant. "And my favorite place to celebrate. The food is excellent, and all the decorations have caused me to forget our case. What's the occasion?"

"Celebrating us with our first real date."

I startled. "It is. I mean it's not a stakeout or sweeping a building or facing the SAC." Laughter hit me from my toes up.

He joined me. We were hysterical. No restraint. My normal introverted, observational self had drowned in the soup.

Gage took a breath obviously to stop the laughter. With little success. "We are going to get thrown out of here," he finally managed.

"But we'll be together," I said.

He waved a finger at me. "One more reason I love you."

Joy tugged at the corners of my mouth, and I rested my chin on the palm of my hand. "I want to hear those three words every day for the rest of my life." I didn't care if I sounded like a hopeless romantic or a child who just received an early Christmas present. "How long do we keep this quiet?"

"Most people already know."

"Who?"

"Jack for one guessed it, and Carson asked me if I was in love with you." Gage chuckled. "Carson went on to tell me I didn't look at you like you were my coworker. I denied both of them until I couldn't any longer."

Our texts sounded at the same time. Jack.

Luke said the person responsible had us blinded.

60

Was it possible to be numb with love while the world exploded in chaos? I thought so because my emotions were spinning like a top. I turned over in bed and saw the Saturday morning's hour hovered over ten thirty. For the first time in days, my body didn't ache from exhaustion, or my heart pierced from grief.

Last night, Gage had held me like I might break and kissed me good night at the door like I'd dreamed about for months.

Now, as I replayed every tender word and sweet memory from last night, I had this woman-in-love optimism going. What would it be like to have his child, a little boy or girl who was a blend of us? I covered my mouth with a chuckle. Heaven forbid, our child would have to line up their closet according to color, use, and the last time they wore it. I crawled out of bed and ground beans for coffee. Today would be a great day. In a few moments, I poured a bubble-topped cup of rich black coffee and walked back to take a shower.

Gage planned to bring lunch around 1 p.m., and we'd work on how to move forward in the Addingtons' baby abduction and the subsequent murders. Until then I needed to focus on the case with the attention the victims deserved.

While I let the hot water pour over me, I thought about the Addingtons, Wades, Phan sisters, Carson, Mercurys, Jack, Luke,

Florakis, the two men locked up on murder charges, and where I fit. What did Jack and Luke have in common with any of them? And why did Luke say the guilty person had us blinded?

A suspicion planted a seed in my brain, and the longer I dwelled on it, the more it grew.

★ ★ ★

Gage arrived on time with two bags from Chick-fil-A. The waffle fries and chicken sandwich with extra of their famous sauce filled my empty tummy. Gage's kisses took over the appetizer and dessert. If we weren't careful, our bodies would take us down a heated path.

Gage tossed the wrappings from lunch into one of the paper bags. "Good thing the camera and bugs are disabled, or we'd be in trouble."

I groaned. "Our secret would be out, and we'd hit the gossip meter."

"'Tis true. Sweet lady, we need to get some work done."

I laughed. "Should we sit on opposite sides of the room?"

He nodded. "We might have to."

I pulled open a drawer containing a legal pad and pen, then grabbed my iPad. He thanked me with a kiss and took a chair in the living room. I grabbed my Dr Pepper and curled up in a chair across from him.

"Want to check on Jack tomorrow afternoon?" I said.

"Yes. According to the nurses' station, he's making steady improvements. I'm hoping by Monday, Duong and Bui will have second thoughts about where they're headed."

"Let's hope Zonner feels the same way. I've been thinking, and I don't know if it's God, but Anna Wright keeps popping up in my mind. We've talked to two of her trusted employees, and nothing's really surfaced. But what are the odds of two instances of baby abductions in two years? Am I fishing for answers and suspecting those who support a Christian woman who loves on those birth mothers like they are her own?"

"Neither one of us are coincidence-believing kind of people."

"I've read and reread the notes, but would you mind going over Jack's and your meeting with Anna Wright?"

61

GAGE

I stared at Risa dressed in jeans and a bright-blue sweater. She had a smudge of yellow Chick-fil-A sauce on her cheek, but I wouldn't tell her, and her hair had been pulled back into a ponytail. No makeup . . . just fresh beauty. I wanted to wake up every day of my life with this woman beside me.

I relayed Jack's and my meeting with Anna Wright. "She cooperated during our interview, very supportive. She phoned Suzi Phan for information about Hai, gave us numbers to contact Suzi, and shed lots of tears when we told her both young women had been killed. She's gone over and beyond what I expected."

"What about the other maternity homes in the city?"

"Nothing yet," I said. "Two of the centers requested the FBI provide a talk to their birth mothers on what to do if approached by someone who wants to buy their babies. I have it penciled in on my January calendar."

Risa moistened her lips. "Ms. Wright's maternity home is one of the largest in the city. Clean. Respected. Faith-focused. Money isn't an issue due to generous donations. But infant abductions creep to where the babies are. She runs a tight ship and is incredibly organized." She paused with a sigh. "Except her desk is always a mess.

Anyway, I know how she feels about the birth mothers because our church supports them, and I've heard firsthand."

Doubts surfaced about Anna Wright's directorship. "Have you been to the facility?"

Risa stared at me wide-eyed. "Once. I was part of a church team who volunteered to make repairs to the home. I should have remembered that."

"Did you spend time with any of the birth mothers?"

Risa tilted her head. "The women worked alongside us. We brought in lunch and later held a worship service. Many had prayer requests, and we did so privately. Some made decisions for Christ, and I counseled them too. Ms. Wright has been on my mind since this morning, something I just couldn't shake. I feel so incredibly stupid about not telling you about my volunteer work there."

"Your reason for helping was mission focused and had nothing to do with a case."

Risa peered at the window behind my chair, staring at something in her mind miles away. Her features darkened, and she touched her mouth.

"Are you thinking the one thing you have in common with Jack and Luke is the maternity home? I didn't enter the picture until the Addingtons' baby abduction."

"Remember Clyde Washington recognized one of Emily Lock's disguises? I suggest we find out more about Anna Wright. I agree she gives all indications of being a strong woman of faith, and the birth mothers all had commendable things to say about her. In fact I've never heard a negative thing about her."

"Any comments made when you were alone with the women?"

"Ms. Wright protested, said we'd done enough, and she could pray with the women and offer discipleship. I shoved aside her objections as humility and appreciation for what we'd done." Risa sighed deeply. "And I could be incredibly wrong to suspect her."

"Or you could be spot-on. The maternity home is a nonprofit. Those supporting the facility are in good standing, and I've already checked them out for discrepancies. Her financials are in order too.

She could easily launder money and route it to an overseas account." I glanced up. "Are we yanking at straws or are we on to something?"

"Think about it, Gage. Based on many of the mothers in a low-income category, she could encourage them to give up their babies, and she takes a finder's fee or more."

"Florakis could work for her, or she works for him," I said. "We could talk to her again. Could be nothing. Could be the answer."

"Add a search warrant. I'm curious about how many former residents chose adoption. Would the information be included in their files? I'd like to find out."

I grabbed my phone for the call, but Risa stopped me.

"Hear me out," she said. "Since I was the original target and we're viewing this from a wild-and-crazy supposition that I could have gotten too close to one of the mothers—I'll visit Ms. Wright on behalf of my church. Remember I resigned from the FBI, so she won't suspect a thing but a woman who is representing goodwill. As a college prof, I'm on break until mid-January. The women I talked to a year ago won't be housed there, but I could ask about them. Others would have taken their place. If Ms. Wright is involved with the abductions, my presence and questions will make her nervous."

I frowned and crossed my arms over my chest. "Might get you on the other end of a smoking gun."

"She wouldn't be stupid." She pointed to her watch. "It's two thirty."

"Risa, are you sure about this?"

"Yep." She eased up from her chair. "I'll keep my phone on record. Won't stand up in court, but her statement could go a long way to prove or disprove her involvement."

"A recording won't save your life. Wait until we have a background or a search warrant."

"Neither will show a thing, or you'd have already interrogated her. I'll give you ten minutes, then I'm on the road. Traffic will be light on a Saturday afternoon, and I'll be there and back in no time."

"Excuse me," I said. "Our work is never 'in no time.'"

Risa made a phone call to someone at her church before she finger-waved goodbye.

"Are you flirting with me?" I said.

"Does it matter? I love you."

"I'm going with you. We're partners."

"Gage, this is a ministry call. You're right. I might be a while, but if I bake chocolate chip cookies with some of the birth moms, I'll bring you one. I'll text you when I arrive. Wait here if you like or lock up when you leave."

"And I'll text you to ensure you're fine."

"I'd expect no less."

"And if you don't respond, I'm calling in the cavalry." I was over-reacting. Right?

62

RISA

I entered Houston Healing and Hope Maternity Care with my senses on alert and caution in my spirit. An instrumental version of "Deck the Halls" played quietly in the reception area, and a modestly trimmed Christmas tree with ornaments of singing angels and clear bulbs hung from the branches. A miniature Nativity scene perched on an unattended desk while the scent of cinnamon filled the air. Festive. Tasteful. Gifts rested under the tree all wrapped the same in red paper and white bows.

"Hello, anyone around?" I said.

Anna Wright bustled in from her office. "Welcome to Houston Healing and Hope Maternity Care. Merry Christmas." Her face brightened "Oh, you're from Mercy Point Church."

"You have a good memory." I stuck out my hand, and she grasped it firmly. Her hand wasn't clammy. "Risa Jacobs."

"How can I help you?" She peered around me. "Are others with you?"

"No, just me." I pointed to the decorations. "This is beautiful."

"Thank you. The girls did the decorations."

"I know you're busy, which is why I'm here. It's Christmas, and I wanted to invite you, the birth mothers, and any staff or volunteers to our Christmas Eve service. It's at seven thirty, and we have shuttles that could transport anyone interested."

Ms. Wright rubbed her palms together. "How lovely. Our driver is off for the evening, and the transportation would be a blessing. I'll check with the girls and staff. I'm sure they'd enjoy ushering in our Lord's birth with a special service."

I'd seen tough women lie their way through interviews, interrogations, and all the way to the witness stand. Some of those leather-hearted women still walked the streets. Others spent their days behind bars. I shouldn't judge, but the diamond on Anna's right hand wasn't purchased at Walmart.

"Gorgeous ring," I said.

"Thank you, Risa. My mother passed recently, and I inherited this beautiful piece that came from her grandmother."

"I'm sorry for your loss. Were you close?" The setting sparkled like new.

"Very much so until dementia struck. She went downhill fast and was often incoherent. I keep telling myself to sell it and put the money into the home."

"I'm sure your mother would want you to keep it. I imagine you had good times to help with your grief. I lost my brother in July. Very hard. Some days are worse than others, and these firsts are difficult—holidays and birthdays. When I least expect it, a memory sends me spiraling." None of my words were fabricated.

Ms. Wright adjusted an angel on the tree. "God is close to the brokenhearted. We'll make it through this season."

"Yes, we will. Is the home full?"

Ms. Wright turned with a glint in her eyes. "Yes. As always, we've planned a Christmas Day feast, and your church has been so generous in contributing food and a gift for each birth mother."

"The faith aspect is one blessing you provide here. Do you hear from past women? I often wonder how they're doing."

"Sometimes they visit, and it's always a joy to see them."

"Can I walk through and wish the residents a merry Christmas? Pray with them?"

"Many of them are napping during the afternoon."

"When would be a good time to come back? Tomorrow afternoon?"

"Risa, you are so busy. It's not necessary."

"I have lots of free hours to do something constructive."

I caught a flicker of anger on the woman's face before a fake smile appeared. "Let's see if any are awake."

"Perfect." I followed her into the common area, where about eight young women in various stages of pregnancy chatted, watched TV, or read.

"Girls, I have someone who wants to meet you." Anna gestured to me. "This is Risa Jacobs and she's volunteered here with the church that supports us in so many ways. She stopped by to see if we'd like to attend the church's Christmas Eve service, and I know several of you would enjoy going."

"Hi." I waved. "If any of you would like to talk, play a game, or pray, I'm available."

A very pregnant young woman raised her hand from a nearby sofa. "I have a hard decision to make about my baby. Prayer would be wonderful. My name is Sara."

"I'd be honored. Where shall we go for privacy?" I turned to Ms. Wright. "Do you have a suggestion?"

"My office is available."

I questioned if Ms. Wright had her office bugged. I turned to the young woman. "Will that work?"

Sara sighed. "I prefer my room."

"Is it presentable?" Ms. Wright said.

"Yes, ma'am."

Two other women requested prayers and preferred Anna's office.

Sara led me to her room. I remembered the setup of the small bedrooms housing the residents. This one was painted pale yellow, and her bedspread carried the yellow with blue flowers. Simple but clean and fresh. But Sara's bright-red hair streaked with purple, a nose ring, and black nail polish indicated the soft colors might have been more suitable for another young woman. She offered me the single chair and sat on her bed.

"Have you been here long?" I said.

"Three months. I had nowhere to go, and Ms. Wright welcomed me with open arms. The God-thing bothered me at first, but I'm okay. From where I come from, this is a huge upgrade, which is why I asked for prayer privately."

"Of course. I'm glad you're in a safe place, and I will continue to pray for you after today. Ms. Wright is a lovely woman, inside and out," I said. "And Myra Cummings is a wealth of resources."

"Myra is like the mom I never had. Love her too. I've been trying to figure out what is best for my baby. Ms. Wright and I have talked." She rubbed her palms on her jean-clad thighs. "I'm sorry. My hormones make me want to cry at the strangest times."

"It's okay." I reached for a tissue from the nightstand and handed it to her.

Sara dabbed beneath her eyes. "I'm thinking of giving my baby up for adoption. Ms. Wright has counseled me about it so I'd be sure to make the right decision. She said allowing a couple who can love and take care of my baby is the best thing I can do for him or her. She's praying for me, and I thought one more person would help me decide. My boyfriend doesn't want me to keep it, but I'm not going back to him no matter what I decide."

"If you keep your baby, do you have means to support yourself and the child?"

"My grandmother said I could live with her, and she'd babysit while I worked."

I moved to the bed beside Sara and took her hand. "What do you want to do?"

She swiped at a tear. "But is it best for the baby?"

"The most important thing a baby needs is love. Have you talked to a private or church-sponsored adoption agency?"

Another tear fell over Sara's cheek. "Yes, a private agency. I've talked to a man and his wife who'd very much like a child of their own. They've been married ten years and feel God has called them to adopt."

"Do you like what you've seen?"

"I suppose. They're in their late thirties. He has a good job. She's blonde, but probably dyed, and he has dark hair. Both have blue eyes, and my baby will have brown." She cocked her head. "They showed me pictures of their home, the baby's room, and a huge backyard."

According to Gage's report, Harvey Sinclair had blue eyes. But so did lots of people.

"God knows what is best, Sara. Let's pray for His will."

Through moistened eyes, the girl nodded, and I prayed for her. At the *amen*, she thanked me. "The people who want my baby are so nice, and I wonder if I'm being selfish. I mean they told me we could have an open arrangement."

"How do you feel about an open adoption?"

"Ms. Wright said the situation could be very emotional, and I agree. Once I gave up my baby, seeing him or her would be horrible. I couldn't bear hearing my baby call another woman *Mommy*."

"When are you due?"

"Three weeks. If I'm going to sign papers, I need to do so soon. Ms. Wright said a midwife could deliver here, and the couple would want to pick up their child right after the birth. They'd even pay the midwife and give me five thousand dollars to help until I got on my feet."

I smelled fraud, but I needed more information. "Is this an opportunity for other birth mothers here?"

"I don't know. Ms. Wright asked me to keep our conversations private. Some of the others might view my decision to give up my baby as wrong, and there was no point in upsetting any of them."

"Where do the potential parents live?"

"I assume here in the Houston area."

How many others had experienced Sara's situation and been duped? "I will pray for the right decision. Why a midwife?"

"Ms. Wright suggested it when we talked about giving up my baby. She said hospitals have lots of paperwork for the birth mother and adoptive parents to complete, and as long as I was healthy, this made the most sense."

"Understandable. Would you feel safer in a hospital environment?"

"If the baby or my health became a problem, a vehicle would escort me to the hospital. It's free."

Clyde Washington had transported a few women to the clinic for appointments, and they didn't return to the van. Had any of them been drawn into a scam? Dare I show her a few pics on my phone?

"Sara, friends of mine got mixed up in an illegal adoption scam."

"How awful."

"She and her husband gave an attorney thousands of dollars to arrange for a private adoption. Then he disappeared, taking their money, and the so-called pregnant woman faked her baby bump."

Sara shuddered. "Ms. Wright told us about a Vietnamese woman who had her baby stolen. Scared us all."

"What would we do without Ms. Wright? My guess is she'd strangle anyone who tried to hurt her birth mothers. Anyway, the family is a friend of mine, and they gave me photos of a few people who might be involved. Do you have time to see if they've been lurking at the clinic?"

"Sure."

I pulled up Emily Lock. Nothing.

Norman Peilman. Nothing.

Peter Florakis. Nothing.

Harvey Sinclair.

Sara studied his pic. "I think I've seen him at the clinic. Not a doctor or anything, just in the waiting room while his wife had an appointment."

"Did you talk to him?"

"Briefly. He said I reminded him of his niece. He wanted to snap my picture to show her, but I refused."

"Smart move," I said. We were getting closer.

The door opened and Ms. Wright stepped in. "I hate to interrupt, but, Risa, there's a call for you in my office."

63

While I wanted to talk to Sara more about the prospective parents for her unborn baby, I bid her goodbye and joined Ms. Wright in the hall. We walked the hallway to her office.

"She's a lovely young woman," I said.

"I agree. She doesn't know it, but her baby's a girl. The adoptive couple is thrilled."

Caution, Risa. "She told me she hadn't decided to give her baby up yet."

The woman opened her door and gestured for me to enter. "Sara has no choice in the matter." She closed the door and locked it behind her.

"Why did you lock the door?"

"Habit, I guess. Often I have work that needs my attention without someone walking in."

"I see. What do you mean Sara doesn't have a choice? By law, she can change her mind after the baby's placed in a home. I admit the reversal would be heartbreaking for the adoptive parents but reality."

"The decision is out of her hands. Have a seat, Risa." Ms. Wright sat behind her desk, and I eased onto a chair opposite her.

"You said I had a call."

"No. I just needed an excuse to free you from Sara. She's quite the talker."

"Why doesn't Sara have a choice?"

She opened a drawer, pulled out a pocket pistol, a Sig P365, and took aim at me. "You see, none of the birth mothers have a choice if I want their baby."

"That's illegal."

"Keep your hands on the side of the chair. I don't need you grabbing your phone."

My phone recorded our conversation, and it lay next to my Glock. But my phone didn't transmit to Gage. "I don't understand. What is going on?"

My phone buzzed with a text.

"Hand me your purse." I lifted it into her hands, and she pulled out my Glock, then set it inside a drawer. She removed my phone and read the text. Laughing, she texted. "It's from Gage, and I'm telling him you are doing great."

"Thanks a lot."

She sneered, and an ugly side of Anna Wright met me. "I learned a long time ago to protect my assets by planting listening devices in my office. Then I got a little wiser and planted them in each girl's room, kitchen, dining, library, game area, and even the small chapel. It's amazing what I've heard through the years."

I refused to show my frazzled nerves. "I imagine the information has paid off in rich benefits."

"Just like this afternoon." She texted someone with one eye on me. "We're about to have company. He's excited to meet you face-to-face."

"Peter Florakis?"

"Smart girl. But we'll wait and see."

"Actually you're the one who's brilliant. This is a sizable operation. Selling babies all over the country to the highest bidder takes good connections." Would Ms. Wright brag?

"And no one's shut us down." She grinned. "Others have tried, which is why I cooperated with the FBI and fingered Zonner. The doctor had abused our relationship, so nailing him labeled me a model citizen."

"The FBI will figure this out. The doctor sitting in prison holds a get-out-of-jail-free card. He's ready to talk."

Wright laughed. "Wrong. He has an ex-wife and sons who are alive because of my generosity. He won't jeopardize their safety. On the other hand, Suzi Phan confided in me about the plan to report the kidnapping to the police."

I shrugged. "Why did you offer to help find Hai and Suzi when you were responsible for abducting the baby? That was a huge risk."

"You're such an idiot. Don't you get it? My heartfelt compassion for their plight removed me from the suspect list. Although I didn't expect the agents to get to the restaurant early. It all worked to my best interest."

"Not hardly. I figured it out. So did Luke."

"And where is he now? But you're just a teacher, one who is short to live on this earth. Too bad you didn't follow directions. Had to tell Agent Patterson, didn't you? Couldn't resist him? I admit, he's hot, but not worth losing your head." She laughed, the sneering unfamiliar sound from a woman who lived two lives . . . two personalities. I'd tell her she was a pathetic simulacrum of a human being, but she wouldn't know the meaning. Had this monster before me given the orders to kill Luke? Had she been there?

Ms. Wright's phone buzzed. "Your escort is here. He must have been close by. Aren't you excited?"

I could hold my own. Now to find out who worked with her. "Hard to wear a party hat when someone is threatening you."

"I want you to stand and walk with me out the front door. Any attempt to run or scream, and I start firing." She waved the pocket pistol at me.

"How do you plan to get away with this?"

"I always have an out."

With her history, she also had a plan. I'd go along until I didn't. An image of Luke's head entered my mind. He had skills too. A stab of fear jabbed at my heart. I wasn't invincible, and until this moment I'd never called myself a fool.

Wright reached for the doorknob and wrapped a scarf around her right hand holding the pistol. "Ready?"

She ushered our way into the reception area. One of the birth moms sat at the desk. "I'm walking Risa out to meet a friend," Wright said. "I've been wanting to introduce them." She shrugged. "I'm playing matchmaker."

It took all my strength not to level Wright and pin her hands behind her back. But those actions had selfishness written all over them when someone might get hurt, and the killer outside would drive away. I nodded at the birth mom and stepped ahead to find the answers behind the murders and baby ring.

A silver BMW parked near the door with the motor running. Wright hooked arms with me, and we ventured out into the chilly air. I wrestled with disarming her, but I needed the identity of the driver.

The power window on the driver's side slowly revealed a man—Peter Florakis. No disguise. His arrogance might be the nemesis to bring him down.

"Hi, Risa." He pointed to a gun in his lap. "Give Anna a hug, and she'll walk you around to the passenger side."

"If I refuse?"

He picked up his phone in the console. "I'm a Boy Scout. Always prepared. A bomb is rigged for the facility behind—"

"Why am I just now hearing this?" Wright said.

"Anna, we always have a backup plan. All I need to do is press a button, and it goes up in flames. How sad for all those birth mothers. But business is business."

No reason to question his sincerity. I gave Anna the required hug, and she jammed the scarf-covered Sig into my ribs. We walked to the passenger side, where she opened the door.

"Buckle up," Florakis said. "You're in for a ride."

64

I left Risa's apartment in a foul mood. Why had I let her take a foolish risk? My confession of love had affected my brains yet again. As soon as this case was officially stamped closed, she and I needed to establish some ground rules. Now I understood the bureau's frowning on fraternization.

Risa Jacobs rode a daredevil wind, and when she had her mind set, nothing stopped her. To make matters worse, she'd left in her indestructible mode. I loved her but she scared me.

I'd drive to the maternity home, but if she'd discovered information about Anna Wright, my presence might mess it up. Risa and I hadn't paid a visit to the home together, and for all practical purposes, she'd resigned from the FBI. Why worry when she'd responded to my text?

Against my better judgment, I drove to the office to make a few calls and follow up on a hunch.

Seated in my cubicle with nothing but quiet, I pulled up photos of Peter Florakis, Emily Lock, Norman Peilman, and Harvey Sinclair . . . the latter might not be his real name.

The Houston Healing and Hope Maternity Care's website showed no photos of Anna Wright, a precaution on her part due to the sensitive nature of her line of work. Many of the birth mothers came from abusive relationships, and the men in those women's lives were out to seek revenge. I searched online until I found a pic on Mercy Point Church's website taken at a fundraiser. From the sideways and somewhat-distorted view, I spotted Ms. Wright. I doubted the woman knew the pic had been taken.

I copied the image and ran it through software with the four known criminals. While it did its magic, I scanned through CARD's investigation as well as other FBI cases for a link to Anna Wright. I saw where she'd fit a few missing or escaped baby ring cases. But the vague connections didn't warrant questioning.

I returned to my original search and drew in a breath. A photo of Peter Florakis and Anna Wright together in a New York restaurant stared back at me. Taken about ten years ago, she appeared about forty pounds lighter and wore a dress that left nothing to the imagination. The caption read "Peter Florakis and Anna Wright announce their engagement."

Other matches connected Wright with Norman Peilman in New York. The ring must have originated there and either expanded or moved to Houston. I'd seen enough to bring her in.

Please keep Risa safe, God. I can't do this without You. I couldn't lose her, and now she faced a killer.

I grabbed my keys and phoned the SAC while racing to my car. Then I'd phone Risa and get her out of there. We needed backup now.

65

RISA

Florakis tuned his car's radio to Rossini's "William Tell Overture" and pulled onto the street. With what I knew of his dark and evil mind, the overture must inspire him. He locked my door.

"Where are we going?" I said.

"East to a special spot where we'll meet up with friends." He flashed his walnut-colored eyes my direction. He enjoyed himself, and that meant torture. From his slight frame, I saw how he could pass for a woman. From the corner of my eye, I sized up his gun in his left hand, making it harder for me to grab.

As though reading my mind, he pointed the firearm in my direction. "You obviously don't trust me. You have a reputation, which makes our rendezvous entertaining."

"I'm so glad for you. Why did you kill Agent Reardon?"

"He got in my way like your brother." He laughed. "That was your fault."

I refused to take the blame for Trenton's death. "You drove the car, not me." I mustered courage. "I asked about Luke Reardon."

He swore. "The man had a nosy streak. Discovered more than I permitted for a man to continue breathing. Took me a little while to detail his demise, but I was pleased with the results."

"Why target Jack in the hospital? You and Lock both failed."

He sneered. "He's next. The man's part cat, but third time's a charm. Reardon said he'd told Bradford about the whole operation, and I'm taking Bradford's breathing personal."

His word choice told me the man had no conscience. Dangerous. "You're the kingpin behind the baby ring?"

"I wish. I take orders and use my own creativity to carry them out."

"Anna Wright?"

"That—? She's like a cheap battery, replaceable."

"What about Emily Lock, Harvey Sinclair, and Norman Peilman?"

He tapped his firearm on the steering wheel. "You FBI types have this curiosity gene."

"I've been told that before."

"Emily is smart, hot, and teaches the master class on disguises and altering handwriting. Harvey gambles but makes sure the odds are always on his side. Norman should have taken driving lessons."

"Who holds the keys?"

He shrugged. "Not my call."

"You don't know?"

Florakis pulled to a stop at a red light. If not for the locked door, I'd fight my way out. I studied his phone in the console. No reason for me to doubt he'd trigger a bomb at the maternity home.

He turned to me. "Rule number one in this organization is ignorance for who's at the top. It pays dividends on a life insurance policy."

"You're saying no one knows who's calling the shots? You keep your life because there's no threat of a double cross?"

"And we all make a lot of money."

A few pieces slid into place. "Genius. Your boss could be anywhere in the world and have more operations than a single baby ring."

He smiled. "Too bad you're headed for elimination. You and I would get along just fine. Start our own operation."

"And just what would we do?"

"Start small and build ourselves up."

"You'll never know if I'm dead. We could make a ton of money."

I needed to stall him, find a way to get inside his head.

He gave me a pout. "Won't ever find out, will we?"

"Just where are we going?"

"Sweetheart, you just asked me that. But I'll fill in the blanks in your pretty little head. We are meeting at Lake Houston for a boat ride. A deserted area during the holidays. While everyone is doing their Christmas joy thing, I'll celebrate with my own plans. I'm an expert with torture methods. King, as a matter of fact."

He planned to end my life slowly and dump what was left in Lake Houston in anticipation of a gator feasting on my remains. I should have fought Wright at the maternity home, but the idea of one more person giving her life for me stopped my move. Those precious birth mothers and their babies deserved a chance to live. Another thought focused on any security cams picking up my abduction. I willingly got into Florakis's car. I didn't have time to analyze it all.

I saw the West Lake Houston Parkway bridge in the distance, and I had an idea where he planned to take me—the same place where Luke's body and car had been found. This could be the day I met Jesus, and unforgiveness for the killer beside me would go to my death. I refused to meet Jesus without doing all He'd asked of me.

I forgive Peter Florakis and anyone else I've failed to show the same forgiveness You have given me.

Keeping my eyes on the road, my mind raced to taking a chance. My wild streak might kill us, but I'd rather die fighting than face Florakis's evil plans.

The car traveled onto the bridge, and I reached deep for courage. Three-quarters of the way across, I released my seat belt. I swung my right fist into his left hand while slamming my left onto his nose.

The gun fired through the passenger-side window. I grabbed his phone from the console and tossed it into the back seat, praying it didn't set off a bomb. I scuffled with him for the firearm.

He fought hard to gain control and the car. But I had determination going for me—and a whole lot of power behind prayer.

He squeezed the trigger again, and the bullet whistled past my right shoulder, taking a little real estate with it. The sting forced more adrenaline into my body.

Florakis pressed the gas pedal, and we headed to the other side of the bridge. Oncoming cars honked and sped around us. A small grove of trees on the left side held my attention. I'd take the chance of hitting them without my seat belt fastened.

We sped across the bridge, and I yanked the steering wheel left, sliding into the embankment, heading to the farthest tree. It could stop us with the impact on the passenger side. Our speed scared me. I calculated the second we'd hit and used all my strength to bash Florakis's head onto the steering wheel.

The impact exploded the airbags, cushioning the crash and jamming the right side of the car into the tree. Limbs and branches scraped the right side of the BMW. My chest ached, and my lungs burned from the chemical release. I caught my breath, noting warmth flowing from my nose. I swiped at the blood with my sweater sleeve, hoping my nose wasn't broken. But it hurt.

Florakis moaned, his head resting against the steering wheel. I yanked the gun from his grasp and pressed the barrel against his temple while opening the driver's-side door. "Get out."

He appeared to be in a semiconscious state.

I unfastened his seat belt and pushed him onto the ground. Then I crawled out over his body.

He reached for my leg, and I shook it off. "Don't even try. Nothing I'd like better than to blow a hole through your head."

Two cars had stopped. Plopping onto the grass, I kept the gun aimed at Florakis.

A middle-aged man in a suit approached. "Ma'am, I've called 911."

I peered up at him, and he backed up at the sight of my gun. "I'm FBI Special Agent Risa Jacobs."

"You're bleeding."

"But I'm alive." I took a breath. "Would you check for a phone in the back seat? It's a trigger for a bomb."

The man held up his palms. "No thanks. I'll let a police officer handle it."

The faint sound of a police car met my ears. More like music.

66

GAGE

I pulled into Houston Healing and Hope alongside three HPD cruisers and two FBI vehicles. Beneath the stately oak shading the curved driveway sat Risa's car. I longed to have overreacted, played like a fool, but my gut said otherwise.

Drawing my Glock, I rushed to the front door and met Wright in the receptionist area.

"What's going on?" Her eyes widened when she saw my firearm.

"Where's Risa Jacobs?"

"I have no idea." Wright wrung her hands, and I didn't swallow her ignorance.

"Her car is here, so where is she?"

"Agent Patterson, she left in a silver BMW."

"With whom?"

"I have no idea. She finished talking to my girls, but when she walked to her car, a man pulled in. They talked, and she got into the car with him."

"Where did they go?"

"I have no idea."

Police officers entered behind me. "Search every inch of the home," I said, "beginning with Ms. Wright's office."

She stiffened. "I demand to know why these officers are here."

"We have questions about evidence linking you to Peter Florakis, who is wanted for murder, and Norman Peilman, a known felon. Both men are connected to a baby ring."

She touched her throat with one hand and slid her other hand into her pant pocket.

"Lift your hands," I said.

The two FBI agents walked in behind me. "Gage, there's nothing suspicious outside," the female agent said.

"I think Ms. Wright may have a weapon in her right pocket. Would you check for me?"

The agent retrieved a pocket pistol.

"Do you have a license to carry this?" I said.

"The home can be a dangerous environment."

"That's not what I asked. Are you ready to tell us the whereabouts of Agent Jacobs?"

"I thought she'd retired."

"She's been working undercover."

A police officer walked into the area carrying Risa's black purse. "Agent Patterson, I found this under the desk."

"Is her phone and firearm there?"

The officer ferreted through the purse. "Her phone but not a gun."

"Where is her Glock?" I said.

"How would I know? She left her purse here, and I placed it under my desk to keep it safe."

"You are under arrest for the disappearance and possible assault of a federal agent."

The officer disappeared into her office and returned with a Glock. "I found this in a drawer."

"I can explain." Wright's flat tone showed she didn't let the worst of scenarios rattle her.

"Begin by telling me the real story about Agent Jacobs."

"I told you already."

"No, I don't think so. Ms. Wright, I'd like to see your security cam for the front of the building."

"Do you have a warrant?"

I smiled, cuffed her, and recited her rights.

"There's nothing on the video," she said. "It's broken." She told me where to find the camera, and I left her with a police officer. The camera had been disconnected from the power source. How convenient.

The women housed at the home showed a mix of fear and curiosity. The female agent asked if they'd seen Risa today. Only a red-headed young woman by the name of Sara had spoken to her. Sara recapped Risa's conversation and Wright's interruption. Nothing said to incriminate anyone.

The SAC phoned me less than five minutes later. "Evacuate the maternity home immediately. There's a bomb threat. Call me back when everyone is out. Bomb squad on the way."

FBI agents and the police officers ushered the women and staff from the building amid questions, tears, and those who wanted to gather personal items from their rooms. Once everyone stood three hundred feet back from the building, the bomb squad arrived to check for a potential explosive device.

I called back SAC Dunkin and reported in. "Everyone's out and the bomb squad is inside."

"Risa and Florakis have been located at the West Lake Houston Parkway bridge," the SAC said. "An accident. Risa said Florakis claimed to have planted a bomb inside the maternity home, triggered by his phone. The phone's in police custody."

"Is she okay?"

"Scraped up and a bullet grazed her shoulder. Two ambulances are en route to Memorial Hermann Northeast Hospital with Risa and Florakis. About a twenty-five-minute drive from the crash site."

"What happened?" My pulse sped into overdrive at the mental image.

"I'll just say it was one of her driving stunts. She'll fill you in."

I inwardly sighed relief. "Is Florakis alive?"

"He's banged up and under arrest. Refuses to talk."

"I have Anna Wright in custody."

"Hold on, Gage. Call coming in about Florakis's phone."

How badly had Risa been hurt? Had the SAC told the truth? I waited what seemed like much too long until SAC Dunkin returned. "HPD has removed the phone's trigger."

That didn't mean the bomb wouldn't detonate. "I'll get back once the search here is completed."

Forty long minutes later, the bomb squad located the explosive in Wright's office and defused the bomb with ten minutes to spare. Florakis had already triggered the activation before leaving the home with Risa.

Twenty more minutes passed before I could assure the residents and staff that it was safe to return. Inside the home, one of the bomb squad officers approached me. "We've found bugs in the office and one of the bedrooms. My guess the whole place is filled with them."

I thanked the officer and relayed the update to the SAC.

"Good work." He gave me the hospital's number.

I thanked him. Even so, I wanted to see Risa's injuries for myself. Then we'd strategize our questions for those in custody. "Once I finish here, I'll check on Risa."

"Give me a report once you're there. If she's worse than she claims, make sure they keep her."

"Yes, sir." I called Myra Cummings and briefly explained the evacuation. "Can you come in to be with these women?"

"I'm on my way, Agent Patterson. Don't tell them the truth just yet. None of those birth mothers need to go into premature labor. I'll explain to them what's happened when I get there."

"Okay. I'll ensure a couple of agents and an HPD officer are here to take statements."

I agreed and made my way back to a meeting room where the female agent and an HPD officer worked at calming the women.

I secured their attention. "Ladies, thank you for your cooperation. HPD and Houston FBI thank you for your patience. Myra Cummings will be here shortly, and you can pose your questions then."

"Has Ms. Wright been arrested?" a young woman said.

"You'll be told more when Mrs. Cummings arrives."

Gasps filled the room, and a few women broke into sobs.

"I'm sorry, ladies. I understand she's a friend and a mother figure to many of you."

I walked out to the entrance and noted the Christmas tree. Gifts didn't have to come wrapped in sparkling paper and bows. Sometimes they came disguised after a difficult trial. *Thank You.*

My worst fear had been losing Risa. It almost happened.

67

I called Memorial Hermann Northeast ER to check on Risa. A nurse said she was conscious and being treated. A three-car pileup had placed Risa's treatment after those hurt in that accident. My mind raced. Couldn't get to her fast enough. Why did the nurse say "conscious"? Had she been hurt worse than a grazed shoulder? Stitches? Internal injuries? Broken bones?

I zipped into an ER parking space and raced to the registration desk. The reality of Risa badly injured hit me like a collapsing stone wall.

After I flipped out my FBI creds, a nurse led me to the area where a doctor examined Risa. I stepped through the blue curtain quietly while my insides tossed with more turmoil than a roller coaster. The doctor glanced at me.

"I'm FBI Special Agent Gage Patterson. The patient is my partner."

He nodded and resumed stitching Risa's shoulder. The urge to call her name and hear her speak nearly won over. But I was a professional . . . yeah, a professional who had a lot of personal stakes with his patient.

I waited with the patience of a two-year-old.

The doctor finished. "Miss Jacobs, you have a concussion, and I want to keep you overnight for testing and observation."

"I'm fine."

"I want to ensure there's not a problem."

"Risa." I stepped opposite the doctor at her bedside. Her face had blue and purple where no makeup would cover, and her left eye had nearly swollen shut. An IV dripped into her good arm. "The SAC asked me to make sure you followed the doctor's orders."

She scowled. "I'm in good shape."

"No, you're not. I'll stay with you."

Her face softened slightly. Then the stubbornness that I'd grown to love flashed across her green eyes. "I don't have anything with me."

"Give me a list, and I'll make a store run."

"How can you refuse a deal like that?" the doctor said, a young guy, and I wasn't so sure I liked the way he eyed Risa.

She closed her eyes. "I hurt too badly to argue."

"Good for you."

She winced.

"Miss Jacobs, I'm prescribing pain medication," the doctor said. "Your body has been tossed around like a beach ball. Consider yourself lucky to have survived the car accident."

I shook my head. "Risa, did you cause the accident to stop Florakis?"

Her mouth curved upward. "Yes. And I'm sure he feels worse than I do. He admitted to hitting Trenton, Luke's murder, and a few other crimes."

The doctor said, "I saw he'd been treated and released to FBI custody."

The doctor and a nurse left the room. She'd be transported to a room shortly. I kissed her lightly, then pulled up a chair to her bedside. "Thank God you're alive."

"Your coloring matches the sheets."

"Probably got my first gray hairs."

She chuckled, but the muscles around her eyes revealed her pain. "What's the status with Anna Wright?"

"In custody. HPD and agents are doing a sweep. Would you believe those two were once engaged?" She started to say something but I stopped her. "Don't talk, honey. I'll tell you what I know. Here are the happenings on my end . . ."

"Thanks. I had so many questions and no answers. Gage, we have Trenton's and Luke's killer."

"Yes, we do. The worst part is over."

★　★　★

While Risa slept, I made a run to Walgreens and Macy's not far from the hospital. She'd given me her size so I could pick up a few things for her, including a toothbrush, toothpaste, deodorant, and pajamas that covered everything.

When I returned, Risa had been transferred to a private room. She roused from sleep the moment I entered the room. "Did you buy out the stores?"

I set the bags on a small sofa. "Not exactly. I have receipts for everything, and a gal at Macy's helped me."

She gave me one of her million-dollar smiles. "Christmas came early."

"It arrived when Anna Wright and Peter Florakis were cuffed."

"For sure. Gage, can I have one or two of your kisses?"

"As many as I want or you want?"

"It's the same number."

I leaned over. How I treasured this woman. Her swollen face caused me to give her a gentle kiss. "I love you. Those are the words I'm supposed to tell you every day. When your face doesn't look like a war zone, I'll collect on a few dozen more."

"Thank you, and I love you too." Her weak smile told me she needed lots of rest. "I have something serious to say." No humor shone from her green eyes.

"I'm listening, honey."

"Just before the accident with Peter Florakis, I forgave him for killing Trenton, Luke, and everything else he's done. The idea of harboring hate for a man so evil made no sense when I believe in a God who will one day make everything right."

I blinked back a touch of wetness . . . me, the tough agent. "I don't deserve you."

"That's how I feel about you."

"One day I'll tell our kids about their brave mother."

"I'd like that. Two of them?"

"Five." I held back a grin.

"Three?"

"Deal." I kissed her again.

"Are you going to show me what you bought?"

"I will if you feel up to telling me about your ordeal with Florakis."

"I'll give you all the details, then you can show me what's inside the bags. I arrived at the maternity home . . ."

"You could have been killed," I said a few minutes later. "But after the semitruck incident, I'm not surprised."

"Good. Honestly, Gage, you don't need to babysit me. Florakis needs an interview and maybe Wright might have more to say too."

"Let them sweat it out until tomorrow."

"Then I'll join you." Her eyes grew heavy. "Now let me see what you brought me before I go to sleep again. By any chance did you pick up a pair of pajamas?"

"All Macy's had were gowns that opened in the back."

"I love you."

Those were the three best words in the English language. While she rummaged through the bags, and she was either pleased or putting on a good front, I considered the likelihood of the two in custody lawyering up.

68

RISA

The doctor released me at ten on Sunday morning with orders to rest and a prescription for pain meds, which I had no intention of taking—until time to sleep. Unfortunately, I felt worse today than last night. Wright and Florakis would get a good chuckle at my poor face, but I'd have the last laugh.

True to his word, Gage stayed with me at the hospital and slept on the pitiful sofa, a little short for his long legs. I slept like a baby, thanks to the doctor, but Gage . . . not so much.

"We're going straight to the office, right?" I said to Gage.

He frowned. "Do you plan to scare the truth out of Wright and Florakis?"

I lifted my chin, causing every muscle in my face to explode. "I'll rest when I'm home and tomorrow. Deal? Please?"

"If you weren't so bruised and swollen, I'd say no."

"Thank you, sweet man."

"Is this how our lives will be from now on?"

I slid him a painful grin. "Maybe. Are you up to it?"

"Challenges are a good thing. I believe my partner has her mojo back. The stress of the past several months has lifted."

"I'm sure I'll still have my issues with grief." I started to reach

across the seat to take his hand, but it hurt. "Some things take time."
I remembered Mom and Dad in Charleston. "Do you mind if I use
your phone to call my parents? I didn't want to alarm them last night
by using the hospital phone and them not recognizing the number."

"Go for it." He picked up his cell from the console and handed
it to me.

I pressed in Dad's regular phone number.

"Gage?" he said.

"Nope. Risa. I have fabulous news. We have those in custody who
are responsible for Trenton's death and the threats."

I heard Dad holler at Mom with the news. We talked for a few
minutes, and I didn't tell them about my wounds. We decided to
celebrate Christmas on New Year's Eve.

At the end of the call, I remembered what the doctor had said
yesterday about feeling worse today. Yet the idea of putting this horrible crime to rest, ending the baby ring, and the strong possibility of
finding Harvey Sinclair and Emily Lock hit the incredibly satisfying
level. If we could get the two in custody to talk.

✯   ✯   ✯

Gage and I interviewed Anna Wright first. I gave her credit for keeping her composure. She'd requested a lawyer, and he'd consult with
her tomorrow. Spending Sunday with a client wasn't on his agenda.
A point for our side if she chose to provide a little information. Now,
sitting across the table from us, she placed her cuffed hands on the
table and smirked as though she had a delicious secret. Gage showed
the pics he'd found online of her with Florakis and Peilman.

"That's not me," she said. "Must be someone else."

"Strange," Gage said, "we have proof of you living in New York
when this was taken, and our techs have identified you as the woman
with Florakis and Peilman. Doesn't appear you two tied the knot."

"Slime." She hesitated. "Florakis planted the bomb in Mercury's
Jaguar."

"Thank you, but it doesn't exonerate you from your charges."

"My attorney will have me out of here in the morning."

"We'll see what the judge says. How do you explain holding Agent Jacobs at gunpoint?"

Wright shrugged. "She misunderstood our conversation." She added syrup to her tone. "Risa, did someone work you over?"

"You should see *him*," I said.

"I doubt it."

I eyed the woman who'd made money stealing and buying babies. "We could talk to the judge if you cooperate and give us the name of your boss."

"No one knows who he or she is. Not another word until I talk to my lawyer. We are finished here." The arrogance in the woman tried my patience. Didn't help that Florakis had made the same claim.

"How do we find Emily Lock?"

"Never met her."

"She'd been a resident at the maternity home."

Wright shook her head.

"What about Harvey Sinclair?" I said.

"Who is Harvey Sinclair? Can't help you there either."

Wright was escorted back to the federal detention center, and thirty minutes later Florakis sat before us. His left wrist matched his splinted broken nose.

Gage read the numerous charges, which read like a grocery list. "How do you plead, Mr. Florakis?"

"Not guilty. My attorney will handle this tomorrow."

I'd need Dr. Looney to sign me up for anger management classes after today. "How do you explain my abduction yesterday at Houston Healing and Hope Maternity Care?"

"You wanted to go for a ride in my car, and then you tried to kill us. You're crazy, woman."

"You admitted to the murders of Trenton Jacobs and Luke Reardon."

"I have no idea who those men are."

"Anna Wright nailed you as the kingpin of the baby ring and a killer. She said you picked out the birth mother, set her up, and walked away with a pocket full of cash. She claimed you ordered the hit on me in July, the murders of Suzi and Hai Phan, the attack on

Special Agent Jack Bradford, and the death of Special Agent Luke Reardon."

"She didn't name me, or she'd be a dead woman."

"You're sending out kill contracts from behind bars?" I said.

"The boss will handle it."

"Name?"

"No one knows. Say, what about my BMW? Do I get my car back after posting bail tomorrow?"

"Mr. Florakis, we can share your charges with your attorney. Your car is impounded, and I doubt if it's drivable. I can guarantee there will be no bail."

Florakis spit across the table. "You have no idea who you're talking to."

"We'll see what a judge says. By the way, we've confiscated several bugs at the maternity home and recordings of you and Anna Wright arranging for birth mothers to give up their babies. Made for great listening."

"Won't be admissible in court when my attorney is finished with you."

69

Gage and I decided my parents needed a Christmas tree before they arrived home on New Year's Eve for our celebration. Gage had invited me to spend Christmas with his family, and the prospect thrilled me, since I'd never met them before. But tonight, December 23, we played holiday tunes, drank hot chocolate, and decorated a freshly cut, nine-foot pine tree. I loved the smell, but poor Gage rubbed his eyes.

We'd dragged the boxes down from the attic and fortunately only had to replace two fuses in the strings of white lights. Mom had eclectic taste when it came to ornaments, which meant boxes of all the homemade and purchased ones that Trenton and I had presented our parents over the years. She also liked crosses and snowmen. If I lived to be a hundred, I'd never understand the combination, but they clung to the branches of the traditional Jacobs tree.

Gage had brought mistletoe, and we stole more than our fair share of kisses and whispers of "I love you." We sang along to the music and *attempted* to harmonize. At completion, we stood back and admired the glittering magic.

What a relief to have the baby-ring case nearly behind us. More work needed to be done to discover the operation's kingpin and locate Emily Lock and Harvey Sinclair. But Peter Florakis, Trenton's and

Luke's killer, sat behind bars, and Anna Wright wouldn't ever convince a birth mother to give up her child again.

I missed Trenton just like in past years. Yet this Christmas I knew where he spent the most important birthday in the universe.

"Here's an ornament we missed," Gage said, interrupting my thoughts.

I didn't recognize the box. "This must be a new one."

"It is. Fits you perfectly."

I took a small box from his outstretched hand and turned it to see the image of the contents. I laughed. "A red race car."

"I bet you'll find the best spot to dangle it."

I opened it and set the race car free from the packing.

I gasped.

A diamond ring hung from the steering wheel. The tree lights picked up the ring's sparkle. "Oh, my goodness." My gaze flew to his smiling face. "Is this what I think it is?"

"Not yet." He bent to one knee and took my hand. "Risa Maura Jacobs, I've loved you since I first saw you. Will you marry me?"

I giggled.

I cried.

I bent in front of him and wrapped my arms around his neck. "Yes! I'll love you forever."

He kissed me lightly, then deeper until we toppled onto the floor.

"Merry Christmas," he whispered. "You are the perfect gift."

70

RISA

SAC Dunkin had scheduled a meeting with Gage and me. My stomach fluttered almost as much as the evening Gage told me of his love. The SAC knew of our upcoming wedding, and he'd congratulated us. We shared with him that we were both willing to transfer to different divisions. Nothing else had been said. We understood our FBI partnership would be sacrificed for our life together. Worth it all. I'd frightened Gage with my wild ways, and if he planned to take on the Risa package, I needed to curb my ways.

I checked off all the requirements of a hopeless romantic. A correct assessment.

Gage and I remained committed to violent crimes against children. I'd return to teaching before I stood by and watched him leave a career he loved. For that matter, I'd direct my passion for helping children to social work.

Whatever the SAC determined, I'd accept. Gage's happiness exceeded mine without hesitation. One thing was for sure—our children, and we wanted several, would have both of us nurturing them.

Anna Wright faced life for her charges, and Peter Florakis received the death penalty. They both refused to provide any details or names of who oversaw the operation. As Wright and Florakis had stated, perhaps no one knew who called the shots. Overseas authorities pointed to the Russian Bratva as responsible for the baby ring. Their operation mirrored a cell structure like what I'd considered to keep the kingpin's identity safe. According to the authorities, the Russian Bratva cut their losses when those within their organization were caught and moved on to another location. The worldwide investigation would continue until the guilty ones faced arrest.

Duong Tuan and Bui Vinh were sentenced to life without parole for cooperating. They revealed a few things about Anna Wright that helped our case. Unfortunately, Hai's baby remained missing. Harvey Sinclair and Emma Lock remained at large.

Myra Cummings took over the directorship of Houston Healing and Hope Maternity Care. My church partnered with her with more financial support. Sara chose to keep her baby girl and had kept in touch.

The Mercury family and Carson Lowell chose WITSEC and new identities out of state. I'd miss Carson, and I believed he'd be successful at whatever he chose to do with his life.

I glanced at my watch. If I didn't take the elevator to the SAC's office, I'd be late. Gage met me at the elevator door and pressed the Up arrow for us. He had his hands in his pant pockets.

"What is this about?" I said.

"We've been demoted to janitor duty." He grinned. "But if we cleaned together, that would be okay."

I laughed. "Oh, why not."

"Great news. Remember Alex and Nanette Wade from Des Moines?"

My eyes widened with the name recognition.

"They're pregnant."

"What an amazing blessing."

He chuckled. "The name will be Risa if it's a girl and Gage if it's a boy."

"We'll need to share that with Dr. Looney at our appointment this week."

The elevator door opened. When the door closed, he turned to me. "A kiss is available upon request."

I wrapped my arms around his neck and touched my lips to his. "Oops. I forgot to make a request."

"You never liked procedure. After this meeting, will we still be like we are now?"

"Not at all. I'll demand two kisses on the way down."

Down the hallway, I stepped into the SAC's office with Gage behind me. SAC Dunkin greeted us and pointed to chairs in front of his desk. "How are the wedding plans?"

"We're about done," Gage said. "We're searching for a house. Mine's too small."

The SAC leaned back in his chair. A good sign. "I have news that affects both of you in your current positions." He paused. "You two have been extremely valuable to the violent crimes against children division. No doubt or question there. You were successful in arresting Anna Wright and shutting down her buying and selling of babies. While she refuses to give us the name of the kingpin, the FBI and all the other agencies working to stop these crimes against children aren't giving up."

He stared at both of us. "ASAC Kendall is retiring, leaving an opening here. Gage, we'd like to offer you the ASAC, but we know you two need to discuss it." He leveled his gaze at me. "Risa, Jack Bradford is retiring too due to his health. Are you willing to partner with another agent? I assume also a matter for you and Gage to discuss. I expect you'll want to think about what I've said for a few days."

I stole a glimpse at Gage, and he took my hand and winked. What a perfect solution. Gage had leadership stamped all over him, and I preferred working in the field.

"Sir," I began, "I'm sure we can give you an answer now. Gage, am I reading you right?"

"Are you sure?"

"Yes. It's a win-win deal."

Gage gave the SAC his attention. "I'm honored to be considered the ASAC."

"And I'm honored to work with whoever you assign," I said.

SAC Dunkin chuckled. "You and Gage will continue to be an asset to the Houston FBI. Maybe marriage will lower the risks you two have taken. But I doubt it. I pity whoever crosses your paths."

Gage took my hand. "We're a formidable team, and we intend to keep it that way for a lot of years."

"At least a hundred." Risa grinned. "We'll need that long to parent those five kids."

DISCUSSION QUESTIONS

1. Have you ever lost someone very close to you? What emotions and behaviors did you experience? What helped you deal with your grief?

2. What actions show Risa's grief? What is the best way to walk through a tragedy?

3. Gage wanted to help Risa in every way possible. Do you think he was ready to give up?

4. Are you adopted or know someone who is adopted? How do you or that person deal with family history? How important is sharing or learning about your birth family's culture or country of origin? How have you gone about that process?

5. Carson suffered with confusion and doubt regarding his relationship with his stepdad. How would you have suggested he deal with what he experienced?

6. Ethan Mercury believed he had no choice but to comply with the blackmailers who threatened his family. What would you have done in the same situation?

7. Are you a proponent of counseling in times of tragedy, or do you think a Christian should rely only on God for healing?

8. Risa and Gage hid their feelings for each other not only to protect themselves but others. How do you feel about a man and a woman working together as partners in any profession with a committed love relationship?

A NOTE FROM THE AUTHOR

Dear reader,

I hope you enjoyed Risa and Gage's story. They believed children are our most treasured gifts and must be protected at all costs. Those who buy and sell children look at the innocent as a commodity. Sad, appalling, and yet true. Risa and Gage, just like all those who advocate for children, were committed to stopping those who abuse children.

Adoption scams are real. If you are seeking to adopt, enlist the proper legal channels and refuse any shortcuts. The child, no matter the age, is worth your diligence and love.

Three of my four sons are adopted, and in the days and weeks following their placement, I feared their birth mothers might change their minds. Sons born of my heart and not of my womb. On July 29, 2021, my husband and I lost one of our adopted sons in a pedestrian accident. In the hours and days following his death, I journaled the intense despair and sorrow. Those emotions became a part of Risa's grief too. If you are going through a loss, seek counsel and allow God to heal your heart. He understands our pain.

Warmly,
DiAnn

ACKNOWLEDGMENTS

Heather Kreke—Brainstorming and all our wonderful chats!

Mark Lanier—Your wisdom and insight always pack power into my stories.

Dean Mills—You're my hero in every story.

Diana Nichols—Thank you for helping me with Gage's name.

Edie Melson—You are my confidence booster.

Leilani Squire—To my dear friend who excels on the list of friends, prayer warriors, super-mom, writer extraordinaire, and encourager.

Lynette Eason—We've shared many suspense tales together.

Susanne Lakin—I value our friendship and the way we encourage each other in our writing and spiritual lives.

Thuong Phan, who helped me with Vietnamese culture.

ABOUT THE AUTHOR

DiAnn Mills is a bestselling author who believes her readers should expect an adventure. She weaves memorable characters with unpredictable plots to create action-packed suspense-filled novels. DiAnn believes every breath of life is someone's story, so why not capture those moments and create a thrilling adventure?

Her titles have appeared on the CBA and ECPA bestseller lists and won two Christy Awards, the Golden Scroll, Inspirational Reader's Choice, and Carol Award contests.

DiAnn is a founding board member of the American Christian Fiction Writers and a member of Blue Ridge Mountains Christian Writers, Advanced Writers and Speakers Association, Mystery Writers of America, the Jerry Jenkins Writers Guild, Sisters in Crime, and International Thriller Writers. DiAnn continues her passion of helping other writers be successful. She speaks to various groups and teaches writing workshops around the country.

DiAnn has been termed a coffee snob and roasts her own coffee beans. She's an avid reader, loves to cook, and believes her grandchildren are the smartest kids in the universe. She and her husband live in sunny Houston, Texas.

DiAnn is very active online and would love to connect with readers through her website at diannmills.com.

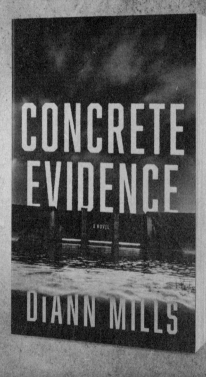

CONNECT WITH DIANN ONLINE AT

diannmills.com

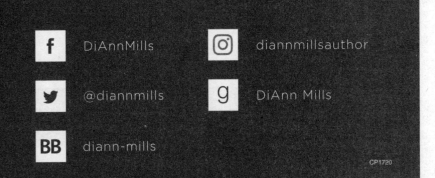